Faces along the Bar

Faces along the Bar

Robert Cranny

WELCOME RAIN PUBLISHERS
New York

FACES ALONG THE BAR
Copyright © 2002 by Robert Cranny.
All rights reserved.

Library of Congress CIP data available from the publisher.

Direct any inquiries to
Welcome Rain Publishers LLC.

ISBN 1-56649-232-7

Printed in the United States of America by
HAMILTON PRINTING COMPANY

First Edition: June 2002
1 3 5 7 9 10 8 6 4 2

For Ava

ACKNOWLEDGMENTS

My sincere thanks to Kathy and to John Weber and Chuck Kim of Welcome Rain, without whom this book would never have happened.

Faces along the Bar

ONE

The bells of St. Catherine's rang out their ancient sound, proclaiming the old mystery. The idea of God was in the air on Sunday mornings, but there was never any certainty. For some of the parishioners churchgoing was habit, insurance. Better to be there than not. For all, it was something parents and grandparents had brought with them from the other side. Something they couldn't ignore at least until they moved away from the neighborhood.

It had a feeling all its own. There was the straightforward pragmatism of working-class people. They respected a man who kept his word and they loved a "character." There were many characters in the neighborhood. Men took care of their families and looked out for their women. Everybody knew everybody the way they do in small towns. You could hear a couple have an argument or a fight through an open window. It wasn't easy to have secrets. On the long summer nights young girls played hopscotch on the sidewalks and the boys played stickball in the street. People sat out on the stoops of the tall dark brownstones. Friends were greeted and strangers were noted. There was always a card game going on, and the smaller children ran when the Good Humor man came around. You could hear Red Barber's voice carry the Dodgers game from Ebbets Field or St. Louis or Chicago. Shouts rang out when they scored and there were curses when there was a bonehead play.

The neighborhood was an island to those who lived in it. There was a safeness and a familiarity. They were all carried along with the notion of a kind of happiness and the unspoken idea of the dream that always told them they could have more. Everything seemed as permanent as the sidewalks and the brownstones and the thin trees that grew out of the sidewalks on either side of the streets. Occasionally, frame houses with small yards in front and back of them broke the monotony of the brown-stones at street endings. On some streets there were apartment buildings that had been built during the boom of the twenties, and the elevated train ran along Fourth Avenue to Manhattan across the river. St. Catherine's stood in the same place for over a hundred years and the neighborhood had grown up around it. Its twin Gothic spires reached to the heavens to remind the Almighty of those of His children whose lives were centered on the streets of the neighborhood. It was their church.

It was always full for the late mass on Sundays. Few of the parishioners were pious. They were realists, survivors, strivers, but they all wanted something better. Their real belief was in holding down a job and taking care of their families. They were willing to work for what they thought would bring them happiness. Father Darcy said the late mass now. He was new to the parish and they were still sizing him up even though it had been over a year since he'd arrived. He was handsome and the young girls wished he weren't a priest. He was tall and slim with dark hair that always fell across his brow. They said he'd be a ringer for Elvis if he let it grow and had sideburns.

When he looked down from the pulpit that Sunday morning, he saw old Mrs. Gallucci sitting in the front pew. Her eyes were closed in prayer as they always were and her black shawl was pulled over her head. Her lips were moving as she held her rosary, and it was as though she alone were staving off all the evil of the world. The other faces peered up at him with little expectation. For them the idea was to get it over with. No surprises. Father Darcy felt his stomach flutter before he began to speak, and all the faces became a blur as he crossed himself. "Dearly beloved," he said. "Someone has written that we live on this earth under a kind of reprieve. That we are here for a while and then this life knows us no more. And sometimes we have to remind ourselves of that in order to set our priorities straight. In order to ask ourselves what is it that is most important to us. As a way of putting some things into perspective. We know the rent has to be paid. The children have to be fed and clothed—educated. Very few have the time or perhaps even the inclination to look into the mystery of life.

"But surely we all have the need to look beyond the daily routine and ask ourselves where we are going. We all want a better life. A chance to do well. To make it better for our children. Maybe even move to the suburbs where all will be wonderful. We all want to be free of worry and fear. We all want to be safe in the world but life always has a way of finding us."

He paused briefly and stared out over them. "And that brings me to what I want to talk to you about this morning. We can't escape reality. As much as we may want to feel safe and free from worry, life will always find us, no matter where we go. No matter how much money we make. No matter where we move to. If you are going to move away from here, then do it for the right reasons. Not because people who may be of a different color than you are moving close to the neighborhood. This is a community. A place where we can all live and grow together. A place that is good for children, a place you can say you are proud to be from. This neighborhood right here in Brooklyn. You have to understand that black parents want the same for their children as you do for yours. And they have the same God-given right to be here."

He paused. He could feel a silent wave of resentment coming toward him from their sullen faces. He immediately felt sorry he had been so direct. Old Monsignor Moloney had always told him to be very careful of what he said from the pulpit. He knew of Darcy's feelings. "Some things you just don't bring up or you'll lose them completely," he had warned him. But the younger priest had nothing of the politician in him. The monsignor did. "You can never point your finger from the pulpit," he said. "You always have to give them a little room to maneuver or they'll never forgive you even if they know you are right."

Darcy had no alternative now but to go on. "Everybody has the right to go after their dreams. Even those who are not like us. Why do we become resentful—indignant when they express the same ambition as us? Some people panic and move away." He could feel himself tremble as he spoke the words, and he wanted to tell them he understood their fears. "But who are we when we root for the Dodgers?" he went on. "Irish, Italian. Polish, black, Puerto Rican? What's the color of a run or a strikeout? Remember how everyone pulled together for Jackie Robinson when he came up? People wore buttons that said 'I'm for Jackie.' Does everybody have to be a ballplayer in order for us not to be afraid? Maybe it's all just a matter of having faith in ourselves. As Mr. Lincoln said, 'to believe in the better angels of our nature.' Love knows no color and fear deadens the spirit. And communities are always about the spirit. The ethos created by the desire to work together for the common good. But unfortunately to some men nothing is sacred. We even hear rumors now of the Dodgers leaving Brooklyn. Hard to believe, but apparently there is some truth to it all. For those of us who live here they are more than a team. They are an institution that brings us all together. Their success is our success and their failure is our failure. Yet one greedy man has put a price on this team that represents something larger than all of us and threatens to take it away if the city doesn't meet his demands. He will be quick to tell us and the courts will agree that he is merely pursuing his right to do as he pleases with his own property. Just as all of you are free to move away from here and never have to look back at what you leave behind.

"And I believe that it is my duty to state the case for the neighborhood. It didn't just happen. It took many years and a lot of sweat and toil to build it. All I wanted to say to you this morning is that I believe in it and I believe in you. I believe in the Dodgers, and I don't want them to go away, either." He crossed himself and walked down the steps of the pulpit. He stood before the altar with his back to them, but he could still feel the dark energy of their resentment moving over him and he felt a sickness in the pit of his stomach.

Kerrigan's stood in the same spot on Fourth Avenue for as far back as anyone could remember, and Johnny Kerrigan and his wife lived over the place just as his father and mother had done before him. He was a tall, handsome man, always meticulous about his dress. He always wore a snow-white shirt and a striped tie held in place with a diamond pin inherited from his father. His long white apron reached from the middle of his chest to the tips of his highly polished shoes.

His hair was parted down the center the way ballplayers used to do it twenty years before. When there was a wedding or a funeral or a christening or a gathering of any kind, everyone always wound up in Kerrigan's. Sunday after church was a favorite time for the regulars and the place was crowded that Sunday. Kerrigan moved behind the bar, calling out greetings and serving up drinks as fast as he could. There was no doubt that bartending was indeed his true calling, because he moved effortlessly and easily kept up with the demand for his services. They were all talking about Father Darcy's sermon and speculating about just how long it would be before Monsignor Moloney got rid of him. Dooney Hanifan worked on the Brooklyn piers. He was in his thirties, short and stocky with an acid tongue, and now he was leaning forward on his stool, asking Kerrigan in a loud voice what he thought of Father Darcy. "I think he's a good guy," he said. "Could have had it easy if he wanted. His old man is a big shot on Wall Street. Mansion up in Westchester and all and here he is at St. Catherine's."

"Well, Jesus! Ain't they always the type," Dooney said. "Wants us all to sit out on our stoops watching the neighborhood fall apart as the coons and the spics move in." He spun around on the stool, looking at the others, and started to laugh, throwing his head back and slapping his thighs. "Yeah, this guy is something else. You wanna know why the Dodgers are pullin' out? Because in a coupla years from now the only ones left to watch 'em will be spics and coons. You better start learning Spanish, Kerrigan, and pull all them Irish songs outta the jukebox. And you better start learning to do the mambo." They were all laughing now.

"Jeez, you shoulda heard what Darcy had to say," Freddie Alcaro said. "Trying to make us all feel guilty. Let me tell you. A priest can be just as full of shit as anyone else and sometimes even more so."

"That's enough, Mr. Alcaro," Kerrigan said. "The man is not here to defend himself." There was a round of applause and derisive cheering up and down the bar. "Kerrigan, you should have been a priest yourself," someone shouted. "Well, my father always told me that being a bartender was the next best thing to being a priest and a very high calling. And I will remind all of you I've played confessor to nearly all of you, listening to your crying and complaining. I know stuff that you don't even know you said. So remember where you are and what you say, or it may all be held against you."

They all laughed again as Red Dahlgren made his way into the bar. They greeted him and he called back to them the way they always did; when he sat at the bar Kerrigan already had a beer in place before him. "And how's it going, Red?" Kerrigan asked him. He raised the beer to his lips, drained most of it, and placed the glass back down on the bar. "Do that again!" Kerrigan filled his glass and Red put it to his lips and took a long pull. He shuddered as he felt the beer course through his body; then he looked at Kerrigan. "I'll tell you how it's going, Johnny. Margo and me just got engaged. We're going to be married. That's how it's going."

"Well, congratulations, my boy! Congratulations!" Kerrigan said. "Hear that?" he shouted. "Red just got engaged." They all gathered around him, slapping him on the back and calling out their congratulations.

Even Kerrigan poured himself a short beer and raised his glass. "Here's to Red and Margo!" he said. "May you have all the luck in the world!"

They all drank and wished him the best.

"You let us down, Red," Bobby Raguso said. "You were the guy always said love 'em and leave 'em, and now the Mick gets himself engaged to a wop."

"Better him than me," Dooney said. "You don't have to get married to get laid these days. Will someone tell the guy he doesn't have to go through with this?"

"You just know a woman is going to be watching over you like a hawk," Raguso said. "She'll even tell you if it's alright to go out and get the *Mirror* and the *News*. And what about turning that paycheck over every Friday. And you'll be lucky if she hands you anything back. Not for me. I like my independence too much. I like to feel I can pick and choose without getting hitched for life."

"Let me ask you, Rags. And be honest now. When's the last time you got laid? Honest, now, and I don't mean with a hooker. That don't count."

"About a month ago."

"Oh yeah? Who?"

"Not someone anyone here would know."

"Right," Red said. "None of us know her because she doesn't exist. Better not let anything happen to that right hand of yours. Best friend you've got."

They laughed, and Raguso lowered his head and stuck his hand out to Red. "You're a lucky guy," he said.

They had broken into smaller groups now, and Red was sitting across the bar from Kerrigan. "Have you set the date yet?" Kerrigan asked him.

"Dunno for sure. Two or three months. Margo wants to move to California. I thought things were going to be a lot better around here after I came back from Korea. Helluva thing to come back and see the shines and the spics moving in. Hell, I got nuthin' against 'em, but let's face it, they're different. They're not like us."

"And what'll you do in California?" Kerrigan asked.

"Don't know for sure. Guess I could always be a cop, but what would be the point of that. I'm sure it isn't much different from what I do here.

Margo wants me to get off the force, anyway. Hell, maybe I'll break into the movies. Good-lookin' guy like me."

"Why the hell not," Kerrigan said. "You know they got some real ugly bastards made it big in the movies."

"Well, the whole thing is Margo's idea," Red said. "She wants to get away from here, especially from her old man."

"The whole thing is to be happy," Kerrigan said. "And you and Margo have to find that for yourselves."

The sun streamed down on the street outside. The Dodgers were playing a doubleheader against the Cardinals, and Kerrigan had just switched on the TV. Red Barber was interviewing Stan Musial. The sound was off, as was the custom.

"The trouble is my mother," Red said. "Haven't told her yet. Don't know how she's gonna take it. She'll have a whole lot to say about Margo being Italian and all. She still wants me to marry a nice Irish girl like Sheila Dolan."

Dooney Hanifan had sidled over and was sitting next to Red. He looked at Kerrigan, catching his eye, then he turned to Red. "Still think you shoulda married Sheila when you had the chance," Dooney said. "Tell me, how does a beautiful girl like that wind up marrying a prick like Harry Cope?"

They were all looking toward Red now, and they knew Dooney shouldn't have opened his mouth. Dooney looked back toward them. "Well, it's the truth, ain't it? The whole damn neighborhood knew she was crazy about Red. Shit, the two of you were together since grade school. You just let that prick take her away from you."

"Fuck you, Dooney!" Red said as he turned to face him. "As usual you don't know what the hell you're talking about." He turned away. "Harry Cope didn't put a gun to her head," he said quietly. "She did exactly what she wanted to do."

"I hate to tell you Red," Dooney said, looking toward him. "But you got it wrong. She married Harry because her old lady made her do it."

"Whatever you say, Dooney," he said. "It's like they say. Everything works out for the best."

TWO

Red walked home from Kerrigan's. Despite the beers he'd had he still felt nervous telling his mother about the engagement. He knew she didn't like Margo and he knew she would go on about Sheila and ask him for the thousandth time what had happened between them. "Geez, I'm a plainclothes cop on the force," he told himself. "Why the hell do I still have to explain myself to my mother?" Margo was so different from Sheila. A difference he loved. She excited him in ways that Sheila never could. She was open and there was a wildness about her. She didn't care what people thought of her. He had loved telling the guys about the very first time they kissed. How she had forced her tongue into his mouth and pressed herself hard against him. She was never tentative. Sheila had always held back as though she were afraid of breaking some rule. Margo had even scared him at first, but now he couldn't see her often enough. She had made him see beyond the neighborhood and Kerrigan's and the job. She was always telling him that there was a whole world out there beyond, and the most wonderful thing would be for them to go toward it together and see it for themselves.

He climbed the stairs to the apartment on the top floor of the brownstone and walked down the long hallway that led to the kitchen. "Hello, girls," he said as he stood in the entrance. His mother and his young sister Annie were sitting at the table having lunch.

"Well, hi there, lover boy!" Annie said, smiling. "How's my big brother today?"

"We expected you home last night," his mother said. "You might at least have given us a call."

"Sorry, Ma, we were on a case. Stakeout. Sitting in the patrol car all night." Annie winked at him. They knew their mother well. "You sure need a shave, lover boy," she said. "I'd never go out with a guy had a growth like that."

"Boy, you're getting choosy. But I know you're just a heartbreaker."

"Not me," she said. "Like you said. I'm choosy."

"You have to be more than choosy these days," Mrs. Dahlgren said. "Especially when it comes to picking the right one for you." Red had often wondered if his mother could see into his head and know what he was thinking. He was convinced she had the ability to know things about him before he told her. He sat at the table and Annie brought him a bottle of beer and a pilsner glass. He poured the beer the way he had seen Kerrigan do it so often and watched the liquid flow into the glass and saw the beautiful creamy head form on the crown. Annie leaned down and kissed him on the forehead. "And I still love you despite your beard," she said. "What about something to eat?" He shook his head. "Not yet." He drank from his glass and wondered how he would tell his mother about him and Margo. He glanced quickly at her and was about to tell her when he hesitated. She was still a handsome woman and there were times when he could still see the beautiful young girl in her face, and the old softness would be there. But it was never for long. She had come to New York from the convent in Galway and took a job right away as a waitress at Schrafft's. That's where she met Pete Dahlgren. All the girls were crazy about him, with his blue eyes and his wavy blond hair, but Margaret Cassidy was the most beautiful woman he had ever seen and he had fallen in love with her the minute he laid eyes on her. And he made her feel that all the sad and lonely days of her life were gone forever. She would be able to forget that she was an orphan raised on the charity of the nuns. Everyone called him "Swede" and she didn't care that he wasn't Catholic. After all, she told herself, this is America. They said he was the best bartender in New York, and he worked in that speakeasy on Fifty-fourth Street, where you had to be somebody to get in. He knew Jack Dempsey and Babe Ruth and even Jimmy Walker himself. They used to say that if Swede Dahlgren gave you the nod from behind the bar, you were in. He was great to be around and loved nothing better than a good time. He loved women and he loved booze and he was a flirt who was never able to stop himself. Women came to him. Margaret pretended not to notice. Some of her friends warned her about him but she didn't care. She always believed in her heart that he was hers no matter what might happen. After they were married she was convinced that he would settle down. He had told her that after they tied the knot everything would be different. He tried hard and she clung to her dream that they would be happy for the rest of their lives, just as it had happened in all of the stories she had read when she was a girl. And she believed that even when he had become a hopeless drunk who couldn't hold a job. She would never allow anyone to say a bad word about him. After Red was born, things did change for a while. He was crazy about his boy who looked just like him. He swore off booze and he came right home after work. There were long stretches when he stayed sober, but it always caught up with him, and Margaret hoped against hope for a miracle. She was pregnant with Annie when her husband died of acute alcoholism.

He had been missing for days before she had to go to the city morgue and identify his body. Then the hardness slowly began to come over her; nearly all her hope was gone. Neither Red nor Annie knew of the radiant young girl who had fallen in love with the handsome man who was their father. There were times when out of the blue the old Margaret Cassidy showed herself like the weak winter sun through the clouds, but then it would disappear as quickly as it had arrived and her face would take on once more the mask of the pain it was trying to hide.

Annie was a senior in high school. She had inherited her father's Nordic good looks, his great smile, and his wonderful sense of fun. There was also a serious side to her that always surprised her mother, and restlessness. She was confident in a way that Red would never be. He had his father's height and build and his mother's Irish face. Even though he was eight years older than Annie, they were close, and he always worried about her. He could see her confidence and her brightness and all those books she was always reading. She already had a scholarship to college, and he knew that she had no fear of moving out into the world. In some ways she was like Margo. She often acted with much more maturity than he did. She knew things about the world and politics and he always knew she would leave the neighborhood far behind at the first opportunity. Somehow she had managed to escape the darkness of her mother's disappointment and sorrow.

There was something in her that left Red and her mother behind, a secretive side unknown to Mrs. Dahlgren, but Red could sense it, even though he wasn't sure what it was.

Mrs. Dahlgren still set the table the same way she did when her husband was alive. And Sunday lunch was the meal he always enjoyed the most. Fresh seeded rye from Marmelstein's bakery, German-style potato salad, and cold roast beef, along with corn beef and pickles and fresh cole slaw. He had shown her how to set the table after they were married. Sunday was still a difficult day for her. She always thought of him, and sometimes she still had the feeling that he would come walking down the hallway and join them. "Aren't you going to eat something, Red?" his mother asked him. "You're usually starving when you come home." He nodded and reached across the table for some rye bread and began to make himself a sandwich. Then he stopped and looked at his mother.

"Margo and I got engaged yesterday. We wanna get married before the end of the year." The words had come out before he could stop them.

"Oh, Red, that's terrific," Annie shouted, then she leaped and rushed around the table to where he sat and hugged him. "And it's about time, lover boy, isn't it, Mom?" She held onto him and kissed him. Then they both looked toward Mrs. Dahlgren. She was slowly and deliberately cutting her sandwich in half. She didn't look up. "You gave no inkling. I didn't know it was that far along." And then she looked across the table at him. "Well, she wanted you, and now she has you. I just hope to God you both know what you're doing."

"I know what I'm doing, Mom," Red said. "It's really what I want."

Mrs. Dahlgren raised her paper napkin to her eyes and bowed her head into it. She blew her nose and dabbed at her eyes. Her two children went to her and put their arms around her. "Margo is a good girl, Mom," Red said. "She's good for me. I know it more than anything. She's good for me."

Annie placed her hands on her mother's shoulders. She kneaded them slowly, moving them gently to soothe her. Mrs. Dahlgren finally forced a smile and then blew her nose once more. And then she reached for her glass and drained it. She looked at her children and shook her head. "I'll never understand Sheila Dolan marrying Harry Cope." She shook her head again to emphasize her bafflement. "He's not half the man you are."

She took Red's hand and kissed it as though he were still a little boy. "So long as you're happy, son," she said softly. "You have to take it the way it comes and enjoy it while you have it." Her eyes filled with tears again and Red bent his head and kissed her on the cheek. Annie was standing between them with her arms around them. "And next Saturday's my sweet sixteen party," she said. "We can make it an engagement party, too. Have a big party for the two of us. Right, Mom?" Her mother looked at her and nodded without smiling. Annie hugged them both and kissed her brother again.

Mrs. Dahlgren lay on her bed in her slip. She could hear the sound of the dishes being washed in the kitchen. She had felt tired after lunch and Annie had insisted she go to bed. For once she listened. She could feel the warmth of the sun on her body as it streamed through the bedroom window and she couldn't stop thinking of Red and Margo.

It seemed that all of the promises of the past had come streaming back to her since Red made his announcement. She remembered how she felt when Pete had asked her to marry him and how sure she was of the future. Now she was overcome with a wave of sadness. She wondered if it was possible to have hope for the future. She remembered how easy it had been for her to let go of her life in Ireland and to believe in Pete and all the fabulous things that could happen in America. She wondered if it was wrong or even foolish to have faith in the possibility of the future. And she realized that all of the strength of the young lay in that promise. Her hand reached out for the rosary on the night table. She held the beads tightly in her hand and tried to pray her way through her loneliness. It had begun for her long before Pete died. The feeling that she had been abandoned once more and that she would never find the joy that came to her when he had first told her that he loved her.

She closed her eyes and she could feel the impatient beat of her heart. It was always prepared for the worst. The same beat that was there during all of those nights she lay awake waiting for her husband to come home, trying not to think of where he was or whom he might be with. And then there was the relief when she listened to his footsteps on the stairs and heard his key turn in the door, when she tried to gauge how drunk he was. And then there was the boozy smell when he came into the bedroom. He would lie down beside her and reach his hand down her leg and kiss her and mumble into her ear. When he touched her it didn't matter where he had been. She would turn to him and open her legs and all of her anxiety would evaporate and be lost in the passion that swept over her like a drug. She would move against his hand and her wetness would come quickly and he would say things to her she had never heard before, things she didn't understand. They were vulgar and rough, but they excited and thrilled her when she heard them.

"I'm going, Ma!" she heard Annie call out. Then she heard the door close and Annie's quick steps going down the stairs. Red was asleep in his room, and she felt the quietness of the house all around her. Sundays always had a special quietness. She faintly heard Red's snoring. She closed her eyes and the memory of Pete Dahlgren came flooding back to her. She knew she wasn't supposed to let these feelings come to her body, but they were so strong. She placed the rosary back on the night table and moved her hand slowly down her stomach and began to move slowly against it. She bit down on her lip to suppress the sigh that was rising up in her. She was transported. Taken away. Far, far away, and she let it happen slowly because she didn't want to come back. She wanted the feeling to last forever. She was floating away and Pete was with her and she was leaning into him. She moaned loudly despite her efforts to contain it and she could feel the shudders moving through her body. Her eyes were moist and she could almost feel the sound of Pete's voice in her ear. She didn't want to let him go. The feelings became deeper and she heard herself cry out, then she was afraid she would wake Red. She moved her hands away from herself and pulled her slip down and covered herself with the sheet. Then she turned on her side, closed her eyes, and fell asleep.

The incessant ringing of the doorbell woke her and she wondered who could be ringing the bell on a Sunday afternoon. She sat up quickly and reached for her robe. She glanced at herself in the mirror of her dressing table and pushed her hair back into place. She still kept it long the way Pete liked it, and it was still lush and red without a trace of gray. She hoped the ringing hadn't woken Red. She hated to be seen in her robe, especially on a Sunday. She had always prided herself on how she looked. When she opened the door, Julia Treacy stood looking at her anxiously. "Oh, Margaret, I'm glad you're home," she said. "I've been ringing so long I thought you were all out. It's Jack. He hasn't been home for nearly HOW LONG and I wondered if he might be here with Red."

"He's not here, Julia, but Red is. He worked last night and he's sleeping now. But come in. Come in." Mrs. Dahlgren led her into the kitchen and they sat down at the table. "I know it's useless to worry about him at this stage," Mrs. Treacy said. "It's just that I have this terrible feeling that they'll find him dead someplace. I can't stop myself from thinking the worst."

"But he always shows up," Mrs. Dahlgren said. "He'll be alright, just wait and see. Just sit there now, and I'll make us a cup of tea."

"Oh, thank you, Margaret," she said. Jack was her youngest son, the only one still living at home. All the others were either married or had moved out. Jack and Red had been best pals since they were children and had been in school with each other all the way from kindergarten to high school. When they were eighteen they had run away together and joined the Marines because neither of their mothers would sign for them. They had gone through boot camp at Parris Island and almost immediately they were both shipped off to Korea, but they were separated when they got there. Jack Treacy had come home after he was severely wounded and spent two years in the veterans' hospital before they released him. After he moved in with his mother he had become a recluse, locking himself in his room most of the time. He left the house only to go on benders when his monthly disability check arrived. It was four years now since he had come home from the war and the routine was always the same. He drank his check each month and never had any memory of where he had been or what he had done. He always went to Manhattan to drink, where he was sure no one would know him. He only came home when all of his money was gone. Sometimes he was mugged or rolled; he even gave it away. It was a good bender when he came home without having been beaten up or thrown in the drunk tank at the Tombs.

At first everyone was sympathetic. They made excuses for him. "If you'd been through what he went through you'd drink, too," they said. He had been awarded the Navy Cross and the Silver Star and two Purple Hearts. He had come home a sergeant, and they had written him up in the *Brooklyn Eagle*. But now they were tired of him. They were saying they should stop his disability check. "When is he going to get on with his life?" they asked. "He's not the first guy to come home from a war all banged up. Jesus, just because he saw some action doesn't mean he has to be a bum for the rest of his life."

Mrs. Dahlgren poured the tea and sat down beside her friend. "Listen to me now," she said. "You just have to stop worrying because it's not going to bring him home. He's in God's hands. He takes care of poor souls like Jack. He's watching over him now. Drink your tea and have a little piece of that cake. I got it fresh in the bakery."

Mrs. Treacy looked at her and her eyes were moist. "Oh, Margaret," she said. "What would I do without you?" She sipped her tea and took a small bite from her cake just to please her friend.

"There's no use trying to wake Red. Once he's asleep you might just as well try to rouse a dead horse. He worked last night and didn't get home until lunchtime. He usually mentions it if he runs into Jack." She wondered if she should mention Red's engagement. She didn't want her to feel bad, but it was all she could think of to change the subject. "But I have something to tell you, Julia," she said. She reached out and took her hand as though to emphasize the importance of what she was about to tell her. "Red just got engaged and he plans to be married before the end of the year."

"That is marvelous," Mrs. Treacy said. "But I didn't know he was that close to anyone. It's a complete surprise, that's for sure."

"Oh, it was a surprise for me, too, Julia."

"Is it someone from the neighborhood?"

"She's from the Bronx. He met her in the city. And to tell you the truth it was she who came after him, but I hear that's not unusual these days." And then she dropped her voice almost to a whisper. "Would you believe she actually came out here looking for him one day? Rang the doorbell and asked for him. She's Italian. Not the way we went about it in our day, is it, Julia? But it must have worked, because she got him. And to tell you the truth, there's no telling how it will wind up."

"Well, if she got Red she's a very lucky girl," Mrs. Treacy said. "He never gave you any trouble. He's decent with a good heart and that's what counts the most. He never forgets Jack. He's not like the others. He's always there for him and I know he wouldn't hear a bad word said against him."

"Seems like yesterday the two of them were little boys playing outside in the street," Mrs. Dahlgren said. "I remember the morning we brought the two of them down to school for the first time. They were so afraid they wouldn't be able to sit together."

"I remember it well. They were like brothers. We never thought then they'd wind up in Korea together."

"Poor Jack!" Mrs. Dahlgren said. "Nobody will ever know what he's been through."

"And for what?' Mrs. Treacy said, her face flushing in anger. "What the hell good did that war ever do anybody? I've asked myself over and over again. Is there anything worth what they put Jack through. I just know in my heart he'll never be himself again. It's as if they didn't send him home at all. The boy that came to me is not my son. He's not Jack Treacy. And when I think of how brave they were going off that morning to join the Marines as if they didn't have a care in the world."

THREE

As his mother worried about him and Mrs. Dahlgren tried to console her, Jack Treacy was walking through Times Square. His hands were stuck deep in his pockets and he clutched the roll of bills that allowed him to continue on his bender. He wasn't drunk and he wasn't sober. There was just enough booze in his system to enable him to function. To those who didn't know him, he appeared to be normal, but his body craved frequent doses of alcohol and he stopped into a doorway and pulled a pint bottle of rye from his back pocket. He removed the top and took a deep slug, then he put the bottle back and moved on. Times Square was an anonymous place. He was a face in the crowd and nobody gave him a second glance. He felt alone and isolated, his mother and Brooklyn were a million miles away. He was lost in the despair he felt inside that he was a failure. And he bore all the guilt of being the only man left in the rifle company he had started out with in Korea. He was sure that everyone who passed him on the street could see right through him. Sure, they could tell what he was up to and knew where he was going, and even in the bright afternoon sunlight he could see the arched neon sign over the doorway that flashed GIRLS-GIRLS-GIRLS.

He walked toward the doorway, opened it, and disappeared from the street. He could feel his breath coming quicker in anticipation as he walked up the steep stairway to the second floor. His hand tightened on the roll of bills in his pocket, his passport to paradise. This was where he wanted to be.

Annie Dahlgren stood behind the backstop in the schoolyard, watching the Sunday afternoon softball game. It was where they all went to be together to hang out and tease and laugh with each other. She laughed as Charlie Gallucci turned awkwardly to chase a fly ball. He tripped and fell and the ball nearly hit him on the head before it bounced away. He struggled to his feet embarrassed and confused, and he could hear them all laughing and yelling at him. He found the ball and threw it feebly to the infield, but the runners had already scored. He watched Annie behind the backstop laughing with the others and he wanted to sink into the ground. He had hoped the ball wouldn't come his way, but it seemed that whenever Annie was watching the game it was almost sure to find him. He saw Toby Walters standing next to her and he was laughing, too. He saw his brilliant white teeth and his handsome black face and he wondered why he was always standing next to her. She seemed to enjoy it. He wanted to make sure that everyone knew that Annie was his girl. Why the hell does Toby Walters always have to stand next to her, he asked himself. She was wearing the ring he had given her. They were going steady. When the next batter came up Annie waved to Charlie, smiling. She was shouting something but he couldn't hear. And then he stood in the outfield watching as she walked away. Where the hell could she be going, he asked himself. "Goddamned nigger," he muttered to himself. He had known Toby since grade school. He was smart and he was going to go to college on a football scholarship. He was great at baseball, too, and got better grades than most of the guys. He knew that Toby read all the time. And Annie read too and he knew they talked about politics and which authors they liked the best. He was really something for a spook, some of the guys said. Then he always told himself that a girl like Annie could never let herself be serious about a spook. The neighborhood would just never let her get away with it. It just couldn't happen. Red would kill the guy and her mother would keep her locked up in the house. It just couldn't be, but he still didn't like that they studied together.

Toby said good-bye to Annie and came back to his place behind the backstop. His father was a super in a building over on Perry Street. They were the only black family in the neighborhood and had known everyone since he was in the first grade. There was just his father and him. His mother had died long ago and he had no memory of her.

Bailey Walters, his father, was a fixture. Everyone knew him. He was a hard worker always ready to do a favor, always smiling and good-natured. The guys used to say that Toby wasn't like a spook at all. He was too smart and he didn't talk like other black guys. People always said he was going to be something. Nobody was surprised when he got the scholarship to Columbia. There were some that were jealous, but no one had said anything out in the open. But something was changing. When other blacks and Puerto Ricans began to move closer to the neighborhood, some of them began to look at Toby differently, too. They used to say he was never a nigger like the others, but now with the scholarship and all he was a bit uppity. Thought he was white and there was no doubt that the girls really liked him. They loved to be around him and some had a secret crush on him. They would talk about him among themselves and tell each other how dreamy he was, but they never talked about him around the other guys. Toby could sense the change that had come over them. He ignored it because he knew he wasn't going to be around the neighborhood much longer. He would be off to college in the fall. There was a whole new life ahead of him in a world where he was sure great things were going to happen. And he knew the world was going to change. He could feel it. There was no doubt about it. He could feel it coming.

And he and Annie were in love. And now she walked through the gates of Prospect Park and looked up at the sky and felt the sun on her face. She could see the high fleecy clouds moving slowly and the clear light making everything and everyone alive around her. She couldn't keep herself from smiling. The park was a huge playground with men and women and children and dogs running and jumping and walking and sitting and laughing and shouting and lying on the grass in their Sunday joy. She walked up a grassy incline and came to a wooded area that was like the remnant of a long lost wilderness with thick bushes and tall spreading trees. It was remote from the crowds in the park. She followed a narrow path until she came to a large old oak, its branches reaching out to make a canopy. There was no sun here, only the occasional beam that reached down through the trees like a spotlight. It was quiet except for the distant cries and shouts of children and the playful barking of joyous dogs.

She looked around, then sat under the huge tree. She leaned back, stretched her legs out before her, and looked toward the small path. She saw Toby coming toward her. There was always such a sureness about him, even in the way he walked. He stood before her now and reached his hands down to hers. She took them and he pulled her to her feet. They kissed and held each other tightly. She was leaning into him and she could feel his great strength. She had always liked Toby because he was different from the other guys. It wasn't about him being black. She loved to hear him talk and she loved to look into his face and see the expectation in his eyes. He could see beyond the neighborhood, he had a sense of awe and wonder and he wanted to know things. They read the same books and they would talk about them for hours. She could share her dreams with him and he didn't laugh. He understood. He was more grown-up than the other guys. They seemed to take everything for granted, but he never did. She felt safe when she was with him. She felt he really knew who she was and that she could see beyond the neighborhood, too.

She had been thinking about the party for her and Red. She wanted to ask Toby, but it would be hard with Charlie hovering around her all the time. He would never let her out of his sight. She asked Toby anyway, but he told her he didn't think it was a good idea.

When they were around each other it was so hard to hide their feelings and so hard for him to see her with Charlie. "I wish you would stop the thing with Charlie," he told her. "I just hate to think of you being with him."

"But don't you see," she said. "What do you think would happen if they knew about us?" She pulled him even closer and he bent down and kissed her. She looked into his face and smiled. "I don't care what they think," she said.

"I just hate to think of you being close to Charlie."

"I'm never close to him. I never even let him kiss me. A peck on the cheek, that's all. I don't even want to waste time talking about it. I just want to laugh at all of them. Why do they make such a big deal about color? I'd just love to walk down the block with our arms around each other and stand right in the middle of the street and kiss you right in front of all of them." "Yeah, and I'd be lynched right before your eyes."

"And I'd be lynched with you," she said. He kissed her again and they lay on the ground together. They moved slowly against each other, then heard the footsteps of someone approaching. He quickly pulled her behind the tree and into the bushes. They watched a young boy pass by carrying a bat and a glove.

"I'm so afraid that something will happen to you," Toby said. "That one of these days you'll lose your temper and just tell them all what you think of them."

"Please don't worry," she said. "I'd never give 'em the satisfaction." She pulled him toward her and kissed him. Her jeans were tight and rolled up to her calves and she dug her fingers into his T-shirt. He heard her sigh. They wanted to make love but were afraid to risk it, but they moved against each other, slumped together, and sat down under the tree.

"Maybe we could run away someplace together," Annie said. "What's to stop us?"

Toby shook his head. "It's no use," he said.

"How much money you got?"

"Just a little."

"We couldn't go very far and then they would all be talking about the nigger and the white girl."

"Can't we just go to a place where they don't make a fuss over the color of your skin?"

"Where?"

"Paris. Lots of black people in Paris. And artists and people who don't worry about it." He kissed her again.

"Or maybe we could just move to the Village," she said. "People don't worry about that kind of stuff there. We could get a little place and we could get part-time jobs and just go to school. Nobody would even know where we lived."

She leaned into him and rested her head on his shoulder.

The sun was going down and the sky was a deep blue streaked with red clouds that stretched across the horizon. The sounds in the park were subdued now and a light evening breeze touched the trees, making a soft comforting sound as if they were aware of the two lovers in their midst. They were waiting for the darkness to come so that they could leave the park together. Annie knew that Charlie would have gone to her house looking for her by now. She was going to tell him that she was at some girlfriend's, studying. He would ask her to stay out with him for a while. She wanted to tell him it was over and give him his ring back, but she knew he would be more of a pest if she did. When she'd start college she would tell him it was over.

They walked across the park together in darkness. They could hear other couples talking and laughing and see them making out on the grass. They could see the main entrance now and the street lights reaching away in the distance.

Just before they got to the gate, Toby pulled her aside and kissed her. They clung to each other as though they would never see each other again. They wanted to run back to their hiding place but they kissed once more and made their way through the gate into the street. They looked around cautiously before they started to walk, then they came to the great monument dedicated to the Grand Army of the Republic. It loomed over them like a great bird and the bearded solemn soldiers of the Union Army looked down at them with the strange rustic faces of another time. The lovers stood in a doorway and kissed again. They couldn't keep away from each other. Annie told him she didn't want to go home. He finally had to step back from her and take her hand to lead her back to the sidewalk before they started to walk again. They didn't notice the car moving down the street. It slowed as it was passing them and the driver peered out through the darkness before it sped up abruptly and moved away. It was only after it was gone that Annie thought she recognized the face of Bobby Raguso. Fear spread through her because she knew that he hung out with Red and the crowd in Kerrigan's.

"What was that all about?" Toby asked.

"Nothing."

"Somebody you know?"

She shook her head. She wasn't sure it was Bobby and she decided not to say anything. She kissed him quickly on the cheek. Then they turned away from each other and walked in separate directions.

Jack Treacy reached the top of the stairs and stood before the ticket booth. The large woman inside stared out impassively, a long cigarette in the center of her mouth, her eyes half closed. "How many?" she asked.

"Ten bucks."

She reached for the roll of tickets, tore off a long strand, and counted them again as she pushed them toward him. The smoke from her cigarette slowly ascended past her face as her thick fleshy arms rested on the small counter. Even though Treacy was conscious of her indifference he still felt a tremor of embarrassment. He moved away from the booth and walked through the beaded curtain to the ballroom. The long room was softly lighted, almost dark. There was a smooth parquet dance floor and banquettes on one side of the room and small tables set up nightclub style with covered candles burning in their center. There was a small bar at one end where three girls sat. They were dressed in evening gowns and they were talking and smoking quietly among themselves. A slow dance number was playing on the multicolored jukebox. Treacy couldn't decide whether to go to a table or sit among the girls at the bar. And then as they all turned and looked at him he realized he was the only customer in the place. He had the urge to turn and leave, but before he could move two of the girls came toward him. They smiled at him and took his hands, leading him to a banquette. They sat close to him and he could feel their legs touching him under the table, then they were calling out to the bartender for drinks. They kissed his cheeks and he tried not to be embarrassed. They took the roll of tickets from his hand and placed it in the middle of the table. And then a thin, expressionless waiter brought their drinks. He was wearing a dirty white shirt and a small plastic bow tie. He put the drinks down before the girls. "Five dollars," he said.

Treacy dug into his pocket and pulled a bill from his roll and gave it to him. The girls moved closer and pressed their thighs harder against him. They kissed him and raised their drinks in a toast. They swallowed them quickly. "Same again," they told the waiter before he left.

"And what are you having?" he asked Jack.

"Bottle of beer." He could feel a hand moving slowly up and down his thigh. The waiter came back with the drinks and Treacy handed him a twenty. The waiter stuck it in his pocket and walked away. He never came back with the change and he was afraid to ask because he didn't want the girls to think he was cheap. They were both moving their hands on his thighs now and he loved the feeling. He wanted to take the two of them out of the place and really be alone with them. The dread fear was slowly beginning to leave him and he was beginning to let himself believe that they really liked him.

They pulled him onto the dance floor and one of them asked him for money for the jukebox. He handed her a bill without looking at it and then he heard Billy Eckstein's voice ringing out through the empty room. "Everything I Have Is Yours." The two of them moved against him and he could feel them through their dresses. He knew he would give them everything they wanted just so they would stay with him. There was no past for him now and no future. Only the warmth he could feel through his body and coming from the girls that was better than any drug. He could smell their cheap perfume and their sweat as they held him tightly and pressed their breasts against him. He wanted to stay with them forever, keep them close and feel the strong womanly assurance that insisted that everything would be alright forever. It would let him feel the way he was before he and Red went off to Korea together. The time when everything was possible. The time before the awful feelings in his head were not there. The time before fear invaded him. Now he could only feel it and bow down helpless before it. It led him around and he couldn't scream or call out for help and he could never explain to anyone else what it was. He pulled the women even closer to him and felt the balm of their presence. He heard a sigh coming from deep inside of him and he moaned. The sound came softly out of him and he moved with them across the floor as if they were angels come down from heaven to bring him home to himself.

FOUR

Charlie Gallucci was sitting on the top step of the stoop as Annie had expected. He looked at her in his sulky way to let her know he was really hurt. She had hoped he wouldn't be there, but when she saw him she ran up the steps and sat beside him. She put her arm around his shoulder and she looked into his face and smiled as if she were trying to humor a little boy. He turned his head away and still sulked.

"What's the matter?" she asked him.

"Where were you?"

"I told you I was studying with the girls. We have exams next week."

"Oh, yeah. Where are your books?"

"I left them with Laura. I marked up a lot of pages and she needed to copy them."

"You were doing homework all this time?"

"Yes."

"All this time? Bullshit."

"Look, Charlie, you can think whatever you like, okay?"

He stood up and pulled her roughly toward him.

"I just missed you, that's all. I wanted to be with you."

He kissed her, forcing his tongue into her mouth. She clenched her teeth and pushed herself away from him.

"Let's go to the garage and we can sit in the car. Nobody will even know we're there."

He moved his hand toward her breast.

"Please, Charlie," she said. "Jesus, we're standing right out in the open here."

"Well, let's go to the garage. Please."

"I can't. Not tonight."

He stared fiercely into her face and she could feel his anger.

"Why can't you come with me?"

"I haven't been home since lunchtime."

"You never have time for me now. Big shot going to college and all. Boy, you really think you're better than everyone else. Guys like me just ain't good enough for you anymore."

"Please, Charlie, you know that's not so."

He moved close to her again. His dark curly hair hung down over his forehead.

"Just hold me, Charlie. Please."

He opened his fly and she felt the heat of him in her hand. He moved against her and kissed her, trying again to force his tongue into her mouth. She stepped back from him, but he came toward her again and took her hand and tried to force her to hold him again.

"Oh please, don't stop now," he pleaded.

She reached back behind her and opened the door to the hallway and then turned and quickly ran up the stairs. Charlie stomped the ground in anger and followed her into the building. He caught her at the top of the stairs and spun her around. His face was flushed with anger and frustration.

"Who're you saving it for? Huh? That damn nigger Toby Walters?"

She drew her hand back and slapped him hard across the face. He looked at her, stunned.

Her heart was beating wildly, and she wondered if he really knew about Toby or was he just taunting her.

"I'm sorry," he said, bowing his head. "I shouldn't have said that."

She could see tears in his eyes and he took her hand and kissed it.

"It's just that I love you so much, I'm afraid of losing you. I'm sorry. I'm really sorry."

"I'm sorry, too, Charlie," she said.

She kissed him lightly on the forehead and went inside, closing the door behind her.

Red was sitting at the kitchen table, smoking and reading the paper. He looked up when he saw her come in and made a show of looking at his watch.

"Getting kinda late there, kid," he said. "I was hoping you'd get home before I left for work."

She leaned against the kitchen door and took a deep breath.

"Gosh, those stairs gonna kill me," she said.

"A kid like you. You should be able to run up and down ten times without taking a deep breath. Kid like you. You gotta be kiddin'."

She came across the kitchen and sat down beside him.

"Where the hell were you, anyway?"

"Doing homework with the girls. We have an exam next week."

"Oh yeah."

"Yeah."

"Doing homework with the girls. Sure you weren't in Gallucci's garage with Charlie?"

"I was doing homework with the girls."

Red shook his head.

"I noticed the poor guy sittin' on top of the stoop like a lost dog waitin' for you. Must be somethin' to have a guy on a leash like that. I think my little sister's a heartbreaker alright."

"I didn't ask him to wait. Mom sleeping?"

Red nodded.

"She took it pretty good today about you and Margo."

"Yeah. I was kinda surprised. I wonder if she'll ever get used to Margo."

"You never know. She'll never get over Sheila marrying Harry. She took it harder than you."

"Why is it so important to her that you're supposed to marry your own kind? I mean Dad was a Swede. She was the only one in her crowd not to marry her own kind. Maybe she figured a Swede was a step above an Irishman."

"I'm really happy for you, Red. And I really like Margo. I liked her from the first time you brought her around. She's for real and she's crazy about you."

"I never felt this way about anyone before. She's just so full of life and she don't take crap from anyone. Mom better watch out."

They both laughed quietly, then Red finished his coffee and got ready to leave.

"Gotta go," he said. He reached behind the chair for his shoulder holster and put it on. Annie watched as he put his jacket on over it and moved his arms up and down to make sure it fit snugly. She always had a tinge of fear when she saw him put on his holster. She didn't like that he was a cop and she could never get him to talk about what he did.

"Be careful," she said as she leaned forward and kissed him on the cheek.

"Never worry about me, kid," he said.

He turned and left and she heard the front door closing behind him. She wished she could tell Red about Toby but she was sure he would never understand. And she knew it wasn't that he was bad or anything. And she even wondered if there was something wrong with her because she loved Toby the way she did, but she always knew that what she had with Toby couldn't be wrong because it made her feel so good. She knew that most people never really thought much about color because they were too busy getting on with their lives and she knew that if they really did take the time to think about it they wouldn't be prejudiced. She hated that she had to keep it hidden and she hated that she had to lie, but she knew there would be hell to pay if Red and her mother found out. She knew they would tell her she was ruining her life. Throwing it all away. So she knew that it was better to lie about Toby than to tell the truth.

As she sat in the kitchen she felt herself tremble. She could feel the silence of the house all around her. It had been terrible with Charlie. He was so jealous and she couldn't get the thought out of her head that he suspected something. The worst part was that there was no one she could talk to. And she wondered if they had been seen coming out of the park. She was almost sure that Bobby Raguso saw them. She got up from the table and went to her bedroom. She paused at her mother's door. It was slightly ajar and she could hear her breathing. Why do things have to be the way they are, she thought. Why can't I tell Mom? Why can't I tell her and she can tell me not to worry that everything is going to be alright.

Earlier that day, Kerrigan had been telling the crowd about Father Darcy coming into the place, asking if Treacy had been there. "Mrs. Treacy calls him, so what does he do but come in here looking for him. God knows where Jack Treacy is, I tell him. He'll show up in a day or a week or who knows. Have a drink, Father, I says to him, but he won't have anything. Can't even get him to take a seat. I mean at a table, not at the bar. Have to keep it respectable." They laughed at the thought of Darcy's discomfort. They had been drinking for most of the day, and they were watching the Dodgers on television. "Tell you something, though, and you can laugh if you like. He's the only priest I've ever known came in here looking for a drunk."

"Aw, for Christ's sake," Raguso said. "Treacy probably owes him money."

"Or maybe he's queer for him," Charlie Wallace said. "Jesus, he's gotta want something from him. Why the hell else would he go looking for him."

"Or maybe he wants him to promise he's not gonna move away from the neighborhood when the niggers move in."

They all laughed again.

"Well, let me tell you something," Freddie Alcaro said. That priest ain't queer. Ever see the way the women look at him. The guy's got 'em all creamin' in their drawers. Ever see the way they all stare up at him when he's in the pulpit. Jesus, you'd think he was Sinatra."

"So do you think he's fuckin' anyone?" Dooney asked.

"Bet your ass he is," Raguso answered. "Only we'll never know anything about it. Goddamn women are better at keepin' secrets than we are."

"Yeah, they just keep it to themselves," Dooney said. "Ever see when they're together in a crowd. Always laughing like they got some great thing they're talking about, and when you look at 'em they go all silent."

"So Father, I says to him," Kerrigan said. "Every time Jack Treacy goes off on his bender we start a pool. Everyone puts five bucks in and who-ever comes up with the day and time closest to when he comes home or shows up in the neighborhood wins the pot.

"See, usually he stops in here before he goes home, to have a beer or two to steady his nerves. And you know, fellas, I had to stop myself from askin' the good father if he wanted in on the action."

They erupted in laughter again.

"Tell you the truth, I think he's in over his head. He just ain't right for a parish like this. Should be up in Westchester or somethin'."

"Naw, I think he just needs to get laid," Charlie Wallace said.

"And how in the fuck would you know?" Raguso said. "You ain't never been laid in your life. You're strictly a hand job."

"Fuck you, Raguso!" Charlie said.

"So you think Darcy is still a virgin?" Dooney asked.

"Well jeez, he sure as hell looks like a virgin."

"Could be fuckin' the housekeeper," Wallace said.

"Naw, he ain't fuckin' the housekeeper. The monsignor's got her staked out," Dooney said. "Been screwin' her for years. They say she's the best blow job in Brooklyn."

They were all shaking with laughter now. "Jesus, fellas, don't get carried away with this. I mean, the guy is a priest, after all, " Kerrigan said.

"Tell you what, though," Raguso said. "I really feel sorry for Mrs. Treacy. I mean what she has to go through every time Jack goes off on a toot. And then when he comes back he locks himself in his room and won't let anyone come near him. Spends every dime on booze."

"Yeah, it's like they say," Dooney said. "Only a mother could love him. And when you think of how he was before he and Red went off to Korea. Coulda had the world by the balls."

"Whatever the fuck he had he doesn't have it now," Charlie Wallace said. "Left it a million miles away in some fuckin' place where nobody ever heard of Brooklyn."

FIVE

Treacy kept checking his pocket to see that his roll was still there. He had left the dance palace with the two girls and now they were sitting in a brightly lit restaurant off Times Square. They still sat close to him as though they had found a gold mine and they were not going to let him get away. He wanted them all to go straight to their place, but they insisted he take them to dinner. He was self-conscious sitting with them because he was sure everyone could tell what kind of girls they were. He wanted them to eat quickly so that they could leave. They were talking to each across him as if he weren't there and laughing out loud so everyone could hear them. He wanted to slide under the table. Even the booze didn't seem to be working for him anymore. He felt frozen and then he wondered if he should go with them. He didn't remember their names and now they were even beginning to look exactly alike to him. He started to tell them he wanted to leave but the words wouldn't come to his lips, and when the waiter brought their food he looked at it and had no idea what he was supposed to do with it. He turned to say something to one of them but again his lips felt like rubber and all that came from him was a low moan. They told him to shut up and eat his food. The restaurant had gone silent on him. He watched the people around him eating and saw their mouths moving in conversation, but he couldn't hear anything. He was in a silent world. He tried to talk again, but no sound would come from him and he began to panic. In desperation he stood and again a long low moan came from him and the two girls pulled him down to his chair and told him to shut up. People around them were snickering. He looked all around him, trying to figure out what was going on. And then one of the girls pulled him close and shouted into his ear. "Pay the bill, we're getting outta here." He finally understood and pulled some bills from his pocket and placed them on the table. They guided him through the restaurant to the door and they were out on the street. Everyone had watched them shaking their heads. Some giggled and nudged each other and others turned away in disgust.

They took him to their small walk-up apartment. Almost immediately they stripped down to their panties and bras and urged him to get undressed, too.

"This is what you wanted, isn't it?" one of them said.

He knew he didn't want to stay. He just wanted them to hold him for a while. They produced a bottle of rye and poured him a large drink and then they were taking his clothes off and pulling him into bed. They knew he would pass out as soon as he lay down. An easy mark. But he kept sitting up, telling them he wanted to leave. The two of them lay close to him and wrapped their legs around him. They kissed him and held him and reached for him, then they tried to pull off his T-shirt and shorts. He tried to resist but they overwhelmed him. He could feel the warmth and the softness of their bodies, then he watched them kissing each other. He reached for his drink and took a long swig and he began to feel awake again. He could hear the sounds of the city outside the window. He moved his hand under the covers and touched one of them and she quickly brushed it aside, annoyed.

"We're all going to go to sleep now," she said. "Lie down like a good boy."

"Let me see you two kissing again," he said.

"Will you go to sleep if we do?" one of them asked.

Treacy nodded and smiled. They leaned across him and kissed and he could see their tongues moving and he was aroused. He was watching them intently and he reached under the covers again and moved his hand on one of them, then they broke their kiss and nuzzled closer to him and kissed him on his cheeks.

"Now we're all going to go to sleep," one of them said.

He took their hands and tried to guide them to his groin but they pulled away again.

"Goddamn it," one of them said. "We've been on our feet all fucking day and we're going to sleep. Get it, big boy? No touching unless we say so. If we thought you were going to be like this, we wouldn't have brought you up here. Now be a good boy and go to sleep. After we've had some sleep you can do anything you want."

He reached for his glass and took another long drink. They watched him, hoping he would pass out. His trousers with his roll were hanging on the end of the bed. He drained the glass and looked from one of them to the other.

"I'm starting to feel good again," he said. "The feeling is starting to come back."

They looked at each other. He lay back against the headboard with his hands joined behind his head. It was the most comfortable he had felt all day.

"I'm beginning to feel like I just woke up," he said.

"Well you can sit up all fuckin' night but we're going to sleep," he was told.

"That's alright," he said. "I'll just watch the two of you sleeping. Just leave me the bottle."

He lay in the dark between the two women, holding the bottle in his hands. He was staring down toward the end of the bed. They were snuggled against him and he was smiling in the darkness. The noise in his head had quieted down and the heaviness was gone from his body. Sometimes it happened like that, he heard himself laughing out loud and he couldn't stop himself and he wondered why it was that he was so afraid most of the time.

"What the fuck are you laughing at?" one of them said. Go to sleep now or we'll send you home." He still laughed quietly to himself and he could feel tears running down his face.

He remembered there was a time when he used to laugh all the time, but that was a thousand years ago. He tried not to let himself think back because it always made him feel so sad. It was hard to believe there had ever been a time when everything was different.

He tried to hold the memory back but he saw himself and Red when they were altar boys together. They would always try to make each other laugh during benediction or high mass. And sometimes they couldn't hold it back and the laughter would come out in a shriek and they would try to cover it up by coughing. Old Father Gallagher would turn around from the altar and glare at them. And one day when they had come off the altar he waited for them and slapped Treacy hard across the face. He just looked at Red and shook his head. He had called Mrs. Treacy down to the rectory and told her that if her son could not behave himself, he would no longer be allowed to be an altar boy.

And he remembered how sure they all were that Red and Sheila Dolan would marry one day. He remembered he had gotten the track scholarship to Fordham and how proud his mother had been. But Red had talked him into joining the Marines and they had gone off to Korea still laughing because only good things could happen to them. And now there was the horror that paralyzed him with fear and made him want to run and run and keep running, but there was noplace to run to. It was inside of him and would always stay with him no matter where he went. And the nightmares made him scream out in his sleep and the movie played over and over again and he saw all the faces of his buddies who were dead and he wanted to be with them. It was not so much about the pain and the horror of what happened but the uselessness of it all. What had it all accomplished? Now they thought they could make it alright by sending him a check every month. Like a tip, or a handout. Why the hell was I there in the first place? When the horror would come he used to panic at first, but he managed to let the memories move across his brain like a movie. No sound, and he had learned to watch it without feeling the terrible reality of its impact on him. He always could see the bloody ponchos with the pieces of bodies gathered up in them. Legs with boots and socks still on them and bones splintered as though the butcher was preparing them for soup. Unrecognizable heads with stricken distorted faces, a look of surprise on them along with a split second of betrayal. *Why?* they asked. *Why have you allowed this to happen to us? What could be worth it? What principle? What cause? What have you done to us?*

He raised the bottle and drank in the darkness. He listened to the two women breathing and then he began to drift off himself with the fears quieted down for a while. But they always reminded him they were there. They made his body jerk and they made his heart pound. But now he was breathing deeply and he had forgotten where he was. The two women sat up together and looked at him. They nodded to each other, then one of them got up slowly and went to the end of the bed. She held his trousers up and put her hand in the pocket, feeling for the roll. She found it and turned and looked at her companion in triumph. She let her fingers move over the money. Still a good-sized roll, then she took it out and began to count it. They were both smiling. Oh, yeah. They had played this guy exactly right. He was a live one, alright. Then they both jumped as they heard an ear-splitting shriek. They turned around and saw Treacy sitting upright in the bed with his eyes blazing with terror. They both dropped the money and screamed.

"I just wanted to see that you still had your money," one of them said.

"You know there are lots of pickpockets on Broadway," the other chimed in.

His heart was still pounding with fright from his nightmare. He still hadn't realized what was going on. He was looking at them holding his trousers and it slowly came to him what they were up to. He lunged across the room toward them and they screamed. They tried to run from the room with the money but he managed to get to the door before them, then one of them picked up a shoe and was pounding him on the head with it.

He punched her and sent her sprawling. She lay on the floor moaning as her friend cowered in the corner. She picked up the bottle from the night table and threw it at him.

It broke against the wall and the smell of booze filled the room. He put his trousers on quickly, picked up the money, and stuffed it into his pocket. He grabbed his jacket, opened the door, and ran down the stairs into the street.

He walked along quickly. He could feel sweat running down his back and he could feel the scratch marks on his cheeks. He tasted blood in his mouth and he realized his lips were bruised. He kicked over a garbage can and watched the refuse spill all over the sidewalk. It had rained and the streets were wet. He could smell the same smell that always came after it rained. The smell of New York streets. And then he realized he wanted a drink. It was late now and he hoped he could find a place. He was still filled with anger and the voice inside of him was urging him to fuck the first woman that came by. Just pull her into a doorway and fuck her. Shit, they're all the same, anyway. Why the hell should he care now? the voice said. They're all just lookin' to get whatever the hell they can out of you. Just let her have it. Young or old. Let them know who's in charge. All the money you spent on those two bitches and what did you get for it? He was frightened and exhilarated at the same time. He was going to find a woman. He would pull her dress off and fuck her right here in the street. Pull her down an alley. Who the hell would care at this time. Any woman out this late is asking for it.

SIX

Annie sat on the stoop with a group of her friends. They were talking about the party and couldn't wait for Saturday night. One of them had brought a portable radio and they were listening to Allan Fried play rock 'n' roll. They danced with each other and they knew all the words to the songs. They squealed when their favorites came on. They wore saddle shoes and penny loafers and their skin-tight jeans were rolled up to their calves. Some of them wore light cardigans over their blouses and had their hair in ponytails. They shared their lipsticks and they swapped clothes. They combed each other's hair and plucked each other's eyebrows. They screamed and giggled together and they always seemed to be breathless. They couldn't talk fast enough and their time had no connection to the past nor to their parents nor any time that had ever been. Theirs was a new world that had no allegiance to anything that had ever been before. That's the way it was in America.

The summer darkness was coming down and it seemed to mute their voices. The smaller children were still playing on the sidewalks and a group of teenage boys stood together further up the block. They jeered and mocked each other and their laughter and their shouts rose up into the coming darkness. The parents had started calling out to the younger children to come home, and they called back pleading for reprieves. And then they were calling out their good-byes, saying they would see each other tomorrow.

Annie and her friends sat close together in the dark now. They agonized, wondering if the boys would come to where they were. They had whispered their secret crushes and they wanted so much to be noticed. Then at last they came to where they were and they pretended they hadn't noticed them. The boys called out their hellos and the girls answered them casually and didn't look at them. They moved closer together and feigned a deep discussion and a disinterest that was far too important to have them even glance at them.

The boys gathered at the foot of the stoop, laughing and jostling each other, always sneaking glances in the direction of the girls. Charlie Gallucci was with them. Annie had noticed him and purposely didn't look in his direction. She knew he would eventually come to where she sat and ask her to go for a soda with him. And she knew that if she did she would have to fight him off afterward. All the girls were crazy about him and he knew it, but he had his heart set on Annie. They all said he was the cutest guy and they all thought he was so shy. And Annie had wanted to tell them the way he was when he was with her, wanting her to do it with him and putting his hands all over her. But she couldn't and they were always telling her how lucky she was to be going steady with him.

Now he stood apart from the other guys and combed his hair. He held a cigarette between his lips and inhaled, letting the smoke out through his nose. When he was satisfied that his hair was just right he put the small comb back in his pocket and touched it above his forehead several times, flouncing the small curls and making them fall away the way he wanted over his forehead. He walked over to the curb away from the others and glanced toward the girls. He drew deeply on his cigarette and blew smoke rings into the air and watched them as though he had performed magic. And then he turned to the girls as though he was sure they had all been watching and waited for the adulation his performance deserved. He was showing off for Annie as if to let her know he could have any of them he wanted. He was so unsure of her and he searched her out, hoping she would smile down at him. He took the comb from his pocket and began to comb his hair again. And then all the girls were looking down, and he smiled, but then he realized they were looking past him. He turned and saw Toby Walters walking by on the far side of the street. Toby waved briefly, then he was gone.

"What do you want, Charlie?" one of the girls called down. "Do you want all of us? You can have us all if you like." They laughed and Charlie didn't know what to say. Annie was laughing the hardest.

"Hate to disappoint you, girls, but I can only handle one at a time," he said. He took a few steps up the stoop and reached out and took

Annie's hand. He led her down the steps and kissed her quickly at the foot of the stoop. Then he looked up at the others.

"I've got the one I want," he said, and put his arm around her waist. They walked down the street together and Annie looked back at them and smiled. They all waved at her and each of them wished he was walking down the street with them.

No woman had crossed Treacy's path after he left the two hookers. His rage left him and he realized his roll had shrunk. It was getting close to the time when he would have to think of going home. Even in his alcoholic daze he shuddered when he thought of what he might have done that night if some unsuspecting woman had crossed his path. His rage had centered itself in his groin and he had wanted to see the helplessness and the pleading and perhaps the recognition of the terrible madness of what had happened in Korea. The worst part always was that there was no one he could talk to. No one who could really understand. The terrible feeling of uselessness was beginning to come back to him and he couldn't bear to think of what they thought of him in the neighborhood. The booze wasn't doing for him what it used to do. It was all beginning to taste like piss and the kick was gone, but he still kept reaching for the bottle in his back pocket and taking long slugs from it in the desperate hope that somehow the magic would come back. He wandered aimlessly through Times Square and he wanted to find a woman now. Some hooker who would just hold him for a while. She wouldn't have to say anything. Just hold him and let him feel her feminine warmth. He felt the money in his pocket and figured there was just enough left for another bottle and a hooker. It was late now. Even some of the giant neon signs had been turned off and Times Square reminded him of a giant empty cathedral after a high mass. He saw the steam rising from the street like incense and he glanced up at the tops of the buildings that reached up to the early sky of a tired new morning.

The breeze scattered newspapers and Playbills and hot-dog wrappers and he saw the statue of Father Duffy gazing south through the square as though he were looking for something that was never going to come. The hero priest of another war giving absolution to the mortally wounded, then dying alone himself. He still looked alone, distant, so far away like all of the dead, and still Treacy could see all of his buddies' dead faces as he lingered in a doorway and drank desperately from his bottle to make them go away.

They had just turned off the giant Camel sign and he saw the last great smoke propel its way out into the emptiness of the street. He could hear the subway rumble beneath his feet and he thought of going home, but he still wanted that gentle woman who would hold him. He told himself it wasn't too late to find her. It wasn't just the sex. There was something else. Something that came from the deep, deep need for a kind of tenderness that embarrassed him. He was ashamed because he thought that a man was not supposed to feel that way. Or maybe it was that he wanted to find some place, it could be a special bar, an after-hours place where he would never even have to try to explain what was happening inside of him. When he'd walk in everyone would know and the woman he wanted would be there. And she would touch that place in him and he would know how to live again. He felt the warm air rush up into the street through the subway gratings and he could smell the steely piss smell that always came with it. The throngs were long gone home. There was no bustle, no merriment, no excitement. The warm hard night hung down and all the brilliant candles had burned out. He started to walk uptown to a hotel he knew on Fifty-fourth Street where he might be able to get another bottle. And maybe the night manager could find him a hooker, too.

He didn't notice the car pulling alongside him. It moved slowly, keeping pace with him, then he heard a voice calling to him. He turned around and the car had stopped next to him. The voice called again and he walked over to the curb. The driver was smiling at him.

"You lookin' to get laid?" the man asked him. Treacy stared at him. "I can take you to some great bodies."

He kept looking up at him, smiling all the time, his white teeth almost sparkling as he kept his eyes on him.

"Come on. All you gotta do is hop in and I'll take you there. Ten minutes from here over on Tenth. And look, I'm not talkin' 'bout colored chicks. Beautiful young white dolls, man. Closest thing you ever goin' to find to a virgin."

He wanted a drink, but the possibility of a woman excited him, especially since he had almost given up.

"Come on," the guy said again. "No kiddin'—have you there in five minutes."

Treacy looked him square in the face and hesitated for a second, then walked around and got into the car. He sat in the front seat and he immediately thought of jumping out.

The guy stuck his hand out. "Clyde Best," he said. Treacy shook his hand reluctantly.

The guy had never stopped smiling. It was as though he knew everything that was going on inside of Treacy. He was in his late twenties and his handsome black face had a kindness in it. He looked Treacy straight in the eye. They sped across Forty-second Street toward the river. Treacy wanted a drink badly. His mouth was dry and he was nervous.

He hated the feeling and he wondered if he should really go where this guy was taking him. Should've gone to the hotel and gotten a bottle, he told himself. They were close to the river now and he wondered when they would stop. They were under the West Side Highway now on the old cobbled streets. The river was directly ahead of them, its dark expanse reaching across to New Jersey where the lights were twinkling above the darkness. A tugboat moved silently down the river, its running lights red in the gloom. They turned away from the river into another cobbled street where there seemed to be nothing but warehouses. They could hear the rumble of traffic on the highway. Treacy was looking for the lights of a gin mill or an after-hours place but he saw nothing. Then Clyde pulled the car over and parked. He turned to Treacy. "I'm going to make sure they're there," he said. He got out of the car and Treacy watched him walking up the steps of a lonely-looking brownstone that was squeezed between a factory and a warehouse. He saw Clyde push the door open and disappear inside. He hoped it wouldn't be too long before he came back. He was trying to stay awake now and he needed a drink. He leaned back in the seat, closed his eyes, and dozed off. When he opened them again he didn't know where he was, then he remembered Clyde. He still hadn't come back. He heard the whistle of a tugboat on the river and he heard the sound of railroad cars shunting in the West Side freight yards. The street was even darker now and looked as though no one had walked up or down it for a hundred years. And now all he wanted was a drink. He just wanted Clyde to come back so that he could go find a bottle. Then suddenly Clyde was opening the door on the other side and got back in the car.

"We were too late," he said. "They've all been taken."

Treacy nodded.

"I'm really sorry, man."

"I need a drink. Just hope I can find a drink. The booze is getting to be like the ladies. Just can't rely on it anymore."

"Well, at least I can help find you a bottle."

Treacy turned his head and looked at Clyde.

"When the booze stops working for me, then I just wanna die. That would be the best thing. All my buddies died young. I'm the only one left. And they keep talking to me and telling me they want me to go with them. 'The endless report that grows out of the silence of those who die young.' Read that somewhere. They keep asking me how come they're all dead and I'm still here. And they won't leave me alone."

"You okay?" Clyde asked him.

"Just need a drink. Or some lady to hold me tight so that I can feel I'm not gonna die."

"I know what you mean."

He reached over and put his arm around Treacy's shoulder and he started to talk to him in a low soothing voice. "I'm really sorry all the women are gone. I really know how you feel. Believe me, I really do. My brother was in the war. All screwed up. We don't even know where he is now."

He moved closer to Treacy and now his head was resting on Clyde's shoulder. He kept talking to him as if he were a child, letting his voice become softer, then he put his hand on Treacy's thigh. He paused to see if his expression had changed. His hand was moving slowly back and forth on Treacy's thigh and he was leaning back in his seat with his eyes still closed and his breathing was becoming deeper. He began to feel himself relax and he slowly stretched his legs out as far as they would go. Clyde had moved even closer and now he had both of his arms around him and his head was resting on his cheek. He pulled Treacy to him and held him tightly and then he felt the weight of Treacy lean into him. They were holding each other now and they could hear each other's breathing. They heard the faint whistle of a tugboat again as if the world was reminding it was still out there, and there was the continuous sound of the traffic on the West Side Highway. The dull hum of the ceaseless flow of traffic that had to be set in motion by God Himself and would surely run for all eternity.

Clyde moved his hands inside of Treacy's shirt and opened it, baring his chest. Then he began to slowly kiss his nipples. Treacy wanted to tell him to stop but he heard himself sigh and he began to feel the warmth passing through him. He was surprised that it could feel so good and he knew he wasn't supposed to feel that way. He wondered if maybe he was queer. Oh God, maybe that's the problem. Oh Jesus! I don't want to be queer, he thought. What if anyone found out? But still it felt so good. So gentle. And it was a man that was making him feel this way. And now his hands around Clyde's head pulling him down to him. He felt himself letting go; Clyde's hands were on his fly and his head was between his legs and he could feel his mouth around him and he had to fight to keep himself from coming right away. Oh yes, he thought. This is what I wanted. It doesn't matter who it is. Just to let go. To feel Clyde's hands move over his body. He was moving with him now and he could feel the delicious warmth washing over him. He heard himself gasp and shudder and he had to stifle the scream that was in his throat and the rich balm of release coursed through him. He opened his eyes and watched as Clyde moved away and opened the door to spit into the street. He watched him wipe his mouth with a hand-kerchief. Then he closed his fly as Clyde started the car, they were heading back toward Times Square. They didn't talk. Treacy kept wanting to say something but he couldn't find the words.

They came to the square and Clyde reached across him and opened the door. Treacy looked at him. He didn't know what to do. He stuck his hand out and Clyde grasped it; they stared at each other for an instant, then Treacy left. He watched the car drive away and almost immediately the loneliness began to come over him again.

He began to feel ashamed. He wanted to go home but he wanted a drink first. He began to feel that they would know what he had done with Clyde. He dug his hands deep into his pockets and started to walk toward the hotel on Fifty-fourth Street. Get a bottle from the night manager. Always had bottles he could sell. Nearly everyone in that place is on a bender. That's how he makes a few bucks. Doesn't charge much over, either. Decent guy. Jesus, hope he has one left. What the hell time is it? Clyde's face came back to him as he walked. The soft smile. The white teeth and the softness in his eyes. He wished they could have stayed together. And then he felt bad for feeling good about it. "What the fuck's the matter with me?" he asked out loud.

SEVEN

D on't buy a present for me," Annie told Toby. "Who would I say it's from? I'd have to hide it." He held her close and looked into her face.

"You know, for someone so smart you really are dumb. What about something you could wear around your neck? You could keep it inside all the time and no one would ever know it was there except you and me." He reached into his pocket and pulled out a small box. "How about something like this. I didn't have time to have it wrapped." He placed it in her hand and even before she opened it she kissed him.

"Open it," he told her.

She lifted the top off the box and gazed down at a small silver Celtic cross and chain. She glanced up quickly at Toby, then looked at the cross again.

"Oh, Toby, I love it, I love it, and I love you."

"Why don't you put it on."

She opened the clasp and held the chain toward him. He took it and placed it around her neck. She held the cross between her fingers.

"I love it," she said again, and she reached out for him and he held her and they kissed.

They were in their secret place in the park. It was dusk and the light was just beginning to fade. "I don't know what to say," she whispered.

"Take a look at the back of it," he told her.

She held it out in front of her and turned it over. It said *Love Forever Toby.*

"I wanted you to have something that came from me so you can look at it and always think of me." She removed the plain ring from her finger and handed it to him.

"No, no, please, you don't have to," he said. "Besides, what would I do with it?"

"You could put it on a chain and wear it around your neck, dummy!"

They held each other and it felt as though the world had gone away and they were the only two people anywhere. They swayed on their feet, moving in a rhythm that came from deep inside them. The darkness was nearly complete now and they were sitting under their tree. Her head was resting on his shoulder. "I want you to come to the party," she said quietly. He held her hand and shook his head.

"It's no good. I just couldn't stand to see you hanging around Charlie all night."

"It's harder for me. All I do is think of you when I'm with him. Why can't we just be together. They make up all sorts of rules and reasons but it's all crazy. None of it makes any sense."

He held her close and kissed her softly.

"I still wish you'd come. It's not as if you've just moved into the neighborhood. You were born here, for God's sake. You have been here forever."

"Things have changed. I'm not a little boy anymore. I'm closer to being a man. When I was a cute little boy there was no problem. They don't come out and call me nigger, but I can feel it. I was never a nigger to 'em, but now I am. And a lot of 'em don't like that I got the scholarship. I'm not one of them and I never will be. I have no illusions about that. I don't care. I'm a full-grown colored guy, get it? And it wasn't just a football scholarship. It was for academics, too. I had to have the high grade average before I got it. For some reason I'm supposed to turn down chances like that. A black guy good at math and science? Why Toby Walters? Black guys ain't supposed to be smart. They'd all feel a lot better if I was pushing a cart in the Garment District. They've put a lot of space around me now. And when the colored and the Spanish began to move closer to the neighborhood the space around me got even bigger. They're just waiting for something to happen with me. Believe me. They'd just love to find out about us, so I ain't gonna risk it going to the party. Jeez, who knows, maybe they know already. I just don't wanna give 'em a chance to start something. I mean, what about that guy that maybe saw us coming out of the park?"

"I don't think he saw us. God, I don't even want to think about him."

She pulled him closer. "When will it be different? Will we ever be able to get away from here together? What's gonna happen?"

"We'll make it. We just have to be careful, that's all. When we get away to school it'll be different. We'll be able to have a lot more time together in the city. It's gonna be alright. Just hold on a little while longer. You just have to believe it's not always gonna be like this for us. You'll see."

Sheila Dolan was surprised when Mrs. Dahlgren called to invite her and her husband to Red and Annie's party. She was Sheila Cope now, but everyone from the neighborhood still called her Sheila Dolan. Her husband Harry's parents still lived in the same brownstone as Mrs. Dahlgren. They had all known each other for years. Mrs. Dahlgren always had a soft spot for Sheila and wanted her at the party for sure. She hadn't thought to ask Red if it was okay with him. She was sure he wouldn't mind. And she wanted Sheila to see Margo.

She wanted to be able to sit with her and ask her what she thought of Margo, and somewhere within her she still held on to the idea that it might be possible for Red and Sheila to finally be able to get together. She still prayed for it and she always told herself that with God all things were possible. She never liked Harry, even though she had known him since he was a little boy. There was something about him, she always said, and she was still mystified as to why Sheila had married him. She had never accepted them being together. It just never seemed right to her.

When Sheila told Harry about the invitation to Red and Annie's party, he told her he wasn't going but if she wanted to go it was alright. She told him the only reason she wanted to go was that Mrs. Dahlgren had asked her. "I've always liked her," she said. "And she has always been nice to me. She sent us a beautiful gift, remember? She didn't have to do that. I'm not going to go by myself."

She was pregnant with their first child and she was close to term. Her belly rose up like a mountain and when she lay down in bed she could feel the baby kick. She often took Harry's hand and held it over her stomach. He was always reluctant to do it, and it bothered her. She never asked him to tell her why it was hard for him. And now he lay back with his hands clasped behind his head staring at the ceiling. She turned toward him and touched his face with her hand.

"Please come with me," she asked him. "It's Annie's birthday party, too, and I've known her since she was a little girl." And Harry remembered how amazed he was that last time he had seen her. He hadn't seen her for a while and he couldn't get over how much she had grown. She was beautiful. She was wearing her school uniform, the Black Watch plaid skirt and the white socks and the white blouse. He noticed how her young breasts strained against the blouse and she was wearing just a touch of lipstick. He couldn't take his eyes off her. She had smiled at him when she realized he was looking at her. Her beautiful young face was lit up with her smile and her blue eyes sparkled with joy and fun. Her blond hair fell evenly down on either side of her face, touching her shoulders.

She had waved at him as she walked by him with a group of girls all on the way home from school, and his eyes followed her as she walked down the street. He was surprised when she turned around and waved at him once more and smiled her lovely smile. Sheila still held him closely and told him once more that she wouldn't go to the party without him. "Please come with me," she whispered. He was still remembering Annie. There was no doubt about it, she had an air about her. Even in her school uniform she showed a sophistication and a confidence as though she knew of a world that was far beyond the neighborhood. There was no reticence in her. She was open, it seemed, and he had wanted to stop and talk to her.

"I'll think about it," he told Sheila. "You know I'm not crazy about that whole crowd. They still haven't forgiven me for marrying you. And the truth is I've never been one of 'em even when we were kids. Why should I give a damn about Red and the crowd from Kerrigan's. You know they're going to be there. Another excuse for them all to get drunk. As if they ever needed an excuse."

"We won't stay long," Sheila said. "I just want to bring Annie a little gift. I'm only going because Mrs. Dahlgren asked me. I don't care what they all think about you or me. You just know they're all jealous of us. They can't stand that we moved away from the neighborhood and bought ourselves a house. I always knew you were not like them, Harry. That's what I liked best about you. You were always a go-getter and you always treated me like I deserved the best." She leaned over and kissed him. He turned toward her and she could feel his hardness against her.

It had been a while since they had made love. She was being very careful about the baby because she had had two miscarriages already and she was so afraid it would happen again. When he tried to move against her she moved away, and he sulked and turned his back on her. She reached across to him and he wouldn't respond. Then she cradled his head on her swollen breasts.

"You're right, Sheila," he whispered. "They're all jealous of us. Goddamn jealous. So let's go there."

"And do you know the nicest part?" Sheila said. "We can leave whenever we want to and then we can drive home together to our own home. Just us, Harry, and we can leave them all behind. They'll never have what we have, and when we have the baby it'll be everything we wanted."

EIGHT

Mrs. Dahlgren always seemed so sure of herself and she made it hard for anyone to see her sadness. She was the manager of an exclusive little antique shop next to the St. Regis just off Fifth Avenue. She had started to work there during the war when her husband couldn't hold a job anymore. He was in and out of hospitals and institutions and his liver was gone. He was sneaking drinks even after the doctors had told him that if he continued to drink he would die. He just couldn't stop. She had long since stopped pleading with him, because she knew it was useless. And she became the sole support for the family. Some rich Park Avenue ladies had opened an antique shop where their friends could donate things and get a tax write-off and all the proceeds went to war relief. She had started wrapping packages and doing the heavy work in the store, but before long she was running the place. The ladies loved her and were thrilled that they had found a "jewel." Mrs. Dahlgren had learned to dress like them and she was even beginning to talk like them. Her accent was still unmistakably Irish, but now there was a touch of upper-class Dublin in it, which endeared her even more to the ladies and their society friends. She had learned to appreciate antiques and over the years had decorated her home with lovely pieces that had come her way through the shop. These were all pieces they couldn't get rid of or had no room for. She had developed an eye for a good piece and she had a flair for decorating. She had learned how to put a room together and she was proud of the new life she had made for herself.

She loved to write the nuns back in Ireland about herself and the shop and all the wonderful things she had discovered in herself. She told them of all the important people she had met and all of the fashionable homes she had been in. There was more than a bit of the snob in her and it seemed to come very naturally. It gave her great pleasure to demonstrate to her friends just how a home should be decorated, and she loved to sit among them and listen to the compliments that came to her. They really admired the way she had turned her life around since the death of her husband. It was as if she had gone to some finishing school late in life, and she wondered how it was possible for these talents to have lain dormant in her for so long. Her friends really liked her and even tolerated her airs. They went with the territory. They were after all still working in Schrafft's and she had been moved into another world entirely, far from the life she had had with Pete Dahlgren.

Annie and her mother got up early on the Saturday morning of the party. They were determined that everything be perfect. The apartment sparkled, the lace curtains were spotlessly white and moved gently in the cool breeze coming through the open windows. The doilies were positioned perfectly on the back of the chairs and the delicate antique coffee table in the living room had decorator magazines carefully placed on it; the glass-doored bookcases were filled with leather-bound editions of ancient tomes that looked as though they hadn't been open for hundreds of years. There were figurines and knickknacks placed around the room. There was no doubt that Mrs. Dahlgren had the loveliest living room in the neighborhood, and she was glad of the opportunity to show it off, especially to Margo's people. She would just as soon not have Red's friends from Kerrigan's, and she expected Margo's people to be common because they were Italians.

Red was anxious, too. He hoped there would be no friction between Margo's people and his own. Margo had told him she cared less how they all liked each other. "It's you and me," she said. "We don't have to live with them, thank God." Red had taken her to Ebbets Field that afternoon. Despite the rumors that the Dodgers were leaving at the end of the season, the ballpark was full. Everyone was sure they would stay in Brooklyn no matter what it took to keep them there. All the powers would come together and everyone would agree that the sacrilege of extracting the Dodgers from Brooklyn would just never come to pass. It would be like moving the Statue of Liberty to Charleston, South Carolina.

They sat together behind first base and Red had his arm around her. They were both drinking from the same container of beer. Red knew for sure as he looked out over the beautiful green of the infield that he probably would never be as happy in his life as he was right then. He was almost afraid to take it in. His father had brought him to his first game when he was a little boy and he still felt the very same sensation that came to him when he looked out over the field for the first time. There was something sacred, clean, clear, and unchanging about the symmetry of the ballpark and the way the crowd sat around it. He thought of his father and the smell of beer brought back the memory of the same smell on his father's breath. There were times when it used to make him feel afraid. But when he was with his father in the ballpark there was never anything to be afraid of.

His father used to tell him stories about the great ballplayers and the great games of the past. Ducky Medwick and Casey Stengel and Uncle Wilbert Robinson and the Daffiness Boys. There was even a game where three Dodgers wound up on third base at the same time. But they weren't daffy anymore. They won the pennant nearly every year now and everybody expected them to. There was no doubt about it. Over the last ten years they were the best they had ever been and two years before they had won the World Series. Beat the Yankees. And Brooklyn went crazy and came together in a way nobody ever thought it could. These were the good times. Why anyone would think of moving the team just didn't make any sense. That's what Red told Margo. There was something in the ballpark that was so separate from the world of the streets. This old ballpark had seen so many changes over the years. Wars and depressions and generations of men and women growing up and maturing around it and sometimes getting their only sense of security and belonging from that ballpark. It was always more than the team and wins and losses. There has to be some permanence. Something that is not going to change just for the sake of changing. And so much was changing now in ways nobody ever would have thought. But no matter what was going on in the world, the game and the old ballpark would always be the same in the very heart of the place that was all around it. Time could stand still in the park and you could feel everything that had ever happened there in the field and in the stands surrounding it. There was a joy. It was about people coming together for something they loved. Something they were sure of. Where you could laugh and shout and call out to your friends. In the ballpark they were all together. Strangers said hello to each other and became friends at least until the game was over. You could have a conversation with a guy you never met before but you knew he was just like you. Decent guys. Everyone's heart seemed to be in the right place. Black guys, too. and there was the feeling you got that you wanted to take outside with you after the game. He remembered his father telling him that the thing about Brooklyn was that everyone came from another place. Parents or grandparents. He had never met his grandparents but he knew they were from Sweden, and his father had promised him that one day he would take him there. They were all immigrants together in Brooklyn, but in the ballpark they were all Americans. There were only two things his father told him he didn't like to see in the ballpark. A smart-ass and a show-off. And he said he didn't like 'em outside the ballpark, either. "Stay away from a smart-ass and never watch a show-off," he said.

Red was never a deep thinker. He always said that, but as he sat with Margo he felt happy in a way he had never felt before. He kept glancing at her as if he had to convince himself that she was really sitting next to him and that she wanted to marry him. He knew that he wanted everything to always be the way it was that Saturday afternoon in the ballpark. He stared out at the field and the afternoon sun lit up the spectacle. The Dodger players, tanned lithe and handsome in their home white uniforms, struck their defensive positions at every pitch, their energy waiting to explode in action, the instant of extreme tension repeated over and over again. He watched them spit and kick the dirt and call out secret instructions to one another with their gloves held up to their faces. And he knew somewhere in his heart that there would always be an uneasiness at the bottom of his joy. He turned to look at Margo again and he heard the crack of a bat hitting the ball; the crowd roared and jumped to its feet and he jumped up, too, pulling Margo up with him. Then he watched Furrillo make the catch near the fence and turn to throw the runner out at third. He made it look so easy, then he simply turned and took up his position again. Workmanlike. Did his job like any good tradesman. That was the way it was supposed to be. Professional. They all sat down again, and he held Margo's hand and she kissed him on the cheek, and he put his arm around her and pulled her close. Her parents were coming to the party along with some of her relatives and they had laughed about the Italians meeting the Irish.

"I just want the time to go by so we can get married and get away from here," she said. "I really don't care about the party. I just want you and me to be together and take off for California."

"Don't bring that up around my mother. She'll try to talk us out of it. When we're ready to go we'll just go."

Margo nodded.

He had been on stakeout again the night before, sitting with his partner in an unmarked car. It had been raining softly and they could see the lights of Manhattan across the river. There was hardly any sound, almost a dead silence, and he began to feel anxious. It wasn't about the job. His stomach had tightened with a fear that just seemed to come from nowhere and he couldn't put his finger on what he was afraid of. Even when he and his partner talked, they had whispered as if they were afraid someone would hear them. They had sat in the car in the same spot for many nights now and it was hard to stay alert. Red could feel a film of sweat on his forehead.

Why should I be afraid now, he had asked himself. Just when everything is going so well. Annie is graduating, and Margo and me are going to get married. But still the anxiety took him and he even began to breathe faster. He lit a cigarette to cover it from his partner. There was the feeling that something was going to happen. What the hell could happen, he asked himself. He wanted to reach out to his partner and tell him what was happening, but he was afraid he would think he was crazy. There was something stirring in the pit of his stomach like a dead weight that had come from nowhere. It made him feel weak and he fought to shake it off. He didn't want to feel it and he didn't want to hear what it was trying to tell him.

And in the ballpark it was still there.

He was able to ignore it most of the time, and he told himself it was just nerves. He wanted to tell Margo about it, but he was sure she would think he was crazy, too. Last night, like all the other nights of the stakeout, nothing had happened, and when the first light of daybreak came creeping in, he and his partner had driven away. The feeling had stayed with him and he had tried to ignore it. He convinced himself he was just nervous about the engagement party and he thought of California and the orange trees and the beaches and the brightness and the whole new life that lay ahead of them so far away from Brooklyn.

NINE

It looked like the whole neighborhood had squeezed itself into Mrs. Dahlgren's apartment for the party. It truly was a neighborhood occasion, one of those nights when it would be a dishonor not to be a part of it. There was the feeling with the way things were going in the neighborhood that it might be one of the last great parties. That was the feeling of the crowd from Kerrigan's.

"Who the hell knows where the hell we'll all be next year or who we might have to live next to," Raguso said.

It was more than a party. It was almost like a reunion or a rally or just a gathering of those who had lived and grown up together for so long. And Annie looked as though she had become a woman overnight. Even her mother found it hard to stop looking at her because she was embarrassed by the tightness of her dress. She was sorry now she had let her wear it. It hadn't looked so tight when she was trying it on. It was pure white satin and now it clung to her. It was cut low and her young breasts burst forth like spring flowers, sensuous and innocent at the same time. She had never looked more beautiful. Mrs. Dahlgren felt the tears in her eyes because she knew that her daughter was gone from her. And it was only now that she realized how beautiful she was. She wore white high-heeled pumps, which gave her an elegance, and her legs beautiful and straight were classic like a ballet dancer's. Her lovely blond hair was done up in a French twist and she wore the single-strand pearl necklace Red had given her when she won the scholarship. One of the older women said she looked like Grace Kelly and someone else said she was more beautiful than Grace Kelly. Her face seemed to glow and her eyes sparkled. She wished Toby could see her. She was only thinking of him when she had dressed and done her hair. It was as though she had been waiting all her life for this transformation to take place. People always said she was a beautiful girl, but tonight she became a beautiful woman. She had surprised even those who knew her well. She had come out of nowhere and they were all awed at this wonderful and unexpected emergence.

But it was Charlie Gallucci who was proudest of all, and he wouldn't let her out of his sight. He wanted to take her away from the party and be alone with her. He danced with her and was trying to fight off anyone who had the same inclination. He found it hard to believe she was actually his girl and the broad smile never left his face. He held her as close as she would let him and his heart was beating with excitement. It was the happiest night of his life. Kerrigan was in the kitchen acting as bartender. His relief man was on duty at his place and all of the crowd were present. Kerrigan's Bar and Grill would be very empty this night. Raguso came into the kitchen and asked him if he was charging for drinks. "They're free to everyone except you," he said. "And don't hang around me tonight. I want to try and enjoy myself. It's rare I get a night off. I want to make the best of it. You always remind me of just how lousy I feel, so for God's sake stay away from me."

"Fuck you, Kerrigan!" Bobby said, and he stomped out of the kitchen. Kerrigan doubled over and some of the others came in and asked Kerrigan what he had done to Raguso. There was loud laughter from the kitchen and Raguso glared over, wondering why they were always picking on him.

Mrs. Dahlgren had asked the monsignor to come by, but he had a very important affair he had to attend in Manhattan and he had Father Darcy go in his place. "They like to see a priest on these occasions," he had explained. "It's a matter of putting in an appearance. Showing the collar, so to speak. You don't have to stay. Have a drink and a sandwich and leave. It will be an opportunity for you to see they're not so bad after all."

"From what I hear, I'm sure I'll put a damper on the evening," Darcy said.

"Father," the Monsignor said. "With all the booze that will be flowing there, even the Pope himself couldn't put a damper on it. You'll be perfectly safe, I guarantee it."

Rock 'n' roll music rose over the party, and Annie and her friends were dancing slowly in the middle of the living room. The falsetto voice of the singer was filled with a strange pleading:

> *Earth angel, earth angel*
> *please be mine.*
> *My darling dearest*
> *love me all the time . . .*

There was a feminine sweetness in the voice and it seemed to come from some magical place where they would never have to grow up. They moved slowly on the floor and held each other tightly as though they were trying to keep out the reality of the world of their parents. There was much more than a generation separating them. The world was going to be a very different place for them. They were looking for a revolution they didn't even know of yet, but they knew that it was going to be different for them. They were feeling the hubris of the newness of their own discovery that they could make life anything they wanted it to be. It was going to be different, that was for sure. They could feel the eyes of the elders on them, and they moved even closer and swayed sensuously.

"Goddamn nigger music!" Kerrigan said. "Jesus, they might as well take their clothes off. They don't leave anything to the imagination. I've never seen anything like it."

Dooney Hanifan laughed at him. "For Christ's sake, Kerrigan! For a lapsed Catholic you're an awful prude."

"I'm no lapsed Catholic, you sonofabitch. I go to the seven o'clock mass every Sunday whether I need to or not. I mean, my God, it's like they're havin' each other right there on the floor."

"Look what happens to you when you get close to some lovelies. You fall apart," Dooney said. "You better not get any closer, you're liable to have a fit."

Kerrigan stomped off to the kitchen, and Dooney moved toward the dancers and tapped Charlie Gallucci on the shoulder. He had his cheek resting against Annie's and he looked up as though he had been startled from a dream. He looked at Dooney as though he didn't know where he came from. Annie smiled at him and reached her arm out to resume the dance, and Charlie stood bewildered, looking after them as they moved away.

And then Margo made her entrance. She led her parents and her relatives through the crowd directly to where Mrs. Dahlgren was sitting. She reached out and pulled her to her feet and hugged her as if they were the oldest friends in the world. She kissed her on the cheek, and Mrs. Dahlgren, not to be outdone in front of her parents, returned the kiss. Then they both turned around, and Margo began to make the introductions. Mrs. Dahlgren kept glancing at Margo as though she couldn't believe what she had done. She greeted Margo's parents with a handshake and her most beguiling smile, then each of the relatives stepped formally as though they were ambassadors presenting their papers.

Mrs. Dahlgren had a way of intimidating people through the regality of her bearing. The antique shop had been a wonderful training ground and the Park Avenue ladies had a willing pupil. She had her hair done at the St. Regis. It cost a fortune, but she hadn't told anyone. It was swept back in that timeless way that only the richest women seemed to be able to achieve, and she wore a black cocktail dress one of the ladies had given her, so simple and so elegant. And like Annie she wore pearls, but hers were a double strand her husband had given her many years before.

Margo's father was a handsome man, tall and dark with black wavy hair turning gray. Her mother was small, with her jet-black hair held together in a bun. She had kind eyes and a lovely smile. She glanced at her husband often as though she were very proud of him, and he always glanced back at her as though he were trying to reassure her. Margo looked like her father and Red knew where her confidence came from. Red had quickly noticed that his mother had assumed her upper-class Dublin accent. There was no doubt she was trying to impress them, and he watched her lead her guests to seats. She sat Margo's parents on the beautiful pale green and white-striped couch she had brought home from the shop and attended them closely, asking them what they would like to drink.

The music had stopped and everyone was looking toward Margo's people. They were in a group by themselves looking very uncomfortable, whispering as though they were afraid to let themselves be heard. Margo's father produced a long black cigar and lit up. The thick smoke wafted across the room, and Kerrigan's crowd were nudging each other. Word had gone out that he was a big guy in the Mob. They all had their eyes on him, wondering if it was true. His suit was expensive. No doubt about that, and Dooney had noticed that his shoes were very expensive, too. And Raguso had whispered that the cigar was no guinea stinker. It had to cost a couple of bucks at least, he said. And Raguso got pissed off because he said it was awful that anyone with an Italian name who had money was always considered to be in the Mob. He said he was getting sick of it. And Dooney told him to shut the fuck up. "What about all the Irish being drunks?" he said.

"Well it's true, isn't it?" Rags said. And Dooney lunged toward him, and the others had to hold him back. Kerrigan told them in a loud whisper to remember where they were.

"Jesus, don't go spoiling this thing for Red," he pleaded. Dooney had calmed down now, and he nodded toward Margo's father. "Look at him," he said. "Don't tell me he ain't a wise guy. And look at the relatives. Jesus, I wouldn't want to meet any of 'em in a dark alley."

"Smartest thing Red could do is to marry into a Mob family," Charlie Wallace said. "Jeez, the guy won't have to worry for the rest of his life. And with Margo being an only child, the old man gets the son he always wanted."

Kerrigan laughed and shook his head. "You guys are way off base. The guy is a contractor. Red told me himself. He's no more in the Mob than Rags here is. He wants Red to go to work for him. Wants to buy 'em a house and all. But Margo don't want any of it. She won't take a thing from him except money." They started to laugh. "Yeah, Red said she's got him twisted around her little finger."

The music started again with a slow number and Margo pulled Red onto the floor. She wrapped herself around him, and they moved together in a gyrating shuffle. This was the new dance called the Fish, and she leaned back and pulled Red into her. Then she moved toward him, and he leaned back, and they moved against each other. Margo didn't care who was watching or what they were thinking. She pulled him as close to her as she could and she kissed him in the lips as though she were staking claim to him in public for all to see. Kerrigan's crowd looked on and there was applause and hoots and whistles of approval.

The dance was over, but Margo held on to Red. She turned to them and smiled and waved. The music started up again and they moved around the floor. Red blushed with embarrassment, but still he knew they would all want to be in his place. Who didn't want a girl like Margo? He was uneasy about his mother seeing them like this. He didn't want her to think he was being disrespectful. He saw her looking toward them. Her face bore no expression but was set in the way that Red knew always hid her feelings. Her Irish look of hidden martyrdom. He hated that look because he knew it so well and he knew it was the face of judgment. She was letting him know she was disappointed in him. She had wanted him to go to college when he came home from Korea. "God knows," she told him. "You have a great opportunity and it won't cost you anything with the GI Bill."

But he went on the cops, always telling her it was just temporary, just something to do for a while. But it was five years, and she was sure there was no likelihood of him ever doing anything else. And now there was Margo. She had wanted to be able to write home to the nuns that her son was going to college, but he had become a cop just like so many of the Irish. There was nothing wonderful in that. He had let her down and now he's out there on the floor in her own house making a show of himself with that girl. And now here they were in her house with all of her Irish friends. Many of them had been in the convent with her in Galway and they had raised their children together, and she felt it a blow that Red had not gone to college like so many of their sons and daughters. They were the Old Guard and they had shared so many of their joys and sorrows over the years. They all knew of the life she had had with Pete Dahlgren and they were so proud of the way she had made a life for herself and her children after he died. And they all knew that the biggest disappointment for her was that Red and Sheila Dolan had not been married. And she wanted to turn the clock back to the time before Red and Treacy had gone into the Marines. Every girl in the neighborhood was running after them. When they walked down the street in their dress blues, it was like they had the world by the tail and they could do anything they wanted to. They would do wonderful things, everything everyone expected them to.

But Red ended up on the cops and Treacy only came out of his mother's house to get drunk. They were never the same after they came back from Korea. Mrs. Dahlgren hated the sound of the name.

Kerrigan's crowd stuck together as though they were all still in the bar. They watched Father Darcy make his way through the crowd and being greeted by Mrs. Dahlgren. She went toward him as if he were a young prince and her face lit up when she was close to him. "I'm so glad you could come, Father," she said.

"I'm afraid I'm a very poor substitute for the monsignor," he told her.

"Oh, not at all, Father. Not at all. We are very glad to have you."

The Irish women gathered around him, beaming. He looked embarrassed, smiling back at them, nodding his head as though he were taking in everything they said. Then Kerrigan appeared as though from nowhere and winked at him.

"Excuse me, ladies," he said. "I've got some church business to discuss with Father Darcy. Do you mind if I take him away for a minute?" They all nodded and moved aside as Kerrigan maneuvered him to the kitchen.

"Can I get you a drink, Father?" he asked.

"I'd love a Scotch if you have it."

"Will White Horse do? I brought it myself."

"That would be great."

"Would that be on the rocks, Father, or would you like a little soda?"

"Little soda, please."

A rock 'n' roll saxophone wailed and the slow incessant beat boomed out. The dancers moved slowly, holding each other closely, their eyes closed as though they were in prayer. Kerrigan placed the drink on the counter before the priest.

"Looks like the whole neighborhood is here," Darcy said.

"Only those who count, Father, and I don't mean in God's eyes." Darcy smiled.

"Whose eyes, Mr. Kerrigan?"

"Our eyes, Father. That's the way it is."

"What about me? Do I pass muster?"

"You're here, aren't you?"

"I was sent here by the monsignor. I didn't have any say in the matter and to tell you the truth I wasn't looking forward to it."

"Why is that, Father?"

"Well, I know my sermon wasn't received too well last Sunday. How do they say it in show business. It appears I laid an egg." He sipped his drink, and he realized the others in the kitchen were listening to him and Kerrigan. He looked at them and nodded in acknowledgment of their stares. He could feel their hostility; he felt he had been set up by Kerrigan and he was annoyed with him. He wanted to get out of the kitchen without making it look as though they had run him. "But I know, Mr. Kerrigan, that you are much closer to the people than I am, so maybe you know more about their reaction than I do."

"Well, Father, I've learned from my experience behind the bar that attacking a situation head-on is not always the wise approach."

"Maybe you missed your calling, Mr. Kerrigan."

"As a matter of fact, I keep a collar behind the bar for emergencies. Suppose you could say I've given the last rites to many a guy who passed out. But they always come to sooner or later, so I could also put in a claim for raising the dead. But of course I'm only a bartender."

"I think you're a lot more than that."

"You do?"

"Yes. You found your true calling, Mr. Kerrigan, and there's a lot to be said for that. Most people never do."

"Then I'm truly lucky."

"You are indeed. It's a great thing to be able to go through life with that kind of certainty. To have that kind of sureness."

"And are you not sure, Father?"

Darcy moved the glass in his hand and watched the liquid rotate as the ice tinkled. Then he put the glass to his lips and finished his drink.

"Well, Mr. Kerrigan, let me just say that I have my moments of clarity. Getting them to last longer is the trick. But much as I would like to chat some more, must make my good-byes and get back to the parish house. As uncertain as I am sometimes when people are in trouble, they don't want to hear my problems."

"The saloon is nearly always open, Father. Come in and have a drink sometime."

"Good night, then."

Father Darcy walked back into the living room and shook hands with Red and Margo. Annie came to where he stood and he smiled at her. She looked directly into his face and Charlie hung back. And then Mrs. Dahlgren stepped forward and urged him to stay a little longer.

"I'd love to, but I have to get back. The monsignor is away, as you know."

"Well, thank you for coming, Father. I'll hope you'll come to the wedding."

"I will for sure."

He bowed his head toward them and left. He was glad to leave. The Kerrigan crowd really annoyed him. They think I'm some sort of a joke, he thought. He knew that Kerrigan was trying to show him up. He was very good at what he did and he had some sort of power over the others. That was obvious. Then he wondered if he should have preached that sermon. Nothing he could do about it now. It was out there and he couldn't take it back. Besides, all I told them was the truth, he told himself.

TEN

They were gathered around Red and Margo now. Red knew they envied him because Margo was the kind of woman they all wanted. There was no need to tell them he was getting laid. He knew they could tell. She stood with her arm around him and he held her close. He relished the envy and the attention. "Why the hell didn't you bring some girls?" she asked them. "What's the matter? You all queer or something?" They bowed their heads and smiled back at her. "And I see you drove the one good-looking guy that was here outta the place. What did you do to that priest, Kerrigan? Jeez, I coulda gone for him myself. Look at my girlfriend Frances over there. She's lookin' to meet some guy. Red told her about all the good-lookin' guys around here. None of you even danced with her yet."

"How about a dance with you, Margo," Dooney asked. "I just wanna prove to you that I ain't queer."

"What do you say, Red," she asked. "Think I ought to take a chance with this guy?"

"Sure, go ahead. Dooney's harmless," he said.

"Well, we'll see about that," she said, laughing.

They watched them move onto the floor. Margo pulled him close and he leaned into her. She winked at them and Dooney placed his head next to her cheek. When they turned again Dooney smiled at them and closed his eyes and shook his head.

"I want one just like her," he called out to them.

"You're too small," Raguso shouted. "You need a stepladder. You have to find someone your own size."

"Oh no," Dooney called back. "It's gotta be someone just like Margo or I'm turnin' queer."

He moved with her across the floor. He was the best dancer; she moved with him and they did some fancy steps and everyone applauded. He flung her out and she turned expertly and he pulled her back into him. She glanced at Red and smiled. She was really enjoying the dance, but she steered Dooney back to where Red stood and she took his hand and pulled him onto the floor. She pulled him close and kissed him on the lips.

"See, that's the difference," Kerrigan said. "When a woman really wants you, man, there's nothing in the world like it. You could dance with her all night, Dooney, but she'll always come back to Red."

"I wasn't trying to steal her away."

"Bullshit," Charlie Wallace said. "You are a sneaky little bastard."

"Hey, listen, you gotta give it a try just to prove you ain't queer."

"Or to cover it up," Raguso said.

As Red and Margo danced, Red saw Sheila and Harry Cope come in. Sheila went directly to where Red's mother was sitting. Mrs. Dahlgren rose up and threw her arms around Sheila as though she were her very own daughter. They hugged and held each other, and when they finally broke apart they reached out to each other again. Mrs. Dahlgren was beaming. Now she was standing back and Sheila was patting her enormous belly. His mother hadn't told Red she had invited Sheila and Harry. He stared across the room toward her and finally caught her eye. He shook his head, then turned away and moved closer to Margo.

He could never stand Harry Cope. It wasn't just because he had married Sheila. He was never really one of the guys. He never got into any trouble. There was that Fourth of July years ago when the cops pulled them all in for letting off fireworks on the block. The only guy they missed was Harry, and he was the guy who went up to Gun Hill Road in the Bronx and bought them back and sold them to the guys. But that was the way it always was with Harry. He couldn't get the clap if he stayed in a whorehouse for a month. He never played ball and some of the guys said he didn't even know where Ebbets Field was. He was a hustler and he always had a job after school. All the mothers used to hold him up as an example. "Why can't you be more like Harry Cope?" they used to say. His family had lived on the ground floor of the same brownstone Red lived in and it was hard to avoid him. And now when he and Sheila came in to visit, they stayed at his parents'.

And still nobody could figure out why she had married Harry.

"You know what it is?" Charlie Wallace had said at the time. "Women will always tell you they want romance, but that's a crock of shit. They want security, so they settle for a lousy lay so they'll have a roof over their heads for the rest of their lives."

"Yeah, that's right," Raguso agreed. "They want the house and the yard and the guy with the steady paycheck and the romance is all forgotten."

"So let me see if I got this right?" Kerrigan asked them. "Because a guy can screw good she shouldn't want all those other things? Is that it?"

"Yeah. If a guy is really good that's all that matters."

"Matters for who?"

"For both of 'em. What's the matter with you, Kerrigan?"

"Oh, there's nothing the matter with me. I guess I just don't get it."

Margo and Red were still dancing, and Annie came and tapped Margo on the shoulder.

"Do you think I could have a dance with my big brother?" she asked.

Red gave her an exaggerated double-take as though he were seeing her for the very first time. He could hardly believe that the woman standing before him was his sister.

"You look fantastic," he said, and he kissed her on the cheek.

"What a knockout!" Margo said. "You have to be careful someone doesn't steal you away tonight."

"We should all run away together," Annie said, and she laughed as if she knew their plans. They glanced at each other. "If I don't dance with you now I might never get another chance. I've watched the way you two hold on to each other."

"You and Charlie aren't doing too badly, either," Red said. "Looks like he doesn't want anyone else to get near you."

"Smart guy!" Margo said.

Annie and Red danced away from her, and Red was still amazed at how she looked. He knew every kid in the neighborhood had to be after her. She seemed to have been transformed overnight. She was like a young Grace Kelly. She was going to be just great at anything she ever did. And she had that scholarship. He felt for sure that his little sister was really going to be somebody. He was very proud of her. Oh yeah, he thought, Annie is going to be just fine. She let her head fall against his chest and he held her almost protectively. Whoever gets her is gonna have to be the best, he thought. Nothing but the very best for my sister.

"I think Margo is just great," Annie told him. "I really like her."

"She's the best thing ever happened to me."

"Mom would still love to see you with Sheila."

"I'm long, long past Sheila, little sister. Best thing ever happened to her was Harry."

As Red and Annie moved around the floor, they saw Mrs. Dahlgren looking at them. They waved to her and she smiled at them. It was her worried smile that they knew so well, and Annie felt bad for Red because she knew well how disappointed her mother was in him. But her big brother had always been there for her, and she had always been able to go to him with her troubles.

And now when she felt closer to him than ever before, she wished she could tell him her secret. She had the urge to pull him into her bedroom and close the door and tell him the whole story, but she knew it was impossible. As much as she loved him, she knew he would never be able to understand. She and Toby were all alone like strangers in a foreign land. There was nobody they could talk to. Nobody they could ever take the chance with.

Red felt a tap on his shoulder, and when he turned he saw Charlie Gallucci waiting to take possession of Annie.

"Okay, Charlie, you can have her back now," he said. Red smiled at her and moved away to where Margo was standing, and they watched them. Charlie glanced at them and blushed. He leaned into Annie and put his cheek next to hers. He closed his eyes and danced as though there were nobody else in the room. But Annie's eyes were open, and when she looked into the crowd standing around the floor she caught the eye of Bobby Raguso. He was staring at her, then she saw him turn and whisper to the others. She felt a spasm of fear in her stomach, and she wondered if he had seen her and Toby that night when they were coming out of the park. If he did, she knew for sure that he would tell the others. But then Red would have heard, and he surely would have said something. Or maybe they didn't tell him because they didn't want to upset him.

She wanted to be with Toby.

She wondered where he was and what he was doing.

She told herself she didn't give a damn about Bobby Raguso and the others. If they knew, they knew. What could anyone do? Shoot them. What the hell could they do about it. It's a free country. This is America. But she knew in her heart it was just bravado and the fear crept back into her. She wanted to tell Charlie to get lost and run out into the night to find Toby. But then the lights were turned down and her birthday cake was carried in and everyone sang "Happy Birthday." She stood before the cake, her face glowing, looking into the flickering candles. They were shouting at her to make a wish; she took a deep breath and blew them out and the lights were turned on again. She felt Charlie's arm move around her waist and her mother was standing behind her, smiling.

Her girlfriends were squealing with delight and someone was taking pictures with a flash camera, and she saw the reflected flashes of the camera like stars in the air all around her. Her girlfriends were giggling and screaming at her to open her presents piled high on the table.

She was trembling with anxiety and excitement and she couldn't stop herself from thinking about Toby. "Later, later," she pleaded. "We'll open them later. I'm just too excited now."

And they were calling out to her to cut the cake, and her mother placed the cake knife in her hand and she pushed the edge down into the cake to cut the first slice. She put it on a plate and handed it to her mother, then kissed her on the forehead. She kept cutting slices of cake until everyone had one. Then she found a corner where she hoped she would be able to get away from Charlie for a while.

The music had stopped and they were sitting in clusters, talking, everyone saying what a wonderful party it was.

"It's just like the parties in the old days when it seemed the whole neighborhood used to get together all the time," Mrs. Treacy said. "And we used to sing all the old songs. Everybody used to bring something and it didn't matter what it was because none of us had much. They were hard times but still we were all together. We all helped each other. We shared everything. That was the time when neighbors were really neighbors."

And then Kerrigan's crowd started to sing one of the old songs that everybody in the neighborhood seemed to know. It was like an anthem, and their voices were joined by everyone at the party and the song rang out full of feeling and pride for who they were and where they came from.

They called her frivolous Sal
A peculiar kind of a gal.
A heart that was mellow
An all-round good fellow
Was my gal Sal.

Mrs. Dahlgren's face lit up as she sang the song with the others. She was thinking of the old days and her happy times with Pete. The voices rose up and wafted through the windows out into the street. There was one old song after another. "Sweet Sixteen" and "Annie Rooney." Even the younger crowd had joined, and Charlie had found Annie and was sitting next to her with his arm across her shoulder. She stood up suddenly and took Charlie's hand and led him outside into the hallway. "Let's go down and sit on the stoop for a while. I want to cool off," she said. They rushed down the stairs together and opened the front door. They sat on the stoop and looked out into the deserted street. The air was cool after the heat of the party and Charlie turned and kissed her on the cheek. It was clear and bright with a three-quarter moon and when they looked up they could see the stars over the rooftops. Charlie snuggled in to her and he could smell her perfume.

She felt so soft and warm, but her thoughts were with Toby. She wondered again where he was and she wished it were him sitting beside her. She wanted to talk about the future. About all the things they were going to do together. There was no one else she could talk to about it except him. And now she stared out into the street, almost forgetting for an instant that Charlie was sitting beside her. And when she had stared into the candles on her cake she made the wish that she could be with Toby. That was all she wanted. She saw them in her mind's eye, running down an old cobblestoned street in the Village. There were crowds of people all around them, but nobody even gave them a second glance.

And they ran up the steps to their place and closed the door behind them.

They were going to make a place in the world for themselves and it was going to be their world. Nobody could come into it except those they wanted. She had always believed they could break away and leave all of the meanness behind. She had never understood it and she was afraid of it. Toby had told her not to even try. You can't understand insanity, he told her.

It wasn't just the neighborhood she wanted to leave behind but that way of seeing and thinking, and something she saw in her mother that always told her that there was no place for real happiness in the world.

She loved her mother but she hated the idea of endurance, that there was some unspoken grace that would come from it that would always be explained as the preferred substitute for joy. She could never just let go and be happy. She had always felt separate from her mother's sadness and pain and sometimes it had made her feel guilty. But not now. Not when she thought of Toby.

They could still hear them singing upstairs. The sound floated out over the street and she recognized the songs she had known since she was a little girl:

> *I'll take you home again Kathleen*
> *Across the ocean wide and wild . . .*

And then the old song that her mother told her was one that Al Smith and Jimmy Walker had sung together once at an affair where her father was the bartender:

> *East Side, West Side,*
> *all around the town,*
> *the kids play ring-a-rosie,*
> *London Bridge is falling down.*

Charlie had started to kiss her neck, but she was still a thousand miles away. She stared across the street, still lost in her thoughts, and he finally asked her if anything was wrong. He took her hand and kissed it. She had never missed Toby so much. Why can't he be here? Why can't he be here, she kept asking herself.

The front door opened behind them and Sheila and Harry Cope came out. Harry looked down at her. "Red's little sister ain't Red's little sister anymore," he said.

They sat on the step behind them and Sheila bent forward and kissed Annie on the cheek. "I haven't had a chance to talk to you all night," she said. "My God, I can't get over how you look. And your dress is fantastic. Harry's right. You're not Red's little sister anymore. Gosh, I remember when you used to sit here watching the big boys play stickball in the street. I'm starting to feel like an old woman sitting next to you."

"Guess I just grew up," Annie said.

"It's good to be back in the neighborhood," Sheila said. "And the party is just like the way it used to be with everybody having a good time."

"But don't you like it out there on the Island?"

"Oh, we do. It's wonderful. We love it."

She looked quickly at Harry. He nodded and smiled.

"It's nice to come back, but it's nice to go home, too. And believe me, the neighborhood's gonna be gone in a year or two," Harry said. He patted Sheila's stomach. "Our kid's not gonna have to worry about who moves in. He's gonna have green grass and lots of space to play in."

"Harry's absolutely sure it's gonna be a boy," Sheila said.

"Only ones gonna be living here will be old people and colored," Harry said. "Even the Dodgers gonna move away. And I'm not a baseball fan, but the writing's on the wall. They know what they're doing."

Annie stood up and reached for Charlie's hand. She wanted to get away from them. "We're gonna take a little walk," she told them. "See you later."

Harry stared at her when she turned around to say good-bye. She felt as though he could see right through her. Charlie held her hand and led her down the steps to the sidewalk, and Harry still stared after them. Even Sheila noticed him staring at Annie and she noticed the tightness of her dress and the way it clung to her.

"She's so lovely," she said.

They watched them as they passed under a streetlight.

"Don't do anything I wouldn't do," Harry called after them.

"Don't embarrass them," Sheila said.

"She is really something," he said. "I mean, overnight she turned into . . ."

"Into what?"

"She's exceptional. I mean. She's like a movie star. Beautiful and . . ."

"Sexy?" Sheila said.

"Sexy. I mean, how does it happen? I don't think she even knows it herself."

"She knows. She knows she has something. She isn't sure what it is, but she knows. It's like an instinct, and I'm sure she's a little embarrassed, so don't be so obvious when they come back inside. Let's go upstairs now."

"You go ahead. I'm gonna sit here and have a smoke."

Sheila went inside, and Harry remained sitting on the stoop, smoking and staring down at the street as though he were trying to find the young couple in the darkness.

ELEVEN

Annie and Charlie had reached the darkened alley that led to Gal-lucci's garage. He wanted her to go with him down the alley but she was hesitant. She had left the stoop just to get away from Harry and Sheila. There was something about them and she still felt that Sheila had not been nice to Red. She knew that if she went down the alley with Charlie she would have to fight him off again. "Charlie, please let's go back," she pleaded, but he held her hand and led her down the alley.

He stopped at the small side door to the garage and pulled her close to him. He was mad for her. He pulled her into him and began to kiss her passionately and he started to move against her. She tried to fight him off but he seemed so much stronger now. He was determined that he wasn't going to let her get away, and she pleaded with him again as she struggled.

"Please, Charlie, for God's sake. Please."

He acted as though he hadn't heard her, and he moved his hand under her dress and tried to pull it up.

She struggled harder to get away, pulling her mouth away from his, but she couldn't break the grip of his arm around her and she could feel him moving against her.

"Please, Charlie, if you don't stop, I'll tell Red, and I'll never see you again. Stop it or I'll scream."

He tried to kiss her again; he was moving faster against her and she heard him groan. He stopped moving and he slumped against her.

"I'm sorry," he said breathlessly. "I just couldn't stop myself. It just happened."

"Dammit, Charlie, you made it happen. God, what do I have to do to make you stop? Is this the way you're going to treat me? I've a good mind to tell Red and he'll beat your ass good. God, look at me. I look like I've been in a fight."

"I'm really sorry. I don't know what happened. I just couldn't stop myself. You feel so good and you look so beautiful."

"And that makes it alright? To hell with you, Charlie."

"Annie, please, I said I'm sorry. I'll never let it happen again. I promise."

She took a deep breath, relieved that she wouldn't have to fight him off anymore.

"It's alright," she said.

"I made a mess," he told her. "It's stained the whole front of my pants. Jeez, I can't walk into the party like this. Even my jacket won't hide it."

"You should have thought of that before."

She started to laugh and she couldn't stop. She put her hand to her mouth but it rose up even more in her and she shook as she doubled over, trying to stop. She was relieved now and she was glad that Charlie was embarrassed.

"What will I do?" he asked. "It ain't funny, you know."

"You'll have to go home and change your pants."

"I hope my parents are asleep."

They walked back down the alley together and when they came to the street they looked up and down to make sure that no one saw them.

"I better go on ahead in case anyone is out on the stoop. I wouldn't want them to see you and me like this. Wait here a minute and then you can walk back."

She watched him as he walked back up the street toward the house, then she started to laugh quietly to herself again. She leaned back against the wall of the alley and she wished she had brought a comb with her. The laughter kept coming back in spasms and she knew she would never have to go through the struggle with Charlie again.

Toby was never like that, she thought. He was always tender and sweet, and he would never make her do anything she didn't want to. He was a man. He didn't act like a boy. It was all just so stupid that he couldn't come to the party, she thought. And she knew for sure that she would never let herself ever be as sad as her mother. That awful heart-breaking sadness that touched and blamed everything and everyone around it. How could she ever know someone like Toby?

And her thoughts went to her father. She wished she had known him. She wished he could have been at the party to see her. But he was always so distant. So far away in another time and he always looked so happy in all of the pictures. She had gone through her mother's album so many times, looking at him because she believed that if she looked at him often enough she would know him, and she loved that he always smiled back at her.

The party was over, and everyone had left.

Mrs. Dahlgren relaxed for the first time all night.

She had finished cleaning up and now she sat in the kitchen drinking a glass of beer. Everything had been washed and put away by her friends, who had stayed to help her. She stretched her legs out before her and stared down at her slippered feet. It felt good to have taken her shoes off.

After they left she sat alone. She felt herself nodding off to sleep but she opened her eyes. She wanted to get up and go to bed, but she was so tired she could hardly move. It was nice to sit and feel the tiredness.

She and Annie had been getting everything ready since early morning, and they hadn't stopped all day. There was so much to do, but it had all worked out so well. She believed that Margo's parents had really been impressed, and she even had the thought that maybe they were not so bad after all. Maybe she could even get to like Margo. And it had been such a wonderful night for Annie, too. She was going to write to the nuns in Galway and tell them about the party and Red's engagement and Annie's scholarship. Annie was the smartest girl in the neighborhood. None of her friends' daughters even came close.

And she was so beautiful.

She was going to be a wonderful lady. She had a refinement that everyone could see, and she was so proud she had given that to her. Then she thought it would have been nice if Annie had helped her after the party. But still, it was her night and she had been so excited. She supposed she was at one of her girlfriends listening to forty-fives and talking and talking. She hadn't even stopped to tell her where she was going and she hadn't had a chance to have a word with her all evening. She hadn't even had time to open her gifts.

She stood up wearily and emptied what was left of her beer into the sink, then she turned the lights out and went to the bedroom. She lay down on top of the covers and closed her eyes.

Time had seemed to go by so fast, she thought. Thirty years in America. She couldn't believe it. It had not turned out the way she thought it would. Everything had seemed to happen so fast. She still had a feeling of expectation. It would come to her and when it did she pushed it back down because she was afraid. She was sure that nothing would ever turn out the way she expected it to. It was tempting God to believe in the future. But still, sometimes she let the feeling linger and for a while she believed that it was possible for something wonderful to happen. She had no idea what it would be.

From as far back as she could remember, the good times were always just around the corner. She was always praying and planning and hoping that everything would turn out for the good. It wouldn't be long now before both Red and Annie would be gone from the house and she would be alone. But even with her children around her she had always felt alone. She knew the feeling from the time she was a little girl in the convent. Always waiting for something or someone who would make everything alright.

She had spent her life trying to do the right thing and she could never allow herself to stop because the nuns would always be watching her and urging her on.

She heard the front door open and she recognized Red's footsteps moving through the house. As he passed her door she called out: "Red, is that you?"

He stopped and opened her door and saw her lying on the bed. He came close and sat down beside her.

"Great night, Mom," he said. "Everyone had a great time."

"I'm really happy," she said. She reached out and took his hand.

"I really hope that you and Margo will be very happy. Just try to do right by yourself. That's what your father would have told you."

He looked at her in the half-light. He wanted to bend down and kiss her but he felt awkward and he hesitated. It had been a long time since they had hugged each other. He bent down and kissed her on the fore-head.

"Good-night, Mom," he said. "I gotta go to work now."

"You must be very tired," she said. "I don't know how you do it. Couldn't you take the night off?"

"I wish I could, but I can't get out of it. Anyway, I'm feeling pretty good. It's been such a great night I don't think I could sleep, anyway. Thanks for everything, Mom. It was the best. Margo was really happy. And, boy, did you see how Annie looked."

"She's more than I ever expected. I'm so proud of the two of you."

"Good-night, Mom."

He slipped out quietly and closed the door behind him.

And Mrs. Dahlgren fell into a deep sleep.

TWELVE

It was six-thirty in the morning and old Mrs. Gallucci stepped out of the house into the alley on her way to the first mass. That was her habit every Sunday for as long as anyone could remember.

She was dressed in her peasant black as though she had never left Sicily. She held her rosary beads tightly in her hand and her lips moved in silent recitation. She prayed so constantly and so intently because she believed that it was only by prayer that the world could be saved. She was always first at the church and she often arrived before the doors were open. In her other hand she clutched her ancient missal, which was battered from constant use and thick with all of the holy cards she had stuck into it over the years. The morning sun shone down with a soft amber light that made her think of Palermo. The memory warmed her and made her smile inside.

She walked slowly down the alley, leaning heavily on her cane, her head held high and her hair pulled back in a twist that gave her a touch of ancient aristocracy. She could hear the birds making their morning calls all around her, busy and joyous. It was her favorite time of the day, when no one was out and nothing was moving and time seemed to stop in anticipation of the day to come. As she made her way down the alley her eye caught something on the ground ahead of her flapping in the light breeze. She didn't pay any attention at first, but as she moved closer she stopped and looked ahead. There was a trail of dried blood that had flowed into a hollow. Her eyes followed the trail and it led her back to the where the breeze touched what looked like a pile of torn clothes lying in the alley. Suddenly she was frightened and she didn't know whether to keep walking or go back to the house.

She crossed herself and moved slowly on as though she were afraid of what she would find.

Then she was standing over the pile. And she looked down and saw the battered and beaten body of Annie Dahlgren.

She thought she was going to faint and her heart hurt her in her breast. She gripped her missal between her two hands and held onto it tightly as though it were an anchor.

There was a pool of blood under Annie's head and her face was bruised and scratched.

Her beautiful dress had been torn off and lay in a tattered pile beside her. She was naked from the waist down.

She looked like a shattered doll that had been flung aside by a bored child.

The old woman's lips moved, but no sound would come out. She wanted to scream, but the sound stuck in her throat and she struggled to catch her breath. She could only stand where she was, as though she were frozen, and she couldn't take her eyes away from the bloodied face that looked up at her. The eyes were wide open, as if she were amazed at what had happened, and her mouth was open as though it were still in the middle of a scream.

Mrs. Gallucci blessed herself again, then she managed to turn herself and she began to walk as fast as she could back to the house. She didn't want to believe that this was the beautiful girl who lived up the street. She remembered that Charlie had brought her to the house and he had introduced her, and she remembered how nice she was. There was no doubt it was her.

The news spread quickly through the neighborhood. Squad cars were parked up and down the block and the alley was cordoned off. Reporters and photographers were all over the place and stopping anyone who would talk to them. They wanted anyone who knew Annie, but nobody wanted to talk to them. Red was in the alley talking to a short detective who was puffing on the stub of a cigar. He had curly gray hair and he was talking intently to Red as though he were trying to persuade him of something, but Red kept shaking his head. Then he broke down and his body was wracked as though he had been hit, and the detective led him back to one of the cars, where he sat in the back. Another cop got in and sat beside him and the detective walked back down the alley.

Everything in the neighborhood had come to a stop. People were crowded around the entrance to the alley, peering down as though they wanted to see where Annie had been killed and see the blood for themselves so that they could believe that it had really happened.

All of Mrs. Dahlgren's friends had come to the house. They gathered around her and fussed and made tea and fried bacon and eggs, trying anything to escape the numbing reality of Annie's death. She really wanted to be alone but she couldn't tell them. She knew they wouldn't let her. They sat around in groups talking to themselves. They had all been there at the party. All of Annie's unopened presents still stood on the dining room table and there was still some birthday cake left. They whispered among themselves and drank coffee. They started to say the rosary and the quiet mantra rose from them, filling the living room, where they had all sung the old songs the night before. They were all in a state of shock and disbelief. None of them wanted to believe that Annie was dead. Least of all Mrs. Dahlgren. When the rosary was ended she looked at her friends and started to smile as though she were seeing them all for the first time.

"There's nothing to worry about," she said. "It's all a mistake. I'm sure it's all a mistake. It wasn't Annie at all. I'm sure she'll be home in a little while." She sat back down and looked at them as though a great weight had been lifted from her. Two of the women pulled their chairs closer to her and each of them put their arms around her and stroked her as though she were a little girl who had fallen from a swing. She looked from one of them to the other, then her grief took hold of her and her face contorted and she slumped forward to the floor. She cried out a piercing scream that could be heard by the crowd, which had gathered in the street below.

Red was slumped over in the back of the patrol car. His partner sat beside him and like his mother he could not bring himself to believe that his beautiful young sister was dead.

A thin veil had covered his eyes when he looked down at her body and allowed himself to hold on to the hope that it hadn't really happened. He could only let himself know the truth slowly, and now with his face buried in his hands the grief broke him. He felt as if he had fallen down a vast chasm that had no bottom, and he fell and fell, and his sobs became deeper and deeper until they reached the place of their origin and went beyond it. He reached the place of utter despair and hopelessness, where there was no sanity, only the monstrous stupidity of the unknown, and he became frightened that if he stayed there he would never find his way back.

Now the sobs started to ease and he felt the hot angry tears stream down his face. He opened the door, got out of the car, and started to walk slowly back up the street. He came to his stoop and he didn't want to go upstairs. He dreaded seeing his mother. The martyrdom of her life would be crowned now with Annie's death. Her inexhaustible capacity to bear pain would be shown once more. He had often thought there was a strange craving in her to overcome the very worst that could happen, as though she were trying to prove that this ability transcended the possibility of joy and happiness. And now she would rise to the occasion as she had always done in the past and take the worst that life could dish out, as if it were the greatest expression of God's will for her. And she would write home to the nuns as though she were in a war and they would tell her she was a hero. She knew no other role. She had learned it so well in the midst of the strange serenity of the nuns.

Red dreaded seeing all those Irish women, too. All of her friends. They would bring him endless cups of tea and they would insist that he eat, and as well as he knew his mother and them they were all like strangers to him. He had started up the steps reluctantly. A cab pulled up and Margo jumped out and came running toward him. She threw her arms around him and he felt himself go limp against her. She lifted her face and looked at him. He was hidden somewhere inside himself. She led him up the steps and they went inside together.

The twelve o'clock mass was crowded that Sunday. Every seat was taken and the overflow lined the sides of the church. There was another throng that could not advance any further than the entrance.

They were kneeling and standing and along with the shock and the sorrow there was a strange tension, as if they were all waiting for something. They had quietly speculated about how it could have happened and who could have done such a terrible thing.

They stared at Father Darcy going through the familiar ritual of the mass. He, too, was feeling the tension. When they stood for the gospel he felt the intensity of their collective attention. He knew they wanted some kind of an explanation. Some kind of an answer, and if it was not forthcoming they were going to explode. There was far more anger than sorrow in the church.

He still hadn't figured out what to say or how to address them. He had asked himself if what he said could make any difference. He dreaded having to climb up into the pulpit, and since last Sunday's sermon he felt even more self-conscious than ever. He could see the petulance, the show-me attitude that looked up at him. How could he speak to the terrible violence of Annie Dahlgren's death and give it meaning. They were angry at this entity they called God. This Jesus, this God the Father, the Holy Ghost, this Prince of Peace. Let nothing you dismay. That's what they always said. Don't worry about it.

Darcy had decided to make it quick. He was not going to stay up there for long. He told himself he would be as honest as he could be. They were angry at God and they had a right to be. He asks so much of us and doesn't tell us anything. He decided to tell them that he was just as baffled as they were. And he would tell them that he was just a man, too. He had no insight to the mysteries of God.

When he looked out over them he noticed there was no coughing. Usually he had to wait for it to die down but on this Sunday morning there was complete silence. He could even hear the burned-down candles sputter and hiss near the side altars where people prayed for special intentions. They stared up at him and he blessed himself and the words were coming from him almost before he was ready.

"All of our hearts and our prayers go out to the Dahlgren family at this terrible time. We are all part of this terrible tragedy that is beyond comprehension. A beautiful young woman who was exceptionally gifted has been murdered right in the heart of where we all live and we all crave an explanation for the meaning of this terrible death.

"We all want to hear some words that will help us to make some sense of this awful violation of everything we nurture and believe in.

"But what words are there to comfort or explain the actions of the madman loosed among us last night who murdered this beautiful, innocent young woman. We can only feel anger and outrage and helplessness because we never become used to madness and evil.

"And we never become used to death, especially that of someone so young and innocent. Still, we say there has to be a meaning. There must be a meaning and the most frightening thing of all is that if God himself were to come before you in this pulpit and explain it to us it would not lessen in any way the devastation or make us feel any less violated.

"Most of you, I'm sure, believe that there can be no meaning to Annie Dahlgren's murder. No meaning at all.

"All we can do is ask how can an act so debased, so devoid of human feeling have any meaning. We might well ask if God has not made some terrible mistake. It is hard not to feel that we are owed some kind of answer to our bafflement. What could be the purpose of inflicting such a terrible death on this innocent girl?"

He paused and shook his head. The doors at the back of the church were open and the early June sunlight flooded in and the summer breeze wafted up the aisles oblivious to the sadness it swept over.

"It is hard to think of having faith at a time like this," he went on. "It is hard to believe in anything in the face of insanity. But then I must ask you all why it is we are all here this morning. And whether we like it or not, the answer is faith. Because ultimately faith is not what we believe in, but it is to be found in how we act. And if we are to keep ourselves free from evil, then it will be our actions that will save us. We will mourn, and we will pray, and ultimately we will try to come to terms with this tragedy which will always defy explanation. You know, I read somewhere that if there were no God we would have to invent one, because it is only by attaching meaning to our lives and our actions that we can go on. And our faith is expressed in how we live. In goodness and in decency. We cannot let the evil of this tragedy take this away from us."

When the mass was over, the crowd streamed out into the street. The squad cars were still there and the alley was still cordoned off. They broke up into small groups and they stood out in the street and on the sidewalks, talking quietly and shaking their heads.

There was no trace of the usual Sunday gaiety and even the small children seemed to cling to their parents. They seemed anxious to be home. Families wanted to be together, away from the uncertainty of the outside. Even the crowd in Kerrigan's was quiet. They spoke almost in whispers and for once the jukebox was silent. The usual clanging bell ringing from the pinball machine was absent, too. They didn't know what to say and nobody wanted to go home. They had all been at the party the night before and they remembered how beautiful Annie looked. There was an unspoken reluctance in each of them to believe that she was dead.

And finally Bobby Raguso banged his fist down on the bar in sheer frustration, knocking over his beer.

"Makes you want to kill someone," he shouted. "Sonofabitch! Goddamn it!" And he banged his fist down again.

Kerrigan looked at him and nodded and then quietly sopped up the spilled beer and poured him another. "Makes you wanna kill someone!" he shouted again. "And that goddamn priest over there. Jesus, anyone know what the fuck he was talkin' about? Gets up in that fuckin' pulpit and says nuthin'. And we're all supposed to walk out of the church like we just have to take it. And that's it. Nuthin' about who did it and what we should do to the bastard. The trouble with these fuckin' priests is that they think we're all dumb. I mean they really think we don't understand anything. Just like the politicians. They really think they have to explain everything to us. They always wanna keep you down. Jesus, no wonder he don't want us to move away. He's figurin' where else is he gonna find a bigger bunch of morons. They always give you the same old shit. This life don't count. It's the next one after you croak. That's when they're gonna pour us the gravy. Then we're gonna have it made. Well, let him tell that to poor Annie Dahlgren. Oh yeah, now we're supposed to hang in here 'til the niggers are happy, too. Well, I'll lay you ten to one some goddamn coon did this. Who the hell else woulda done somethin' like that? Who?"

Kerrigan shook his head. "Naw! This was someone outside the neighborhood. You can bet your ass on that."

"Jeez, I'd like to get my hands on him," Charlie Wallace said. "I'd bring him up on a roof and drop the sonofabitch and watch him splatter on the sidewalk. And no cops need come around askin' questions, either." He lifted his glass to his lips and drained it.

Kerrigan had been quiet through all of their talk. He had kept himself busy replenishing stock as if he didn't want to be a part of their speculation. Freddie Alcaro watched him as he filled the lockers in back of the bar with bottles of beer.

"What's the matter," he asked. "You've said nothing all morning."

"What the hell do I have to say. Bad enough I have to listen to you guys." He climbed on to his stool and stared out listlessly. He looked weary. He lit a cigarette and blew the smoke out before him, then he lowered his head and began to move it slowly from side to side.

"Poor Red," he said. "Jesus, he was so happy last night. And his mother. I mean I saw her go through all that stuff with Red's old man." He poured himself a short beer and took a gulp. "She raised Red and Annie by herself and Pete Dahlgren was always the best bartender in New York, I mean the best, but what a fuckin' character. Everybody loved him, but the sonofabitch couldn't stay sober. Served and drank with the Who's Who of the city, especially the ballplayers. They used to tell him everything. Father confessor like he was some fuckin' sage or somethin'. The poor guy couldn't find his own way home. Used to fix 'em up get 'em laid and everything. Head bartender at the St. George. Great pal of Durocher's. Pete used to steer him to the big stakes card parties and the floatin' crap games. Only thing was Pete never had any money. Always in hock. Durocher used to ask him to watch out for his wife while he was playin'. Boy, what a looker. And the story goes she and Pete had a thing together. But women were always crazy about him. And I mean women. I ain't talkin' sluts and bimbos. They used to say that when the Dodgers went on the road Pete Dahlgren never came home. Four or five of the wives were taking care of him. Or he was taking care of them. That's what they were sayin' and knowin' about Dahlgren, some of it had to be true. Durocher was a jealous bastard, and that's why he asked Pete to watch out for his wife when they were on the road. She was one beautiful woman and she's still makin' movies and the story goes she had it bad for Pete Dahlgren. Jesus, what is it with guys like that?"

They had never heard Kerrigan talk like that before and they had stopped calling out for refills even though their glasses were empty.

"That's the way it is with some guys, you know," he went on. "They just have it, and they don't even realize it. He was the smartest guy and so good-lookin'. And if you ran in to him on the street he'd always tell you about all the bad breaks he was havin'. Everybody crazy about him and never had two cents to rub in his pocket. And Jesus, his own wife! A ringer for Maureen O'Hara. I swear to God. She's still a lovely lookin' woman. Men were always crazy about her, too, and after Pete died there were lots of guys came knockin' on her door, but I don't believe she ever went out with another man. That was it."

He got off the stool and came down the bar and replenished their drinks.

"Can't get my mind off that beautiful little girl. Jesus, who could have done such a thing. The way she looked last night when she was dancing. I remember looking at her and Red when they took a turn together. I was thinking that things have a way of working out. Red is getting married and Annie's got herself a fancy scholarship. Pete Dahlgren would have been braggin' all over the neighborhood."

He shook his head and climbed back on the stool.

"They gotta find the sonofabitch did this," Dooney said. "They gotta find him and make sure they lock him up good before we get ahold of him."

They all nodded and drank their beers.

THIRTEEN

Jack Treacy opened his eyes and listened to the pounding on the door of his room. He heard his name being called and he didn't know where he was. He was trying to find his memory and he stared up at the ceiling, trying to focus his eyes. The knocking on the door continued, then it slowly came to him that he was home in his own bed and he recognized his mother's voice. He shouted at her to go away.

"Please, Jack, please," she called. "Please open the door."

He raised himself up and searched the night table for his cigarettes. She was knocking on the door softly now. He lit a cigarette and took a long drag, then he began to cough. He couldn't stop and the tears were running down his face. The back of his throat felt as though he had swallowed acid and his mouth was dry.

"Jack, please," his mother pleaded again. "It's about Annie Dahlgren. They found her dead in Gallucci's alley this morning. She's been murdered. Poor Mrs. Dahlgren. What in the name of God is she going to do?"

He stared at the bedroom door unsure of what he had just heard. He felt as though he hadn't slept at all. "I'll be out in a minute, Ma," he called out. He heard her footsteps as she walked away. He couldn't remember when he had come home. His trousers were lying on the floor beside the bed. He reached down to pick them up and he rummaged through the pockets to see if he had any money left. He found two single dollars and change. He got out of bed and stood groggily, then he sat down again and took another long drag from his cigarette. He could feel the shakes move through his body and he began to tremble. The old unnameable fear gripped him and he fought to keep himself from yelling out to banish it away. He reached under the bed for the bottle he had brought home. He put it to his lips and drained what was left. He hoped it would stay down and make his shakes go away. Then he began to sweat and shake even more and felt as if he were freezing to death. He pushed his hair straight back with his two hands and buried his face in them. He was really more afraid than ever before because the booze wasn't working for him the way it used to. There were times now when he couldn't get drunk and he couldn't get sober. He folded his arms around himself and tightened them, holding on. "Oh Jesus, let this fucking thing go away from me," he whispered. "God almighty help me."

The past few days were a blank to him. He had no memory of where he had been or how long he'd been away. He stood slowly and walked to the bathroom. He stared into the mirror and saw his dirty bearded face staring back at him and he saw the fear in his bloodshot eyes. Then he noticed the scratches and bruises on his face, and when he raised his hands to inspect them he saw that they were scratched and bloodied, too. He stood and stared, hardly able to move. He had no idea what had happened. He pulled off his T-shirt before to get into the shower and he saw the welts and scratches all over his body. But he was always bloodied or beat up when he came off a bender. He felt sore all over and he stood under the hot shower, letting it cleanse him. And again he tried to bring back the memory of where he had been, but he could remember nothing. He got out and dried himself off and brushed his teeth and combed his hair. It had been a long time since his body had been washed. He walked back into the bedroom. He picked up his shirt and trousers off the floor. There was a huge bloodstain on the front of his shirt. The dried blood was brittle to his touch and his trousers were stained, too. He held them out before him and he saw they were stained heavily with blood around the top of the legs and the fly. He became frightened and he began to shake. Jesus, how did it get there, he asked himself. What the hell sort of a fight was I in? There were always a few bruises and scratches but never as much blood as was on his clothes this time. He went to the closet and found his old Marine Corps seabag and stuffed the clothes into the bottom and put some dirty laundry on top to cover them.

Arnie Meyers was always thought to be the best detective in Brooklyn and some even said on the entire force. He was Red's boss and he wanted to make sure they found the killer as quickly as possible. And now Red was with him as they led Charlie Gallucci out of his house. His parents stood at the door watching and his grandmother sat inside still clutching her rosary. A tall cop opened the door of a waiting patrol car and Arnie Meyers got in beside Charlie. Red sat on the other side of him. A crowd stood on the opposite side of the street, watching silently as the car pulled away.

"I don't want you worrying about this, Charlie," Arnie said. "We just want to bring you down to the station and ask you some questions. Tell us exactly what happened between you and Annie. We'll have you back home in no time."

He caught Red's eye and winked.

"We're not arresting you or anything like that and there are no charges. You understand that? We already told your parents there's no need for a lawyer or anything. It's you doing us a favor. Do you understand that, Charlie?"

He nodded and stared straight ahead, trying to hide his fear.

"There's nothing to be afraid of. We just want to go over everything with you in detail and get it all down on paper because every little detail is very important to us," Arnie said.

Charlie kept telling himself that he never should have left Annie that night. And he felt a terrible guilt because he knew that if he hadn't acted the way he did there would have been no need for him to leave her and go on ahead.

"And you know, Charlie, there are some questions we have to ask you that I know would be hard for you to answer in your home with your mom and dad nearby. We understand that. Know what I mean?"

He nodded again. "You see, Charlie, we have to know exactly what happened between you and Annie in that alley. You're gonna help us find whoever did this."

He caught Red's eye again and nodded slightly.

Arnie settled back in the seat and pulled newspaper from his pocket. He flipped it over to the back page and read the headline aloud. "Giants to quit Polo Grounds. Jesus, did you see this?" he asked the driver. "Stoneham's gonna move the Giants to San Francisco."

The driver nodded. "And O'Malley's gonna keep the Dodgers in Brooklyn."

"Well, let me tell you something," Arnie said. "You can bet your ass that if the Giants go the Dodgers go, too. No doubt about it. O'Malley's in back of all of this. He's such a lyin' bastard. I mean why the hell doesn't he just come out and tell us the truth? But he won't because the sonofabitch wants us to keep going to the ballpark until the end of the season. Then he'll make his announcement. But he'll keep up everyone's hope until the very end. Milk every fuckin' dime and then take off. Brooklyn makes the guy rich and now he's gonna take off with our team. Wonder what it takes to make a guy like that?"

Charlie heard the words but somehow they didn't make any sense because he couldn't concentrate and he couldn't believe where he was. He couldn't believe Annie Dahlgren was dead, and he was just beginning to realize that there were some people who believed that it might have been he who killed her. He was afraid of Red because he had seen the way he looked at him. He knew Red would blame him for what happened. He might even think it was he who had murdered his sister.

When they reached the precinct house they walked Charlie to a small windowless room. Arnie whispered something to Red and left. Then Arnie sat him at a small table and sat opposite him. He was chomping on the unlit stub of a cigar, looking down at some papers. Charlie noticed that Arnie's lips were brown from the cigar and there were stains on the corners of his mouth. He wanted to bolt.

Arnie's eyes seemed so small in his head and there were ash stains on the front of his shirt. Then the detective looked up from the papers and he was smiling at him. His wispy hair was uncombed and his teeth were stained amber, and Charlie wondered how this guy could be the best detective in Brooklyn. Everybody had heard of Arnie Meyers. He made Charlie think of the old man who owned the Chinese laundry on Fourth Avenue. His teeth were stained yellow.

"So how long were you and Annie Dahlgren going out together?" Arnie asked.

"We started going steady about six weeks ago."

"But you knew her for a long time before that?"

"We grew up together."

Arnie removed the stub from his mouth and threw it in the wastebasket. He reached into his shirt pocket and pulled out a cellophane-wrapped cigar. He opened it and put it into his mouth, rolling it from side to side as if he were trying to find the right place for it. When he found the spot, he lit a match and made circles with it around the end of the cigar while he puffed and sent a cloud of smoke swirling over his head. Then he leaned back in his chair and wriggled until he was comfortable. He looked at Charlie again as though he were seeing him for the first time. He was glad Red was not there with them.

"I want you to tell me about last night. Now, as I understand it, you and Annie left the party together. What happened after you left?"

"Well, we really just wanted to get a breath of air and cool off a little, so we sat on the stoop for a while."

"How long?"

"Not long. Some people came out and we left and walked down the block because we wanted to be by ourselves."

"Who were the people who came out?"

"Harry Cope and his wife."

"So you left right after they came out?"

"Well, we talked for a minute or so and then Annie took my hand and we left."

"So they saw you walk down the block?"

Charlie nodded.

"Were they the only people to come out just then?"

"As far as I know."

"Was there anyone else outside. I mean, what about across the street? Did anyone else see you?"

"I don't think so."

"So you walked down the block. What happened then?"

"We went down the alley next to my parents' house."

"That's where the garage is?"

Charlie nodded.

"Any other kids from the party go down there?"

"No. We were alone."

"Anyone see you go down the alley?"

"I really don't know. I don't think so."

"What about the Copes. Did they see you?"

"I don't think so."

"Did you tell them you were going there?"

"No, we just said we were going for a walk, and Harry Cope said that we shouldn't do anything he wouldn't do."

"What did he mean by that?"

Charlie shrugged.

"That what Harry said? 'Don't do anything I wouldn't do'?"

Charlie nodded.

"So how long did you stay down there?"

"Not long."

"How long?"

"Ten . . . fifteen minutes."

"And then what?"

"I went home."

"How come you didn't go back to the party?"

"I was tired."

"Bullshit. Young guy like you couldn't get tired if you tried. Annie Dahlgren had to be by herself down that alley when she was attacked. What happened? Where the hell were you? Jesus Christ, you are her boyfriend, aren't you? Where the hell were you? How come neither of you went back to the party? What happened between you two? From what I hear you wouldn't let her out of your sight all night and then you leave her alone in the alley. Now look. Why don't you tell me what happened?"

Charlie bowed his head and looked up at Arnie. He was just about to say something when the door opened and Red came in. Arnie looked at him, annoyed. He stood up and they went outside into the hallway. He closed the door behind him.

"For chrissake, Red, the kid is terrified of you. Can't you see that. I've gotta have some time alone with him. Anyway, you belong home with your mother."

"She's got all her friends around her. She don't need me."

"This ain't good, Red. It ain't good at all. You're too close to this. There's no way you should be here and you know it."

"Arnie, I'm going crazy. You gotta let me be here. You gotta let me do something."

"You know the rules. You wanna get my ass in trouble?"

"Fuck the rules, Arnie. I wanna find whoever did this. Jesus, I gotta keep myself from going crazy."

"I can't let you do it. It's personal for you, Red. Can't have you going off half-cocked. You know your temper. For chrissake, it's gotten you in trouble before."

"Look, I'm gonna find whoever killed my sister whether I'm on the case or not. And you can have my badge right now if you want it."

Arnie looked at him and shook his head. "Look, you sonofabitch, don't you think I know how you feel?"

"Please, Arnie. You can't expect me to stay out of it."

"Okay, okay, but get this. You don't leave my side. You ask me if you wanna go take a piss. If you ain't with me I gotta know where you are. That's it. You do nothing on your own and if you fuck up on me, you hand in your badge. Got it?"

"Thanks, Arnie, I won't let you down."

"I'm going back in and talk to the kid. He's scared shitless of you so wait out here 'til I come and get you. I gotta play him out a little."

Arnie sat across from Charlie. He relit his cigar and puffed, filling the small room with smoke. "So tell me, Charlie, how come neither you nor Annie Dahlgren went back to the party?"

He stared down at his feet and didn't answer.

"Look, kid, what the hell happened between you two? From what they tell me, you and her were together all through the party. Couldn't stay away from each other. Am I right?"

Charlie nodded.

"What happened between you two in that alley?"

Charlie looked at the detective, and Arnie could see the fear in his eyes.

"Come on, kid, tell me what happened."

He bowed his head and looked at the floor.

"You're not gonna tell me or you just gonna clam up on us? Here we are trying to find out who killed Annie Dahlgren and you can't even answer a few questions. What the hell's the matter with you? Well, I'll tell you what. Maybe it's me. Maybe I need a little help. I was hoping to keep Red out of this 'cause I know how mad he is."

He stood up and went to the door and brought Red back in with him. And now they both were staring at Charlie and they could see him tremble.

"What the hell you so scared of?" Red asked. "Why the hell won't you tell us what happened in the alley? Why didn't you go back to the party? What the hell are you covering up? You know what I think, Charlie? I think it was you killed my sister."

"No! No! I swear to God I didn't. Oh God, Red, you can't think that. I swear on my mother. I didn't do it. I didn't do it."

"Then why the hell won't you tell us what happened? What the fuck's the matter with you?"

Charlie was sobbing now, and he pulled a handkerchief from his pocket and wiped his eyes. "I didn't kill her. I swear I didn't," he said through his sobs.

"If you didn't do it, then why the hell can't you tell us what happened?"

Charlie's face was buried in his hands now.

"I'll tell you why you didn't go back to the party. Because you made it with my sister, you sonofabitch! Ain't that it? She didn't want you to, but you made her, you lousy little prick!"

Charlie was shaking his head, moving it from side to side, and his face was wet with tears.

"You couldn't wait to get her out of the party. I saw you. You got pissed off if anyone else asked her to dance. You didn't even want to let her dance with me. Christ, her own brother! Oh, you had plans alright. You couldn't wait to get down that alley and when you got her there you forced her to make it with you. She didn't want to, but you didn't care. You forced her. You held your hand over her mouth so she couldn't scream, and you banged her head against the wall, and you knocked her out. And then you pulled up her clothes and you did it. You fuckin' coward. Didn't you? Didn't you. And when you were done you went into the garage and you got a knife and you stabbed her over and over 'til your hand hurt, didn't you?"

Charlie jumped up and started to shout at them. "That's a fuckin' lie. You're a liar. You're a goddamn liar. I didn't do it. I didn't do it."

Red rushed out from behind the table and lunged toward him. He pushed him back down in his chair and stood over him. "And you left her there bleeding to death. You left my poor little sister bleeding to death."

He was staring into his face and Charlie leaned back as far as he could, desperate to get away from him.

"Ain't that the truth, you little wop bastard? For Christ's sake, you been sniffing around her for as far back as I can remember. What the fuck she ever saw in you is beyond me."

"Aw, Red, please believe me, I didn't kill Annie. God, I was crazy about her. I would've died for her." Red reached down and grabbed him under his chin and held his face. He slapped him hard and yanked him to his feet. "You're a goddamned liar. You killed her and you know it. Go ahead, say it. Say it. Tell the truth."

Red had him by the throat and Charlie was fighting for his breath as Red pushed him back down into the chair.

"Red, please—for God's sake, I didn't kill her. I didn't know anything about it 'til I heard my grandmother." He looked toward Arnie, imploring him to intercede, but the detective sat impassively rolling his cigar around his mouth as if Charlie weren't there. He started to tremble as Red finally went back to the other side of the table and sat down.

"So why don't you tell us what happened," Arnie said. "Like how come you didn't go back to the party?"

"Be . . . because we'd been making out and I made a big stain on the front of my pants. I couldn't go back because everyone would see it. Annie was laughing at me. She thought it was funny. I didn't make it with her. I couldn't stop myself from . . . letting it happen. It was my fault. Annie didn't want to make out. I hardly held her and it happened."

"So what happened then?"

"Annie said I should go home first in case anyone would see us. I mean in case we ran into anyone."

"So you left her in the alley by herself."

"But she was only going to stay there a minute or so."

"Why didn't you let her go back to the party first?"

"I don't know. She told me to go ahead."

Arnie stood up and pushed his chair back. He came around the table and stood next to Charlie. "Tell me something, kid. Was she seeing any other guys? She ever date anyone else?"

"She had my ring. We were going steady."

"So she wasn't seeing anyone else? Was she friendly with any other guys in the neighborhood?"

"She liked to talk to Toby Walters. I mean, they read books together, and they talked a lot because they both got scholarships and all."

"Toby Walters."

"Yeah. She really liked to talk to him and I know he liked to be around her."

"You're sure nobody else saw the two of you go down the alley?"

"I don't think so."

"What about when you were on the way back? Did anyone see you?"

"I don't think so."

"Did anyone else know you were going down the alley?"

"No. I mean, when we went out on the stoop it was just to cool off. We hadn't planned to go down the alley. It was only when Harry Cope came out that we walked away. Annie said he gave her the creeps."

"Why did she say that?"

"She said he always had a weird smile when he looked at her."

"Did he see you go down the alley?"

"I'm pretty sure they couldn't see from that far up the block."

"Well, somebody had to know she was there. Somebody had to be watching."

FOURTEEN

It was late afternoon when they brought Charlie Gallucci home. There were still clusters of people standing around talking quietly and they watched Charlie go down the alley and enter the side entrance of the house. He went straight to his bedroom and locked the door. His parents stood outside knocking and asking him if he was alright, but he wouldn't answer them and he wouldn't let them in.

"You're lettin' that little bastard off too easy," Red said. "I don't believe a fuckin' word he told us."

"Look, Red," Arnie said. "Charlie Gallucci didn't kill Annie. First off, there wasn't a mark on him, not a scratch, and she put up a helluva fight. She was fightin' for her life. I'm really surprised nobody heard anything. Whoever did this didn't get away without a mark on them." They drove on and Red stared straight ahead.

"I think whoever it was was from the neighborhood," Arnie said, "somebody who knew her and was watching her for a long time."

"Jesus, who in the neighborhood would kill her? Who the hell would do that to her? I mean, I know everyone. I don't love 'em all, but I can't think of anyone who would've killed my sister."

"Something I learned a long time ago. You never really know anyone. I mean we all have a secret self. All of us. Doesn't make us bad, but we all have it. So what I mean is, you can't eliminate anyone when it comes to something like this." He turned and looked at Red. "Now remember what I told you, kid. I don't want you going off half-cocked. First time you get out of line, I get your badge. You do nothing on your own. You uncover anything, you come to me right away. Nothing on your own. You got it?"

Red nodded.

"Jesus, I mean the whole precinct knows you're working with me. Even the brass. So they got their eye on this, too. Don't go behind my back. Lotta people got their ass on the line for you. And leave the Gallucci kid alone. State of mind you're in, you're liable to kill someone. I can understand that."

Toby Walters wasn't home when Arnie and Red asked his father where he was.

"Don't know," Bailey Walters told them.

"Did he come home last night?" Arnie asked him.

"Yes, he did."

"What time?"

"Don't know."

"Did you hear him come in the house?"

"I really don't remember."

"Then how do you know he came home last night?"

"Because he was in his bed when I got up this morning."

"What time was that?"

"Six."

They looked around the small basement apartment. It was clean and neat and the walls were painted white. It lacked a feminine touch. It was the home of a father and son.

Practical, no frills. No adornments. Bailey Walters's wife had died when Toby was a baby and his father had raised him alone.

"What time did you go to bed last night?" Arnie asked him.

"Late. Had some buddies over to play cards. Went to bed after they left."

"What time was that?"

"Around one o'clock."

"And Toby hadn't come home when you went to bed?"

"Nope."

"Did you talk to him this morning?"

"Nope. Guess I was out when he got up."

"Do you know where he went?"

"No."

"Do you mind if we take a look in his room?"

"What do you want with him? Why don't you tell me what this is about?"

Arnie looked at him and paused before he answered.

"I believe he was a friend of Annie Dahlgren, the young girl who was murdered last night."

Bailey Walters nodded and shook his head slowly.

"Did you know her, Mr. Walters?" Arnie asked.

"They used to come here to study. They were real close friends. They were interested in a lot of the same things. She was a lovely young lady."

Red looked at Arnie and caught his eye. Mr. Walters still sat with his head bowed at the table. "Could we see his room?" Arnie asked again.

Mr. Walters stood up and they followed him into the small narrow bedroom. They both spotted the small framed picture of Annie on the night table. Red picked it up and looked at it. It was a picture he had never seen before. She smiled out at him as she stood under the huge old oak in Prospect Park. Her blond hair was pulled back in a ponytail and she wore a white sleeveless blouse and blue jeans turned up to the calves. She wore a bandanna around her neck and it looked as though she was gesturing to the picture taker. She was as happy as he had ever seen her. He placed it back down on the night table. He had heard Toby's name mentioned in the neighborhood and he remembered watching him at the softball games on Sunday mornings in the schoolyard. And now he was putting his face together with Annie. There was something he had heard about them being friends, but he had never given it much thought.

The secret that Annie and Toby had tried so hard to keep was all over the neighborhood now. It was still gossip and a rumor neither confirmed nor denied, like the stories of the Dodgers leaving. "I knew there was something going on between 'em," Raguso said as he hunched over his beer. "Saw them coming out of the park together that time and no one believed me. Remember, Dooney? I remember sayin' that the guy has lived in the neighborhood so long he thinks he's white. So he thinks he can go out with white chicks."

"Annie was his friend, that's all," Kerrigan said. "What the hell's the matter with that?"

"Tell me the truth," Dooney said. "Do you think anyone could just be friends with a girl as good-lookin' as Annie? I mean, a spook. Come on."

"Sure he could. Why the hell not? I mean, he's smart and bright. Worked his ass off since he was in knee pants around the neighborhood.

Neither he nor his old man ever took a nickel from anyone without working for it. And that scholarship he got ain't just for runnin' track and field. He's a damn smart kid, and there's a lotta people jealous of him. How come a colored kid got so much going for him? I mean he's not supposed to amount to much. Some people be happy if he was just to keep delivering groceries for the rest of his life."

"Aw, for chrissake, climb down off your soapbox," Dooney said. "That kid is so goddamn arrogant. I mean, you can see it. Just the way he looks at you. Really thinks he's hot shit. Too good to play with the rest of the kids down at the schoolyard. Always carryin' a book with him just to let us all know how smart he is. Don't kid yourself. You can see the way he was around Annie Dahlgren. It was more than just friends. And you know what? Nobody wanted to say anything because they were afraid of what Red would do if he found out. Shit, the night of the party I saw the kid standing across the street from the house staring up at the window, jealous because he couldn't be there. All he wanted was to get her pants off. You know what it means to a coon to get a white chick's pants off? He's no different than the rest of 'em."

"Right—and all the Irish are drunks," Kerrigan said.

"What the hell do you mean by that?" Dooney asked.

"Well, that's what they say, but we know it ain't true. You're saying every black guy wants to get a white chick's pants off."

"Yeah—that's what I'm sayin'. Biggest thing ever to happen for a spook."

The others murmured in agreement.

"Jesus, you guys look like you're ready to string the kid up right now. No proof, no nothing except that he's black."

"Why the hell are you stickin' up for him?" Charlie Wallace asked.

"Well, Jesus, someone better stick up for him before you guys have him lynched."

A quietness came over them and they drank their beers silently as though the mention of the word had opened up its possibility. Kerrigan was looking at them as though he really hadn't known them before.

"How come I never heard any talk in here about those two kids being friendly? Jesus, if that was the case nobody seemed to mind before."

"The trouble with you, Kerrigan, is that you can't see what's in front of you," Dooney said.

"That kid's been headin' for trouble for a long time because he was walkin' around here like he was white or somethin'. And everyone forgot he wasn't. Even when Rags told us he saw them together coming out of the park, no one paid any attention. That's what you call arrogant. I mean did he think he was going to be with her and no one was going to say anything?"

"I really like to ask you Dooney, because maybe I just don't get it. What the hell is wrong with two kids spending time with each other. And why the hell is it any concern of yours? In case you've forgotten—this is America. We are in Brooklyn. We are not in Alabama, for Christ's sake. Look—two kids get friendly because they're scholars. One of 'em happens to be black and that makes him a killer? Can't you do anything better than come up with a scapegoat?"

"Jesus, Kerrigan, you're beginning to sound like Darcy across the street there. Why you never went to the fuckin' seminary is beyond me. Shit, you woulda been a bishop by now."

They were all looking at him, laughing, and he folded his arms across his chest and shook his head as he smiled back at them.

"We're talking to everyone who knew Annie Dahlgren," Arnie told Bailey Walters.

"Been livin' here a long time and I ain't never heard of anything like this," he told Arnie.

He shook his head. "I think she was the sweetest little girl I ever met, and those two got along so well together. They just talked all the time like they could never shut up. Loanin' each other books and bring pieces from magazines to read. And when they got on the phone you couldn't get 'em off it. Talked about college and what they were gonna do. Life couldn't happen fast enough for those two."

"And you haven't talked to your son since Annie died."

"No, I haven't."

"Does he know what happened?"

"I don't know, but I guess he's gotta know by now."

"You've got no idea where he might be?"

"No, I don't."

"Look—we'll be back. Just wanna talk to him, ask him a few questions."

Arnie handed him a card. If you need to reach me just give me a call."

Bailey Walters sat down at the kitchen table after they left. He still couldn't believe Annie was dead. He was so fond of her, and she had always been so nice to him. He had always been afraid for Toby and he knew how it was between them without them ever having to tell him. He had always known that something would happen and now it had, and as much as he liked Annie he always believed it wasn't a good thing to mix with white folks. Toby knew what they would say about him. And now he was caught between his heartbreak and his anger and he knew for sure they would come after him.

They had to find someone, and Toby was it. He was on the way home when he saw the car pull up outside his building and watched Arnie Meyers and Red go in. He had hidden in the basement across the street, and when he saw them leave he had dashed across the street into his apartment. He knew they would be coming back and he ran past his father in the kitchen and went straight to his bedroom. He pulled down the old battered suitcase and began throwing clothes into it. His father stood at the door watching him.

"Hey, what you doin'?" he asked.

Toby was reaching for some of his books and was putting them in the suitcase. Then his father came into the room and put his hand on Toby's shoulder, but Toby just kept packing. Bailey Walters spun him around quickly. "Look, son—you don't have to run away," he said. "You ain't done nothin'. That detective told me they just wanted to ask you a few questions 'cause that little girl was your friend. They talkin' to everyone who knew her."

Toby stood straight up and looked into his father's face. "Pop—once they get hold of me they ain't never gonna let me go. Believe me, I know that. Unless they find someone who confesses and they got the goods on, they ain't gonna let me go. 'Cause they gotta find someone, and guess what? I'm the colored boy was hanging out with Annie."

Bailey Walters nodded and looked into his eyes.

"Look, son. I've lived right here for over twenty years. Everybody knows me around here, and they know you since you was little. We ain't some of those folks just moved in. You grew up here. If you did nothin' wrong, then you got nothin' to run from. I mean, they talkin' to everyone. They been all over the neighborhood."

"Everyone else is white, Pop. That's the difference. We live here, but we ain't part of them. That's the difference. We're different. We're black.

They think all I ever wanted to do was to make it with Annie. They wanna believe that. What other reason would I have to be with her? If they can't find anyone else, then they always have me."

He left the bedroom and went into the kitchen. He looked out of the basement window.

He wondered if they might have someone watching the house. His father watched him.

"I still think you ought to wait for those detectives to come back. Or you could just go down to the precinct now. Just walk in. That way they'll know for sure you have nothin' to hide. You run away now, they won't stop 'til they catch up with you."

"I got nothin' to hide, Pop, 'cept I can't hide the color of my skin, and that does something to them. Sure, I grew up here, but guess what? I'm still a nigger. It was alright when I was little and cute, but now I'm a man. And I'm smart and I got a scholarship. And they got all these coloreds movin' in all around them. Who're they gonna take it out on? Who?"

"Still think you got it wrong, son."

"Oh, Pop, you always made it seem like they were doing you a favor when they gave you the privilege of working your ass off for them. You never talked back to anyone and they figured you for a good nigger."

Bailey Walters closed his eyes briefly as though he had been stung. He moved away from Toby and looked through the window, then he came back and sat at the kitchen table.

"You can think whatever you like, but all I ever wanted to do was to make a home here for the two of us after your mamma died. Only thing that mattered to me was you, and the only person I ever answered to was myself. Anyone ever treated me badly, I just never went to work for them again. Easy. I always figured I was a man. And bein' a man is what you think of yourself, not what someone else think of you. Never cared a damn what anyone else think. They call me a nigger, I can't help that. I don't have to be what they call me. Most people treat me nice. Most folks is good. Never had to kiss no one's ass, and I still think you got it all wrong."

"Pop, I didn't mean any disrespect. You know how I feel about you. It's just that no matter how long we live here, we'll always be black. We're not supposed to get ahead. They'd like for us to keep our place. Pop, you know what I'm talking about." He moved to where his father was standing and he put his arms around him.

"You're the best, Pop," he said in a whisper, because he could feel the tears rising up in him and he was afraid he was going to be overcome. "If I was to live to be a hundred I'd never meet anyone like you."

They held on to each other and they both knew that something had changed, that somehow nothing was ever going to be the same and neither of them wanted to say it.

Toby went to the window again and looked out into the street, then he went to the bedroom and snapped the locks shut on the suitcase. He carried it into the kitchen and his father looked at him, knowing he was helpless to stop him.

"Please, son—I still think you should go down to the precinct. Let 'em know you have nothing to hide. I mean, as soon as they figure out that you've taken off they won't stop 'til they've found you."

"I ain't no Jackie Robinson. I ain't no ballplayer hitting home runs. I'm a black kid had the nerve to go out with the white girl. That's all they can see. I mean Annie's brother is a plainclothes cop. They're gonna get the smart-assed nigger went out with his sister."

"Ain't nuthin' I can do to stop you. I know you got your mind made up."

He went to his bedroom and came back with a roll of bills. He tried to hand them to Toby, but he wouldn't take them, then finally he stuck them in Toby's pocket. He reached his arms out and they held each other again. Then Toby was out the door, bounding up the steps to the street. His father saw his feet move quickly past the basement window and they were gone.

Toby walked quickly toward the elevated subway on Fourth Avenue. A breeze had sprung up and the sky was darkening. A thunderstorm was moving in fast. It had been warm and muggy, and now even as he hurried along he could smell rain coming. When he approached the station he saw two cops standing near the stairs.

They were talking with their backs turned to him and he decided to cross the street and take the stairs on the other side. He kept glancing at them to see if they might look toward him but they were oblivious. It was nearly as dark as night now under the elevated, and the stores had all turned their lights on. The passing cars had their lights on, too, and there was a brilliant flash of lightning and an ear-splitting roll of thunder, immediately followed by another flash of lightning, and the rain began to fall in torrents. It flowed down the gutters and the streets glistened and great streaks of water splashed down from the el, hitting the sidewalk with great force. A train passed overhead, roaring into the station, and its brakes screeched as it came to a halt. The traffic in the street had slowed to a crawl and it seemed that all of a sudden everyone had disappeared. The sidewalks were empty and people were standing silently in doorways and under awnings. The rain fell as though it were the fulfilling of a prophecy and would last forever. It all seemed appropriate to Toby, as if the gods knew of his flight, and he wondered if he was making everything up in his head. Am I really running from the cops, he thought. He felt the suitcase in his hand and he knew that he was going to take the train into Manhattan, where he could easily disappear. Catch a bus out of the Port Authority and head south or west or wherever the first bus was going. Or maybe just head upstate and stay in one of those little towns with an Indian name that nobody ever pronounced properly. It seemed to Toby that those places were still located back somewhere in history. Modern times had not reached them yet and he knew that nobody would ever find him in a place like that. And he decided that's what he would do. Take a bus north. The Adirondacks. He had read somewhere that they covered a vast area and some parts of them were still hardly explored at all. Hard to believe. Just a hundred and fifty miles north of the city. He could stay there until they found whoever killed Annie, then he could come back home and go to school. He was terrified the cops would find him and take him in and never let him go. He knew of all the pent-up anger of the neighborhood even before Annie was murdered and he knew it would explode and they would only see that he was black and it would reach out blindly for him. It was always there behind the smiles and the handshakes and the pats on the back. There was the false camaraderie that hid the lie behind the anger. He had lied to himself, too, denying that it really was there because he didn't want to believe it. He always knew in his heart that he was never really included. The anger just needed something to let it come rushing out like a sudden storm and now they had their excuse.

It wasn't the kind of thing he could articulate to his father. It didn't come from something he could figure out and it wasn't just from observation. It came from a feeling deep in the gut where the truth always lay. He was outside of the pale and he was tolerated. The insults came not in words but in false attitudes and manner, and no matter how well he tried to understand, it baffled because it was all based on a kind of insanity.

He knew that what was there between him and Annie was beyond the comprehension of the neighborhood and yet it was as simple as the coming together of kindred spirits. An awareness of each other they were powerless to resist that had made them feel older than everyone around them.

He stood in a darkened doorway, waiting to make his way up the stairs to the subway.

He had a feeling that they had to be looking for him now. The cops on the corner had been joined by two more. They had moved back and they were standing under an awning as the rain still poured down. They were wearing the black oilskins that reflected the lights, and flaps hung down over their shoulders from their caps, making them look like French foreign legionnaires. He suddenly left the safety of the doorway and started to walk quickly toward the subway stairs. He could hear a siren wailing in the distance and he felt a spasm of fear in his stomach. It was coming closer and he looked over his shoulder in fear, then he saw the lights of the speeding patrol car. He saw it stop under the station. He told himself he was crazy and he should have listened to his father. What the hell am I running away for? Jesus, I should go to the precinct and let them ask me anything they want. Then he heard voices shouting. He started to run up the steps two at a time. He was afraid to look back in case it was him they were after, then he heard his name being called. He knew his father must have told them he had left. He heard a commotion behind him and he looked back and two men were running after him. They called out to him, warning him to stop, and now he could hear more sirens. They seemed to be coming from every direction. The rain was still coming down relentlessly and the thunder sounded like the heavens were being pulled apart.

He dropped his suitcase and flew up the steps. He hoped that he would catch a train as it was just pulling in to the station. Sometimes you get lucky, he thought. Then the miracle happened. A Manhattan-bound train pulled in just as he reached the top of the stairs. He leapt over the turnstile and ran up the stairs to the platform. The train was still in the station as though it were waiting for him. He raced toward the open doors and just as he got there they closed slowly. He reached through the doors desperately trying to open them. The train started to move out of the station gathering speed, and he was forced to release his grip on the door. He heard shouts down near the token booth and he could hear the cops coming up the stairs to the platform. They had their guns drawn, and when the last car of the train had passed he jumped down to the tracks and made his way to the other side of the station. They were shouting for him to halt and he saw two men leap down to the tracks to follow him across. He ran down the length of the platform stairs and leaped down them and he heard the sharp crack of gunfire. He was still on the stairway leading to the street and just as he came near to the bottom the figure of Arnie Meyers was standing before him with his gun drawn. He barreled into him, knocking him over and sending him sprawling on the sidewalk. Arnie's gun went flying and he hit the ground so hard he couldn't catch his breath. He tried to raise himself but he slumped back down to the pavement.

Toby ran on blindly, not knowing where he was going. They were firing after him now and he felt anger replace his terror. The bastards want to kill me, he thought. They're not going to give me a chance. They kill me now and they've got the whole thing wrapped up. They would never even have to look for the real killer. He felt tears of frustration mingle with the pelting rain spitting in his face. The thunder rolled across the black sky and the lightning flashed its electric madness as though all of the world had gone crazy, and when he looked over his shoulder he saw the vicious muzzle flashes of the cops' guns firing at him. And then suddenly he fell spread-eagled on the ground. He managed to get to his feet quickly and he was running again. He could feel an awful pain running through his body and it seemed to settle in his shoulder. He wondered if he could be having a heart attack, but he knew young guys like him didn't get heart attacks. But the pain throbbed and wouldn't go away. Then he saw the huge bloodstain on his shoulder, and he realized he had been shot. A huge childlike sob came from him and took his breath away. His arm had lost all feeling and he couldn't raise it and he knew he couldn't go on much longer. He was off the avenue now, running up a quiet street with houses on either side of it. He had grown up in the neighborhood, but he didn't remember the street. It was different. No apartment buildings, just houses with grassy spaces leading down to the sidewalks. He wanted to sit down, close his eyes, and go to sleep. He wanted to reach out to someone—anyone—and tell them all of the terrible wrong that was happening. He wanted to hear someone say it shouldn't be happening at all. He could hear sirens wailing all around him and he could hear shouts in the distance behind him. He leaned against a tree planted at the edge of the sidewalk but he knew he couldn't stay there for long. He looked at his shoulder and saw blood oozing from the wound and he felt weak and wondered if he was going to die. Part of him didn't care anymore. It told him to slide down to the ground and let himself sleep, to close his eyes and let the world fall away, to drown the noise of the sirens and the shouts and let himself slip into that peaceful place where the world would leave him alone. But he forced himself to move on.

FIFTEEN

Word had spread quickly through the neighborhood that Toby Walters had run away and the cops were hunting him down. Raguso slammed his fist down on the bar in Kerrigan's and shouted, "What the hell did I tell you? What the hell did I tell you? Jesus, didn't I tell you. I knew it had to be him." They were all there for the Sunday evening ritual of commiseration before the dreaded Monday morning and the return to work. Dooney Hanifan, Fat Charlie Wallace, Freddie Alcaro, Tommy O'Connor, and the rest crowded together around the bar as though they had won a victory. They raised their fists and shouted at one another. They were almost jubilant. It was all turning out the way they believed it would, and Kerrigan moved down to the end of the bar as he always did when he was at odds with them. "You know, we ought to find that sonofabitch ourselves," Raguso shouted. It seemed hard for him now to keep his voice down. "We could save the cops the trouble. They say there was a shootout at the subway station on Fourth. He's got to be somewhere in the neighborhood. Whadaya say? Let's go find the coon. Jesus, we owe it to Red, don't we?"

"Vigilantes went out with Wyatt Earp," Kerrigan said. "The cops are gonna chase you guys off the streets if you try that. Jesus, Rags, what the hell's the matter with you? Dooney, for God's sake, talk to him." But they didn't seem to be listening to him.

"You're all crazy," he shouted at them. "You lay a finger on him, you're all in deep shit."

But they were all over by the door and the window, looking out into the street as though they couldn't stop themselves. "You're gonna go out there in the pouring rain with half the cops in Brooklyn looking for him with cars and radios and everything. How the hell are you guys gonna find him?" They didn't answer him.

"Listen to me," Kerrigan pleaded again, but they were standing outside now on the sidewalk in a group with the rain pouring down on them. He watched them through the window. They were shouting and gesticulating like children on the way to a birthday party. Their glasses still stood on the bar and the place was empty except for the few old men who always sat in the back. The crowd outside was arguing among themselves about which direction they should take. The thunder and lightning were gone but the rain still poured down heavier than ever through the darkness.

They started off toward the avenue, taking up the entire sidewalk, laughing and shouting the way they did on the way to a ballgame. Fat Charlie Wallace struggled to keep up with them. Windows were opening and people were looking out into the street and the crowd was beckoning and shouting at them to follow. "We're going to get Toby Walters," they said. The crowd kept getting larger even as the rain poured down relentlessly. The sidewalk was too narrow to contain them now and they spilled over into the street, holding up traffic. They linked arms like a great wave sweeping aside anything or anyone who got in their way and they shouted out for all niggers to leave the street.

The march swelled and gathered momentum. People were coming out of their houses to join. They wore raincoats and carried umbrellas, and when they reached the avenue they halted and Dooney and Raguso told them to break up into groups and cover the whole neighborhood. They ran off into the night, calling out to each other and shouting Toby Walter's name. "And don't forget," Raguso shouted. "Whoever finds him brings him back here. Right here."

Patrol cars with their lights flashing sped up and down the avenue, and some of the crowd had gotten their cars and were cruising around the streets, using flashlights to peer into alleys and yards and spaces between the houses. They checked doorways and basements, shouting and calling to one another as though they expected to find the fugitive at any minute. The plan was to bring him back to Gallucci's Alley, where Annie Dahlgren had been murdered. The police were trying to disperse the crowd. They called out to them with their bullhorns, telling them to break up and go home, but they didn't pay any attention. Arnie Meyers sat in an unmarked car with Red watching the mob running and shouting, stopping cars in the street and harassing people coming off the subway. Arnie had been walking with a limp since Toby knocked him over. Red had urged him to go to the hospital but Arnie was determined to find Toby. He chewed on an unlit cigar and looked at the mob through the window. "I've never seen anything like it," he said, turning to Red. "I've been in this precinct for a long time. I thought I knew the people and the neighborhood well. Jeez, they're all ordinary working stiffs like me. Decent people. But look at 'em. They want blood. What the hell happens to people?"

They had put a guard around Bailey Walters's place in case the crowd got nasty and decided to go after him. Arnie had visions of them dragging the old man into the street and beating him up or lynching him on the spot. He was determined it wasn't going to happen, but he knew when the mood was ugly the mob had a life of its own. Red was surprised, too. He had seen Dooney and Raguso and all the crowd from Kerrigan's leading them on. All it ever took was a couple of hot-heads who bore out all the fear and frustration of the crowd. But he was numb. It seemed that every feeling he ever had was taken away and he felt nothing. There was a part of him that still refused to believe that Annie was dead. There was an ache in him under the numbness that he couldn't let himself feel because he was afraid it would rip him apart if he let it reach his heart. Arnie knew from long experience that crimes like this were usually the result of some unexpressed anger, a chip on the shoulder or a smoldering resentment that finds its way to the loins and expresses itself in the most violent act that vitiates the evil energy. Someone had told him once that when you bury anger you bury it alive. The problem is, you never know when it's going to erupt or in whom. But now it seemed that all of the repressed anger and fear of the neighborhood had been unleashed and it looked like the cops could do little to control it.

Father Darcy was standing outside the church, holding an umbrella, and the whole neighborhood seemed to be out in the pouring rain. There were shouts and even laughter and a strange electricity in the air. Everyone was anticipating the capture of Toby Walters and they couldn't wait to get the good news. Rumors were rampant and they changed by the minute. Some said they had already found him and others said they were closing in on him. Darcy heard cheers go up and die down again and he wondered if anyone had any idea what was going on. There was an army of cops of in the street trying to get everyone to go home but they weren't succeeding. No one was paying any attention to them and there was even a strange gaiety in the night as though they were in the midst of a block party. The rain was not defusing their energy nor their desire for the capture of Toby. Some of them waved when they saw Darcy standing on the steps, calling out to him to come down and join them. He saw that the cops had given up trying to disperse them. They were just going through the motions. "Please go home," he heard himself shout at them. "In the name of God, please go home and let the police handle this. You can't take the law into your own hands." He ran down the steps of the church into the street. "Please go home," he shouted. "Let the police do their work." He stood in the middle of the crowd now, shouting into their faces as they ignored him. He shouted at the cops, too, but they laughed and turned away. He wondered if this was what the cops wanted. They had to want it. They could break it all up if they wanted to. The wildness of the crowd frightened him and he had to fight his way back to the sidewalk. He started to run toward the avenue. Sirens were still wailing and the black and green squad cars were darting back and forth like messengers at the edge of a battle. There was a huge red-faced cop directing traffic at the intersection and he went up to him and asked him who was in charge. The cop tipped his cap to Darcy in the respectful manner and pointed to an unmarked car parked under the elevated. He ran toward it and looked inside. He saw Red sitting in the driver's seat and motioned to him to open the window.

He nodded to Darcy. "I'm trying to find out who's in charge," he said.

"This is Inspector Meyers," Red said, turning to Arnie. He looked at Darcy.

"What can I do for you, Father?" he said.

"I want to see the streets cleared of those people. They're like a mob. God knows what they'll do. Can't you break it up?"

"We don't have enough people."

"I just hope they don't get to that boy before the police do."

"Well, I wouldn't worry about that. We just had a report that they're closing in on him. Woulda been a helluva lot easier if he hadn't tried to run away."

Darcy shook his head. "Hard to believe what's happening. Who would've thought it would have come to this."

"It only takes a few jerks to get it rolling, but that's the way it always is."

A train rumbled over the elevated, making it impossible to talk. Darcy bent down to the window again after it had passed.

"Do you think the boy did it, Inspector?"

"I don't know, Father, but you have to wonder why he chose to run away. He hasn't made it any easier on himself."

"I'm sure he panicked. He's scared to death and with good reason. I mean the whole neighborhood wants to believe he's the killer and they're out in the streets ready to lynch him."

"He's our only suspect now, and he's trying to run away. If he didn't do it, why is he running? Nobody else we've talked to has tried to run away."

The car radio crackled and Red started the car in response to the message.

"I wouldn't worry about it, Father," Arnie said. "We'll find him, and if he didn't do it he's got nothing to worry about."

Darcy stood up and moved away from the car and watched it speed down the avenue. Red glanced at Arnie as they drove.

"Jeez, that guy loves to stick his neck into everything. You should hear him on Sundays. Tellin' us how to run our lives. Thinks we should all stand back and welcome the shines into the neighborhood. We're all supposed to act like good Christians. The trouble with guys like him is they could never make it in the real world. *Do we think Toby Walters really did it?* Is he kidding? Who the hell else did it? Who else would want to do it? You know what, Arnie? Soon as all this is over I'm getting as far away from here as I can. Let the shines have it. They'll never have what we had. Watch it. A year after they take over, the neighborhood won't be fit to live in. But Darcy would like us all to stay. But you see, Arnie, Darcy comes from some rich family up in Westchester. His old man is some sort of big shot. Don't mean a damn thing to him that my sister's dead. He's more concerned about that coon than he is about me and my mother. And imagine—the guy was in our house at the party last night."

Arnie stared straight ahead and nodded.

Mrs. Treacy had waited so long for Jack to come out of his room that she had almost given up, but when she heard the shower running she began to put his breakfast on the table. She believed that if he ate properly and got enough rest all would be well with him and he would become his old self again.

"Hurry up, Jack," she called. "I've got your breakfast on the table and I made some lovely Irish soda bread. And the eggs are soft-boiled, just the way you like them. Come and sit down before everything gets cold."

Treacy had showered and shaved now and he was wearing clean underwear for the first time in nearly two weeks. The awful smell had left his body, he had used lots of deodorant under his arms and he had splashed aftershave over his face. He saw himself in the mirror and the shakes swept over him for an instant. He felt himself shiver. He gritted his teeth to keep them from chattering and he began to sweat. He saw his arms and he looked at the long red scratch marks and felt the bruises and welts all over his body. There was a purple bruise under one of his eyes and there was another long scratch mark on his neck. He pulled his shirt on and buttoned it all the way to cover it up. He wiped the sweat from his face with a towel and he thought of his bloody clothes sitting on the bottom of his seabag. Again he tried to remember where he had been and what had happened. He held his hands out in front of him. They were shaking as though he had the palsy and they were scratched and bruised and raw looking. He finally came out of the bathroom and sat at the kitchen table. His mother leaned over him and kissed him on the cheek. Then she sat in her chair and smiled at him. She poured him a cup of tea and passed the cup and saucer down to him. She still made it the old way, letting the loose tea sit in the pot and pouring the boiling water into it. She always covered the pot with a tea cozy to keep it warm. And she had cut off the tops of his eggs and served them just the way he liked them. There was the plate of Irish soda bread heavily buttered. He had always told her it was his favorite meal in the whole world. She looked at him, seeing his bruised and cut face. She had long since learned not to ask him any questions. It was always the same when he came home. For her the miracle was that he was home. That he could never tell her where he had been or what he had done was an accepted part of his homecoming. As long as he was safe and sound it all didn't matter. He would be home with her now for a few weeks until the dreaded check came. It was supposed to help him but it was killing him. The government was rewarding him for his service and valor by allowing him to drink himself to death.

To his mother, he was still her little boy and he always would be. And it was she more than anyone else who understood what had really happened to him. It broke her heart that there seemed to be no way to reach him. And now she smiled at him and urged him to eat. He drank his tea slowly and ate some soda bread, and she began to tell him what had happened to Annie Dahlgren. She started to cry as she spoke, dabbing at her eyes with a tissue. "What's the world coming to at all?" she said. "That beautiful young girl. My God, how could anyone do that? And poor Mrs. Dahlgren. With all she's been through and the terrible time she had with that poor unfortunate husband. Oh, Jack, if you could have seen how beautiful she looked at the party. And so smart and so bright. You have to wonder the way things happen. Why, I keep asking? Why do things happen the way they do? Why does God let them happen? Right here in the neighborhood where she lived. Hardly a stone's throw from her own house."

Treacy bowed his head. He didn't want to believe what she had told him. Annie Dahlgren. How could it be? Red's beautiful sister. He loved to see her walking down the block. Countless times he had watched her from his window. There was something about her. He couldn't eat anymore, and the shakes hit him again and he had to hold on to the seat of his chair with both hands to keep from letting his mother see. And then the fear welled up in him. He thought of the blood on his clothes and the scratches on his arms. He fought to hold on and he bit his lip.

"Do they know who did it?" he asked.

"Everyone is saying that Toby Walters, that young colored fella, had something to do with it. I don't know. There's all kinds of rumors going around. I can only think of poor Mrs. Dahlgren. My God, what she must be going through."

He sipped his tea and poked at his egg. He needed a drink badly and he remembered it hadn't been working for him. Wasn't doing for him what it used to do. Jesus, he thought, if the booze don't work, what the hell am I going to do?

"The poor little girl was lying in the alley half the night bleeding to death. They say it was a terrible sight. And raped. How could they do it? Not only have his way with her but kill her. They say they couldn't count all the stab wounds. What sort of animal must he be? My God, what's happening to us? A poor innocent little girl never hurt anyone in her life. What sort of man would do that?"

Treacy could only shake his head and look at her.

"Are you going to eat your eggs?" she asked him.

He shook his head slowly and a feeling of panic began to come over him. He glanced at his hands again and the sweat on his neck made the scratches sting. He couldn't get his mind off the bloody clothes, and much as he tried to keep it away the terrible thought came to him: *It could have been me. Maybe it was me.*

"I'm not feeling well, Mom," he said as he stood up. He moved around the table and kissed her on the cheek and went to his room. She was used to him. This was the way it always was when he came home. He locked the door behind him and he sat on the edge of the bed and buried his face in his hands. Then he stood up and went to the closet and took out his seabag. He unlocked it and reached down into it and pulled his shirt and trousers. He threw them out onto the floor and looked at them.

They were stiff with dried blood. He picked them up quickly again and stuffed them into the bag and locked it. He sat down on the bed again and tried desperately to remember where he had been and who he'd been with. He could hardly remember coming home. Did I get home last night or the night before? he asked himself. Was it before or after they had found Annie Dahlgren? He got down on his knees and reached under the bed for the bottle, but when he pulled it out he saw it was empty. He couldn't get Annie out of his mind. He wasn't afraid for himself, but the thought that it could have been him who killed her was unbearable, and no matter how hard he tried he couldn't relieve himself of the possibility. There was a part of him that wanted to convince himself that it was him. He sprawled on the bed and broke out in a sweat, then he jumped up and unlocked the door and ran to the bathroom to examine himself in the mirror, looking at every scratch and bruise. *How did they get there? Where did they come from?* He had a vague memory of being with two women who tried to roll him but he couldn't remember if he had fought with them. And he swore again that he would never drink again. He wanted to talk to someone, but he couldn't think who. He had no pals anymore. It was ages since he had a long talk with Red, and he remembered how close they used to be, and he knew he couldn't talk to him about this. He wished he could find someone who would tell him that it wasn't him who killed Annie. But his whole life was a kind of secret now. He tried every day to avoid himself and reality. And now he was afraid the world was going to find him. And it would confirm all of the worst feelings he had about himself.

SIXTEEN

Toby Walters opened his eyes and didn't know where he was. And for a minute he didn't remember the chase or that he had been shot. He felt a comforting numbness enveloping his body. It felt as though the world had gone away and decided to leave him alone. But then he began to feel the throbbing pain in his shoulder and the ache began to pierce his numbness. He heard sirens away off in the distance as though they would never stop, then he felt the rain falling on him and he realized he was soaking wet. He shivered and tried to raise himself up, but he found it hard to move. It was pitch-dark and he could hear the brooklike sound of water rushing down a drain, and somewhere through the darkness there was the ever-present hum of the night, the current of life moving through it. Then everything came back to him. He reached up and felt the wound in his shoulder and the blood was still oozing out of it. He felt as weak as a baby. There was no feeling in his legs.

He managed to raise himself to a sitting position and through the darkness he could see he was close to the side of a white frame house that was surrounded by trees. There was a low hedge shielding him from the street and the sidewalk and he began to realize that he was not far away from where he had started out. And now he could feel the coldness of the ground under him. Then a wave of terror swept over him and he wondered if he was going to die. He heard voices coming from the street and his stomach heaved in fright. He lay down behind the hedge, barely daring to breathe. The voices came closer and now he was lying flat on his back, staring up into the blackness of the night with the rain falling on his face. The voices were in the middle of the street now out in front of the house. And they began to shout and argue among themselves.

"For chrissake, we're all soaked. Let's go back. I've had enough of this shit," one of them said.

"Yeah, the hell with that nigger," someone else said. "Maybe the sonofabitch has bled to death by now."

"Let the goddamn cops get him," another chimed in. "Shit, we're outta beer, anyway."

And then he heard them laughing as they moved away and he heard a loud belch. He knew they were all drunk. And he knew they had stopped again and they started to argue among themselves. Some of them wanted to go back and continue looking for him. Then they started on their way again.

He knew he couldn't stay where he was. It would only be a matter of time before someone would find him. He managed to stand up and a wave of nausea and dizziness hit him and he nearly fell back down again. He wanted to just lie down where he was and wait until they came for him. He was sure he couldn't go on. Then he heard shouts down the street and he knew he had to go. He managed to steady himself and his legs began to move as though they had a life of their own. He was surprised. It felt as though some power had taken over and was propelling him along. He even smiled and felt giddy, then he heard sirens and voices again. He stopped in a doorway and looked up and down the street. He could see an old redbrick building standing on a corner. It looked like an armory or an old castle with a turret on one end. He didn't recall ever seeing it before. There were stained glass windows that reflected the streetlights.

He stared at it and wondered if he was dreaming or if it was really there. He edged out of the doorway, cautiously making sure there was no one on the street, then he began to walk toward the building. He felt drawn to it. He stood before the front door and tried to open it, but it wouldn't budge. He looked up and down the street again, and then he moved around to the side of the building and saw a small side door with a light over it.

He reached for the handle and turned it. Miraculously, the door opened. He walked in slowly and listened. There was absolute quiet. He moved slowly down a long corridor, keeping to the wall for support, and suddenly he could hear voices speaking in unison as if they were chanting. He stopped and listened. He had never heard anything like it before, and he didn't know what it was. He walked on until he came to a door with a stained glass panel of Mary holding the infant Jesus. Her gentle, innocent face looked at him and he stared back at her. He opened the door and passed through it and the chanting voices were closer. They moved in unison, repeating the same phrases over and over, and then he came to another door. The voices seemed to be coming from beyond it. He opened it slightly and peered inside. He was looking down the length of a small chapel and he saw rows of nuns kneeling with their heads bowed. He opened the door enough for him to squeeze through it and then closed it quietly behind him. He was feeling faint and a terrible blackness was closing in around him. He struggled to stay on his feet, and he hoped nobody would turn around and see him, but they were totally absorbed in their prayers. He could smell the church smell of candles and incense and he felt an unexpected comfort. There was an unearthly serenity in the chapel, and he had to lean back and rest against the wall because he thought he was going to faint. He spotted a small curtained confessional off to one side and he began to move slowly toward it as quietly as he could. When he reached it he pulled the curtain aside and sat down in the darkness. His head slumped to his chest and he couldn't keep his eyes open. He listened to the rise and fall of the voices as they moved through the prayers, repeating and repeating the words like water moving over a falls, moving as though to stop would precipitate some terrible catastrophe:

> *Hail Mary, full of grace;*
> *The lord is with thee*
> *Blessed art though amongst women*
> *And blessed is the fruit of thy womb, Jesus.*
> *Holy Mary, Mother of God;*
> *Pray for us sinners now and*
> *At the hour of our death. Amen.*

He could feel himself sinking, falling through a deep dark hole, moving faster and faster as though he were being pulled by a magnet.

He stretched his arms out desperately to find some kind of hold that would save him from falling deeper and deeper, then he heard himself cry out in terror and there was only the blackness.

When he opened his eyes he saw two nuns staring down at him. He was lying on a narrow bed in a small room that looked like a cell. There was a crucifix on the wall opposite him. He had the urge to jump up and run but he could only lie there helpless and weak. His shoulder was throbbing with pain and he could hear his heart beating weakly in his chest. The older of the two nuns was kneeling at the side of the bed. She took his hand and held it gently and smiled down at him. "It's alright," she said. "It's alright. There's nothing to worry about." He noticed her eyes looking directly in his. They were soft and blue. He realized they had taken his shirt off and his shoulder was bandaged.

The other nun stared down at him with a question in her eyes, but they were soft, too, and he felt a strange comfort coming from her as though she knew something that was beyond time and the world. He began to realize that he had passed the convent so many times and had always wondered what it was like inside.

His eyes wanted to close but he fought to keep them open because he was afraid of the darkness he saw when they were closed. He was afraid he would die and he would not be able to tell. He wanted to ask the nuns if he was dying, but he was afraid of how they would answer. He was moving in and out of consciousness and it was hard for him to tell the difference. He thought of God and wondered if he would see Him. He hoped he wouldn't because he knew that if he did he would be dead for sure. He thought he heard his father's voice calling out to him, then he was sitting with him at the kitchen table.

He had never talked to him about God and he never went to church. When he opened his eyes the nuns were still there and the older one was pulling the bed covers up under his chin. The younger one placed a cold washcloth over his forehead and held it gently in place. She smiled at him and he thought that she didn't look much older than Annie.

Her skin was beautiful, so white it almost glowed. She looked like Mary in the panel he had seen on the door. The older nun whispered something in her ear and left. Through the haze of his pain and fever, he thought he heard the urgent wail of a siren. It seemed to come closer and closer and finally it stopped nearby, and he wondered if the cops knew where he was. A spasm of fear ignited in his stomach and ran down his legs, and he felt as though he were paralyzed.

SEVENTEEN

Father Darcy had fallen asleep in his clothes. His trousers were still damp from the rain and he had tried to finish reading his breviary but hadn't been able to stay awake. The prayer book had fallen from his hands and lay on his chest, rising and falling with his breathing. The phone had been ringing several times before he heard it. When he picked it up he heard the soft voice of Sister Immealda. "I believe the boy is the one they're looking for," she said. "He's very badly hurt, Father, and he's lost an awful lot of blood. To tell you the truth, Father, we don't know if he's going to live. I don't have the heart to call the police. I don't want to do anything 'til you get here yourself. He'll have to be taken to a hospital."

"I'll be right over, Sister," Darcy said. "Don't do anything else 'til I get there."

The rain was still falling as he left for the convent and the streetlights were reflected on the pavement. It was quieter now. The mob had dispersed but still the wail of sirens continued. He knew he would have to get Toby to a hospital and then the police would have him. He wondered why it was that the whole neighborhood was convinced that Toby was the killer. Nobody seemed to question it. When he came to the convent it always appeared to him as if it had been placed down in the street from another time. Its redbrick structure with its round turrets could have come from Camelot and he had always wondered how a place like it could have been built in Brooklyn. There had to be a story to it. He had never liked playing priest to the nuns. Their simple serenity tended to irritate him, and when he went there they treated him like he was an emissary from the Pope himself. They made their way quietly through the vale of tears, and as much as they knew of the harshness of the world that surrounded them, it never came between them and their belief in the ultimate goodness of God.

Sister Immealda led him inside. "I'm so glad you're here, Father," she said as she walked ahead of him and led him to where Toby was. The younger nun was still sitting at the side of the bed. "He's getting weaker," she whispered as Darcy came in. Toby lay with his eyes closed. The young nun removed the washcloth from his brow and dampened it again from a small basin of water nearby. Toby mumbled something as Darcy peered down at him. He looked so young and he really wasn't yet a man. He opened his eyes and saw Darcy and he could see the fear in his face. Tears welled up in Toby's eyes and rolled down his cheeks. The young nun moved close to him and brushed them away with a small white handkerchief. Toby wasn't a Catholic but he knew from living in the neighborhood that priests always showed up when someone was about to die. Darcy forced a smile and Toby could tell. He was convinced he was going to die and Sister Immealda looked at him with all of the concern of the mother he never knew.

"Am I going to die?" he managed to whisper.

Darcy shook his head. "Don't worry. We'll take care of you," he said. "There's nothing to be afraid of."

He pulled a chair close to the bed and sat down. He leaned over Toby. "Try not to talk," he said.

"Everyone thinks I killed Annie," he whispered. "I swear to God I didn't. I loved her. How could I kill her?"

He tried to raise himself up to get closer to Darcy but the blackness closed in again and he slumped back and closed his eyes. Sister Immealda was standing close to Darcy and she motioned to him to move to a corner of the room with her.

"He is getting weaker," she said. "We need to get him to a hospital right away. Should I call the police now?"

Darcy hadn't taken his eyes off Toby and he knew he was telling the truth. "Father, he's still losing blood and his pulse is fading. We don't have much time."

Darcy knew there was no choice and he nodded to her to make the call.

"Please leave me alone here for a minute, Sister. I want to pray over him. The nuns left, and Darcy moved back to the bed. He stared down at him and prayed silently. He felt awful that they had to give him up to the police because he knew they believed he was guilty, too. He walked to the door and went outside. Sister Immealda was waiting.

"Is there anything more we can do for him here?" he asked. Couldn't we take care of him here?"

"We're not doctors," the old nun told him. "He's got to get to a hospital."

"Alright. Call the ambulance. I'll call the police."

He asked for Arnie Meyers and they told him he wasn't there. "This is Father Darcy. I'm at the Convent of Mercy on Gibbons Street. Tell him there's an ambulance on the way to take the boy to Saint Gregory's. And be sure to tell him that no one else is to know. We don't want that mob descending on the hospital. The kid is very weak and has lost a lot of blood. Tell him he needn't worry about him trying to make a break."

Almost as soon as he put the phone down he could hear the siren of the ambulance as it approached. It arrived just ahead of Arnie Meyers and Red, and they watched as the attendants carried Toby out on a stretcher. He was unconscious. Darcy followed Toby into the back of the ambulance and he was surprised when Arnie got in beside him. They had already attached a transfusion drip to Toby's arm and a young doctor was kneeling over him with a stethoscope, listening to his heart. Arnie was chewing on the stub of a cigar and as Darcy watched him he could feel his anger rise up. He knew that nothing surprised Arnie anymore. He had been too long on the force for that. There was very little he hadn't seen. The madness of people was the norm for him.

"I think he would have died if he hadn't found the convent," Darcy said. "Guess he's lucky the mob didn't find him. The whole neighborhood out in the night hunting him down like an animal. Bloodthirsty. And the police did nothing to break 'em up."

He was fighting to contain his anger.

"Father, you don't know what you're talking about," Arnie said quietly. "I suggest that we not let our emotions run away with us. I don't want to embarrass you but the word is out all over that you are a minority of one. We haven't received any complaints. You shouldn't talk about things you know nothing about. The kid brought everything on himself when he tried to run away. What are people supposed to think? We didn't start chasing 'til he started running."

"And the fact that he's black has nothing to do with it, either?"

"Color's got nothing to do with it. Cops don't choose the victims. Killers do that and we do our job regardless. Now I respect the cloth and all that but really, Father, you are way off base. This kid is the prime suspect in this case because his actions point to it. Black's got nothing to do with it. You're the only one keeps saying it has. We have no alternative but to place him under arrest. That's the law."

When Harry Cope heard what was happening in the neighborhood he drove to Brooklyn through the rainstorm. He told Sheila he wanted to be in the hunt for Toby Walters. She begged him not to go but he was determined. She kept asking him why and he told her he had seen Toby across the street looking up at Annie's apartment the night of the party and he knew he was up to something. "Besides, I never liked that kid, anyway. There was always something about him. Looked at you like he was better than you. Jeez!"

"When did you see him?" his wife asked him.

"When we were out on the stoop."

"How come I didn't see him?"

"It was after you went back inside. Remember I stayed to have a smoke."

Harry had come to despise the old neighborhood since he bought the house on the Island.

He secretly despised Kerrigan's crowd and the people he considered suckers who would be caught up in the huge change that would happen when the blacks started to move in.

But when he got to the neighborhood that night he found the core of the mob and became one of them. He was in a group with Raguso, Charlie Wallace, and Dooney Hanifan. They were all surprised to see him because he was giving up a night's work, too. That was a lot of money for a printer on the *Daily News*. He told them he just had to do it because he had known Annie since she was a little girl, and he told them that if it wasn't for the goddamn niggers moving in he never would have moved away from the neighborhood. And he told them how he had always felt about Toby Walters. "Never liked him," he said. "Too big for his boots." Well, he was going to get his comeuppance now. And besides, he told them, "I'm almost sure I saw him standing across the street from the Dahlgrens' house the night of the party. I was out on the stoop having a smoke and I saw him behind a car. He didn't think anyone spotted him, but I did. He was looking up at the windows. I mean, you could hear the music and people having a good time. He musta been really pissed off. Annie had been out on the stoop with Charlie Gallucci. Toby Walters had to see them. I mean it doesn't take much figurin' out to see what happened. Just hope we get to him before the cops do." They tolerated Harry and he knew in his heart he would never be one of them. He knew they still saw him as the guy who stole Red's girl away when he was in Korea. That was never going to change. And they knew, too, that Harry Cope always had an angle. That's the way he was since they were kids. He never did anything out of the goodness of his heart.

It was eight in the morning and Red sat alone at the bar in Kerrigan's. The place wasn't open yet but Red hadn't been able to sleep all night. He had knocked on the door and Kerrigan had let him in.

"Jesus, you look beat," he told him. And then he reached under the counter and pulled out a bottle of brandy. He filled an old-fashioned glass and pushed it across to Red.

"Get some of that into you," he said. "Do you good."

Red raised the glass and took a long swallow. He felt the warmth moving through his body and he lit a cigarette.

"So they got Toby Walters?" Kerrigan said quietly.

Red looked at him, surprised. "Jeez, you got a wire to the station? No one's supposed to know that yet."

"Tommy Kane that walks the beat stuck his head in the door twenty minutes ago and told me. Said Arnie Meyers thinks he did it for sure."

"It's alright with me. I just want it to be over. Don't even wanna think about it."

"What about you?"

"What do you mean?"

"I mean do you think the kid did it."

"Ran away, didn't he? Why would he run unless he did it?"

"Maybe he just got frightened. I mean he coulda panicked when he knew everyone was gonna find out about him and Annie. That wasn't going to go over big, especially with what's happening around the neighborhood."

"Look, his old man tried to get him to go to the precinct. His old man. And the kid packs a bag and runs. What are we supposed to think?"

"Well, you know, Red, Annie was a pretty bright kid. Lot of confidence. I don't think she would've been with a guy who . . . well you know."

"Look, it's like I said. I just want it to be over. Doesn't make any difference who did it. My sister isn't coming back."

Kerrigan poured himself a cup of coffee.

"So how'd they catch him?"

"He wound up in the convent off Fourth Avenue. He'd been shot. He passed out and the nuns found him. They called Darcy and he got in touch with us."

"So he's really hurt bad?"

"Sonofabitch was bleeding to death when the nuns found him. They fixed him up."

"Can't figure this guy Darcy out," Kerrigan said.

"Yeah—he's gotta be buckin' for Cardinal or somethin'. Loves to act like he knows what's best for everyone."

"I don't know. I think he's for real, believe it or not."

"Sure likes to stick his nose into things. Should mind his own business. Some things he should just stay the fuck out of. I mean the guy's a priest. He gets his three squares a day and a roof over his head. What the hell does he have to worry about?"

Kerrigan didn't answer him.

"You shoulda seen him at the hospital when they bring the kid in. Goes right in the emergency with him and he stays with him while they operate. And then when they bring him to the room he stands in front and won't let anyone else in. I thought Arnie was going to blow a gasket." He was shaking his head slowly. "I mean the guy really believes we wanted to take him because he's colored. Jesus, Johnny, we see colored around here every day. I've know 'em for as far back as I can remember and I never hated them. Never had any reason to. Just don't wanna hang out with 'em, that's all. Something wrong with that?" He paused and Kerrigan poured him some more brandy.

"And the truth is, Johnny, whether you like it or not they are different than us. They talk different, they laugh different. Throwin' their heads back and slappin' themselves. It's like they're all in on some joke they all know and we don't get."

His eyes were red from tiredness and his head was bowed as though he didn't have the strength to hold it up. He sipped his drink and looked across the bar at Kerrigan.

"I don't know. I'm just so goddamn tired, and I'm afraid to lie down and go to sleep. And I don't wanna go to my mother's house."

He raised his arms over his head to stretch and his mouth opened in an interminable yawn. He shook himself and leaned forward, putting his arms on the bar for support.

"I remember when we were coming home from Korea," he said. "Was like we were on that goddamn ship forever. You never saw anything so crowded in your life. It was like the fuckin' subway except you couldn't get off. All the black guys used to hang out together. Every day you'd see them up by the forward cargo hatch playin' cards and laughin' and jokin'. These guys wanted to be by themselves because that's what they were used to. You could never really get to know 'em. And there's this guy Smitty. Big sonofabitch and black as the ace of spades. He's our platoon leader and he's a good one, too. Trust him with my life, but when I see him with those other black guys I knew I didn't know him at all. It's like he knows somethin' and he sees right through us. Always half a grin on his kisser. I mean he's real smart. Been to college and all. When I'm alone with him he's a different guy than when he's with the others . . . I don't know. I know I ain't prejudiced. I don't hate 'em; I just don't wanna be with 'em, that's all, and if I'd known about Annie and Toby Walters I woulda stopped it dead. No question. No way they could ever be together. Just the way it is. Don't know what the hell ever got into her."

"You ought to go home and get some sleep."

"Can't go into that house. Jesus, Johnny. Somethin' happens to me when I look at my mother and see all that fuckin' pain in her face. I feel so goddamn helpless around her. I know it's terrible, but, Jesus, it's like she was born to mourn, do you know what I mean, Johnny?"

"You need to talk it out with someone, Red."

"What the fuck do you think I'm doin' here?"

"I'm a bartender, Red. Jesus, what the hell do I know about these things?"

"I don't give a fuck what you know or don't know. I just want you to listen."

"That's easy, Red, but I was thinking about that chaplain they got there in the precinct."

"What the hell is some priest gonna tell me. It's God's will? She's in a better place now? She's with the angels? I know all that bullshit. Priest. Jesus! I need Margo. I'm gonna go home and call her."

"You should try talking to Darcy. Now don't get mad at me. He's not like the others."

"You know, Johnny, you have this thing for priests. You workin' on commission or somethin'?"

The phone rang and Kerrigan walked to the end of the bar to pick it up. He listened for a while, then he nodded and hung up and came back to where Red was sitting. He poured himself another cup of coffee and took a sip.

"Know who showed up last night and joined the vigilantes?" Red shook his head.

"Harry Cope. He musta thought there was a reward—guy'd do anything for a buck. Drives in all the way from the Island. Jesus!"

"The fuckin' guy's nuts."

"They all came back here last night after they gave up the search and goddamn if Harry didn't walk in here with 'em. Shoulda seen him. All prepared for the weather. Big yellow oilskin like he's going deep-sea fishin'. He's buying drinks for everyone and you know how tight with a buck he is. And he doesn't wanna give up the search. Pleadin' with everyone to go back out again. You shoulda heard him."

"He never comes around here. What the hell's the matter with him?"

"And he keeps going on about Annie. How he'd known her since she was a little girl and they had to find the black bastard killed her."

"What the fuck's up with him?"

"Beats the hell outta me. But you shoulda seen him. Wouldn't leave the guys alone. Pestered the hell out of 'em and kept wanting to buy 'em drinks."

Red shook his head and stood up. He placed his hands on the bar and stretched back.

"None of this makes any sense," he said. "I feel like I'm dreamin' all of it. I think I'm gonna walk home and open the door and my little sister is gonna ask me how I'm doin' and I'm gonna tell her I'm fine. I can't believe she's not at home."

He stood by the bar and his head bowed into his chest and he started to sob. He tried to hold back his tears but they flowed from him and ran down his cheeks. He pulled a handkerchief from his pocket and covered his face with it. Kerrigan watched him and let him cry until he wiped his face and his eyes and put the handkerchief away. He finished the last of the brandy and looked at Kerrigan.

"I don't give a damn who did it, Johnny. It ain't gonna change anything and Annie ain't coming back."

"Just go home, Red, and go to bed. Sleep will catch up with you."

"No, Johnny, just let me sit in one of the booths. I can't go back to the house."

EIGHTEEN

Bailey Walters had gone to the hospital but the cops wouldn't let him see Toby. He sat alone in the lobby. He had always been a patient man and never gave anyone any trouble. He was well liked, had a smile for everyone, and there was a gentleness about him that even left some people a little embarrassed. He had a courtliness they never expected, probably because he was black, something in him that when they got close always surprised them. He found it hard to sit in the lobby, and when he couldn't sit he paced back and forth. He had told himself a thousand times that he never should have let Toby take off so easily. Would have been better, he thought, if he had locked the door to the apartment and called the cops himself. And then he began to realize that they were out to get him, anyway. Toby was unarmed. They would have caught him eventually. He never could have gotten away. There was just no need to shoot him but they did. An unarmed boy who never hurt anyone. He began to realize he was not going to see Toby and he walked out of the lobby and down the corridor to the entrance when he saw Arnie Meyers walking toward him. He was limping and as usual there was a stub of a cigar stuck in the corner of his mouth. There were two cops walking behind him and his face was flushed and unshaven. He looked exhausted and he stopped walking when he saw Bailey Walters.

"Your boy's in a lotta trouble," he said. "They fixed him up good. He's gonna be okay. They tell me it was touch and go for a while. Just lucky they got him to the hospital in time. The doc says if he lost any more blood they wouldn't have been able to save him."

"They won't let me up to see him," Bailey said.

"Don't worry; I'll take care of that."

He called one of the cops over and whispered something to him and the cop went to the reception desk and spoke to the nurse.

"Now, when you go up there," Arnie said, "you tell him he's got to co-operate or we're gonna be very tough on him. Tell him all he's got to do is answer the questions we ask him. And be sure to tell him that it's gonna do him no good to hold anything back. I wanna know what went on between him and the Dahlgren girl, you understand?"

He removed the cigar stub from his mouth and looked at it to see if it was worthwhile putting back. "All I know is the girl is dead and your boy's got a lot of talkin' to do. If he's got nuthin' to hide, then he's got nuthin' to worry about."

Bailey felt a tremor of anger pass through him.

"My boy didn't kill that little girl," he said.

"Well, he'll just have to prove that, won't he? So when you get up there you better talk some sense to him." And then he turned abruptly and walked away, leaving Bailey standing where he was. The two cops followed Arnie.

When he came to where they had Toby, he showed his pass to a huge cop who guarded the door to his room. The cop opened the door for him and he walked inside slowly. Toby was propped up on pillows and he was sleeping. He didn't want to wake him. He saw the tubes coming out of his nose and the drip attached to his arm. He moved to the head of the bed and looked down at his son. He still could see the little-boy face and he looked peaceful. He kissed him on the forehead. Toby's upper body was bare except for the huge dressing covering his chest and shoulder. He saw Toby open his eyes and the tears running slowly down his face. He fought to hold back his own tears but he couldn't, and he brushed the tears away and smiled. He felt Toby's free hand take his.

He tried to keep smiling.

"How you doin', Pop," Toby asked. Bailey stood up straight and struck a boxer's pose, raising his fists up and down and punching at the air in the classic way.

"I'm doin' great, son. Just great. And what about you? How you doin'?"

"Better."

"They didn't think you was goin' to make it."

"I'm weak but I'm okay. Still got the pain. Still hurts, but I'm okay."

"I know you didn't kill that little girl, son. Never doubted you for one minute."

"They been in here wantin' me to confess, Pop. They want me to tell 'em I killed Annie."

"All you gotta do, son, is keep tellin' 'em the truth. That's all you gotta do."

"They don't care about the truth, Pop. They just want me to tell 'em I did it."

He looked directly into his father's face, then he reached out and pulled him closer.

He glanced quickly at the door to make sure the cop wasn't listening and he whispered, "I'm not gonna let 'em keep me here. I've gotta find a way out. You've gotta help me, Pop."

"If you try to get away from here they'll kill you for sure, son. You didn't do it, so the best thing is for us to get a good lawyer. That's the best way. We get a real good lawyer. Somebody knows what he's doin'. Someone knows his way around. They got guys like that. We don't want one of them court-appointed fellas. We get a fella knows what he's doin'. A fella really believes you didn't do it. And once you talk to him he's gonna believe you for sure."

The cop came into the room and told Bailey his time was up. Toby held on to his father's hand because he didn't want him to leave. He bent down and kissed his son on the forehead.

"Don't worry, son," he said. "I'll be back here every day. We gonna win. Don't forget it." He turned away slowly and made his way out of the room.

Toby watched him as he left. He had never realized how much he loved his father and he felt ashamed of all the things he didn't like or understand about him. He didn't like the way he talked and dressed and he didn't like what looked to him like his servile manner.

And even his gentleness made him angry. The felt hat always perched squarely on the back of his head even when they sat at the kitchen table together and the way he moved as if he had all the time in the world. He never got ruffled or spoke back when some of the tenants were nasty with him. He remembered when he had carried him on his shoulders into Ebbets Field so that he could see Jackie Robinson, and he had told him that things would never be the same again. Change was gonna come fast now, he said, and he wasn't sure what his father had meant. The fans were wearing buttons that said, "I'm for Jackie." Everyone was wearing them, not just blacks. His father had bought him one, and he remembered he still had it somewhere. "You are seeing the beginning of something," his father had told him.

For a very long time he hadn't understood that he was different, that he was black or that it meant very much. It had all seemed to change suddenly and he knew there was a kind of wall around him. He realized he was the only black in the neighborhood. No one had ever said to him, "You are different because you are black." But all of a sudden he had found out that he was black and he was different.

Toby's friends used to come over to his house all the time. They were all white and Bailey Walters knew it would be different one day. There would be a parting of the ways. They and Toby would see the reality of the way things were. Toby would begin to see that there were two worlds in America. One white and one black, and it seemed that that was the way everyone expected it to be. Black people didn't count the way white people did. Black people's hard times were just something they were born for and they were the best at going through them. They were meant for getting by and smilin' through and being weary. They were the great mistake of American history. Everything would have been fine if they just hadn't been brought here in the first place, and people acted as if they weren't here at all. Invisible and ever present at the same time. Cleaned houses, shined shoes, and raised white folks' children. Their tragedies just didn't measure up to white folks' tragedies. They were the stuff of movies and the theatre and the great novels.

Blacks were able to handle their tragedies so well. Never made a fuss. They just seemed to be blessed with unlimited patience and understanding. They didn't need to concern themselves with the great possibilities of life. The American Dream wasn't for them. White folks would do that for them and the black folk could look with pride on the role they played in bringing about the white folks' happiness. That's the way it is. Toby had never expressed his inner feelings about the reality of black and white and he knew for sure he wasn't like his father. He couldn't be, and it scared him and excited him at the same time. He would never bow his head in servitude or supplication. He assumed his freedom was his because that's the way it was. He took it for granted just like the white folks did.

Margo found Red in Kerrigan's. He had fallen asleep in a booth and she couldn't wake him up. He hadn't known where he was and she was angry at Kerrigan for serving him.

"He was hurting, for God's sake," Kerrigan told her. "And I can't stop him from taking a drink if he wants to."

"You shouldn't have served him when he was drunk."

"For God's sake, woman, can't you see he's more exhausted than drunk. All I did was give him a glass of brandy. I've known Red since he was a kid and one thing I do know is my business. What he needed was brandy."

"You think you know him, but you don't. None of you. You're all a bunch of goddamn drunks spending half your lives in this place."

"That's a disgraceful thing to say to an honest bartender."

"Do any of your crowd really know what's happening in the world?"

"All too well, Miss Margo. All too well."

"Well, I think you all have your heads up your asses, if the truth be known."

"I'm far too polite to reply to you the way I'd like to."

"You can say any damn thing you like."

Kerrigan was twisting the bar cloth in his hands as though he wanted to strangle it. *Fuckin' wop bitch*, he thought. *Why the hell doesn't she learn to sit down and have a drink like everyone else. What's the matter with her?*

The others were looking at her now and they winked at each other as they sipped their beers. Margo had her arm around Red and was trying to get him to his feet.

"Stand up, honey," she was saying, as he twisted away from her and sat back down in the booth again. She got him to his feet again and she put her arm around his waist and started to walk him toward the door, but Red stopped and pulled her close to him and started to kiss her full on the lips. She ducked her head and started to walk him to the door again. They were all grinning at each other and Kerrigan could see that Margo was embarrassed. His impulse was to go to her and help get Red out the door, but he held back because he wasn't sure if she'd let him. He was thinking that she should have let him sleep in the booth and come back later to get him. That was the usual procedure, but Margo had a mind of her own and as far as Kerrigan was concerned she was letting them all know who was boss. *Fuck her,* he thought. *He's her problem now. No Irishwoman would ever try to run her old man out of a bar. No sir. Goddamned spoilt bitch. She's got the poor bastard by the balls.*

She managed to get Red out of the bar and onto the sidewalk. Kerrigan went to the window and watched as she moved slowly up the street with Red. She was a handful, alright.

He wanted to go to the door and yell after her, but he stopped himself because of Red. The word was that she was just like her father. He was supposed to be one tough sonofabitch who never gave anyone a second chance. All the talk was that he was connected to the mob, but that's what they said about all the goddamn wops.

Some of the others were looking out the window with Kerrigan, laughing as they watched Margo and Red struggling to make their way home.

"You should never let guineas in the place," Dooney Hanifan said. "And if you want to see a place go to ruin in no time flat just start lettin' 'em in."

"Fuck you, Dooney," Raguso said. "If it wasn't for the wops around here the place woulda folded years ago."

"Well, we can say good-bye to Red," Kerrigan said. "It's all over for that poor sonofabitch. He was the last guy I ever thought would let a woman lead him around by the nose. Jesus, he coulda had 'em all. Any broad around here he wanted."

"Yeah," Dooney said. "Anyone except Sheila Dolan."

"Jesus, when you think of him and Treacy and all the women they coulda had and now look at 'em. Treacy's a drunk and Red's being led around by the nose. Some couple of Micks," Charlie Wallace said. "Red's gonna be wearin' an apron before he knows it. Oh yeah. Margo will fix him up. She'll be movin' him to a nice little place in the suburbs away from all the bums like us. He'll be just like Harry Cope. Walk the dog and water the plants. Take out the garbage and mow the lawn. You need a real man to do all that."

They were laughing as they moved away from the window and took their places at the bar. Kerrigan was laughing, too. And he thought it odd that they were all laughing about Red and Margo when Annie Dahlgren had just been murdered. We're a strange goddamn bunch, he thought. And he kept on laughing, then he heard himself calling out.

"Come on, boys, drink up. Next one's on the house. To hell with that goddamn guinea bitch."

"You know, Kerrigan," Charlie Wallace said. "I still don't know why you let guineas drink in here, especially Raguso. You oughta get a sign for the door. No wops. Period."

"You know, you're right," Kerrigan said. "But I think we ought to be democratic about it. I think we ought to take a vote."

"Fuck all of you," Raguso said as he jumped off his stool and walked out the door. Before he went out he turned back and gave them the finger, then bumped into Jack Treacy as he was coming in. They watched as he walked to the end of the bar away from the crowd and sat in the corner by himself. Raguso was still standing by the door looking after Treacy.

"Well, maybe we ought to let Raguso stay," Kerrigan said. "I have to admit, Rags, it's bad for business when you're not here. See, you're the kinda guy when somebody looks at you they wanna take a drink."

The crowd laughed, and now even Raguso smiled. He walked back to his place and Kerrigan filled his glass.

"And tell me this, you bunch of Irish pricks," Raguso said. "How come this bastard wants to take the Dodgers to Los Angeles is a Mick? Tell me if he ain't." He sipped his beer and looked at them, waiting for an answer. When nobody answered, he drained his beer and placed his glass down on the bar loudly.

"Enough said," he almost whispered.

"Well, if the truth be known," Kerrigan said, "O'Malley is not a Mick. He's a guinea. He was never an Irishman to begin with."

They looked at him and started to laugh.

"Now let me take care of Mr. Treacy and I'll tell you the story." He went to where Treacy sat and asked what he wanted. They had all noticed that Treacy was clean-shaven and neat. They were all surprised to see him because he hardly ever came into the place anymore.

"Gimme a cup of coffee, Johnny," he said.

Kerrigan went to the back and brought him a cup and poured his coffee.

"Are you alright, Jack?" Kerrigan asked him.

"Yeah—sure. Just needed to talk to you for a minute."

"I'll be right back," Kerrigan said, and he went back to where the crowd sat.

"Now, as I was sayin', O'Malley was never an Irishman to begin with."

They looked at him and started to laugh.

"It's true as sure as I'm standing behind this bar."

They looked at Raguso and he glanced at them, shaking his head. "Go ahead," he said. "I can't wait to hear this one."

"You know who told me this story? None other than Red's old man. That's right. And let me tell you there was nothing he didn't know when it came to the Dodger organization. The truth is this Irish family took in this kid whose parents were wops because from the time he was born he was driving them crazy. They were so desperate they had him in a sack on the way to the river one night and some stupid guinea priest persuades them to put the kid up for adoption, and a family in Red Hook name of O'Malley gets him. They had gone down to the ASPCA to get a dog and they couldn't find one they liked. They run into this guinea priest who couldn't find anyone to adopt the kid and they take him off his hands. You know Irishwomen. Suckers for priests, even wop priests. They say the husband nearly went cockeyed looking at the kid, trying to figure what the fuck it was. Now this is a guy never took a drink in his life. Took the pledge years before and from the day they take the kid he never draws a sober breath. Story goes he threatened to jump off the Brooklyn Bridge a hundred times. The kid won't eat nuthin' but spaghetti and guinea bread and he's eatin' 'em out of house and home. The wife has to go out and get a job just to keep 'em in groceries. The old man works the night shift so he's home all day with the kid. And one day the wife comes home early and catches the old man with his hands around the kid's throat. He's just a breath away from croakin' him, but typical of a woman she shows up at just the wrong time, and the little bastard lives. And that little guinea bastard is Walter O'Malley, who became an accountant and stole the Dodgers out from under the owners and now is moving them to Los Angeles. The only reason that man is breathin' today is because some poor miserable Irishwoman came home from work early because she had a headache. And that's the way it goes."

They were all looking at Raguso, waiting for him to say something.

"I don't know why the hell I drink in this place," he said. "I really shoulda listened to my old man. 'Watch out for the Irish,' he told me. 'They're nuthin' but a bunch of bullshitters. Drink with 'em,' he said.

'You could even fuck their women but for the love of God don't ever believe a word they say because they're the one race of people on the planet don't even believe themselves.' And my old man could hardly speak English but he could always tell when he was talkin' to an Irishman and he knew that the only thing ever came out of 'em was bullshit."

They applauded him and clapped him on the back, and Kerrigan filled their glasses once more.

NINETEEN

Treacy sat hunched over the bar, sipping his coffee. He paid no attention to the crowd. They glanced down at him furtively and some of them nodded, but he didn't acknowledge them. They were feeling uncomfortable and it was clear he did not want any of their camaraderie or their boisterousness. They spoke among themselves. There was still a trace of the respect they once had for him and nearly all of them had brought him home drunk at least once since he had come back from Korea. They had helped carry him up the stairs and rang the bell on the front door and waited for his mother to take him in.

They had been in the apartment and seen the framed picture of him and Red standing together in their dress blues that was taken just before they went off to Korea together.

He had never talked to anyone about what happened to him in Korea. They had all tried to pry him open, starting with the doctors and the psychiatrists, the chaplains and the physical therapists. Red had spent hours with him after he had come home, too, but Treacy would never talk about what happened to him in Korea.

Red had snuck bottles of booze in to him but the mention of Korea seemed to have the power to instantly sober him up. And when he got out of the VA hospitals he started going on benders. Everyone made excuses for him at first and they were sympathetic and tolerant, but as time went on they began to lose patience with him, even his mother. She threatened to throw him out of the house, but she never did. It broke her heart to see him become a drunk who didn't seem to care what happened to himself. She was always there for him and she always believed that one day he would be alright and be the same as he always was. But there were some who said he was faking the whole thing. Just an excuse for him to drink. "Jesus Christ, haven't guys come back worse off than him?" they said. "And what about the poor sonsabitches who never made it back? Lying over there in the ground thousands of miles from him. Shit, they can't even complain. The truth is some guys don't know when they have it made. Look at Treacy. Full disability and everything taken care of and he walks around like the poor soul. He knows what he's doing, don't kid yourself."

They never said any of this in front of him, and they never let Red hear them, either. There were all sorts of stories about Treacy and what he did when he was on one of his benders. How come he never stayed in the neighborhood when he was on a bender? Some said he was queer. That was his real problem. The thing is, they said, when you put on an act like that you can get away with anything. They didn't say too much in front of Kerrigan, either. And now Treacy caught Kerrigan's eye and motioned him to come to the end of the bar. He leaned toward Kerrigan because he didn't want anyone to hear him.

"I hear they've got the Walters kid," he said. "Do you really think it was him?"

"I don't, but what difference does it make. Everyone else seems to think it was."

The others were looking toward them and trying to act as if they weren't. Kerrigan pulled his stool closer to the bar and looked into Treacy's eyes.

"What's the matter? What are you scared about?" he asked him.

Treacy shivered and placed his hands on the bar to steady himself. The tremor passed and he held his coffee in both hands and sipped it. Kerrigan could see beads of sweat on his forehead and he took a handkerchief from his pocket and wiped it. He folded the handkerchief and put it back in his pocket.

"Do you want a shot? Looks like you could use one," Kerrigan said. "Looks like you've got the shakes."

"It ain't that. I'm over the bender. Just got this awful feeling that won't go away. Came over me when I heard about Annie Dahlgren. Got this awful feeling in my gut, Johnny. Feel like I wanna die."

"Maybe you ought to check yourself into a hospital."

"You know how many goddamn hospitals I been in? They don't know what they're doing. They've got a pill for everything. Got all the answers and tell you nothing."

He wiped his face again. The others were talking in whispers and were trying to hear what the two men at the end of the bar were talking about. Treacy raised his head and looked toward them. They turned their heads away, and Treacy kept looking at them.

Kerrigan watched him as he eased himself off his stool and walked slowly down the bar. Then he was standing before them and they turned their eyes away from him.

"What the fuck is it about me you'd like to know?" he asked them. They remained silent and turned back to the bar and stared down at their beers.

"Come on back and sit down, Jack," Kerrigan said. "Come on. Sit down and drink your coffee."

"No, Johnny. I ain't sitting down. These guys might know something about me that I don't know. I mean, I've seen the head shrinkers and the doctors and the priests and none of 'em can tell me what's wrong. So I figure maybe it's time I asked them. Whadaya say, fellas? I mean, if you got the answers, I wish the fuck you'd tell me. I mean you've solved all the problems in the neighborhood. How about solving mine?"

They glanced toward Kerrigan.

"Come on, Jack," he said. "Let's finish that cup of coffee."

Treacy stood staring at them. He was breathing hard and sweat was running down his face.

"Look at these fucks," he said, and he turned to Kerrigan.

"They're sittin' on the same damn stools they were on before I left for Korea. It's like they haven't moved a muscle, and they couldn't wait to get their hands on Toby Walters last night. They love the smell of blood, but not their own. They always have to have the odds stacked for them. I didn't see 'em volunteering when the war was on. Every one of 'em looked for an excuse to get out of it. But they know every fuckin' thing. They even know for sure it was the black kid killed Annie Dahlgren. They're so goddamn sure they would've killed the kid if they'd found him last night. See—these guys know everything. Fucking neighborhood coming apart, but these guys know everything.

"They even know what's the matter with me, right guys? I'm a fuckin' queer, I drive my mother crazy, and I'm a lazy bum don't wanna work, right, guys? I'm an ungrateful sonofabitch because I came home alive with a one hundred percent disability pension, and I drink it up every month. Is that it, fellas? Do I offend you, you fine upstanding citizens?

"You fuckin' fine examples of red-blooded American manhood. You bunch of fuckin' cowards. Still be in here sippin' your beer when they pull the lever on that kid. And you'll all be sittin' here when the Dodgers play their first game in Los Angeles."

Kerrigan came out from behind the bar and put his arm around Treacy. He led him back to the far corner of the bar and Treacy sat down on the stool. The others watched. They looked into their beers and looked at each other. They shook their heads and shrugged their shoulders. "Fuckin' guy is crazy," one of them said quietly. Kerrigan looked down the bar toward them and poured Treacy another cup of coffee.

"You're lucky they didn't turn on you," he said.

"They don't have the balls," Treacy answered.

"I wouldn't be too sure about that. They have the stomach and the balls for a lot of things."

"I meant every fuckin' thing I told 'em."

"Look, why don't you do yourself a favor and go and see that Father Darcy. He ain't one of those by-the-book fellas. I mean, he ain't gonna tell you to get down on your knees and ask God for help. Three Hail Marys and all that shit. The guy's for real."

He looked into Treacy's face.

"I wish I could make it easy for you, kid. I just don't want you doing somethin' to hurt yourself." He tapped Treacy lightly on the arm and moved down to the other end of the bar. Treacy finished his coffee and went home.

He lay on the bed in his room with the door locked. His hands were clasped behind his head and he held a cigarette between his lips. He inhaled deeply and blew the smoke out across the room. He looked at the LP moving around on the Victrola and listened to the tenor sax of Lester Young as he played under the plaintive voice of Billie Holliday singing "Ain't Nobody's Business If I do." She sang all her songs as though she were trapped in the circumstances of her life. Gotta just let it all play out, nothing you can do to change it. And now for the first time in a long time he wanted out of whatever held him. It frightened and surprised him, and he didn't understand the feeling. He had listened to that song a thousand times and he always heard the defiance and the futility and the longing on the way to destruction. At least allow me the dignity of my own demise. It doesn't matter how it looks to you. Who can understand that once you have lost something you can never get it back. Life tells you you have to do it differently and that's just too much work—with no guarantee at the end of it.

He could feel the sweat on his face and along with the voice of Billie Holliday there was the sound of the small rotating fan that sat on the bedside table. He watched the cigarette smoke swirl around when the breeze from the fan touched it and from the street he could hear the wailing sound of a sanitation truck and the clatter of the empty garbage cans as they were thrown back onto the sidewalk.

It seemed so long ago since he and Red had left together, but it really wasn't so long. Six or seven years now. It was the time when he believed he could do anything he wanted to. The time of incredible possibility. But that possibility had been gone for a long time. And the question plagued him all the time since he had come home.

What am I afraid of?

And he could never find the answer.

What was it that brought that terrible sense of impending doom? He reached under the bed for his bottle and when he pulled it out he saw that it was empty. He wanted to feel the warmth of it coursing through his body like a magical balm that took all his torment away. One of the shrinks had told him once that pain was habit, a way of seeing and feeling, and that there was a way to make it stop. He had leaped up from the deep armchair and run out of the building and never gone back. They all are telling me I'm doing it all to myself, he had told Kerrigan.

He rose from the bed and went to the closet and unlocked the door. And then he took a key from his pocket and opened his seabag. He had kept all of his old uniforms. He had always told himself he was going to thrown them out but he never seemed to get around to it. And now he pulled out all of the bloody clothes he had stuffed in there and spread them out on the floor. He had the strange hope that he might have dreamt it all, but when he looked down at them the dull maroon stains were still there.

They were on his white shirt with the Mister B collar and on his light gray slacks. His mouth went dry with fear and he fell to his knees and cringed, holding hands to his face and biting down on his lip. Panic began to take hold of him and he glanced around desperately, then he jumped up and gathered the clothes, stuffed them back into the seabag, and locked it again. He put the bag back into the closet, locked the door, and went out into the street and walked toward the church.

TWENTY

Margo had brought Red home. One of Mrs. Dahlgren's friends had opened the door and when they went inside Mrs. Dahlgren came toward them.

"Don't worry," Margo said. "I'll take care of him." Mrs. Dahlgren looked at Margo and Red as though she had never seen them before. Red was grinning at his mother like a little boy hoping she wasn't going to scold him. He was so much like his father, she thought—always helpless before a woman, especially when she paid him a lot of attention.

She felt there was something tough in Margo. Her jet-black hair reached her shoulders and her spiked heels made her taller than Red. Her bust strained against her white blouse and her skirt was so tight, she wondered how she could walk. She could see the determination in her and she knew that Margo was one of those women who would always get what she wanted because she would let nothing stop her. And she knew there was nothing she could do to stop her from having Red. She could see a lot of herself in her and she wished that she might have had some of her strength earlier on in her life.

In place of strength she had buried her fears and her sorrows and her orphan shame. The nuns had given her manners and her sense of duty that had always determined her place in the world. What had become the driving force in her life was her desire not to let the nuns down. She had always told herself that she owed them so much. She had also buried her innocence and hardly dared to show it to herself. She had carried it inside of her like an unborn child for so long and now it cried for release. She had pleased the nuns for far too long, always wanting them to see what a good mother and wife she was. Wanting to convince them of how far she had come in America. She put money in the envelope every time she wrote them, even when she didn't have it. What would they think of her if she didn't send money?

"He's really just exhausted," Margo said. "I don't think he's slept at all. Kerrigan said he didn't drink much at all."

Mrs. Dahlgren wanted to tell her to get out and leave Red and her alone, but she couldn't. She didn't think it right that Margo should bring him to the bedroom, but she nodded and went back into the kitchen, where her friends were sitting around the table, drinking tea.

They knew how she felt and they reached out and clasped her hands across the table.

She stared down and stifled a sob, pushing it back with all of her strength, then she reached for her pocketbook and took out her rosary. She wrapped it around her fingers, squeezing it until it hurt. She felt the movement of her tears inside of her, but they wouldn't come. She wouldn't let them. She lifted her head and stared across the kitchen at the open window. She was looking at the red bricks of the house across the yard. She heard the starlings in the trees and the sound of Margo's laughter coming from the bedroom. She heard the click of the door being locked and Margo laughing again. She knew Red was drunk, but even so . . .

Then she heard his laughter, too, and she thought, my God, this woman can make him do anything. How dare she? How dare she?

Then she heard the thump of Red's discarded shoes hitting the floor. Margo was playing with him as if he were a little boy. It seemed like it had all happened before. Long ago when Red was a little boy and Annie wasn't even born. She remembered her husband. He would have liked Margo. Never too late for a party no matter what the circumstances. She still stared expressionless at the brick wall through the window and she remembered the night long ago when she had heard her husband coming up the stairs talking and laughing. He had someone with him. She thought it was one of his drunken buddies, but when he came through the door a pretty young woman followed him. She had smiled at her as though she had nothing to do with the whole thing, and she was drunk, too. Pete Dahlgren stood and grinned at his wife as though he were a little boy coming home after school. She smiled at her, too.

"She had no place to go," he said as he put his arm around the girl. All she could do was stare at her husband. She didn't know what to do. She didn't want a scene, although she wanted to scream at her husband. But she didn't want the neighbors to hear anything. She felt helpless. And she didn't have the strength to fight him. And she was never able to stay mad at him for long. She watched him take the girl into the bedroom, and just before he closed the door he turned to her to tell her he just wanted to settle her down.

He apologized for days afterward. "Oh, Margaret, you know it meant nothing to me. Jesus, I was drunk. If I had to do it all over again I'd never let it happen. I don't know what gets into me."

She liked it when he was contrite. It meant that at least for a little while he might behave himself and stay off the booze for a while. And it was then that she knew for sure that she was still the apple of his eye. He would love her the way he did when they first met. Things were good when he was trying to make it up to her. He would come straight home from work and climb into bed beside her. It was around that time that little Red had his tonsils taken out and Pete had lost his job again. He had taken Red to the hospital that day and when she came home from work he had dinner ready. And after dinner he told her he wanted to take a walk around the block. She was sure he would go drinking but he came back a little later with a quart of vanilla ice cream and served it in the tall, wide-brimmed glasses he had brought home from the hotel where he worked. And they took Red into their bed that night and he had slept between them. When Red fell asleep he had reached across and took her hand and kissed it softly. He turned out the light and promised her it was going to be different. They would always be happy together, no matter what. The drinking was over for good. He was going to change. He was going to find a new job, a good one that he would keep, and every night would be like it was that night. He told her he would try to get away from the bartending business. He would come home a regular time like everyone else. And every night they would sit at home and listen to the radio together.

And he had kept on kissing her that night. That way he had of kissing her that always drove her crazy. The way he moved his lips back and forth over hers, and she heard herself sighing. When he moved closer to her she was afraid little Red would be crushed between them.

She could feel his hand on her breasts and she reached down and picked Red up and placed him behind her. Then they moved toward each other quickly like magnets and she was breathless. It had been a long time since they had been together like this and she wanted him inside of her. Her breasts were taut and she wanted him to kiss them the way he always did. Then she was on top of him and she had him in her hand, guiding him into her. It felt wonderful and she wanted to scream, but she was afraid they would wake little Red. He was moving quickly and his hands were on her breasts and she had the feeling coming over her, moving out from the center of her being. Her breath came so quickly and she felt herself convulse, and it went on and on and she bit down on her lip to stop herself from crying out. Then it began to recede like the tide moving out but leaving its mark long after it is gone. She heard little Red crying for her and she turned around and held him close to her. Pete moved away and fell asleep. She was so happy, she couldn't close her eyes for a long time and she smiled out into the darkness that surrounded them.

That was the night Annie was conceived. Pete was gone a long time. And now Annie was gone, too.

One of her friends had placed a cup of tea before her but she didn't notice. She was lost in her thoughts and felt a sadness so deep it had taken her beyond feeling. She wondered if it was true that some people are born under a dark star. It seem to her that her dark star had followed her ever since she was a little girl. It had made her an orphan and brought her to the convent in Galway along with all of those other little girls who had been born under the same dark star. They all knew it but they never mentioned it to each other. They had all wanted so much to be good little girls and the nuns had shown them how hard it was to be good. So many of those same little girls had gone to America when they had grown up and they had always stayed close to each other even after they were married and had families of their own. They had never had it easy. There was always trouble of one kind or another, but they were always there for each other. And they always remembered their time in the convent together. They always found something to laugh at.

Their own children knew they came from a world that was totally alien to theirs. They had all heard the old stories so many times that they could tell them backward, and Ireland and the convent was this magic mystical place where there was no reality. In some ways they were strangers to their children and the children were strangers to them. They each truly came from different worlds. To the children their parents would never be Americans. They were Irish. They wondered if things had been so bad for the parents back there, why did they laugh so much every time they were together?

And the parents had all hoped their children hadn't been born under the same dark star. They all wanted to believe there was no dark star in America. Only good things could happen in America.

But Margaret Dahlgren knew for sure that the same dark star shone down on her children, and she wondered why it was so. There was nothing she could do about it. After all the prayers and masses and novenas it was still there and she was afraid there was something bad in her and she was ashamed. She would always be Margaret Cassidy who had never known her father or mother. In all the time she had been in the convent she had never had a visitor or a letter from anyone. She had never been good at laughing, but Pete had been able to get it out of her. It was as if he had found her in the convent and taken her away. And everyone had told her that only good things could happen to her in America. When she had met Pete she believed that it was all going to change. He made her laugh and told her she was beautiful. And he said America was the place. It was where all the good things were going to happen.

The bedroom door opened and Margo came out. She stood by the kitchen door looking in.

"He's asleep," she said. Then she shook her head as though she had completed a great chore and took her lipstick from her pocketbook and started to do her lips as she looked into a small compact mirror. Mrs. Dahlgren stared at her. There was something about Margo that fascinated her because she never seemed to doubt herself. She did what she wanted to. There was no turmoil in her.

She would never let Red get away with anything the way she had let Pete do for so many years. There was strength and sureness in her. She was nothing other than what she appeared to be and it was plain that she didn't much care what anyone else thought about her. And Margo knew what Red's friends must have said about her. She loved him and that's all that mattered for her. And Mrs. Dahlgren could see how Red changed when he was with her. She could see that there was something between them they never had to talk about. It was just there. A connection.

She was so surprised at Red. He was like a little boy coming out from behind his mother's skirts because he had Margo to protect him. Tears finally came to her eyes as she looked across the kitchen toward Margo. Margo put her compact away and moved to her. She bent down and put her arms around her and held her face close to hers. Mrs. Dahlgren could smell her perfume and she was looking into Margo's face. She was surprised to see the softness in her eyes; she pulled a handkerchief from her pocket and blew her nose and wiped away the tears, but they kept coming as if they contained all the sorrow of her life. And then Margo was standing behind her, kneading her shoulders, moving her hands back and forth. Mrs. Dahlgren wanted to tell her to stop but she felt herself let go and feel the warmth of Margo's hands.

"You've had a terrible time," Margo said. She kept moving her hands slowly back and forth. The tautness was beginning to leave the older woman. She had felt brittle but now she was beginning to relax. She leaned back into Margo and she sighed.

"It's alright," Margo said. "It's alright."

The other women were looking at her fascinated.

"Red told me they caught the colored kid," she said. "He's in the hospital. They shot him when he was trying to get away."

Mrs. Dahlgren didn't say anything.

"I just want you to know I'm here for you," Margo said.

She was standing before her now. She could see the natural color in Margo's dark face.

She had beautiful skin and her lips were full and sensuous. Her teeth were perfect. She was surprised to see that Margo was wearing no makeup except for lipstick. Her jet-black hair was full and lush and fell to her shoulders. She had always believed that Italian women were always heavily made up.

The sound of Red's snoring reached them from the bedroom.

Margo smiled.

"I wonder if I'll ever get used to his snoring," she said. "You know, he's a lot like you. He'll only rest when he can't stand on his feet anymore."

"He was always very stubborn, too," Mrs. Dahlgren said. "But we are all stubborn. Annie, too. Neither of them ever listened to me. They always did whatever they wanted to. They would only come to me after they had already made up their minds. They are both like their father. He'd promise the stars in Heaven. Always making promises, and the trouble was he always meant to keep them."

Margo nodded her head and smiled.

"Oh yes, they were both like their father. Dreamers. Annie more than Red, but with Annie I had the feeling she would do what she said she was going to do. She was determined. A dreamer with her mind made up. She didn't think I knew her the way I did, but I did. Children always think their parents don't know them."

She paused, surprised she was opening up to Margo. She had pulled one of the kitchen chairs close to her and she had reached out and took her hands in hers. She saw the tears welling up in Mrs. Dahlgren's eyes, then they were running down her cheeks. She groped for her handkerchief and Margo fought to hold back her own tears. She told herself she needed to be there for her now. She watched the older woman dab at her eyes and blow her nose. She sat up in her chair and took a deep breath.

"I was always the most frightened when I found a little happiness," she said. "I always knew for sure it wouldn't last. It would always be taken away. I have never trusted it. Somehow I think it is always meant for others. Something I couldn't afford. When it comes I let my guard down, and then something bad is sure to happen. It's just too hard when it's taken away."

Margo didn't know what to say. She held Mrs. Dahlgren's hands tighter and looked into her face and saw the frightened eyes of a little girl looking back at her.

Red's snores were becoming louder and came in the steady unbroken rhythm of deep sleep. Red sounded just like his father and Mrs. Dahlgren held her handkerchief to her eyes again. All of the sadness of the past was in the kitchen with them, along with the pain of Annie's death. It sat over them like the dark star that would never go away.

Annie had always hated her mother's sadness and the heartbreak that seemed to attach itself to her. She had listened to so many of the stories of the convent and the nuns. She had begun to realize that her mother was waiting for something that was never going to happen and all of the other women were like that, too, and she was determined that she wasn't going to be like them. Ireland was in the past. She had come to believe that it must be a terribly sad place, even though when they all gathered and told the old stories they always laughed and looked at each other in sadness as though they had all been cast out of the Garden of Eden.

She had always looked beyond the neighborhood across the river to Manhattan. There was a whole new world beyond the East River, and across the Hudson there were places like Michigan, and Illinois and Kansas and Idaho and California. She only knew them from books and movies but these places were totally different from Brooklyn. There was Los Angeles and San Francisco and all of those glamorous places she saw in the movies where people lived in big houses and had swimming pools. A whole different way of living, a different kind of freedom that didn't carry all of the pain of the past with it. She wanted to go there. She wanted America and everything good that could happen. And sometimes she became so excited at the prospect of going away that she could hardly sit with the excitement of it. But it was something she could never allow herself to share with her mother. And then there was Toby, and he felt the same as she did.

She had recognized something in him even before she knew him. She used to watch him play softball in the schoolyard when she went with her girlfriends to watch the guys when they played after church on Sunday. She had giggled with the other girls when they saw him and they all said how cute he was. They could never mention him when any of the guys were around. It was just something among themselves, but for Annie there was something else about him. She could see how confident he was. It was like he knew something the other guys didn't. From the very first time they caught each other's eye they had recognized something in each other. They felt they knew each other before they met, and that they had had a history together and they were meant to resume something they had started long long ago in another time. They were careful right from the beginning to guard their secret from everyone else. That's why she had accepted Charlie Gallucci's ring when he had asked her to go steady. She had known him since they were children. When she wanted to give it back to him she was afraid to because he was so possessive. She knew he would follow her all the time and never give her a minute's peace. She had to create some kind of diversion. Charlie was it. She and Toby always arranged to meet away from the neighborhood. When they were at the schoolyard watching the softball games they made it a point to avoid each other. He never gave her a second glance and she acted as if he weren't there. But Prospect Park was full of secret places where they could meet. They had found a huge old oak tree at the bottom of a grassy hill. There were smaller trees and bushes around it and they were able to stay hidden and still tell if anyone was coming close. It was their favorite place and they loved to sit under the tree together. They could hear the sounds of the park and the city off in the distance. It was where Toby had first kissed her, and they had both felt the same frightening thrill coming over them because they knew that whatever happened they would always be together. Being together was their joy. They knew in their hearts without ever having to say it that they would never leave each other. Their love was like the city itself, strong and so vulnerable at the same time. It came crashing down on them like a Christmas tree knocked over by a drunk. And like the city with all of its stark irrational violence that could flash like lightning and be gone just as quickly.

There was always the eternal expectation. The search for a new kind of happiness that could never be taken away. American happiness and American certainty. The guarantee for life. But all of the problems of the world had come to America with the immigrants and they had collided with all of the problems of the new land and the new people, and for some it seemed as though a terrible trick had been played. But still, with all of the madness, the possibility of something better never went away.

And Annie and Toby could always feel it, especially when they were on the bridge. There were angels moving through the lights with them always ready to bestow their favors on those who believed in them. America was always on the brink of some uproarious change. The threat of it was always in the air. It would always happen and even the angels couldn't stop it.

Sometimes they climbed up into the tree and they could see the huge expanse of the park laid out before them and the monument at Grand Army Plaza. Toby told her it looked like the Arc de Triomphe in Paris. It celebrated the victory of the Union Army in the Civil War.

Sometimes they met under the Brooklyn Bridge at night. They walked on the old cobblestoned streets and they looked at the factories and the ancient warehouses that had been there since Lincoln's time. Now they stood silent and neglected and forgotten. They would sit on the old wooden jetty that reached out into the river and they could hear the lapping of the water under them as it brushed against the pilings. They looked across the dark expanse of the river at the lights of Manhattan on the other side, the buildings reaching up into the night sky as though they were touching the heavens. And they looked up at the bridge high above them and they could feel its power as it stretched across the river. But still the lights of the city beckoned as though they held the secret to life itself. Looking at the lights was like looking into a treasure chest. So many sparkling flashes to see all at once, and all you had to do was cross the river, and you could stand and reach your hand into the chest and take anything you wanted. There was the feeling that everything was possible. When you walked through the streets you were caught in the chaos of its mad energy. The possibility of what could be didn't go away. It was in the streets and in the faces of the crowds. There was the excitement of a great hunt, a great search that never lost its allure.

Some nights they had walked across the bridge together in the darkness. They always held hands, staying close to the guardrail as the traffic sped past them. There was an urgency in the speed of every car, as if each one was on a mission. Speed was all that counted. Their drivers forgot they were high above the river on a great wondrous span. They just had to get where they were going as though they were condemned to speed through the night for all eternity.

Toby and Annie had stood close together and looked down toward the mouth of the harbor. They could see the Statue of Liberty bathed in light and they saw the curve of the FDR Drive like a ribbon around the city. There was always the feeling that it had sprung up overnight like magic and could disappear just as fast. It bore all of its newness like a beacon and still there was the feeling that it was really very old. And its newness would never run out. It was new every day. The inventions and the innovations would keep coming no matter what and those who couldn't keep up would be left behind. It took its past with it but didn't pay much attention to it. There was the unspoken belief in the idea of happiness rising. Nobody ever seemed to think it was possible for happiness to fall down on them. To come silently like a visitor in the night to those who were not looking so hard. All you had to do was look hard enough, was the word. The eternal expectation. In America everything is possible.

But there was always the stark violence ready to strike. The startled wailing of sirens rushing to the violence and the tragedies. The executive's heart attack that caught him with his pants down, or the beautiful young woman leaping through the lights and the mad energy to her death, convinced her happiness was never coming. They would both be stories for one edition, then forgotten forever. Change would always come. And then it, too, would be hardly remembered, filed in the invisible history of the metropolis.

TWENTY-ONE

The funeral procession sped up the highway toward the cemetery at Valhalla, north of the city. It was bright and sunny with a high blue sky. Mrs. Dahlgren sat in the back of the limousine between Red and Margo. She wore her best black dress and the lovely strand of pearls her husband had given her years before. The death was still an abstraction, an oddity that had no connection to the brilliance of the day outside. Another blow to be mystified over. In the days since the murder she had heard so many times from so many of her friends that God had called Annie and that she was in a far better place now. She had gone home. It made her want to laugh and then it made her angry. What kind of god was this? This god of the dark star? What kind of god picks on certain people and lets things happen to them, leads them on, brings them to the brink of happiness and then takes it away. Or flashes happiness before them in the darkness of their confusion and doubt when all seems lost, gives a brief respite, shows them what it could be like, then closes the door again? What kind of god is this? She had nodded her head at every expression of sorrow and concern by her friends, and when she was alone in her room she had cried quietly for herself and her frustration.

In a way she recognized that she was in a much tougher place than Annie. She had to live. That was the thing. Living is hard, she wanted to tell everyone. There was a long low moan inside of her that bore all of her pain but she was afraid to let it go. Every time she had felt it coming she closed her mouth tightly and pressed her small white handkerchief to her lips to help push it back.

But now as the limousine sped up the highway, a sob broke from her and the deep moan of pain that came from the very center of her being reverberated inside the car.

Red and Margo were startled and held on to her as though some other force was trying to pull her away from them. All of the years of anguish and disappointment broke from her like a torrent. She heard sounds coming from her that she had no control over. The high keening that was like the cry of a lost child. She was a lost child, like her daughter.

The sobs racked her, then they finally subsided and her head rested on Red's shoulder. She felt like a broken doll. Her eyes were closed and she looked as though she were sleeping. They sped along the highway at sixty miles an hour with the hearse ahead of them. Annie's coffin was surrounded by flowers. There was a large wreath from Red and his mother resting near the head of it.

They drove through the gates of the cemetery. The headstones and the monuments stood up before them, stretching as far as the eye could see. Thousands and thousands of deaths and every one of them inexplicable. It was like entering an insane asylum trying to explain everyone's madness. All they could do was to try to put a good face on it. It was the same with death in a cemetery. All they could do was try to make it look good.

There were statues of angels poised like ballet dancers with strange benign smiles on their faces. Faces of madness in a place full of death. They arrived at the gravesite, and the coffin was in place above the grave, ready to be lowered into the ground. Father Darcy stood between two altar boys holding the book of the liturgy. Their white surplices were blowing in the breeze.

It was a day made for a picnic and now they were listening to Darcy's voice rise and fall on the wind as he read out the prayers in Latin. Nobody knew their meaning. They all stood sullenly as they did in church on Sundays. They wanted it to be over. The terrible oppressive reality hung over them and there was the tension of the approaching finality when Annie Dahlgren would be laid to rest and buried, gone as though she might never have trod the earth.

For some there was a nearly irresistible urge to laugh or to shout. Anything to break the tension. To just get it over with so they could all get out of there and get on with their lives. Where the hell was God, this unseen bastard Darcy was trying to conjure up for them? Kerrigan's crowd was looking across the grave at him with unconcealed scorn. What was that story about Lazarus? Raising the dead, my ass! Where are your miracles now? And this is the guy wants us all to stay put in the neighborhood and wait for the niggers and the spics to move in. Let him show his god to us now. None of us have ever really believed this stuff.

TWENTY-TWO

Toby felt well enough to sit up. He had slept for a very long time and now he felt stronger. The weakness had left him and there was hardly a trace of pain in his shoulder. He had begun to let himself feel that maybe there was a way out. How could he convince them he hadn't killed Annie? Then he remembered it was the day of Annie's funeral. He had talked to his father about sending flowers and they had both agreed it wasn't a good idea.

He still couldn't believe that she was gone, that he would never see her again. Part of him wondered if she had ever existed at all. It had been such a short time for them. They didn't know each other just a short time ago and now the whole world wanted to know about them as if they had always been together.

He heard voices outside in the hallway, and he saw Arnie Meyers come limping through the door. He was wearing a white short-sleeved shirt that looked like it was too small for him. He sat down heavily in the straight-backed chair. He took a stub of a cigar from his shirt pocket and put it in his mouth. He moved it back and forth with his lips and he pulled his chair closer to the bed. He turned around and motioned to the cop who was standing by the door and the cop left, closing it behind him.

"You're looking a lot better," he said. "But you're lucky to be alive in the first place. You came very close to getting yourself killed."

Toby lowered his eyes and avoided the detective's gaze.

"If you'd been hit half an inch further down, you'd be a goner. You wouldn't have a thing to worry about."

He reached forward and placed the stub on the edge of the small chest next to the bed.

"Woulda saved us all a lot a trouble. Everything woulda been nicely wrapped up. Case closed. Everyone gets to go home. Woulda been nice. But you didn't get killed, so here we are."

He smiled at Toby.

"Now I don't want you to think I wanted you dead. I mean a young guy like you got a lot to live for. Amazing how life or death can be just a matter of inches. That's what they say about baseball. A game of inches. Bang-bang plays. Umpire's call. Sometimes it's got nothing to do with the truth. It just the way a certain guy on a certain day sees things. Call goes against you one day, and the next day you get a break. Who's to know? That's the way it goes. Ain't a helluva lot you can do about it.

"Thing is, I have to find out who killed Annie Dahlgren."

"If I was a white guy, I wouldn't be here," said Toby. "I'd be out there with everyone else looking for whoever did it. If she could, she would tell you I didn't kill her. How come you didn't lock up Charlie Gallucci? He's the guy was last with her. How come? He's the last person to see her alive. How come you're not holding him?"

Arnie looked at him.

"Maybe it's because he wasn't tryin' to run away. He didn't have a bag packed, ready to leave town. He cooperated with us. He didn't have half the cops in Brooklyn out chasing him."

"Sure he cooperated. What did he have to lose? If he runs away he's in more trouble than me, right?"

"Fact is he didn't run away and besides we got nuthin' on him."

"What have you got on me? Nothing, but I'm here with a guard on me. Only reason I'm here is I'm black. That's what you got on me."

Meyers took a small crumpled pad from his pocket and started to flip through the pages.

"I wanna know where you were last Saturday night from eleven-thirty on?"

Toby leaned his head back and closed his eyes and said nothing.

"See, the way I figure it is this," Arnie said. "If you don't wanna answer questions, then you have something to hide."

"I got nothing to hide."

"Then why won't you cooperate?"

"I want a lawyer."

"You can have all the lawyers you want after I talk to you. Look. It all comes down to this. You, Toby Walters, are all we've got. We don't have another suspect. You, my boy, are it."

Toby held out his arms in a gesture of helplessness.

"See, I've got a boss I have to answer to and then there's the borough president and all the politicians. I don't know if you've been reading the papers. A lotta people wanna see you in the chair. Now the way I see it is that it's up to you to tell us the truth. Take advantage of the opportunity to prove you are innocent. My boss screams and yells a lot, especially when the politicians are on his ass, see, and then he gets after me. It's nothin' personal between you and me. I'm just doing what I have to do. I'm an easygoin' sort of a guy. I mean, you nearly killed me when you ran over me. Leg still hurts, but I'm not mad at you. In my job these things happen. With me it's never personal."

Toby opened his eyes and looked at him.

"See, there are certain facts in this case which point to you. They are all reasons to have you here under guard. Besides those, there is resisting arrest, aggravated assault, and a whole lot of other things. Now, you are not on trial but you have to tell me why you shouldn't be. It's up to you."

Toby looked at him.

"I didn't kill Annie and don't tell me that me being black has nothing to do with me being here."

"Listen, kid. You better forget about being black because the facts ain't black or white; they are what they are. You were seeing the girl secretly. You were seen on the block that night around her house. And you were jealous. We have witnesses. That's a fact."

"So I was on the block. So what? Everyone who was at the party was on the block. What the hell does it have to do with me? Is there a law says I can't be on the block?"

"You were seen standing across the street from her house looking up at the windows."

"Is that why I'm here under guard? Because I looked up at the windows? I was invited to the party. Annie asked me to come."

"Why didn't you go?"

"What do you think?"

"Because you both wanted to keep your secret." Toby was looking into Arnie's face. "But it was killing you that she was up there dancing with

Charlie Gallucci. You wanted to stay but you couldn't. You were hanging around outside the whole night. You didn't miss a thing. You saw all the comings and goings. You were seen. And you were there around the time it happened?"

Toby shook his head vigorously. "Not true. Not true. I passed by once and went home."

"You were angry as hell that Annie Dahlgren was with Charlie at the party. She was up there dancing with him and you were standing down there in the street. And then you saw them going down the lane together and you couldn't stand that. And when you see Charlie coming out of the lane alone you went after her and you killed her."

"You're crazy. Crazy. Look—Annie and me were afraid that maybe they'd found out about us. That's why I didn't go to the party. How do you know Charlie didn't do it before he came back out of the lane? Why not Charlie, or is it that white guys just don't do that sort of thing?"

Arnie puffed his cigar and looked at him.

"So you're standing across the street looking up at the window trying to catch a glimpse of her. Weren't you afraid someone might see you?"

"In the first place, I wasn't scared for myself, I was scared for Annie. She didn't care if anyone knew about us, but I did. We thought that maybe we'd been seen together in the park a couple of times. Nobody ever came up and said anything, but we knew there might be rumors so I was really staying away from the block."

"But you did go there the night of the party?"

Toby nodded.

TWENTY-THREE

Darcy droned on. The prayers were interminable. Mrs. Dahlgren was standing between Red and Margo. They held her arms to support her, but they could feel her body tremble. Darcy's voice seemed to go on forever. Kerrigan was standing next to his wife, and Raguso stood next to him surrounded by the others. Fat Freddy Alcaro, Dooney Hanifan, Charlie Wallace, and all the others. Harry Cope and Sheila stood together. Her light summer coat wouldn't close around her enormous belly and she leaned into Harry for support. He had his arm around her waist. He was staring down into the grave at the coffin, his face impassive.

And now Darcy was sprinkling holy water and the wind scattered drops of it among them. They were all hoping now that he was coming to the end of the readings. But there was always more and the words droned on.

Kerrigan's crowd was getting impatient just as they did in church on Sundays. They were always true to themselves. There was a part of them that didn't believe at all in the church. This was stuff their parents and grandparents had brought with them from the old country. They had a reluctant loyalty to it because it was theirs. They were true to the ritual, but they didn't believe in it anymore. Darcy was wearing the right uniform but he wasn't one of them. There were spics and shines that were Catholics but they weren't Catholics in the way they were. The shines should stay with the holy rollers, shouting and clapping their hands, having a party like they always do, rockin' and rollin'.

All the stuff that was on the radio now. Nigger music. Everyone going crazy down there at the Brooklyn Paramount like they used to do for Sinatra. What the hell is happening?

Arnie Meyers placed a fresh cigar in his mouth and lit it, holding a match to it, making small circles around the end of it. Clouds of smoke swirled around him and Toby waved his hands in the air to fan it away.

"Smoke bother you?" Arnie asked him.

Toby didn't answer him.

"Did you stay away from the party because of Charlie Gallucci?"

Arnie was looking at him, waiting for him to answer, but he said nothing.

"How did you feel about your girlfriend being with Charlie? Didn't it bother you?"

"Sure it bothered me, but I wasn't going to kill anyone over it."

"No—you were angry as hell. Your girlfriend is at the party with some other guy and then you see them come out and go down the block to the alley. So you follow them and when you saw Charlie head back you go down the alley and you're so angry you kill her."

"You're crazy. Jeez! Why the hell do you keep saying that? Do you think saying it makes it true? Why would I want to kill someone I love?"

"Jealousy."

"Look, I wasn't jealous. There was one thing I was sure of in my life and that was how me and Annie felt about each other. Her being with Charlie didn't bother me."

"Bullshit."

Sheila caught Red's eye and she smiled quickly. There was still something in her look that pulled him to her, but now there was a feeling in his gut. The old resentment of her rose up in him. He could never forget that she had rejected him. He hated that she was standing next to Harry. Of all the guys in the neighborhood she had to marry him.

He looked at Harry and he saw the ever-present smugness. His superiority. He could never be just one of the crowd. He saw Red looking at him and they held each other's gaze. Finally Harry moved his eyes and Red was sure he saw just the trace of a smirk on his face. It was always hard to tell with Harry. Sometimes he looked as if he were smiling when he wasn't.

Red was never happier to be with Margo. He knew she could give him more than Sheila ever could and he knew in his heart that Margo was so right for him. But on the day he arrived home from Korea he had gone straight to Sheila's house looking for her. Her mother had answered the door and told him she was working. He spent the afternoon in Kerrigan's. They were all glad to see him come home safe and he was a little drunk when he went back to her house after she had come home from work. He had brought her a pure silk kimono from Japan. He had bought it in Tokyo when he was on leave and he had carried it in his pack for months.

When he knocked on her door again, her mother opened it. She looked at him without saying anything, then she called Sheila and closed the door. He could hear her steps as she ran to the door and opened it, her face flushed. She threw her arms around him and hugged him. He kept looking for her lips but she held him in a hug, and every time he tried to break away to find her lips and kiss her she moved her head. Finally she let go and stood back, looking at him. He moved toward her to kiss her, but she turned her cheek to him.

"I'm a little high, but I ain't drunk. You can kiss me," he told her.

And then he saw Harry Cope standing behind her. He stuck out his hand to Red.

"Welcome home," he said. "Glad you made it back."

Red didn't get it at first, then it struck him. He looked at Sheila and she looked back at him and she didn't know what to say. For a moment he thought she was going to cry.

"Harry and I are engaged," she finally said.

She spoke so softly he could hardly hear her.

But he didn't have to hear. He knew her letters had not been lost when there were none. She just had stopped writing, and now she was engaged to Harry. They both stood looking at him. He held the package with the kimono in it tightly in his hands, then he stepped back and flung it toward them. It bounced off Harry's chest and fell at his feet. Sheila bent down and picked it up. She moved toward Red, holding the package.

"I'm sorry," she said. "Please, Red, it's not the way you think. It just happened. I'm sorry. Honest to God, Red, I'm really sorry."

Red felt tears coming to his eyes. He didn't want to cry in front of them and he turned to walk away. He really wanted to run. Sheila held the package toward him. He shook his head.

"Please, Red, take it," she said.

He shook his head. She thrust it toward him and he knocked it out of her hands and it fell to the ground once more.

"Fuck the two of you," he shouted. "I hope you both die."

Sheila's mother was standing behind them now, peering out at Red.

"Come inside now," she said to them. "Let him be. Let him be."

"And fuck you, too, you old bitch," Red shouted at her. "You tried to break us up from the start. Keep your precious daughter."

"Now that's enough, Red," Harry shouted. He moved toward Red with his hand thrust forward.

"No hard feelings. Look, Red, it just happened."

Red swung. He caught Harry on the side of the head and sent him sprawling on the ground. Then he jumped on him and began to pummel him. Sheila and her mother were screaming and windows began to open up and down the street. The two women were trying desperately to pull Red off Harry. A crowd had gathered around them now. Harry had finally managed to get out from under Red. He was bigger and he rolled on top of him, then sat astride him.

He began to punch Red unmercifully in the head and face. Both their noses were bleeding. Someone had called the cops and they could hear the approaching sirens and somehow they were pulled apart. They glared at each other, too winded to talk.

Harry went back into the house with Sheila and her mother and Red limped away in the direction of Kerrigan's. The package with the kimono still lay on the ground where he left it.

Darcy had finally raised his hand in the final blessing, making the cross in the air, then he stood back as the coffin was gently lowered into the ground.

Mrs. Dahlgren moaned in her grief, and Margo tightened her grip on her arm.

Then they led her away from the grave.

They had all dispersed now, and Darcy was left standing alone by the grave with the two small altar boys standing at his side. He was looking down into the grave and when he raised his head again he saw Jack Treacy standing across from him. He hadn't noticed him before, and now as he and the altar boys walked away Treacy walked beside him. The rows of graves on either side of the pathway rose and fell on the hilly ground. Flowers and small flags fluttered in the breeze with a strange gaiety and the birds sang all around them. There was an unnatural peace.

Something not quite true about it, Darcy thought. A sly illusion. The dead weren't around to feel this peace. It was only felt by the living, and it was only quiet because the dead didn't make noise. It was as if all those lying in their graves had been part of some great practical joke they could only share among themselves. There were thousands of graves with tombstones springing up like crops as far as the eye could see. Hard to imagine they had all been alive once. There was a time when they were all walking around alive and well. They had been loving and hateful and joyous and angry. They had taken advantage of and been misunderstood and they had come home late. They had loved and abused their wives and husbands and their children. Done a whole lot right and a whole lot wrong. They had been divorced and remarried and been loyal and deceitful and strong and weak. They had ridden the subways and been stupid and brilliant and maddening and serious, silly and secret and alone in their hearts. And there was nothing they could have done to stop themselves from dying. Senators and movie stars. Ballplayers who hit .300 and plumbers and children and very, very old folks who seemed to be around forever.

All their energy was gone now. Dissipated. No more. Where was all of that energy now? All of their anger gone. Disappeared into the air with all of their sorrows and joys. No trace of their lives except in the memories of those who loved them. They were names and dates now. When they came in and when they went out. All individuals, separate and distinct. Who could reach them now? No one could ask them what it was like where they were. And now everyone in the group that was leaving to go back to Brooklyn had had at least one fleeting thought of what it was like to be in the ground. None of them had let the thought linger.

Death was not the thing to ponder at a funeral.

Darcy, Treacy, and the altar boys were approaching the roadway where the cars were parked, and they watched them pull away and head back to the city. Treacy lit a cigarette, then he heard Darcy asking him if he could have one and he turned and offered him one out of his pack of Luckies. He held a match for Darcy and watched him puff.

"I need to talk to you, Father," he said.

"How's your mother doing?"

"She's okay."

"Let's sit," Darcy said.

He told the altar boys to wait by the car and he and Treacy crossed the roadway and walked up the pathway leading to another section of the cemetery. They came to a bench and they sat down.

"What's up, Mr. Treacy?"

The tall conical cedars moved gently with the breeze and they looked as if they would remain in place until the day of judgment. Treacy was gazing out over the rows of graves. He looked as though he wanted to say something but couldn't find the words.

He stared down at his hands and turned to Darcy.

"I don't know how to say it but I have a terrible feeling it was me killed Annie Dahlgren."

"What in the name of God would make you think that?"

Treacy shook his head. "I don't know, Father. Maybe I'm just crazy. Maybe I shouldn't even have brought it up, but I'm going crazy."

"What makes you think it was you?"

Treacy took a deep drag from his cigarette; then bowed his head and stared at the ground.

"I've just come off a bender. I was on it when she was killed. I've been in and out of blackouts for the past week. I remembered nothin' until my mother told me Annie had been murdered." He paused and shook his head again.

"I was in bed when I came out of a blackout, and I've no idea how I got home or where I'd been. But that's the way it always is, Father. Nothin' new about that. But I saw my clothes lying on the floor in my room where I left them. There were bloodstains all over them, and I've no idea how they got there. Scares the hell out of me."

He held his hands out to Darcy. "Look at my hands. They're full of scratches and bruises. And my arms, too. Looks like I did something terrible. Jeez, I feel like I wanna kill myself. And look at my face, scratches and marks all over it."

Darcy put his hand on Treacy's shoulder.

"But you go on these benders all the time. Your mother told me. And you always come home looking like this. Am I right?"

Treacy nodded.

"Looks to me like you're assuming an awful lot. You come home after a bender, and you don't remember anything except you're bloodied. Not the first time that's happened, is it?"

"No, Father."

"I'll bet dollars to doughnuts it wasn't you, but for your own peace of mind you should go down to the precinct and bring them the clothes. They'll send them to a lab and make a few tests. I guarantee it wasn't you who killed Annie Dahlgren."

"But what if it was me, Father? What do I do then?"

"We'll cross that bridge when we come to it. The first thing we have to do is find out if that's Annie's blood on your clothes. I doubt it."

"I don't care for myself. I just couldn't see my mother have to go through it."

"Look, we'll bring your clothes to the precinct. Believe me, it will all be alright."

"They have that colored kid in the hospital and they could have the wrong guy."

"Tell you what. Call me tomorrow morning and I'll go down to the precinct with you. How's that?"

Treacy looked at him and nodded.

"I don't think it was the colored kid, either, but you have to do this for your own peace of mind," Darcy said. "You can't go through your life looking to pick up guilt wherever you find it."

TWENTY-FOUR

Arnie Meyers puffed on his cigar, looking at Toby. He leaned back in his chair and stretched his legs out in front of him.

"So you spent all your time that Saturday night in the vicinity of Annie Dahlgren's house."

"No, I didn't. I got there just before eleven-thirty."

"Where were you before that?"

"I went to the city because I didn't want to be around when the party was on. I wanted to get her off my mind. She had begged me to come to the party, but I told her it would be harder for me to be there. I went to the city. To the Village. I wanted to hear some jazz. I went to a couple of places, but I couldn't stop thinking about her. I guess I felt . . ."

He bowed his head and looked at Arnie.

"You felt what?"

"I guess I felt lonely. Left out. I wanted to be with her. I don't know how to describe it. I was lonely and angry, I guess."

"What were you angry at?"

"That things had to be the way they were, but I don't expect you to understand that."

Arnie had been writing in his notebook, then he stopped and looked at Toby.

"Try me."

"Well, I guess I was asking myself why it was that I had to stay away from the party. I mean, I grew up in the neighborhood. Everybody knew me, and I thought this is crazy. And then I figured to hell with it. Let 'em all see me."

He shook his head and put his hands over his face.

"I mean, Annie and me wanted to leave all that old stuff behind us. Guess we just didn't know. We knew that no matter what we did or didn't do there were always some people who would always be pissed off. Guess when I was walking around the Village, I began to get angry. It all began to get to me. Just because I happen to be black, everything changes. There would be no problem if I was white. Guess I'm not supposed to feel certain things, especially around white girls. Long as I kept my place, there would be no problem."

Arnie went on writing in his notebook.

"So you decided to come back to the neighborhood."

Toby nodded.

"Then what?"

"I walked down the block past the house and went home."

"I think you're fulla shit."

Toby gripped the sides of the bed with his hands and squeezed tightly. He wanted to leap from it and grab Arnie by the throat. He fought the feeling until he thought his chest would explode, then the door opened and a nurse walked in.

"Please, you must leave now," she said.

Arnie stood up slowly, keeping his eyes on Toby. Toby leaned back and closed his eyes so that he wouldn't have to see him.

"I'll be back," Arnie said.

He turned away slowly and followed the nurse out of the room. Toby opened his eyes and stared toward the door. He told himself that somehow he was going to get away. He rose slowly and edged himself off the bed. He walked toward the window, pulled up the blind, and looked out. It was the middle of the afternoon. People were walking and traffic was moving back and forth as it always did. Life was going on. He opened the window and looked down. It was a long way down to the ground. He could hear a radio playing and he recognized the voice of Red Barber. Someone was listening to the ballgame. The voice was so sure, so real and so familiar. There was an assurance in it as though nothing would ever change. He closed the window and moved slowly back to the bed. He nearly fainted, and he discovered he was far weaker than he thought. His shoulder began to throb again. He lay back on the bed, looking toward the window. He could see a small patch of blue through it and he could still hear the faint sound of Red Barber's voice and the muffled roar of the crowd as someone got a hit. And then he drifted off to sleep, exhausted.

They had all come back to Mrs. Dahlgren's house after the funeral. They drank coffee and tea and whiskey and beer and they ate sandwiches, German potato salad, and cole slaw.

They told stories and laughed the way they always did as they joked and kidded each other. It was hard to believe they had just come from a funeral, but they were all clinging to something together. They shouted and laughed and shook their heads at each other's words as if to assure themselves that life was going to go on for all of them.

Nobody talked about Annie's death. She could have been away at summer camp.

Harry Cope was sitting by himself as he always did, with an attitude that rarely invited anyone to come close. Sheila was near Mrs. Dahlgren and the other women. Red and Margo sat together holding hands. Sheila's belly protruded like a huge ball under her dress. Her face was full and glowed in pinkish health. She caught Red's eye once more and they looked at each other. She turned away quickly as though she were embarrassed.

Red was anxious to get away because he wanted to get down to the precinct to find out what was going on. He was hoping the black kid would have confessed by now, then they could get the whole thing out of the way so he and Margo could start their journey to California. The neighborhood was the past. It held all of his mother's sadness and his father's drunkenness, his disappointment with Sheila, and now Annie's death. What reason could there ever be for staying there? The neighborhood's going, anyway. Just a matter of time. Harry Cope was right after all. What's gonna be left here? Nuthin' but spics and niggers. He was so glad he had Margo. She would never let anything or anyone stand in their way, and he knew for sure he didn't want to be a cop anymore.

There was a whole other world out there that was as new for him and Margo as coming to America had been for his mother. With Margo he could do anything he wanted. Harry Cope might be a prick, but he knew how to go after what he wanted. He had to admit that. But he knew that he and Margo would go farther than Harry ever dreamed of. They were going to go to California. Or maybe even Seattle. But he liked how Los Angeles and San Francisco sounded. He only knew about these places from the movies, but still he felt he had been to all of them already. It was all about getting what you wanted. That was the thing.

He looked across the room at his mother's friends. He had known them all since he was a little boy. They would never change. There was too much of the old country in them. They were still telling the same stories they told thirty years ago. They were stuck. Stuck with the neighborhood and stuck with themselves. They were a sad crew, he thought. All they ever wanted, it seemed, was to be with each other. They had come so far from the old country and they never seemed to want to go any further. He had the feeling they didn't know America at all.

Darcy had arranged to meet Treacy at the precinct house, and now as he waited he wondered if he would show up. It was after ten now and he was late. He had not really expected him because he knew how fearful he was. Or maybe he had gone off on another bender. He figured the whole thing was alcoholic paranoia and a terrible desire to keep on punishing himself. He was sitting on a bench just inside the door and he was curiously watching the comings and going of cops and lawyers, and petty criminals, some handcuffed, some looking as though they had slept in their clothes, and some shouting across the room at people he couldn't see. Three men in handcuffs were sitting on the bench opposite him. The cops looked bored, as if nothing could ever faze them. They had seen it all before. No more surprises for them.

Darcy lit a cigarette and stood up. He walked down the hallway to the main door and looked down the steps to the street.

He was sure Treacy wasn't going to show up and he felt relieved. He hadn't really wanted to go through the ordeal with him but he felt the least he could do was make the offer to go with him. He told himself he'd give it five more minutes, and he wondered if he should call Kerrigan's to see if Treacy was there.

He looked down the steps again. Then he saw Treacy walking toward him, carrying a brown paper shopping bag. He nodded when he got to Darcy. The priest led him inside to the desk sergeant and he asked if they could see Inspector Meyers. The cop picked up the phone and mumbled into it, then he repeated himself.

"There's a Father Darcy here to see Arnie."

He paused, holding on, then he nodded and placed the phone on the hook.

"Walk down the hallway. It's the fourth office on the right."

They walked down the hallway together and just before they went into the office Darcy paused. "Best thing to do is get this over with. I'm sure you don't have a thing to worry about."

When they went into the office they saw Arnie Meyers leaning back in his chair. The ever-present cigar was in the center of his mouth, unlit. He looked at the two men and rocked slightly in his chair, barely nodding an acknowledgment of their presence. Red Dahlgren was sitting in a chair at the side of the desk, looking on.

Treacy hesitated when he saw Red. How could he say what he had to say in front of Red?

"I'll give you odds you came down here to see if you could spring the colored kid. Am I right, Father?" He smiled as he removed the stub from his mouth and placed it precariously on the edge of the desk. He looked up at Darcy, waiting for him to answer.

"Well, as a matter of fact I've come down to talk about Jack Treacy here. I know he and Mr. Dahlgren here are old friends." Red and Treacy looked at each other awkwardly. They nodded and didn't know what to say.

"What's this all about?" Arnie said, looking irritated.

"I'd like to talk to you alone about it," Darcy said.

"Why is that?"

"It's a delicate situation."

"Anything to do with Annie Dahlgren's death?"

"It may or may not have. That's why I'm here."

"Well, Red here is working on the case with me, so whatever you have to say you can say it in front of him."

"Look, this is a really difficult situation. It's hard to present to you what we want to in front a member of Annie's family."

"Red is not here as a member of the family. He's on the job. A working plainclothes man."

"All the same, I wonder if you would just let me and Mr. Treacy talk to you alone."

Arnie looked at them exasperated and shook his head in annoyance.

He turned and winked at Red. "Do me a favor, Red. Would you mind stepping outside for a minute."

Red stood up and shrugged. He looked at Treacy and the priest, then he walked out of the office and closed the door behind him.

"This better be good," Arnie said. "I don't have a lot of time to waste."

He picked up the stub of his cigar, placed it in his mouth, and began to light it.

"Shoot!" he said.

Treacy glanced at Darcy. He was sweating heavily and he reached into his pocket and pulled out a large handkerchief. He wiped his face and shifted his weight from one foot to the other. There weren't enough chairs in the small office for them to sit.

"This is Jack Treacy," Darcy began. "He lives on the block where Annie lived. He and Red grew up together and they were in the Marines together. He came home from Korea in very bad shape. He was badly wounded, but he suffered even more in a psychological way. He's been through a lot, and he has a problem with drinking from time to time."

"Him and a lot of other guys. So what are you tryin' to tell me?"

"Well, he was on a bender over the weekend that Annie was killed. He woke up at home in his own bed, and he had no recollection of where he'd been or who he'd been with."

"Oh, yeah," Arnie said. "That's so unusual. I'm sure this wasn't the first time something like that happened to him."

He looked at Treacy and noticed the scratches on his face.

Darcy was feeling embarrassed, but he forced himself to go on.

"And when he came to, he noticed that his clothes had extensive bloodstains on them and there were bruises and scratch marks on his face and arms. He has no idea how any of them got there and he doesn't remember being in an altercation of any kind. He came to me at Annie's funeral and told me he was afraid that there was a good possibility it could be him who killed her in a blackout."

Arnie leaned further back in his chair and tilted it back. He kept his gaze on the desk, not looking at the two men in his office. Then he joined his hands behind his head and swung his feet up onto the desk. He looked directly into Darcy's face as though he were letting what he had just heard sink in and was in the process of selecting the appropriate reply. He was making it obvious that he was allowing himself a wide range of choices, opening and closing his eyes and moving his head in small gestures from side to side. He moved the cigar stub from his mouth and looked into the priest's eyes.

"So, you have brought me the real killer, Father?" he said. "That's very nice of you, and I'm sure young Toby Walters will be very happy. Very civic-minded of you, Father. And you, too, Mr. Treacy, for coming forward like this. I must really commend you both. Yes indeed. I must really commend you."

Darcy glared back at him.

"Look, we don't need your cynicism. Jack Treacy came to me of his own accord. And just for the record, I don't believe for a minute that he had a thing to do with the death of Annie Dahlgren. The reason for coming here was to help him get rid of his own fears. God knows the man has suffered enough in his short life. All I wanted you to do was to test the blood on those clothes to see if it matches Annie Dahlgren's. That's all. What do you have to lose. Indulge me, Inspector, please. There's more to life than facts. If that's all it is, then it doesn't amount to much. You act as though you have the toughest job in the world. Wanna try mine for a while?"

Arnie allowed himself an ironic grin.

"That might not be a bad idea," he said. "Except being a rabbi would be more in my line. But maybe you'd like to try my job. Maybe you've got a bug for this kind of work."

He turned and looked at Treacy.

"So, you believe you're the man killed Annie Dahlgren?"

Treacy wiped his brow again and nodded.

"Let me see if I've got this right. You get home after a bender and you don't remember a damn thing. Nothing. Where you were. Who you were with. And from what I'm led to believe, this is the norm for you, is that right? Do I have that right?"

Treacy nodded.

"So you come down here with all of your guilt and remorse and we're supposed to make it all better for you. Look, Father, drunks like him live off this stuff. Do you how many of 'em I've had in here telling me the same story. There's always a least a dozen people out there want to confess to a killing."

He reached into his desk drawer and pulled out a stack of letters held together with a rubber band. He took off the band and spread them across the desk as if he were playing solitaire.

"Every one of these is a confession. A lot of people wanna die for murders they didn't commit. You want my job? Indulge you? I can't afford to waste time with these clothes."

"Please, Mr. Meyers. I know he didn't do it, but for his sake, could you arrange to have the blood tested. This man has been through so much. Just to ease his mind."

"You know, I've got the borough president on my can, not to mention the newspapers. I just can't afford to waste the lab time. I can't do that for anyone. Everyone wants results and it's my rear end hanging out there. I just can't do it, Father. I mean, you want me to send this guy's drinking clothes to the lab because he's suffering from a hangover?"

He stood up quickly and went to the door and opened it.

"Red," he called. "Would you mind escorting these two gentlemen out of the building?"

He turned away from them as though he were dismissing them like schoolchildren. Then he sat down and started to write on a yellow pad as if they weren't there.

Treacy stared at him and he started to tremble. He reached down into the paper bag and started to pull out the clothes, then he flung them across the desk at Meyers. Darcy and Red grabbed him and tried to restrain him but he leaped across the desk and started to throw punches at Arnie.

"You fuck," he yelled. "You smart-ass sonofabitch! I been dealin' with bastards like you for a long time now. I've seen good men killed for no reason because of assholes like you. So goddamn sure of yourself, but you're more about your fuckin' pension than gettin' at the truth."

They were struggling to pull him off Arnie, and two more cops burst into the small office.

They grabbed Treacy and locked his arms behind him.

"How the fuck do you know it wasn't me?" he shouted.

The hallway outside the office was crowded now with cops trying to find out what was going on.

"Lock the colored kid up because it's easy. No fuckin' effort in that."

They put handcuffs on him and had him lying facedown on the floor. Arnie was standing behind his desk, trying to catch his breath, and Red was pushing everyone out of the office. When the cops left, Red and Darcy were looking at Arnie, waiting for him to say something. Darcy's impulse was to apologize, but he couldn't bring himself to do it.

The bastard brought it on himself, he thought. Then Red was standing over Treacy, shaking his head in disbelief.

"Jesus Christ, Jack, what the hell's the matter with you?"

Then he turned to Darcy.

"You know, Father, you got some nerve bringing him down here," he said. "What the hell's your game? It's hard enough going through this without you bringing my buddy down here to tell us he killed my sister. Don't you know he's been screwed up since he got back from Korea?"

Darcy shook his head and was about to say something when Red spoke again.

"You know, they were talkin' about you yesterday in Kerrigan's. Standin' up in the pulpit there tellin' us we're bigots because we don't like what's happenin' to the neighborhood. I just wanna tell you that collar you're wearin' don't mean a thing to me right now. You come in here with this guy I've known since the first grade, went in the Marines with and fought in Korea with. You're gonna change everything, ain't you? You don't know anything about us. All you wanna do is embarrass us. We've got the guy killed my sister. We got him dead to rights. So leave us the hell alone."

He looked down at Treacy again.

"Jack, you gotta stop listenin' to this guy. How the hell you ever get it into your head you killed Annie? Jesus, Jack, why do you do it to yourself? You don't have to carry all the guilt of the world because you didn't get killed in Korea. Jesus, enough guys died. Some of us had to come home. Maybe we gotta make it up to those guys by living."

He turned back to Darcy.

"Why don't you bring him home and maybe buy him a drink. Jesus, it's the least you could do."

Arnie Meyers pushed the bloodied clothes off his desk.

"And take these with you," he said. "I'll leave Mr. Treacy here in your custody. If he gets out of line in any way I'm holding you responsible."

Darcy bent down and picked the clothes off the floor and put them back in the bag. Red helped Treacy up off the floor and unlocked the handcuffs.

"Father Darcy was only trying to help me," Treacy said. "He came down here for me because I asked him to. Trouble with you, Red, is you never did any thinking for yourself. Someone else always had to do it for you. That black kid didn't kill Annie. Count on it. It just all works out nice and handy to have him around to pin it on."

"Listen, Jack," Red said. "If I really thought for a minute it was you killed Annie, I'd blow your head off right now. I'd be more than happy to hang for it."

"You got it all figured out, don't you?" Treacy said.

"Yeah, I got it figured. Don't take much figurin'. It's like I said: Just because you were the only guy left standin' in your outfit, you have to blame yourself for everything. You're to blame for every bad thing happens anywhere. How many goddamn times you have to be told?"

"You don't know a fuckin' thing about me, Red, and you never did."

"I know enough."

"You know shit. You're so goddamn sure about those clothes even before you test 'em, looks to me like you and Meyers want the kid hung no matter what."

"You two just better get the hell outta here before I have you locked up," Arnie said.

Darcy picked up the paper bag, put his arm around Treacy's shoulder, and guided him out to the street. The sun had gone down and the air was still thick with humidity.

They were both tired and Treacy was fighting the tremors that were beginning to run through him. He felt dizzy and had to lean inside a doorway. His shirt was soaked through with sweat. What is there for me to count on now, he thought to himself. There was no relief anywhere.

"Do you need a drink?" Darcy asked him.

He shook his head. "The booze don't do it for me anymore, Father. Don't know what I'm gonna do. Sometimes I think I'm gonna shake right outta my skin."

"Best thing is to go home and get some rest. When your system is clear of booze, you'll be okay. Go home and go to bed and put all those notions about Annie Dahlgren out of your head. You did what you had to do. It's not up to you anymore."

"But what about the colored kid?"

"Nothing we can do about that right now."

"They'll give him the chair for sure. The bastards can't wait."

They walked on together, and Darcy didn't know what to say.

He walked down the pathway to the side door of the rectory. He opened the door and went to his room. The housekeeper was gone for the day and the monsignor was at a function in the city. He sat down in his armchair and he felt like a fool. He knew the crowd in Kerrigan's would soon have the story. It would be all over the neighborhood.

He leaned back and closed his eyes. In this parish they don't call you a fool; they call you an asshole. But he knew in his heart he did the right thing. And he knew that when the monsignor heard it he would come down on him. Tell him to mind his own business.

Arnie had sent Red home after Treacy and the priest left.

"Look," he said. "We'll have this whole business wrapped up in no time. We got the kid where we want him. There's nothing much for you to do here right now. Go home and be with your mother. We'll have a confession out of him soon. Believe me, he ain't gonna hold out long. Just a matter of time. It's not a good idea for you to be there when I'm talking to him. You know what I mean."

Margo had been staying at Mrs. Dahlgren's. She was there when Red got home. He was surprised at how well she was able to handle his mother. The older woman was slowly letting her in and had begun to like her being there. The Irish ladies had stopped congregating in the kitchen now that it seemed that Margo was running things. When Red came in the door she unashamedly threw her arms around him and kissed him full on the lips. Mrs. Dahlgren looked at them, then turned her head away, and when they broke apart Red was embarrassed. He looked toward his mother but she was leaning over the kitchen sink with her back toward him as though she hadn't seen them. He went to her and kissed her on the cheek. She turned around, surprised. He didn't usually kiss her. She smiled at him, then at Margo.

Much as he was thrilled to see Margo, he wanted to go to Kerrigan's and tell them about Darcy and Jack Treacy coming to the station. His mother knew Treacy since they were kids and he didn't want to say anything about him in front of her. Red wanted to tell them there would be no more benefit of the doubt for Darcy. Christ, to use poor Jack Treacy the way he did. He believed that even Kerrigan himself would be convinced that Darcy had his own agenda. He would never be with them. He was surprised at himself for the way he felt about the priest. He had never been religious, but this guy was really rubbing him the wrong way.

TWENTY-FIVE

As Red had arrived home, Arnie Meyers showed up in Toby's room. Toby's heart sank when he saw the detective walk in. He was not the kind of man he would have ever wanted to know under any circumstances. This was the guy everyone said was the best detective in Brooklyn. He pulled the chair close to the head of the bed and looked at Toby. Toby always had the impulse to close his eyes whenever he saw him because the small ferret face always repulsed him. The small head with the thinning shaggy hair that was never combed, always looked dirty. Arnie looked dirty. It looked as though he wore the same clothes every time he saw him. It was just that everything he wore looked the same on him and he had no eye for style at all.

"So you said you came home from the city and walked down the street past Annie's house. You just stayed for a while and then you went home. Is that what you told me?"

Toby nodded.

"But you didn't go home, did you?"

"Yes, I did. I walked down the block and then I went home."

"You walked down the block alright, but you didn't go home. Just as you were looking at the house you saw Annie and Charlie Gallucci come out on the stoop and then they walked toward the alley and you followed them. You knew why they were going there and you couldn't stand it.

"You mean to tell me you weren't jealous when you saw them walk down the street together. You really thought she was true to you but here she was walking down to the alley with Charlie and he had his arm around her waist. They were very close together. Nobody would have mistook them for anything but lovers. I mean that's the reality of the situation."

"She was true to me. She never would have done anything with Charlie."

"Oh sure. She was true to you. Then what the hell is she walking to the alley with him for?"

Toby didn't know what to say.

"Listen, it's just between us. But didn't you feel the least bit betrayed?"

Again Toby was silent.

"For Christ's sake, there's nothing wrong with feeling betrayed. Any guy with red blood in his veins would've felt the same way."

"You don't understand. We knew we had to play this game. She had to act as if Charlie was the guy she really cared for."

"Bullshit!" Arnie shouted. "You really expect me to believe that her deception included going down the alley with Charlie."

He shook his head and smiled broadly.

"Boy, did she take you in. She really pulled one on you. Yes sir. You, my boy, were had. Clear as day. I mean, what do you take me for? This is the girl you are supposed to be crazy about and she's with this other guy about to make out with him and you don't follow them. You just wait till they pass without seeing you?"

"You ever been with a black woman?" Toby shouted.

The smile quickly left Arnie's face.

"No, goddammit, I haven't."

"Well, what if you had and your friends found out about it. How would you feel?"

"Don't be so goddamn smart!" he said angrily. "Besides, I'm askin' the questions here. You know that's what they told me about you. They said you were a smart-ass."

"Think about it," Toby shouted at him. "If the neighborhood found out about Annie and me, what do you think would've happened? Maybe it's time you started looking at reality. It ain't exactly the land of the free and the home of the brave around here, despite Jackie Robinson. When you're black, they still play by different rules. And they ain't your rules, law and order and all that. Whatever might happen to me what would've happened to her. I mean, who knows. Maybe whoever killed her knew about us and it was their way of takin' care of business. Of course, you haven't given that possibility a thought."

"You don't know what the hell I'm thinkin'. It's my job to look at every possibility."

"Look—I'm telling you the truth. I didn't like her going down the alley with Charlie, but I swear to God I didn't kill her. See, I trusted her. I knew she could handle Charlie."

"The truth is you just couldn't stop yourself. It's called passion. It's not the kind of thing you can rationalize. It's when something else takes over in you and you hardly have the awareness of what you are actually doing. I've seen it up close for years. And most courts see it as being understandable. Crimes of passion are looked at differently than calculated premeditated crimes. You were caught up in passion and jealousy. You were not the first and you won't be the last."

Toby closed his eyes in frustration.

"I'm sure you're not a killer in your heart," Arnie went on. "But sometimes circumstances just take over and people get out of control. I've been through this sort of thing more times than I care to remember. It's always the same. I mean, I can look at you and I know you are not a killer in your heart. It's really a very sad thing because it happens to good people. People who nine times out of ten wouldn't act the same way. Experience tells me that the best thing for you to do at this stage is to admit the truth.

"Stop fighting your own denial. There's a part of you that doesn't want to believe that you actually killed Annie Dahlgren. The thought is so monstrous you can't bring yourself to face it. But sooner or later you will have to because we've got all the proof we need."

Toby stared straight ahead. His mouth was dry and his heart was beating furiously in his chest. He wanted to jump up and run from the place. He did not want to ever see the face of Arnie Meyers looking at him again. It sickened him. It was a horror that belied everything he had ever dreamed of. A corruption. An insanity. That ferret face with the yellowing teeth and the sureness of him. He never doubted himself. He was so sure of everything.

"I'm a lot older than you, son," Arnie said. "You are in the time of your passion. That's probably the biggest part of the whole thing here. Passion changes as you get older. Things that you used to feel so strongly about don't bother you anymore. Like this whole thing about the Dodgers moving. Everybody's all upset, but you know what I say? I say let 'em go. The hell with 'em. If they don't appreciate my support all these years, then let 'em go. The hell with 'em. See, everything changes all the time. And you know, I believe you had a right to feel the way you did that night when you saw your girl with Charlie Gallucci. You felt betrayed. Now, they say you can't be hung for what you feel, and I'm sure that if you had to go through it again you'd have acted different. What you need now is to go give yourself a break. Let go and admit you killed her. That's all you need to do and you'll feel better."

"There's nothing to admit. I didn't kill her. I didn't follow them down the alley. I went home. Ask my father."

"I did. He said he was asleep and didn't hear you come home. Now, I believe him because he's an honest man. See, the problem we have is there is no one to back up your story. See, your story will only count when it's backed up. When there is someone to confirm what you say. It has to be corroborated. And the thing is, Toby, we have a witness who is willing to swear you were seen coming out of the alley that night around the time Annie was murdered. Someone who can positively identify you. No mistake."

"Well, your goddamn witness is a liar," Toby shouted.

"Oh no. Oh no. The truth is, you were clearly identified."

"But let me give you the kicker," Red was saying to the crowd at the bar. He looked down toward Kerrigan to make sure he would hear what he had to say.

"We've got a witness who saw Toby Walters coming out of the lane."

Kerrigan didn't look up and continued to wash glasses and rinse them in the sink under the bar.

"Oh yes, Mr. Kerrigan," Red went on. "We have a witness and you'll never guess who it is. I figured the sonofabitch had to be good for something and damned if he didn't come through for us." He turned at looked at the crowd now.

"Our witness is none other than our good friend Mr. Harry Cope, my old sparring partner."

"Jesus Christ! Harry Cope," Raguso shouted. They moved in closer to Red.

"He came to Arnie himself. Says he saw the kid coming out of the alley, then he looked up and down the street and ran like hell."

"Well, what do you think of that Mr. Kerrigan," Dooney said, smiling at him.

"How come he never said anything the night we were all out hunting for Toby?"

"What the hell difference does it make?" Charlie Wallace said. "He saw the kid, didn't he?"

"So, when our good-lookin' priest comes down to the station with Treacy, we already have the witness and he's trying to pass off poor Jack as the patsy. Jesus, I coulda killed him. So what do you have to say now, Mr. Kerrigan?"

They all looked down the bar at him and he came slowly toward them, wiping his hands in his apron.

"Still bet the place he didn't do it. That's what I have to say."

"You're fulla shit," Dooney shouted. "You can't see the truth when it hits you right in the face."

"All of a sudden, Harry Cope, the guy everybody loves to hate, is a hero around here because he says he saw the kid coming out of the alley. Christ, next thing you'll all be cheering for Walter O'Malley."

"Fuck you, Kerrigan!" Dooney said. "Remember, you're the bartender around here. Just get some drinks up on the bar."

"You go on like that, Dooney, and you're cut off. You're out of the place. I don't need your monkey Irish ass around here."

"What the hell do you mean, monkey Irish ass?"

"You heard me. I said your monkey Irish ass because you act like a dumb-ass monkey. A dumb Irish monkey."

Dooney lunged toward Kerrigan and the others had to pull him back.

"Maybe I'm outta here, anyway. I don't need his shit."

"Fine with me," Kerrigan said. "You can leave anytime you want."

"Fuck you, Kerrigan, I ain't leavin'."

Then they were all laughing and shouting again and Kerrigan was busy filling their glasses.

TWENTY-SIX

Sheila Cope had started bleeding, and they were afraid she was going to lose the baby. Harry brought her back to her mother's house in Brooklyn so that she could be closer to the hospital, and he was working nights at the *Daily News*.

She was back in the house where she grew up, in her old room, which had hardly changed since she had left to marry Harry. All of her old pictures were still there and even some of her records and her old Victrola. She had always meant to move them to the house but she had never gotten around to it. She wanted a baby more than anything in the world; now she was close to the time when she was due and she was very much afraid she was going to lose it.

Everything had been fine up to now. There had been no problems at all, but now she had a feeling that something terrible was going to happen. But she was happy to be near her mother. When she looked around her old bedroom she couldn't believe that the time had flown by so fast. It seemed like yesterday that Red and Treacy and the whole crowd were in high school growing up together. They had all been so close and now so much had happened since those days when they thought they would always be together.

It was five years now since she had married Harry. She had always known how the guys felt about him, but she knew they didn't know him the way she did. He had always been so good to her and treated her so well. And yes, he wasn't like the other guys, but in a lot of ways she was thankful for that.

She lay on the bed with her back resting against the headboard and she couldn't stop herself from thinking about the old days and the way things used to be. She thought of Red being with Margo and she was surprised that Red would have chosen her because she didn't seem like his type at all. She had often thought of what it would have been like if she had married him. She knew for sure that if she had, she wouldn't have the house on the Island nor the car nor all of the wonderful things Harry had given her.

She was looking at the old grade-school picture that still sat on top of her dresser. She was sitting between Red and Jack Treacy and the three of them were smiling out at the camera as if they would be smiling together forever. Now the whole neighborhood believed she was so lucky to have Harry. They all said he was a great provider, the best guy a wife could have. And everyone knew how happy she was that they were going to have the baby.

But there were some things she had never talked to anyone about, not even her mother. Something had changed with Harry, and it was so hard to talk about. He had been so good to her for so long that she found it hard to complain, and she had asked herself if she was making too much out of something that was really nothing.

She had fought to banish her thoughts about him. She remembered Mrs. Dahlgren and the way things used to be when they were kids. She remembered Red's father stumbling down the block drunk, handing quarters out to the kids, and Red running away ashamed. Her mother had never liked Red and Sheila always believed it was because of his father. She remembered sitting with him in Prospect Park. He was crying because of the way his father was and she had put her arm around him and told him it was okay. And she remembered that Treacy had found them in the park and they had all sat together and made a pact that no matter what happened they would always be together. And now she wished there was someone she could talk to. There were things she just couldn't tell anyone. She knew they would never believe her because they all thought she had such a wonderful life with Harry.

"There is absolutely no doubt about it," Arnie Meyers was telling Toby. "You were clearly identified. We are one hundred percent sure. No doubt at all. It's airtight, and we have the motive. You would make it a lot easier on yourself if you would just drop the bullshit and confess. Whether you do or not you will be formally charged in a day or so and you will be transferred from here to the house of detention. The doctors say you are up to it now. That's the deal."

"Your witness is a liar," Toby said. "Nobody saw me come out of that alley because I never went down it. That's the truth. If I confessed to you I'd be lying."

"I'll tell you what happened," Arnie said. "You followed Annie and Charlie to the alley. You made sure to stay back a bit so they wouldn't see you. You saw them go down the lane and you waited until you saw Charlie coming back by himself and then you figured this was your chance to be with Annie. You were hiding in a doorway and you watched Charlie go back up the block to the party. You couldn't figure why he had left her there by herself or why she hadn't come back with him. I happen to know the reason, but I can't tell you. You hesitated at first because you couldn't tell if maybe Charlie might come back. But you decided to take a chance anyway because you were desperate to see her. You couldn't have stopped yourself even if you wanted to. You were mad to get to her so you walked down the lane and found her standing in the side door to Charlie Gallucci's house."

Toby was moving his head slowly back and forth as though he couldn't believe what Arnie was telling him.

"Is this what your so-called witness told you?"

Arnie smiled. "You were so jealous, you were driven. Chances are you would have gone down the alley after them even if Charlie hadn't come back, but now you knew she was there by herself and you were mad as hell. You felt betrayed and you were going to take it out on her. I mean, here she was with Charlie and you knew she didn't have to go down there with him, didn't you? She could've made him stand on his head if she wanted to. But she went down the alley with him. Why? It pissed you off real good. You knew Charlie wasn't like you. He wasn't going to college. He didn't read books and poetry. He wasn't interested in politics. Just another kid on the block, but she goes down the alley with him. He wasn't even smart like you. He'll be lucky if he graduates, for God's sake. But he's white. He doesn't have to hide or sneak off to Prospect Park and he can go to all the parties with her. Don't tell me that doesn't piss you off. You've already told her she's got to stop this thing with Charlie once and for all, but it keeps going on and on and you are getting madder all the time. She's been telling you all along the thing with Charlie doesn't mean a thing, but you don't believe her. You call her a liar. And then you see them walk down the lane together. And you walk after her that night. You walk down the lane and you see her standing in the doorway. She tries to walk away when she sees you but you won't let her. You push her back into the doorway and that's when you start to lose control. Believe me, I've studied it. I know exactly how it happens. Seen it hundreds of times. Something inside of you takes over. All of the jealousy, frustration, and anger gathers in one place. Right in your gut and then it begins to rise until it hits you right in the front of your brain and you're blinded. It takes over and you are left standing outside of yourself, looking at this madman. You're holding her and she's struggling and screaming out that you're hurting her but you don't even hear her. And then you punch her."

He stopped and poured himself a glass of water from the pitcher on the nightstand.

Toby watched him, fascinated and terrified. He couldn't believe that Arnie would go to all this trouble to make up such a story. He felt sick. It was all so wrong. It just could not be the way Arnie said it was. And he felt tears of sorrow and frustration welling up in him.

"And you knock her unconscious. You have to hold her up now because if you don't she'll fall to the ground. You are pressing yourself against her now and there's no resistance. You feel her body. She's been wearing that beautiful dress to the party. This is the one that caught everyone's eye. They all said she was a knockout. You yank the dress up and you pull her underwear aside and you rape her. There is still no resistance. And now there is no more hiding. No more frustration. Now you can have her and even after you've finished you can't lose the feeling that has come over you. You still feel betrayed and frustrated and now they are all going to pay the price for what they have done to you. For always looking at you because you're different. For being a nigger. And that's what you hate most of all. Not being a part of the whole. And now she is still unconscious and she is leaning against you. You pull out the knife you always carry with you for protection and you start to stab her in the chest over and over and over. You can't stop yourself. It feels good to get it all out, and you only stop when your arm is so tired you can't raise it anymore. She slumps to the ground and even as she does you still don't realize what you have done. Because you can't let yourself know.

They wouldn't let you have her, so you killed her. You left her lying there in the lane until old Mrs. Gallucci found her the next morning."

He took a fresh cigar from his shirt pocket and removed the cellophane, crinkling it in his hand. He lit it as though he were giving himself a reward. Toby watched the smoke gather around Arnie's head. It smelled like old socks. He looked at his browned stained lips, plump and moist, and he wanted to leap out of the bed and put his hands around his throat and strangle him. He hadn't known what hatred was until now. He knew he would not be able to breathe if the feeling didn't go away. Now he began to understand what Arnie had been trying to describe to him when he was talking about Annie. Arnie stood up and limped to the window. He pulled the blind up and looked down, then he leaned back and stretched his arms over his head. He was puffing on his cigar, then he turned and caught Toby's eye for a split second and limped back to the chair beside the bed. He held on to the back of the chair with both hands and looked down at Toby.

"They're going to book you for murder, so whatever you have to say you can save for your trial. Denying the truth is not a defense."

He turned away and walked toward the door, then he was gone. Toby was seized with a spasm of terror. He got out of the bed and went to the window. He just had to see the world outside to make sure it was still there. There had to be a way out, he told himself. He knew that if they took him off to jail he would never be free again. He stared out the window, trying to see if there was a way to climb down, then it occurred to him that he didn't even have any clothes. There had to be a way to get them, he thought. And now he began to feel weak. His legs trembled and he began to sweat. Oh God, he thought, there just has to be a way out. They were never going to believe he didn't kill Annie even if he could prove it a thousand percent. They wanted it to be him, that did it. They didn't want anyone else. It had to be him. He moved slowly back to the bed and lay down.

The terror wouldn't leave him, and he began to go through the names of everyone in the neighborhood, trying to figure out who it was had said they had seen him come out of Gallucci's alley. Why would someone say they had seen him? It was a lie, but why? Why did they want to hang him for something he didn't do?

He longed to see his father's kind face looking at him with total love and acceptance as it always did. Then he started to cry. A soft breeze rattled the blinds and he looked toward the window again. He told himself it was his only bet. He had to find a way to get out. It was late evening now and night would be coming soon. He had come to hate it because now it was full of nightmares, and when he lay awake all he could see was the terrible vision of Annie being stabbed over and over again by a figure he could never identify.

Night had come to Brooklyn, and Darcy lay asleep in his easy chair. His breviary lay at his feet and his reading glasses had slipped down his nose.

Red Dahlgren was making his way home from Kerrigan's, and all he could think about now was getting away to California with Margo. He could not face his grief over Annie's death. He had managed to bury it somewhere deep inside of him. He was thinking of Los Angeles and Hollywood and palm trees and everybody smiling and tanned. He imagined Margo and himself living in a house with a swimming pool. The skies would always be blue and they would be able to see the beach from their house and the perfect waves of the Pacific breaking clear and sparkling. When he approached his mother's house he dreaded the thought of being there. He didn't want to be around her. It was harder to contain the reality of Annie's horrible death. He wanted Margo and the sun with Brooklyn far behind him. But Margo was in the house waiting for him and she held him when he came in. She would hold him all through the night. And she would whisper to him that they would soon be leaving and they would always be together. "We'll always be in the sun," she had whispered to him. "We'll always be warm together."

When Monsignor Moloney came home that evening after attending a political function in the city, he went to Darcy's room and knocked on the door. When he sat up in his chair he saw the door opening and he turned on the light, then he saw the monsignor come into the room.

"Didn't mean to wake you," he said. "Thought you might still be up. Just getting back from that affair at the Waldorf. A long night, Father. A long night. I'm getting too old for this sort of thing. I thought the speeches would never end. Just be thankful you don't have to go to them. And the cardinal. My God, I thought the poor man would never stop. God bless him, but he doesn't have the gift of keeping people's attention. He was tough with them, though, in his own way. Whatever he might be, he's no patsy, that's for sure. It was a good night no matter the length of it. Some things you have to endure for a good cause."

He sat down near Darcy and now his jovial expression left him. "I know it's late, Father, but to tell you the truth I'm really disturbed," he said.

"Now, I know you bring a lot of passion to your work and that's all to the good, but when you start taking on drunkards with illusions and hallucinations, then I think I have to step in and draw the line."

He reached into his pocket, pulled out a pack of cigarettes, and put one in his mouth. He lit it using a silver lighter.

"I'm smoking far too much," he said. "But I had a call tonight just before I left for the city. Somebody down at the precinct. Seems they were very disturbed by you bringing this fellow Treacy down there with a paper bag full of bloody clothes. To tell you the truth, Father, I can't say I blame them. I mean this Treacy chap is a known drunk, something wrong in the head. It seems nobody can do anything with him. His poor mother has come to me a dozen times. So he comes to you with a cock-and-bull story and the clothes and you have nothing better to do than to bring him down to the station. I mean, he's not all there. Anybody in the parish could have told you that. I know he's a veteran and all that, but he's made himself into terrible nuisance."

"He came to me, Father. He was in a lot of anguish. He was convinced he had killed the Dahlgren girl. He hadn't been drinking when he came to me. I brought him down to the station house because I thought he could be relieved of his anxiety. I acted as his priest."

"Well, you succeeded in making us look awfully bad down there. Those men have a job to do. A tough one at that. You could have advised him to go down there by himself. Why did you have to go with him yourself? I mean, a known alcoholic. A troublemaker. They tell me there was a terrible ruckus and you had no small part in it yourself. Now, Father, there is no excuse for this, and I don't like it one bit. Here we are trying to hold a parish together, and you go down there and make us look like fools. Believe me, this episode is all over the neighborhood by now, and I can only ask you what in the name of God got into you? I won't have you making us look like fools."

"A man came to me who was suffering. He was in a great deal of pain. He was at that point where I really think he might have been thinking of doing away with himself. I knew there wasn't much I could do for him, but he came to me and told me what was troubling him. He really was terrified it was him killed the young girl. All I wanted was to bring him to the station and I thought they would go along with me and just reassure him and send him home, but it ended up that they just went to great lengths to humiliate him. It wouldn't have taken much on their part to just go along and mollify him. After all, Red Dahlgren was there and he and Treacy grew up together. Were in Korea together. It took a lot for Treacy to come to me and so I felt it was the least I could do for him. It wasn't a big deal. If the cops had shown just a little bit of humanity, there would have been no problem at all."

"You know, Father, I've seen priests driven out of their parishes because of this sort of thing. It's like that affair I was at tonight. Politics. What's most important is the way people see you. How they perceive you. They don't like do-gooders or second-guessers. They don't like to be embarrassed or shown up. You can't spring surprises on them. I just wish you would talk more to me. It's like that sermon. I mean, it seems you go out of your way to antagonize people. For God's sake, come to me before you let these situations get out of hand. You can't go at them head-on. And what will get you in the most trouble is spiritual idealism. It doesn't work. There are areas we should never go into. Now, I don't want any more of your interjecting yourself into the work of the police. No more embarrassments. Will you give me your word on that?"

Darcy nodded, but he didn't mean it

"We'll say no more about it, then. But I have your word."

The monsignor left and Darcy sat in his chair with the light turned off. He wondered why he had ever become a priest. It always amazed him when he thought of the incredible variety of men he had come across since he had entered the seminary. In many ways it was no different than the outside. And maybe it was just politics after all. Some old priest had told him that every life is a mystery looking for a mystery. True communion was when men brought their pain to one another.

When they shared their own mystery. And they didn't have to do it in God's name. It never had to be made official. But he knew he could never talk to the monsignor like that. And he knew the monsignor wasn't looking for answers. He wanted things to move along without any turbulence. Keep it all moving along nicely, even if it meant he had to ignore what was really happening.

TWENTY-SEVEN

Jack Treacy's body twitched and shook as he lay in his bed. His mouth moved in an incomprehensible monologue as he struggled in his nightmarish sleep. It was the same dream that haunted him over and over.

He was walking through a snow-covered landscape that terrified him. He could see an endless column of trucks and jeeps, vehicles of all kinds and files of men on either side of a winding road. They moved slowly, doggedly through the snow, weighed down by their packs and their fatigue. Their faces were gaunt and bearded, expressionless. Some carried litters with the wounded, who lay so still. The walking wounded struggled alongside, blood showing through bandages wrapped around them like pennants. The bitter cold wind whipped them like a cruel master urging them on.

Treacy hated his dream because it was true, there was nothing he could do to change it and it would never go away. It was like watching the same movie over and over. The retreating columns of men and machines always led to the same place. Even in his sleep he was always able to tell himself that it was a dream, but it was real, too. A memory that was played out over and over again. And he watched it knowing what was going to happen and he cried out in his sleep to be released from its horror. His mother, sitting in the kitchen, heard his cries and the terror in his voice, she covered her ears with her hands as she had so many times, and she hoped it wouldn't last long.

He watched the column approach a bend in the road and the dread ran through him. He was trying to shout at the column, to warn them, but they always kept marching on doggedly toward the bend. He could never find his voice no matter how hard he tried.

Then he heard the thump of mortars and saw the black earth erupt out of the snow, and he saw bodies rise up into the air and fall back down like pieces of broken dolls. He could hear the terrifying sound of machine-gun fire.

And the screams of the men who were hit and the shouts and the curses. He saw the snow turn red with blood, and the Chinese were suddenly charging down the sides of the hills and they were caught in an ambush.

All he could see was death, and he heard the Chinese soldiers blowing their bugles and screaming like banshees in a mad cacophony, their terrible dedication making them completely oblivious to the terror they evoked. They flung themselves at the column as though their bodies had no value and death meant nothing. They acted as if they were celebrating.

Treacy felt himself falling to the ground. His head hit the hard-packed snow and he was barely conscious. His body seemed to respond of its own accord. A Chinese soldier was on top of him, screaming, and Treacy rose up and punched him off him, then beat him with the butt of his rifle. The soldier was on the ground now and he was looking into the face of a young boy who looked back at him, his eyes pleading even as Treacy smashed the rifle into his face, breaking his skull apart. The blood spurted up at him and the stock of his rifle was covered in it and pieces of bone were stuck to it. He was covered in blood and he plunged his bayonet into the boy's chest. Long after the firing had ceased he kept plunging the bayonet. It wasn't until he fell in utter exhaustion that he stopped. They had to pull him away and he sat on the side of the road and couldn't move. The blood had frozen on him. He could smell its sweet smell and he could hear cries and moans all around him. His breath hung like vapor in the bitter-cold air. He felt as though he were suffocating and he couldn't breathe. He woke up from his nightmare with a cry of terror in his throat.

Margo held Red close to her. He could feel her breasts pressing against him and he knew he never wanted to leave her. He loved her warmth and her softness and she kissed him again and again. Mrs. Dahlgren was still taking the sedatives the doctor had given her and she was out to the world in her bedroom.

"I want us to get away from here as soon as we can," she said. "Far away. I'd leave tomorrow if we could, but I suppose we have to wait until it's all over."

"It's not gonna take long," Red said. "We've got that black kid nailed. Soon as the trial is over, we'll take off."

"The sooner the better. Do we have to wait here for the trial?"

"If it wasn't for my mother I wouldn't wait. Nothing's gonna bring Annie back.

"Whoever would have figured Harry Cope would wind up being the star witness. Got the coon kid dead to rights. Saw him coming out of the alley. Had to be him. Arnie's the best damn detective in Brooklyn. Nobody's gonna put anything over on him."

"I just wish we could leave now. I don't want you hanging around with that crowd down in Kerrigan's. They really make me sick."

"They're all jealous of me. You should see the way they look at you."

"I've seen the way they look at me, and I know they've all got just one thing on their minds."

"To tell you the truth, I don't blame them. I mean you are so fantastic looking. I just feel like the luckiest guy in the world."

She kissed him again.

"I saw the way Sheila looked at you at the funeral. She didn't look very happy. I know she was trying to catch your eye. She's got to be sorry she ever let you get away. Bet she's sorry she married that guy."

"Naw—she's really attached to him. He gives her everything she wants."

"Bet she's not getting what she really wants."

"Be nice. She's pregnant, isn't she? He must have been giving her something."

"I can tell she's not happy, believe me."

"Frankly, my darling, I couldn't care less."

He kissed her and then he could feel her hands moving over him and then she was on top of him. He heard her sigh and then she was opening his pants and forcing them down his legs. She guided him inside of her and then they were moving together and she was making noises in her throat and Red felt as if he was being taken away with her. She was in a frenzy and then he heard her gasping and he exploded inside of her and she was breathing as though she had run a race.

"I want us to be together like this every day," she said.

They could hear Mrs. Dahlgren's snores, and Red felt she was a stranger. An intruder he had never really known. He knew the way she had loved his father, but what they had was theirs alone. She had been so close to his father and yet distant from him and Annie. She was always in a world of her own and only came out of it when she had to.

Margo kissed him softly on the lips.

"I thought of so many things at the funeral," Red whispered. "Things I hadn't thought about for a long time. How close Annie and me used to be. I really was her big brother. She used to tell me everything. And she used to drive me crazy asking me questions all the time. But something changed. Don't know why but it did."

He closed his eyes and bit his lip.

"Did she ever tell you about Toby Walters?"

"No, she never said anything."

"You had no idea?"

"I thought Charlie Gallucci was her boyfriend."

"Guess she had a lot of people fooled."

"Guess she did, but now when I think about it I'm not surprised. She always did exactly what she wanted to do. She used to always tell me her secrets and make me promise not to tell Mom. When she first started to wear makeup I let her hide it in my room because Mom wouldn't let her go out with it on. She used to ask me about our dad all the time. I hardly knew him myself. I mean I remember him, but I didn't know him. I was just a kid. And I used to make up stories about him for her just so I'd have something to tell her. My mother was always telling us how wonderful he was. How hard he worked and how lucky I was to have had him for a father."

He took his cigarettes off the coffee table, gave one to Margo, and put one between his lips. He lit them and they both inhaled.

"You know the old man musta really been a piece of work. He was always dodging someone. Always someone coming to the house looking for him." He shook his head.

"Don't know why I'm talking about all this old stuff."

He put his arms around her and held her close to him.

"Jesus, I hadn't thought it for a long time but there was this one guy used to come to the house looking for him. Tough-lookin' guy. And my mother used to know who it was as soon as the bell rang. She'd send me down the stairs to tell him there was no one home. This happened a couple of times and he always looked at me like he knew I was lying. He'd have this little smile on his face like a sneer, and one day after I told him there was no one home he said, 'Why don't you go out and play, sonny boy, and I'll take a look for myself.'

"I didn't know what to do and I just stood there and then he reached into his pocket and pulled out a quarter and gave it to me and told me to go off and buy myself some candy. I walked down to the candy store and I bought some bubble gum and a comic book. I can still remember looking at the baseball cards. If I think hard enough, I can remember who they were. And I knew I should wait for a while because I didn't want to go back to the house when he was still there. But after a while I would walk back slowly up the block. I knew something was happening but I didn't know what it was. And I'd walk up the stairs to the apartment and I'd knock on the door. My mother would open it and she'd never look at me and she would always tell me never to tell anyone about the man coming to the house. I found out a long time later the guy was a bookie and he came around to collect on the old man, but he was always off on a tear. And I think the sonofabitch always knew when the old man was off someplace. Always knew when she'd be there by herself."

Margo leaned over and kissed him.

"No good looking back now," she said.

"The old man got away with everything and she always stuck up for him right to the end. Everyone thought the world of him. They kept him on at the Saint George Hotel even when he couldn't stand because all the ballplayers liked him. He used to get 'em their booze and their broads. I found out about all that stuff after I went on the force. I'd meet guys and they'd say, 'You Pete Dahlgren's kid?' Everyone knew him. A real character. They told me he used to play poker with Durocher and George Raft. They all loved to gamble. It was great except the old man never had a nickel. He wasn't in their league but he didn't let that stop him."

"It's okay, baby. Stop thinking about it. It's all behind you now. It's just me and you. We're gonna leave all this crap behind us. It'll be like none of it ever happened. Like this neighborhood never was. Everything will be brand-new. No looking back. We won't even come back for a visit."

They held each other tightly.

"And we'll be like this every day?" Red said.

"Every day," Margo whispered.

Sheila Cope couldn't sleep. She heard Harry turning the key in the front door and she hurried back to bed and pulled the covers over her. She lay on her side as though she were asleep, then she heard him coming into the bedroom. He undressed quickly and got into the bed and lay beside her. She felt his hardness pressing against her. She could never stop herself when he wanted to have her, even when she knew it was too close to her time. She had always wanted to please him, but when the bleeding had started the doctor had told her to refrain from having sex. He sulked like a little boy and no matter how hard she tried he wouldn't come out of it until he was ready. She felt that he was punishing her. She was surprised and shocked at the way his anger had come out when she had refused him the last time. He had turned on her with a terrible sneering anger and said awful things to her. He told her she cared more for the baby than him and that she had tricked him into getting her pregnant. He told her he wasn't ready yet to be a father.

"What about us?" he said. "Aren't I enough for you? Don't I give you enough? Goddamn it, what more do you want?"

"But I'm bleeding," she had pleaded. "The doctor says we shouldn't."

She had turned away from him and he exploded. He had grabbed her arm and flung her to the floor. She was screaming, pleading with him to stop, and she had tried to run out of the house. She got out of the room and reached the top of the stairs, but he was right behind her and she tripped and fell all the way to the bottom. She lay moaning in pain and she was sure she had lost the baby. Harry was full of remorse and had carried her back up the stairs and laid her on the bed. She had reached down and was amazed to find that she wasn't bleeding.

When she went to the doctor she told him she had had an accident and he told her not to worry, that everything was alright. He told her to be careful. No sex, and she must stay in bed as much as possible.

Still, she was baffled by Harry's behavior. He had never shown that side of himself before. He was never like the other guys, loud and arguing. He hardly ever took a drink. It was true what they all said about him. He was a great husband. Sheila was very proud of him and basked in his attentiveness. She couldn't ask for a better guy. What happened? He was always taunting her about Red now, saying she still had the hots for him. She had never intended to become pregnant and even after she knew she was afraid to tell Harry. But now, more than anything, she wanted to have her baby.

She lay in bed with her back to him and she could feel him moving slowly against her. She reached around and took him in her hand and moved back and forth faster and faster until she heard him moan and she could feel his wetness. Then she lay awake until she was sure he was asleep. She drifted off herself, feeling the baby kicking inside of her.

TWENTY-EIGHT

Arnie Meyers called Red and told him to meet him at the hospital the next morning. They were going to book Toby Walters for the murder of Annie Dahlgren.

When they came into his room, Toby was sleeping. They stood on either side of the bed while a uniformed cop booked him. He was to be arraigned as soon as he could leave the hospital. He was determined now that they would never take him to jail. Arnie had told him there was no possibility of bail and he knew that if they locked him up he would never be free again.

Afterward Arnie and Red walked out of the hospital together.

"This thing won't take long," Arnie said. "Open and shut. All be over before you know it. The thing now is to get on with your life. And to tell you the truth I didn't think it was going to be so easy, but you know—sometimes you get lucky. How's your mother doing?"

"She's alright. She's got her own way of dealing with it. Stays in her room most of the time and goes down to the church to light candles. Cries and sleeps. Her friends come over and they always have a lot to talk about. All that stuff back in Ireland years ago. Jesus, they never stop talking about it. Must be some fuckin' place."

"You should try to get away. I mean, this thing is wrapped up. Take some time off. I know it's been tough. Won't be long now before it's all over and that kid's on his way to the chair."

As they came out of the hospital, Arnie saw Bailey Walters coming toward them. They noticed each other and their eyes met. Arnie turned away as though he hadn't seen him. Bailey went inside and took the elevator, then walked down the long hallway to Toby's room. There was a huge cop sitting on a chair outside. Bailey gave him the pass and the cop frisked him and let him go into the room. Toby was sitting up and he smiled when he saw his father.

"Hi, Pop," he said. He had the urge to jump from the bed and throw his arms around him, and he fought to hold back his tears. They reached out for each other as Bailey came closer, and he bent down and hugged Toby for a long time before they finally let go of each other.

"They've booked me for murder," Toby said. "I'm going to be arraigned in a day or so. They're gonna take me out of here and lock me up."

"I know you didn't do it, son," his father said. "I know you didn't kill that little girl."

"But they believe I did, Pop."

"We're gonna find you a good lawyer, son. Don't worry. I'm gonna get the best. I promise you. Good lawyer have you outta here before you know it."

He pulled the chair close to the bed and sat down.

"They think they got the whole thing wrapped up, Pop. Doesn't matter what you or the lawyers do. Won't make any difference. They want it to be me. They're gonna make sure it's me. They're not looking for anyone else. I'm it. The nigger kid had the nerve to go out with a white girl."

"You gotta stop thinkin' like that, son. This is Brooklyn. We ain't in Alabama or Mississippi. They can't get away with that stuff here."

"They can do anything they want, Pop."

Bailey Walters shook his head. He didn't know what to say.

"I'm not gonna let 'em kill me, Pop. I'm gonna find a way to get out of here, and I gotta do it fast 'cause they're planning to move me out of here in a day or two. They gonna bring me to the house of detention. Put me in a cell, then I get arraigned. That's it. No way out after that. They put me on trial and I'm convicted. All over. They want this black boy in the chair."

"Hold on. Hold on, son. You're goin' way too fast. You got yourself convicted and dead and you ain't even had a trial yet. They can't control a jury, son."

"It's like I keep telling you, Pop. They can do anything they want."

"I'll tell you, son. You try to get away from here and you're dead. How you gonna get out of here? Tell me that? How you gonna do that? Ain't no way you gonna get outta here."

"You gotta help me, Pop. You gotta bring me some clothes."

"I can't do that, son. I ain't gonna stand around and watch you be gunned down."

"They're gonna kill me one way or the other. If I make a break at least I have a chance. The other way it's over."

Bailey Walters shook his head.

"Listen, son, you gotta calm down. You're gettin' way ahead of yourself. Now, I know what's goin' on with you and I understand it, but ain't no use panicking. No use doin' somethin' stupid. Best thing you can have goin' for you is a good lawyer. The law is the law, son. They can't mess around with that. And a lotta things can happen between now and the trial. There's always a way, son. You gotta believe that. First thing we gonna get you bailed out of here."

"They're not gonna give me bail. It was all over when they booked me. They say they got a witness saw me coming out of the lane where they found Annie. I was nowhere near the lane at the time they're talking about. No one coulda seen me because I wasn't there. It's a setup. You should see the way that detective looks at me. He made me the guy before he ever asked me a question."

"Son, you bein' silly. Tell me just how you goin' get outta here? Huh? You think you gonna just pass right by that cop on the door? You wouldn't be here if you hadn't run away in the first place."

He stood up and walked around the room in frustration, then he sat down again.

"I pleaded with you. You lucky you ain't dead already, and now you wanna run away again. Believe me, you just makin' it look like they got the guy who did it."

"You gonna help me or not?"

"I ain't gonna help you kill yourself."

"Well, I'm gonna make a break for it whether you help me or not."

"Oh, son, for God's sake, please don't talk that way. Make 'em prove it was you. They can't railroad you."

"They got all the proof they want."

Bailey Walters didn't know what to say. He didn't want to believe that his son was right.

He wanted to believe that Arnie Meyers was an honest cop doing his job. Surely they wouldn't go after Toby just for their own convenience. Because he was a Negro. Not here. Not in Brooklyn. They couldn't just make him their scapegoat. If that was true, then Toby wouldn't have a chance in court. But could they do this? Why would they want to do it? Things aren't the way they ought to be, he thought. Look at Jackie Robinson.

Lotta things changin' since Jackie came up. You could feel it. It was in the air. He remembered how it was now when he went to the ballpark. Everybody pulling together for the Dodgers. When Jackie stole home, they didn't care that he was black. How could all that change when it came to Toby? And it was true what he said. They weren't looking for anyone else. It all stopped with him.

"Will you help me, Pop," Toby asked him again.

Bailey Walters lowered his head and looked at Toby with a look of pain on his face.

"You can't get away from here, son. How you gonna do that?"

"The window."

Bailey turned in his chair and looked at it.

"God Almighty, son, do you know just how high up you are? You ain't never gonna make it down from there."

"Just bring me some clothes, Pop, and you've gotta do it right away 'cause I don't know when they're gonna move me from here."

"I ain't promisin' nuthin.' But the first thing I'm doing is gettin' a good lawyer."

"Save your money, Pop. No lawyer's gonna do me any good. Just bring me the clothes."

Bailey Walters stood up and shook his head slowly. He moved close to Toby and held him, then he turned away and walked out.

The papers announced the next day that Toby Walters had been booked for the murder of Annie Dahlgren and that he was to be arraigned as soon as he left the hospital. There was a picture on the inside page of the *Daily News* of Arnie Meyers coming out of the hospital with Red just behind him. There was just the trace of a smile on Arnie's face, looking as though he might just have made a quip to one of the reporters. Retirement was near now, and this was a good way to go out. No doubt about it. Arnie was pleased at how fast he had broken the case. Now he was going to go out on the top of his game, just like DiMaggio. Class. That was the way. Everyone sorry to see him go. Still the best detective in Brooklyn.

The regulars were taunting Kerrigan as they read the paper to him.

"So Kerrigan, who the hell do you think did it," Raguso asked him.

Kerrigan shook his head and leaned back against the shelves, a position he rarely took.

It was a signal to them to leave him alone.

"Looks like you guys got all the answers. Papers say Toby Walters did it."

"You don't get away that easy," Dooney said.

Kerrigan walked to the other end of the bar.

"Look at him," Dooney said. "Arnie Meyers, the best goddamn detective in Brooklyn, books the kid. Has him dead to rights. And Kerrigan can't come up with another name because there is no other name. Ain't that the truth, Mr. Kerrigan?"

"Let's skip it," Kerrigan said.

"Oh, now he wants to skip it. We should all just shut the hell up about it. Is that it?"

Kerrigan flung his bar towel down in frustration and they broke into laughter.

Charlie Wallace was the first to see Harry Cope.

"Well, Jesus Christ, the star witness!" he said, and they all turned and looked at him.

Harry looked at them awkwardly, an embarrassed smile on his face.

"Give this man a beer," Charlie called out to Kerrigan.

"Come over here, Harry," Dooney shouted. "Tell Kerrigan here who you saw coming out of Gallucci's alley the night Annie Dahlgren was killed. Go ahead. Tell him."

Harry lifted his beer and held it with his two hands around it. He looked around at all of them.

"Go ahead, tell him," Dooney shouted.

Harry took a long sip from his beer, closed his eyes quickly, then opened them again.

"Same guy I told them down at the station," he said.

"Yeah, but tell him who."

"Toby Walters."

Kerrigan stared at him and their eyes met.

"Let me ask you something, Harry," Kerrigan asked him. "Did Toby Walters see you?"

Harry shook his head.

"How come?"

"What the hell are you, the district attorney?" Raguso said.

They all laughed at Kerrigan. Harry hadn't answered Kerrigan. He wanted to ask him again but instead he poured himself a short beer and leaned back against the shelves.

"What the hell are you doing here, anyway?" Dooney asked.

"Well, Sheila's expecting any day now and we're staying at her mother's to be close to the hospital."

"How's she doin'?" Raguso asked.

"Okay."

"So you gettin' ready to pass out cigars?" Charlie asked.

"Well, I just hope it's a girl," Dooney said. "Imagine having another copy of this guy."

They all laughed, and Harry laughed with them because there was nothing else he could do.

He drank his beer and let himself feel he was one of them. The door had opened a crack for him and he was letting himself in. He had never been a drinker and the distance between him and them had been there for as long as he could remember. Even though he had never been one of them, they had always had a grudging respect for him. He was a guy who knew how to get ahead and they had to admire him for that. He knew how to put money away. He was a real steady guy. Never seemed to need anyone, and he was sure of himself. Went after what he wanted. That was the thing about Harry. Charlie Wallace had said once that O'Malley, the owner of the Dodgers, must be a guy like Harry. That kind of a guy. If Harry owned the Dodgers and he thought he would make more money by moving 'em, he'd do it without thinking twice.

"That's the kind of a fuck he is," Charlie Wallace had said.

Raguso had started as a runner on Wall Street and was still little more than a glorified messenger.

Dooney worked in a sheet-metal shop in Queens.

Charlie Wallace worked on the waterfront, shaping up every morning for a day's work.

They all had a profound lack of interest in their jobs, believing that the necessity of having to hold them prevented them from really pursuing the American Dream. There was a sign at the back of the bar that read WORK IS THE CURSE OF THE DRINKING CLASS. They were a strange proletariat, loyal to their working-class roots yet always eager to leave them behind. The promise of America hung over them like a judgment, always reminding them of how far they had to go. Best thing that could happen to a man was to hit the number. Took care of everything. They were the sons of the Great Depression looking for the Big Rock Candy Mountain where they would all be safe and secure and their mind-forged manacles would be broken and the beer would never stop flowing.

They didn't believe the dream was in the neighborhood anymore.

It had shifted beyond to a new standard that was telling them that living there and getting by with your friends in the neighborhood wasn't enough. The once proud appellation of Worker wasn't where their pride was now. There was this new expectation. The old battles for rights and decency and dignity were forgotten. Something was leaving them, fading into the past. The old neighborhood stuff didn't apply anymore. They were trying to catch up to something new. A new kind of certainty. They saw it in the movies and on television and they heard it on the radio. That America was out there beyond the neighborhood and each of them was wondering secretly how they could get there. They all wanted what Harry Cope had.

"But who would've figured that Annie Dahlgren was seeing Toby Walters on the sly?" Raguso was saying.

"Can you beat that? Jesus, and keeping Charlie Gallucci on the string to cover it up."

Harry Cope was nodding.

"It's a free country, ain't it?" Kerrigan said. "At least it was the last time I checked."

"Aw, come on, for Christ's sake," Dooney said. "Would you let your daughter go out with a nigger?"

"If he's a decent guy, black or white, it's alright with me."

"Get the fuck outta here," Charlie Wallace said. "You mean to tell me that you'd let her bring a nigger home with her?"

He started to laugh.

"You know, Kerrigan, I don't believe a fuckin' word you say. You just do it for the sake of argument."

"And what would your wife have to say about it?" Dooney asked.

"She feels the same way I do," Kerrigan said.

"Bullshit!" Dooney shouted.

"Jeez, a coupla years from now that's all you'll have here," Charlie Wallace said. "Nuthin' but niggers. And you'll have nuthin' but that fuckin' jungle music on the jukebox. You'll be sellin' rotgut and Wild Irish Rose."

"Yeah, he'll have to hire a bouncer. Nothin' going on in here but knife fights. Dem bones, dem bones, dem dry bones! You're gonna have a great time, Kerrigan."

They were all laughing and banging their glasses on the bar and Harry joined in. He was laughing, too, having the time of his life.

"Why do you think I moved out?" he asked them. "Life's tough enough without having to worry about spics and niggers."

They looked at him and nodded.

"How could such a bright young girl like Annie Dahlgren wind up with a coon?" he asked. He shook his head slowly.

"Times have really changed," he said. "She had every young guy in the neighborhood after her, and she winds up with him. And nobody knew about it. That's the kicker. How the hell did they get away with that?"

"Well, there were rumors," Raguso said. "I think people were afraid to say anything on account of Red. You know, I think I might even have seen 'em together myself once. Just came back to me since it all happened. It was on a Sunday late in the evening, nearly dark. I was in the car and I see Annie with this guy. I was across the street from them and I thought it was Toby. I don't know if they saw me or not but they ducked into a doorway and when I drove past I couldn't see. It was nearly dark, but knowing what I know now I'm sure it was Toby Walters."

"Well, he was always too fuckin' smart for his own good," Dooney said. "The guy always thought he was better than everyone else. Always tryin' to show everyone how smart he was. But that's the way they are, you know. Show the white guy he ain't the boss. Hey, now look, I'm for equality and all that, but you know what the problem is? They're never satisfied. Give 'em an inch and they take a mile, and pretty goddamn soon they'll be runnin' everything. And that's just the way it is. It ain't got nuthin' to do with prejudice. Nuthin' to do with that."

"Still can't get over her goin' out with that guy," Harry said. "Now, I'd never say it in front of Red or his mother, but you know, maybe she was too smart for her own good, too."

"And maybe Toby Walters had what the other guys didn't have," Kerrigan said.

"Oh yeah—and what's that?" Charlie Wallace asked with a smirk.

"Well, let's see. He was good-looking. He was really smart. Scholastic scholarship and an athletic one if he chose it. He could play any kind of ball better than anyone. Maybe that's what it was."

"Jesus, Kerrigan, it sounds like you had the hots for him yourself," Dooney said.

They looked at him, waiting for him to react. He shook his head and walked to the far end of the bar and poured himself a short beer. He came back slowly and filled Harry's empty glass again, knocking on the bar with his knuckles to indicate it was on the house.

"Harry, it looks like you might be acquiring a taste for this stuff."

"Well, right now, it takes the edge off. I mean with Sheila ready to give birth any minute and all that time I had to spend down at the precinct. I thought that guy Arnie Meyers would never stop asking me questions."

"How did they know you saw Toby coming out of the lane?" Kerrigan asked him.

"They didn't. I told them when they came around after they found the body. One of the cops brought me over to Arnie and he brought me down to the precinct. There wasn't much to tell except that I saw him coming out of the lane that night. Sheila and I had gone to sit out on the stoop to catch a breath of air and Annie was already sitting there with Charlie Gallucci. They left after a while and walked down the block toward the alley. Sheila went back up to the party and I sat there for a while and then I went down to the avenue to get some smokes. When I was walking back up the block I saw Toby Walters coming out of the alley and that's what I told Arnie Meyers."

"Yeah, that's why he's the best detective in Brooklyn. The guy don't miss nuthin.' I mean things you and I would never think of, he's able to put it all together. If Arnie booked Toby, then you just gotta know it was him that did it."

TWENTY-NINE

Bailey Walters walked home from the hospital. He wished he could avoid having to meet all the people he knew in the street. They didn't talk to him now. They just bowed their heads and walked on past him as if he weren't there. All the warm hellos and the bantering were gone. He felt like an outcast. He had been a fixture in the neighborhood for so long.

But now it was as though nobody had ever known him. He was wondering if he would have to quit his job and just move away. It would be terrible to have to start all over again. That would be hard. He wasn't a kid anymore and good jobs, especially as a super, weren't easy to come by. He felt tired. He could hardly lift his legs. He stopped into the diner to get a cup of coffee and the counterman hardly acknowledged him. He drank his coffee quickly and left. To hell with them, he told himself, but he could feel the hurt. Maybe Toby is right, he thought. How could they all change so quickly. They had all condemned him even before he had had a trial. Then he realized there was nothing he could do to change it. But he wondered if Toby was right. That maybe his only chance was to try to get away. Would they give him a fair trial? Could they give him a fair trial? It all seemed to be a foregone conclusion that Toby Walters had murdered Annie Dahlgren, and Arnie Meyers and the cops were not looking for anyone else.

They want my boy to die, he thought. As he was walking past the church, he thought of the young priest who had arranged with the cops to have Toby brought to the hospital. He wanted to talk to someone and he walked up and down outside the church. He had never been inside. He knew the young priest had helped Toby before. He told himself that at least the priest would talk to him.

He rang the bell to the rectory and the housekeeper came to the door. She looked at him with the stern look of a mother superior that she must have been born with and she asked him what he wanted.

"I want to talk to the young priest," he said.

"The young priest?"

"Yes—my name is Bailey Walters. The priest got my son Toby to the hospital when he was hurt."

She looked him over, then opened the door wide.

"Step inside," she said. "I'll see if he's available."

She went away and left him standing inside of the door. A large crucifix hung on the wall opposite him and he stared across at the stricken Jesus. He felt uneasy. He had never been that close to a cross before and it seemed that the blank eyes of Christ were staring at him. He had the urge to quietly tiptoe out the door and into the street. He could smell the faint odor of incense. He had always heard that the Catholics were very mysterious and they believed in magic and miracles. It looked like the figure on the cross was begging him to do something, then Bailey began to imagine that the lips were moving. He thought he must be going crazy. He was about to go out the door when he heard footsteps coming toward him. The figure of Father Darcy was standing before him. The priest smiled and he knew right away who Bailey was. He could see Toby in his father's face.

"You must be Mr. Walters," he said.

The older man nodded and Darcy stuck out his hand, then he asked him to follow him inside. They sat in the priest's study facing each other. Bailey had removed the plaid cap he was wearing and held it tightly in his hands. He looked at Darcy and he didn't know where to start. He was beginning to feel warm and there were beads of perspiration on his forehead.

"Can I get you a glass of water?" Darcy asked him.

Bailey nodded and Darcy left and came back with the water. He drank it down, closing his eyes in relief.

"I don't really know why I came here," he said. "I ain't been on the inside of any church for a long time. I was passin' by on the way back from the hospital. It's hard now since they got my boy. Everybody turns their eyes away when they see me like I'm some kinda leper or somethin'. People I've known and worked with for years."

He shook his head again. "All I know is they got my boy and they all want him dead. They gonna kill him first chance they get and that's the truth. They all full of hate. I see it in their faces. They not gonna give him a chance. I got no one to talk to and I gotta get him a lawyer. A good one. Not one of them fellas they give you. I got money. I can pay. God knows, I ain't got much but I'll pay everything I have."

Darcy sat back listening to him, letting him talk on.

"Toby wants to try to make it out of the hospital 'cause he believes they ain't gonna give him a chance at the trial. He wants me to help him get away. He asked me to bring him some clothes. He says that once they lock him up he ain't never gonna be free again. And I know he didn't kill that little girl."

Darcy thought it strange that he had never met Bailey Walters before and here he was opening himself up to him. He was tempted to invoke the old standby. What was referred to as the wisdom of God. To tell him that he should leave things in God's hands.

Maybe that's what the monsignor would have done, but he knew in his heart it would be wrong to talk that way. Yet this was another situation like Treacy. Better to say nothing than to toss out the old clichés, he thought. Anyway—what place did God have in all this madness, he asked himself. He was beginning to understand that in the world of men you had to deal with men and not with God. He remembered reading somewhere that God had let go of the whole thing a long time ago. And if that was true, it was a frightening prospect. We had to climb out of the shit by ourselves. Maybe when you reach the top of the pit, God might be waiting to pull you up. Jesus had never given anyone an explanation for madness. For the irrationality of men. Who or what determined what came out of men? Darkness and light. He knew for himself that what he felt most of the time was a kind of confusion. A not knowing in the face of the action that had to be taken. He couldn't explain Annie Dahlgren's death and he couldn't explain why they all seemed so intent on making Toby Walters the scapegoat. It was all so easy to do that.

Arnie Meyers putting an end to the investigation was outrageous. Everyone knew it. They had to know it, but the unspoken conspiracy had taken hold of them and had buried their doubts and silenced their hearts. The tragedy had to be given its finality before they could all move on. They had made themselves separate a long time ago.

"He's got no clothes. They took his clothes away," Bailey Walters said. "I got to get some clothes to him. Gotta do it quick 'cause they gonna move him any day now. They gonna lock him up. But he been gettin' stronger."

"Why have you come to me, Mr. Walters? How can I help you?"

"Don't know for sure. Just don't know."

"I could certainly help you get a good lawyer."

"I ain't thinkin' 'bout a lawyer right now. I think Toby's right. No matter who we get, Arnie Meyers gonna beat 'em all. They got it stacked. They all want it that way."

"But think about it, Mr. Walters. If he makes a run for it, it's all over. If he goes to trial there's always the chance he'll be acquitted. If you want my advice, I'd have to tell you not to do anything to help him run."

"Know what they say 'bout this detective Arnie Meyers? They say he just never gets it wrong. No sir. He so good he can't afford to be wrong. And that's what the trouble is. How's my boy gonna fight that?"

He bowed his head and slumped in his chair. Darcy was looking at him, trying to think of the right words to say. Then he saw Bailey pull a large white handkerchief from his pocket and wipe the tears away from his eyes. He blew his nose and mopped his brow. He looked at Darcy with a half-smile of embarrassment. The priest looked at his dark face, so African and so American. So familiar. So much a part of the daily vision of American life. There was a look of bewilderment in it as though it had just been removed from his native village in Africa. He saw the experience of all those who had gone before in Bailey's face.

The surprise at being removed was still present. It had been carried down through the generations. The event over which they had no control. It was like Job all over again. What was God trying to prove? How many Gardens of Eden have to be emptied? What was He after? What was He testing? Or was He paying any attention at all. One injustice after another. He remembered the monsignor telling him that you had to go through many dark nights of the soul. You had to do it over and over again. And somehow he could not bring himself to believe that the monsignor had ever had a dark night. For him there was always the political solution. Let's get together on this. Whose back has to be scratched.

The earthly solution never allowed the grace of God to move in. Darcy wanted to believe that despite all evidence to the contrary the world made sense. And that's what faith was. It wasn't something you believed in. It was like a grace. A persistence that let you overcome your own deadness. It was what you believed in and how you acted. Faith was a millimeter away from despair. And he knew that sometimes even despair was a kind of grace. The willingness to appear to be a fool to other men.

He stood up and walked around the room. He offered Bailey a cigarette and they both lit up. He looked at the older man and was about to say something but hesitated. He went to his chair and sat down again. "I don't know what to tell you," he said finally. "But I want to help you and I want to help Toby."

Bailey Walters nodded. "Then I gotta do it, don't I? I gotta help him get away."

"If I thought it would do any good I'd go down to the station again and talk to Arnie Meyers, but I know he won't listen. I still think your best chance is the trial. Even if he did get away they'll hunt him down until they find him. Look, Arnie and the cops have a lot of power, but surely they can't fix a trial. I mean, not in this day and age."

"They can fix anything they want. Always been that way. They got no evidence against my boy 'cept what they make up. Don't you know that. Don't you know they can do anything they want to."

"But they can't pull that stuff here."

Bailey leaned forward in his chair.

"Believe me when I tell you they can do anything they want."

"So you don't believe there's any way he'll get a fair trial?"

"Maybe if he was white. But he ain't."

THIRTY

They had never seen Harry Cope drunk. He sat drinking and grinning at them. He had bought drinks for the house, and they had all bought him drinks back and they were all standing on the bar before him. He knew he could never finish them all. He was swaying on his seat, mumbling something they couldn't understand.

"Look at this fuck," Raguso said. "What the hell's gotten into him. Guarantee Sheila ain't gonna be happy with him tonight."

"All that good livin' got you goin' crazy, huh, Harry?" Charlie said. "Had enough of the fresh air and the green grass. Must be terrible out there on the Island with not a nigger in sight."

Harry looked at him and grinned incoherently. He couldn't seem to form words and he had no idea what they were saying to him.

"You better give him a cup of coffee," Dooney said. "The poor bastard will never make it home. Jesus, his poor wife. Imagine this bag of shit fallin' in the door. She could be going to the hospital any minute and him drunk as a skunk. That tells you the truth about this guy. Where the hell is he when she needs him?"

"What the hell are you talkin' about?" Raguso said. "You ever been married? Ever had a kid?"

"Fuck you, Rags," Dooney said.

"He never even got laid, forget about getting married," Charlie Wallace shouted.

They were all laughing now and Harry lifted his head from the bar and laughed with them.

"Fuck you, too," Dooney said. "You know what I think? I think he's a goddamn queer."

"No he ain't," Raguso shouted. "The guy's married and his wife's expectin' a baby. Look at Dooney here. The sonofabitch is still a cherry. Or maybe he's queer himself. Can't even get himself a date."

"Listen," Dooney said. "I get dates, and I get laid, too. Thing is I don't come in here braggin' about it. And I ain't queer, 'cept for Rags here. I just love his little Italian ass."

They all laughed harder then ever and Harry was looking at them, trying to keep his eyes open with a silly smile on his face.

"Dooney, you're fulla shit," Charlie Wallace said. "You ain't never got laid and I'd like to know when's the last time you had a date? And who was it?"

Dooney lifted his glass and drained his beer.

"Think I'm gonna tell you guys?"

Now they were all nodding at each other.

"You can't tell us Dooney Hanifan 'cause it never happened. You're too goddamn cheap to pay for a date."

They laughed again and Dooney called out for another beer.

"Even a goddamn hooker wouldn't take him on," Raguso said.

"Why don't you get lost," Dooney said.

"The hell with you, too," Raguso shouted.

"Truth is you ain't never been laid and it ain't never gonna happen 'til you get a face-lift."

Kerrigan was at the far end of the bar reading his newspaper. He had heard it all before.

He heard a thud and when he looked around he saw that Harry had fallen off his stool and was lying on the floor. He was smiling up at them as if he had done something wonderful.

They picked him up and sat him in a booth across from the bar. His head lay on the table and he started to sob.

"Oh, sweet Jesus," Charlie said. "The fuck is on a crying jag now."

Harry was crying and mumbling and moaning and they all moved back to the bar and left him in the booth. They could hear his moans as Kerrigan gave them refills.

"For Christ's sake, shut the fuck up, will you, Harry," Raguso shouted.

"You are looking at a man who is supposed to be happier than us," Charlie said. "Jesus, look at him. That's what married life will do to you."

"Why don't one of you take him home," Kerrigan said.

"Jesus, you know what would happen then?" Dooney said. "Sheila's old lady'd give us hell for getting him drunk. Blame us like they always do. Let him sleep it off. He just ain't used to it, that's all."

The moans suddenly subsided and Harry fell asleep. They turned back to their drinks and Kerrigan stuck his face in the paper. They were talking quietly among themselves and they could hear an occasional snore from Harry.

It had started to rain, falling lightly at first, but now they could hear the sound of thunder erupting and through the window they saw blinding flashes of lightning.

There was a strange quietness at the bar and the nickels in the jukebox had run out. No one had thought to put more money in.

The thunder seemed to shake the bar itself and now they were all turned toward the window, looking at the downpour pelting into the street. Then in the midst of the storm they heard a loud groan. It started low and began to rise in pitch.

They had all turned around. Now they were looking at Harry. He was leaning back in the booth with his head upraised and his mouth wide open. The cry was disgorging itself from deep inside of him. They thought he might be having a seizure or a fit, but they could only watch and listen to the awful cry coming from him.

When he had emptied himself, he turned and looked at them. He started to shake and he shrunk back into a corner of the booth with his arms wrapped tightly around himself as though he were trying to get away from something. As if he were in the throes of some terrible nightmare.

"What the fuck's the matter with him?" Raguso said. "Jeez, I'm glad he don't come in here all the time. You could never have a drink in peace."

"He don't drink enough to be having the DT's," Dooney said. "Last time I saw a guy go through somethin' like this was Treacy, but he's a lush."

Kerrigan came out from behind the bar and went to the booth.

"Are you alright, Harry?" he asked.

He looked at Kerrigan, terrified, and shrunk further back into the corner of the booth.

"How about a cup of coffee?"

Harry was staring at him and he started to moan again as though he was in great pain.

"Give him a shot of Bushmill's, for Christ sake," Charlie Wallace said.

Instead, Kerrigan went back to the bar and poured out a glass of brandy. He brought it over to the booth and placed it down on the table before him.

"Come on. Drink this up, Harry," he said.

Harry looked at him and then at the drink. He buried his face in his hands and began to sob.

"It's alright, Harry," Kerrigan told him. "It's alright. We'll get a cab for you. Take you right home. Come on, fellas, help me get him into a cab."

Dooney and Raguso came over to the booth. Kerrigan reached down and pulled Harry to where they could lift him up, but he wouldn't take his hands away from his face and he was sobbing like a baby.

"Jesus, he's gonna be feelin' real good in the morning," Raguso said.

"Yeah, I'd like to be there when he wakes up. Never seen this sonofabitch with a hangover. Like to see him suffer for once."

"He ain't much good to his wife now, is he?" Charlie Wallace said.

"Be just like a woman to have the baby when her husband is all fucked up."

"I think one of you should go with him," Kerrigan said.

They stood him up finally and walked him out the door into the street. It was still raining but the thunderstorm was gone. They could hear it rumbling away in the distance. The street was deserted and silent.

They could hear the click of the traffic lights as they changed. It seemed the night was standing still.

Nothing was moving. They had seen no traffic at all. Not even the sound of a car in the distance.

It was going to be hard to get a cab. It felt like they had all gone home for the night. Raguso and Dooney stood in the doorway with Harry as Kerrigan went out into the street to look for a cab.

"Harry shows up one night and he's nothin' but trouble," Raguso said. "And he's the one guy would never go out of his way to help anyone. Why the hell don't we just dump him here on the sidewalk."

Kerrigan spotted a cab on the avenue and he put his fingers to his mouth and whistled. The shrill sound pierced the night and the cab turned and sped toward them.

"One of you should go with him," he said.

"You're the good Samaritan, Kerrigan. You go with him," Dooney said.

"Jesus, you know I can't go," Kerrigan said.

He reached under his apron into his pocket and pulled out a bill.

"Look, here's five bucks," he said. 'Why don't the two of you go with him."

Reluctantly, they led Harry to the cab and pushed him inside. They sped off into the night and Kerrigan stood in the doorway looking after them.

"Here's what we do when we get there," Dooney said. "We bring him up to the front door. We ring the bell. And we run like hell."

Raguso nodded. "No waitin' around for someone to open the door."

Harry was seated between the two of them, still sobbing and moaning. Occasionally he would mumble something, but they didn't pay any attention to him. Then he started to talk as if he were having a conversation with someone. His voice was becoming clearer and louder and then he was shouting.

"Shut the fuck up," Dooney told him.

Harry paid no attention and he was still shouting and getting louder all the time.

"The guy's crazy," Raguso said.

Harry suddenly stopped shouting and looked around as though he didn't know where he was. He held Raguso's arm and looked into his face. "Jesus, Rags, I don't know what to do. I got fired two days ago and I'm afraid to tell Sheila. Goddamn boss had it in for me for a long time. Waited 'til Sheila was due and then he pulls the plug. Sonofabitch! Baby's due any day. I can't bring myself to tell her."

Dooney and Raguso looked at each other.

"How come he fired you?" Dooney asked.

"God, I'm going crazy with this," Harry said. "What the hell's gonna happen to us?"

"I thought you was union and you couldn't get fired."

"My last promotion took me out of the union. I'm management now. That's how the sonofabitch was able to fire me. Figured I was after his job. Guy never liked me."

"Bet you was, too."

"Oh fellas, don't kid around with me. I don't know what to do. That's why I been drinking. Had to get away from the house. Went chasin' after Toby Walters. Jesus, it took my mind off it. I don't even want to go home now."

"You're gonna have to tell her sometime. She's gonna find out, anyway," Dooney said.

"Jeez, I can't tell her when she's just about to have the baby. I don't want her worrying."

"Look, Harry, she's gotta figure somethin's wrong. She ain't never seen you drinkin' like this, right?" He nodded.

"Jesus, I feel so ashamed. We got the house and she loves it. It's just the way she wants it for the baby. It has all the things she wanted. And the baby's room is ready whether it's a boy or a girl. She was so happy about everything."

"You'll get another job, Harry. I hear you're real good. One of the best."

"Ain't a lot of jobs around like mine. Might have to start lower even if I'm lucky. Jesus, and all the expenses we're gonna have."

"Hey, I know it's tough, but you ain't the first guy to get fired. You got something put away, I bet."

Harry nodded.

"See, I knew," Dooney said. "And you get unemployment, don't you?"

"That ain't much."

"It's better than nuthin'."

"Jeez, I don't wanna go home. I can't stand looking at her. She knows something's up. She's probably driving herself crazy wondering what the hell's wrong. Why don't we turn around and go back to Kerrigan's."

"Because you been eighty-sixed."

"He'll let me back."

"Hell he will. He paid for the cab to take you home. And Sheila's worried sick about you and she's just about to deliver. You can't do that to her. And you ever hear of this thing for better for worse. That means you gotta stick together no matter what," Raguso said.

"That's right," Dooney said. "Fuckin' smart guy like you ain't gonna have trouble findin' a job."

Harry's head fell to his chest again and his eyes were closed as if he had passed out.

"This fuckin' guy's nuts," Raguso said.

Dooney shook his head.

The cab drew up outside the house and they pulled Harry out. They walked him into the building and rang the bell. When the buzzer sounded they pushed him inside the door and ran back to the cab.

"The guy ain't broke up over Annie Dahlgren. He ain't never been broke up over anyone but himself," Dooney said. "Sometimes when a guy gets loaded all sorts of stuff comes out. Never seen him loaded like he was tonight. Guess he's feelin' the pressure. Must be somethin' when your old lady's gonna pop any minute. I figure he's got a right to tie one on. Better than sittin' home with Sheila's mother. Remember how she used to hate Red?"

"Do you think he really ever got over Sheila?"

"Yeah, and Margo's the one that did it for him. Took him a long time, though."

The cab sped back toward the bar through the silent streets. It was still raining and the lights were reflected in the streets.

"He sure was crazy about her, though," Raguso said. "He would have married her. No doubt about it."

Sheila's mother helped Harry down the hallway to the bedroom. She pushed open the door for him and said good night. She pulled the door closed behind her. It was the first time she had ever seen him drunk and she was surprised. But it didn't diminish her admiration for him. After all, a man's entitled every once in a while, she told herself.

Harry stumbled about the small bedroom, and Sheila sat up and looked at him. She couldn't remember ever seeing him drunk, either. She was surprised. She had often wished he would go out and tie one on. Anything was better than those terrible silences and the rage that came out of him. She was afraid of his rage.

He sat on the edge of the bed with his back to her.

It took her a while to realize that he was crying quietly. She moved closer to him and put her arm around his shoulder.

"What is it, Harry?" she said. "What's the matter?"

He just kept shaking his head.

"It's alright," she told him. "You've been working so hard. I know it hasn't been easy for you. I'm not mad at you. Why don't you get into bed. Get some sleep, and you'll feel better in the morning."

He stood up and walked to the dresser and looked at himself in the mirror.

"For God's sake, Harry, it's alright. You're making it seem like you did something terrible. You got drunk, that's all. You're with me now. It's alright. Come to bed. Come over here and let Mama hold you. Let Mama hold you the way you like her to."

He turned and looked at her. His face assumed the look of a little boy. He came slowly toward her, then he was standing over her. She rose up and began to undress him.

"Remember how you always want me to be the mommy. Let's pretend again. I'm the mommy. And we're going to get little Harry ready for beddy-byes, aren't we?"

He nodded and smiled at her.

"And Harry's not a bad boy, is he, now?"

He shook his head again.

"Harry is Mommy's good boy, isn't he?"

He nodded again and now he was naked before her.

"Come on into bed now and you can lie next to Mommy."

He smiled eagerly and nodded.

"Doesn't baby want to lie next to Mommy?"

She reached her hand out to him and he took it in his. She pulled him in beside her. She pulled him close to her, cuddling and kissing him.

"It's alright now, baby," she whispered. Her hand reached down for him and she held him and started to move it back and forth slowly.

"Is this what Mommy's little boy likes?" she asked. Harry nodded.

"He likes Mommy to play with him, doesn't he?"

She heard him sigh and he moved closer to her and buried his face in her breasts. She moved her hand faster now and then she felt him convulse against her.

"That's better now for Mommy's good boy, isn't it?" she whispered. "And now Mommy's baby is going to go to sleep like a good boy, isn't he?"

His eyes were closed and she listened cautiously to his breathing. She was relieved when she knew for sure that he was asleep. She thought of the change that had come over him.

She felt the baby kicking inside of her. That was the most important thing in the world to her now. She placed her hand over her belly and felt the tiny kicks.

Harry turned in his sleep and moved closer to her. Everyone thought he was so strong and such a good husband. How could she explain how frantic with fear he was at the prospect of their baby coming into the world.

She felt a tenderness toward him she couldn't explain. They didn't know the little boy in him the way she did. She found herself thinking back to the time when she and Red were together before he went to Korea. Everything was so simple then. They had all believed things were going to be a certain way, that each of them would always be the same.

But everything had changed and so had each of them.

And now as she lay next to her husband she sensed that everything was changing again. Thank God for the baby, she whispered to herself. The most important thing was to have a healthy baby. She was not going to let anything stop that from happening. She would have her baby and love it and let the rest of the world take care of itself.

THIRTY-ONE

Jack Treacy walked through the summer heat of Prospect Park. His clothes were stuck to his body and sweat poured down his face. Even in the heat he felt a tremor and a chill ran through him. He hadn't shaved for a few days now and it had been a long time since he had had a haircut. He stared straight ahead as he walked but he had no idea where he was going. He was just walking, forcing himself to move. He felt that if he stopped he would never move again. He had the *Daily News* stuck in his back pocket and he had seen the picture of Arnie Meyers coming out of the hospital after they had booked Toby. He had felt anger come over him the same way it had when he went to the precinct with Father Darcy. He wondered why nobody was asking questions. How they had just accepted that Arnie and the cops had found their man. Why were they all ready to hang Toby? His own bloodied clothes were still on his mind and he still agonized over how they got that way. He wondered still if he had killed Annie Dahlgren himself.

Still, what am I gonna use in place of booze? Tell me that. That other stuff don't appeal to me. Don't want to stick needles in my arm. Too much trouble and hard to come by. Booze was easy. No complications. Drink your drink and that was that. Someone had mentioned AA to him once. He said he didn't want to sit around in some dark place with a bunch of old lushes. Story is they place a bottle in the middle of a long table and they all sit around betting on who'll be the first guy to reach out for the bottle to take a swig. Then when the guy reaches for it, they wrestle him to the ground and they all sit on top of him until he's calmed down. Then they all go back to the table and start over again. There was always some poor fuck reaching out for the bottle even when he knew all the power was long gone out of it. Jesus, imagine having to do that for the rest of your life. Life should be like a movie. Pay your money. Go in and sit down and if you don't like it you can get up and walk out and go find another movie. One you really enjoy. One that has everything in it to make you happy. One you can watch over and over again and never grow tired of. It always turns out exactly the way you would like it to be. Just goes on and on. Happy forever.

He was used to the comforting feel of a flat bottle in his hip pocket and now he reached around unconsciously to find it and it wasn't there.

I don't wanna die, he told himself. Too scared to die. Don't want anyone to die. Saw too many people die. They said it was for a good cause.

I don't want anyone to die even if they committed murder. Don't want to see it anymore. Don't want anyone to die. In his heart he knew he hadn't killed Annie Dahlgren. He knew he never could have done it. He hated death. It didn't give those guys back in Korea enough time. Just came and took them, and someone said they died for some kind of freedom. All they knew was that they died because they were there. Nobody ever asked them what freedom they died for.

He had a vision of Toby Walters being led to his execution. The long walk to the place where the chair is waiting. He forced it out of his head. It kept coming back. It just wouldn't go away. Nobody wanted to talk about the mystery of life. That's what had affected him the most when he came home from Korea. It was never so much what happened to him as it was that he could never impart to those who weren't there the horror. And the pure sweetness of the camaraderie of men who were truly together in a way they would never be again.

He stopped and bought a can of soda from a hot-dog vendor and swallowed it in a few gulps. He couldn't stop sweating. He was looking at some children trying to get a kite off the ground. He sat under a tree at the edge of the vast stretch of grass and watched them. The children ran and ran and the kite rose, and just when it seemed it was ready to soar, it came crashing down to the ground. They never seemed to be disappointed. They laughed and ran into the wind again, always more hopeful than the time before. He wondered what it would be like to feel like a child again. He knew it was still in him someplace along with the sweat and the nightmares. And he felt the tears of his sadness, but as he kept looking at the children he knew it wasn't all sadness. There was a possibility that things could change. They were running into the wind again and the kite was making its way slowly, shakily into the air. They were running as fast as they could to try to give it more life, and now it was higher than it had been before. They were shouting for joy, encouraging each other, then one of them fell and the others tripped over him and the kite came tumbling down once more, and they rolled over in the grass laughing and shouting.

It was cool under the tree. Treacy pulled a handkerchief from his pocket and wiped his face. A slight breeze made the leaves rustle. There was a comfort in the sound. It was beyond cars, and men and airplanes and bridges. Then the tremor came over him again and he shivered. He folded his arms tightly around himself to stop from shaking and he leaned back into the tree and stretched his legs out before him. The tremor passed and he began to sweat even more than before.

He had felt the first glimmer of hope in himself since he had come back from Korea. It had come to him like a grace. He never expected it and he wondered if he could trust it. Maybe it was just part of the DT's.

He stood up and began to walk again slowly, and as quickly as they went away, the old fears came trotting back like old friends. So natural and so familiar, like vultures spotting a carcass. He fought to hold on just a little longer to the little piece of hope that had come to him. The tiny grace with the pale delicate light that was so fragile. And away off in the distance now he could see the small figures of the children still trying to get the kite up into the air. He would always think of them. Maybe they could help him hold on to his little bit of grace.

He came out of the park and found himself walking near the hospital where Toby Walters was. He saw the rows and rows of windows and he wondered which room Toby was in. It was a redbrick building and the window frames were painted white. It had a cheerful look about it and he saw groups of white uniformed nurses passing in and out of the entrance.

He thought of Arnie Meyers and Red and the way they had thrown him out of the precinct.

And he remembered Darcy. He had stuck up for him. He was a good guy. He wasn't like a lot of the other priests he had known. At least he tried. He was alright. Just like Kerrigan said he was. He wished he could talk to him now and tell him about the feeling he had. He wanted Darcy to tell him it was true. A true feeling. That it was possible for things to change. Was it possible that one day he wouldn't hate himself?

Was it possible that one day all the guilt would go away? Was it possible to have some peace? Was it possible that he wasn't just bad? Was it possible that he was worth something? As he walked on he looked up into the sky to see if by some chance he might see the children's kite flying up there. But there was only blue sky, empty and clear.

THIRTY-TWO

Bailey Walters pulled out the drawers of the dresser in Toby's room. He rummaged about, taking out clothes and throwing them on the bed. Shirt, underwear, pair of pants.

That's all he'll need, he told himself. How the heck am I gonna get 'em in there, he wondered. "Goddamn it, I must be crazy," he whispered to himself. "They'd just shoot him down if he tries to get away."

All I ever wanted was to be left alone, he thought. For people not to mess with me. I don't care if you don't like me. Just treat me like a man. Wanna feel better than me? That's alright. Go ahead. Just don't bother me about it. That damn Arnie Meyers is so sure nobody in the world is as smart as him. Just the way he looks at me tells me he's got somethin' to hide. He ain't as smart as he thinks and he's scared someone's gonna find out. He just don't wanna hear nuthin'. Only thing I can do is bring Toby his clothes.

Let him take his chances. If they gonna kill him one way or the other, then at least let him be free when they do get him. Don't wanna give 'em the chance of hangin' him. I'd rather kill him myself. He stood up and took the clothes off the bed. I just gotta do this, he told himself. I just gotta do it.

Red Dahlgren looked at his mother and realized how much she had aged since the death of Annie. She had lost so much weight, her clothes just hung on her, and she didn't bother to wear makeup anymore. Her lovely angular face was gaunt, skeletal. Her eyes had a distant look as though she were always somewhere else deep inside of herself. She could hardly bear to be in the world anymore. She had withdrawn into herself and when she spoke, her voice was little above a whisper. She stayed in her room, lying on her bed with her rosary beads clutched tightly in her hands as if she were afraid that if she let go she would fall apart completely.

Red wanted to tell her of his plans with Margo. They had made up their minds that they were going to go away as soon as they were married. They were going to go to California. Los Angeles, three thousand miles from Brooklyn. A whole new life. He wanted her to tell him that she thought it was all wonderful, but he knew she wouldn't do that. But he wanted her to be as excited as he was. He wanted to say look, Ma, look what I'm doing. He wanted her to be happy for him.

As he looked at her sitting across from him in the kitchen he couldn't find the words to talk to her. He went to the icebox and brought back two cans of beer. He poured hers into the tall Pilsner glass she loved to sip from. She loved a good head on her beer and she always allowed it to stand for a long time. She had learned that from her husband. She had loved the way he always poured her beer for her.

She lifted the glass to her lips and sipped gently, moving her head back slightly. She felt the cold beer invade her, then she gently placed the glass back down on the table. Her face flushed a little and her eyes watered. She wiped her lips with a paper napkin.

Red drank from the can and looked at her. She was always after him to drink from a glass, but now she didn't bother anymore. It didn't matter now. She knew that anything she had to say would have no effect on anything. He saw that her spirit seemed to be gone. He wished she would chastise him the way she used to for not using a glass. Now she stared past him as if he weren't there.

He encouraged her to drink her beer. He thought it would loosen her up a little and maybe remove the awful mask of sadness and despair from her face. But no matter how she looked she would keep her will. She would always be able to take care of herself no matter what. She would die standing up. That was her way. She would never give in no matter how badly she felt. All her Irish friends would rally around her just as they always had for each other since their days together in the convent. They were all on the raft of life together, paddling toward the same place. They loved their husbands and their children in their own way but they never really needed anyone else because they always had each other. They were of another time and another place. A world apart.

A place they could really never leave. They had something that had been formed when they were orphans and that bond would never fail them. The allegiance of the dark star had brought them all together.

Mrs. Dahlgren could tell when Red was nervous, no matter how well he tried to hide it. She knew he wanted to tell her something. He filled her glass again and looked admiringly at the head he had put on her beer. He smiled at her as she raised her glass and took a sip.

"You know they booked the colored kid," he told her.

She nodded.

"Arnie's sure it was him. He has no doubt."

She nodded again as though it made no difference to her.

"And you won't believe it, Ma. Jack Treacy goes to see Father Darcy because he found some blood on his clothes after he came off his bender. He tells him it must have been him killed Annie. My God, I couldn't believe it. So Darcy brings him down to the precinct to have the blood tested. Arnie ends up havin' to throw the two of 'em out of the place. What the hell kind of a priest is that? Tells Arnie his investigation has been too narrow. I mean he's talkin' to the best detective in Brooklyn."

"What difference does it make now? Nothing's going to bring her back," she said.

She paused and took a sip from her beer and brushed back a wisp of hair from her brow.

"Did you know about Annie and Toby Walters?"

She shook her head.

"You had no idea at all?"

"I knew she was seeing someone besides Charlie Gallucci. She was a very smart girl. I knew there was something going on, but I didn't know what it was."

"But what made her do it? I mean she coulda had anyone she wanted."

"She always knew what she wanted. She wasn't afraid of life. She was going to go after everything she wanted. She was never going to have much patience with anyone who couldn't keep up with her. She was never afraid like me. Your father was afraid, too. He had everything but he held it back and I never knew why. There was no dark star hanging over Annie."

She bowed her head and Red saw the tears well up in her eyes. He came to where she sat and put his arm around her and put his cheek close to hers. Then he turned and kissed her.

"It's alright, Ma. It's alright," he said.

"And they've got that young boy and they'll hang him for sure," she said. "What's the sense of it? She was happier than I'd ever seen her. She was so alive. So alive. They must have had something good together. When I remember how she was at the party. Everyone was looking at her. They couldn't take their eyes off her."

"It's okay, Ma. I know. I can't even let myself think of her now."

Then they were holding on to each other. Red felt his own tears rise and he fought to hold them back.

"I just want you to be sure you're doing the right thing," she said after a while.

"What do you mean, Ma?"

"I mean that you're sure about Margo. I like her. I really do. She's been very good to me. And there is something about her."

She paused. "To tell you the truth, I worry that's she's so different than Sheila. As God is in heaven I know you and Sheila were meant for each other. To this day, I don't know what changed it all. Whatever she saw in Harry Cope, I'll never know. I had my heart set on you and her. She used to come to me with her troubles, such as they were. She's not happy now. I can tell you that. There's something wrong there. There's more to it all than just providing for someone. A man has to do more than that. I always thought it must have been her mother. If you hadn't gotten into that fight with Harry it might have been different. You never went after her."

"Oh, Ma, why do you still bring all that old stuff up? Please, Ma. I love Margo. We really have something."

"Maybe the good thing is the way she went after you. She really knew what she wanted and she went after it. A lot to be said for that."

"I'm glad she did. I'm glad she did."

He moved back to his chair and stared down at the table, unable to look at her. He knew exactly why he was with Margo. She was so unlike his mother. She was warm and she believed in him. She held him close and made him feel good. She wasn't afraid. She was free and she never gave a damn what anyone thought of her. She knew what she wanted and she wanted him. She and Annie were a lot alike. She never told him how disappointed she was in him and she didn't have that fuckin' Irish blackness. There was no dark star hovering over her. She didn't have a goddamn tragedy. There was more life in her than in that whole crowd down in Kerrigan's, and maybe the best thing was that she wasn't Irish. And he was supposed to feel bad that she wasn't. Jesus, you'd think she was a spook. She's Italian. What the hell's that got to do with anything? She wasn't a wop like that asshole Raguso. And she was smart. She'd tell those guys where to go and they knew it, too.

To hell with Sheila.

To hell with Harry Cope.

To hell with the whole damn neighborhood.

Me and Margo will be gone. Far far away from this place. No more "Mother Macree." No more "Who Threw the Overalls in Mrs. Murphy's Chowder?" No more "Galway Bay" and all that shit. Somebody hits the number once and they believe in God all over again.

"I'll always worry about you," Red said. "I know you would never come to California."

She shook her head.

"You'll always be welcome and I know Margo would love to have you."

He couldn't believe what he was saying to her. It was just coming out. It wasn't what he had wanted to say at all. But he was sure she would never go west with them. He felt guilty about wanting to get away. There was so much to leave behind. It was time to move out. It was a huge country, after all. It really was bigger than Brooklyn.

Mrs. Dahlgren knew that Annie and Red would never know the world she had come out of. There would always be a world of difference separating them. Without ever saying it, they understood this of each other.

How many times had he turned to look expectantly into her face for the hint of the approval he always wanted, just the glimmer of a smile of recognition, but she just didn't know how to give it.

Margo, though, gave it to him. She brought the warm feeling to his gut. She made all of the unspoken things fade away so they couldn't strangle him. Thank God for Margo, he told himself, and now he was more anxious than ever for the two of them to get away from Brooklyn.

Bailey Walters placed a pair of blue jeans and a shirt in the bottom of a large shopping bag. He put some T-shirts and underwear over them and he put some apples and oranges and bananas on top of them. He picked up the bag and held it as though he were weighing it. Then he crossed the room and picked up the phone.

"Hello, Reverend, it's Bailey Walters," he said.

"Hello, Mr. Walters," Darcy answered. "What can I do for you?"

"I've got the clothes all put together for Toby and I'm gonna take 'em down to him."

There was silence and Bailey waited for him to say something. The priest didn't know what to say.

"I gotta do it. I can't let my boy down," Bailey said.

Darcy still didn't know what to say.

"Can you hear me, Reverend," Bailey asked.

"I can hear you, Mr. Walters," he said.

"It's like I said before," Bailey said. "He's got no chance if they try him. No chance. I got no choice. I gotta try to help him get away from there."

"I wish you hadn't told me, Mr. Bailey. You should really think about what you're doing. He's not going to get away. The odds are all against him."

"They all against him the other way, too. I have to do it."

"I can't tell you what to do, Mr. Walters. I have no right one way or the other. It's a terrible choice you have to make, but I can't tell you to go ahead. That's up to you."

"I want you to go down there with me, Reverend."

"Do you realize what you're asking me to do, Mr. Bailey?"

"Look, they give me a hard time every time I go there. I ain't askin' you to do anything. Just figure if you're with me they'll back off a little bit."

"Then I'd be helping Toby escape."

"No, you wouldn't. You'd just be going up there with me, that's all. You wouldn't be helpin' me do nuthin'."

"What are they going to think when they find out he's gone? You can be sure they're going to come looking for you and me."

"They not goin' to know nuthin'. They gonna find a bag with fruit and underwear in it. That's all. What's that gonna tell 'em? Please, Reverend, I got nobody else. I got no one I can turn to. I want you to walk in the street with me. You'll see how people are looking at me now. I did so many favors for so many of them people. Now they don't wanna know me. I'm afraid to walk in the street. Look, I never asked much of anyone but I need some help now."

Darcy was silent because he still didn't know what to say. He knew it was useless to try to talk him out of it. His desperation came through the phone.

"Do you think what I'm doin' is a sin, Reverend?"

"No, Mr. Walters, I don't believe it is, but it's breaking the law."

"I ain't breakin' God's law, am I? And if I ain't, then that's all that matters. Will you come with me?"

He heard Darcy sigh into the phone and he waited for him to answer.

"Okay," he heard Darcy say. "Meet me at the rectory in half an hour."

Darcy hung up the phone and stayed sitting in his chair. Maybe I can reason with him while I'm walking him to the hospital, he thought. I've got the parish to think about, too. And the reputation of the church. My God, if the monsignor ever got wind of what I was up to, he'd have me defrocked. He lit a cigarette, went to the window and looked out into the street. It looked the same as it always did and would stay that way forever. He could hear the voices of kids further up the street playing stickball. There were shouts and arguments and the derisive laughter of the winners lording it over the losers. He heard the sound of the broom handle dropping on the asphalt and the distant sound of the elevated as it screeched to a halt in the station. And there was the tinkling of the bells of the ice cream truck as it drove into the block. Everything was normal. He withdrew from the window and sat down heavily in his chair.

He felt scared and he had an overwhelming sense of loneliness.

He wondered why he had not been more blunt with Bailey Walters. Just to be able to say right out that he wouldn't go to the hospital with him. Then he thought of calling him back. Where the hell does he live, anyway, he thought. I don't even have his number.

THIRTY-THREE

The two men walked down the street together, Bailey Walters carrying the large brown shopping bag with the clothes in it, and Father Darcy beside him. They could feel the eyes of the passersby looking curiously at them. They wondered what Darcy was up to now, going off with Bailey Walters. They looked straight ahead, not allowing themselves to see the stares. They were on the far side of the street from Kerrigan's and as they passed it, Darcy couldn't resist a quick glance across the street. He saw the faces in the window looking across at them. Some of them were standing in the doorway. They looked at them silently, curious, as though they had been given a problem to solve.

Where are they going? What the hell are they up to now? Kerrigan himself watched them through the window. He wasn't surprised to see Darcy with Bailey Walters. He figured they were on the way to the hospital to see Toby, but he didn't say anything to the others.

"You just know that sonofabitch is up to something," Dooney Hanifan said.

"You're goddamn right he is," Raguso said. "Headed for the hospital to try to talk the cops into letting the kid go home."

"The guy don't know when to give up," Charlie Wallace said.

"Takes a goddamn priest to go against his own people. Sidin' with a nigger. What the hell else is new? He goes out of his way to throw it up in our faces. Really makes you wonder what the hell he's up to. What's he doing it for? What the hell does he get out of it?"

"Fucked if I know," Dooney said. "But you can bet your ass he's gettin' somethin'. You know what it is? Some guys like to be martyrs. They think there's something noble in takin' the side of murderers. If they were holding the devil himself, Darcy would be down there trying to bail him out. How do you figure a guy like that?"

"Tell you what it is with this guy," Raguso said. "His old man's a big-shot lawyer down on Wall Street. Plays golf with Ike and all that. His picture's in the paper every time you turn around. Always raisin' money for someone, but Darcy's got it in for him. He just wants to embarrass the old man, make him look bad in front of his big-shot pals.

"Fuck him," Raguso said as they turned away and went back to their places at the bar.

Bailey Walters was glad Darcy was with him. The more they passed people in the street and saw their faces, the more convinced he was that he had to help Toby get away from them.

It was terrible to feel all of their hatred and hostility. He had made up his mind that he would move away himself now. He would give his job and the apartment he had lived in for twenty years. He wondered where he would go and how he would make a living. He had some money saved but that wouldn't last very long. And he had brought some money with him to give to Toby. He knew it was all crazy. All upside down. None of it made any sense. It all came out of the blue. It just happened and now nothing would ever be the same. It was as if madness had dropped down out of the sky on them and there was no way to stop it. That's why he had to help get Toby out of it. How could he be heard in the midst of all the insanity. It wasn't the same neighborhood he had moved into twenty years before, even though they were nearly all the same people. What happened, he kept asking himself. Why couldn't they all sit down together and really find the truth? It didn't take much to see that something else had taken over. What had come over them all? They had all been as proud of Toby as he himself was when they had heard about his scholarships. They had always been honest, hardworking people.

He remembered how elated he was when Jackie Robinson had come up with the Dodgers. The great separation was coming to an end and all of Brooklyn was behind Jackie. Everyone wore buttons that said "I'm for Jackie," and he had bought one for Toby. It was still in the house somewhere.

And Harry Truman had integrated the armed forces after the war.

There were going to be great changes, but now as he and Darcy walked down the street on their way to the hospital, Bailey Walters felt a kind of outright hostility he had never felt before. There were the same people who had always been decent and given him work and respected him. He was afraid, and he unconsciously moved closer to Darcy. He knew they were all for Jackie as long as his brothers and sisters didn't move into the neighborhood. As long as they didn't forget their place. As long as they didn't want to go out with anyone's sister. All Jackie had to do was make the double play and steal home when the Dodgers were a run behind. As long as he kept his mouth shut. As long as he didn't forget the favor they were all doing him. As long as he doesn't forget he's a nigger.

Darcy felt the hostility, too. He knew he was on thin ice with them to begin with and he wondered if they ever really heard anything he had said from the pulpit in the way he had meant it.

Maybe religion was just a sort of habit that had no relevance to the reality of the world around them. Theirs was the world of jobs and bosses and children and shoes and the need to make more money and the wife going back to work. Striving and the unspoken anger. Goddamnit. We deserve more. This is America. There was always a dark unspoken resentment and now it all seemed to be coming out and they had to turn it on somebody. Darcy had felt it as soon as he arrived at the parish. He didn't understand it at first but it began to come to him slowly. They were angry. A malignant, cynical anger that was hidden, covered up even from themselves, but with the death of Annie Dahlgren it had burst forth and found its focus. And now even as he walked down the street with Bailey Walters he knew he had to be with him. He knew he had never really understood what being a priest meant, if it had any relevance anymore. Was he with Bailey because he was a man or was it because he was a priest. Freud had said he was looking for a new kind of man, one who was neither priest nor doctor, a listener. A fellow traveler who wasn't concerned with fixing or judging, someone who celebrated the mystery of every man. Someone who could plumb the depths of himself and not recoil at what he found. Someone who knew intimately the inherent guilt of men. Ontological guilt. It was there waiting for you when you came out of the womb. Someone who knew we were not going to find the answers. Someone who knew that pursuing happiness was madness. Someone who understood that chaos was the natural order of the universe. What was the price we paid for chasing the American Dream. He couldn't prevent a slight smile coming to his lips. And someone had said that you couldn't take anyone any further than you had taken yourself. So much for priests and psychiatrists. He felt that he had not come very far at all. And he knew that the truth was that you had to find the way yourself. We are ultimately alone and no one wants to know that.

Harry Cope had slept late. He had barely moved since he had closed his eyes the night before. He was still in the fetal position, his feet drawn up into his chest and his head tucked into his shoulder.

Sheila had slept on and off through the night. The baby was very active. She had felt it kicking more than ever before and she had the feeling that the birth was going to come very quickly. Her bag was packed with everything she needed to take with her to the hospital. There had been no bleeding for a while now and she was very relieved. She believed in her heart now that everything was going to be alright. She was going to have a lovely healthy baby and she believed that once the baby came into their lives everything would be okay again. Harry wouldn't be so anxious. He would be happy to have a son. Or a little girl. It didn't matter. They would really enjoy their lovely home and Harry would put up a swing and a jungle gym in the backyard. She pictured him out there on a lovely bright sunny day playing with his son. He already had a camera and he loved to take pictures, but when the baby came she knew there would be no stopping him.

She really wanted him to be happy and she wanted to be a good wife to him. She wanted the old comfort she had used to feel with him. She had been so proud when they were able to buy the house. And he had worked hard to get them the things they had wanted. He was the youngest foreman on the job and he deserved it, and he was going to college at night. Everyone always said there was no one who worked as hard as he did.

She told herself it was just a phase he was going through. She was sure that all men went through it. It was a big adjustment, having a baby. It scared a lot of men. But now everything was going to be alright. He had pleaded with her not to tell anyone he had hit her. He told her he just didn't know what came over him. She was surprised he had slept so long. It wasn't like him. He was snoring and still in a deep sleep. Her mother came up behind her and looked in over her shoulder.

"Poor Harry," she said. "You know, I always believe it's worse on the men than the women when their time is near. The poor things go half-crazy not knowing what it's all about. We know what we have to do but the men don't have a clue. They all act dopey and feel helpless. No wonder they get drunk, although I have to say for Harry, he's better than most of the men around here."

She placed her hand on Sheila's shoulder. "He's a far better man than your father ever was. I envy you, and I don't mind saying it. What I would have given to have had a man like Harry. He put you up there on a pedestal and never took you off. The best thing you can do for him is to give him a healthy baby. Wait 'til you see. He'll be a wonderful father. I can't tell you how glad I am you married him. You'll never have any cause for regret."

Sheila closed the door and made her way back to the kitchen. She poured herself a cup of coffee. Her mother followed her and sat down beside her.

"The best thing for him is to sleep," her mother said. "At least he's not walking around here dopey with anxiety. You should let him sleep as long as he wants."

Sheila nodded. She sipped her coffee, then she suddenly gasped in pain and stretched herself back in her chair. Her mother rushed to her and clutched her hand.

"What is it? What is it?" she said.

"I think it's started," Sheila said. "I think it's coming. I hope I'm not bleeding."

She gasped in pain again. "You better call Dr. Rosen," she said. "I think it's time to go. You better wake Harry up, too."

"Now don't worry," her mother said. "Everything's going to be alright. It's all going to be fine."

She ran back to the bedroom and opened the door. She went over to the bed and shook Harry gently on the shoulder.

"Harry, Harry, wake up," she said.

He opened his eyes and looked at her.

"It's Sheila," she said. We've got to get her to the hospital."

He remained in the fetal position, staring at her. His head hurt and his eyes wouldn't focus.

She heard Sheila gasp again and she ran to the kitchen. Harry stared at the open door and he felt a cloud of fear descend on him. He wanted to crawl back under the covers and never come out. He heard Sheila's mother calling him again.

"Come on, Harry," she said. "You have time for a quick cup of coffee."

He stumbled out of bed and made his way to the bathroom.

He ran the faucet and threw some cold water on his face. He wet his hair and brushed it straight back.

The sight of his face frightened him. He saw the fear in his own searching eyes. He had no idea of how he got home. He had a vague recollection of being in a taxi and he thought there was someone with him but he didn't know who. He knew he had been in Kerrigan's and he was sorry he had been there. He wondered what had possessed him. He was afraid of what he might have said. What the hell am I afraid of, he asked himself. He had always played it very close to the vest and it wasn't like him to confide in anyone. He could never stand the Kerrigan's crowd, and yet he had gone there.

It scared him that he couldn't remember how he got home. He heard Sheila's mother calling out to him again to hurry up. He went to the kitchen and saw Sheila sitting back in a chair with her hands clasped over her stomach. She smiled at him and reached for his hand as though she wanted to be reassured. He looked at her and forced himself to smile despite the fear in his stomach. Sheila's mother poured him a cup of coffee. She poured milk into it and added sugar just the way he liked it. He had always liked the way she catered to him. He used to kid her, saying that if he had met her first he would have married her. She loved to dote over him. They were able to communicate with just a glance and a meeting of the eyes. She was convinced that her daughter had gotten the best man in Brooklyn and she never hesitated to let Sheila or anyone else know it.

As far as she was concerned, there was no one else like Harry.

THIRTY-FOUR

Jack Treacy walked past Kerrigan's. He was on his way to talk to Darcy. When he glanced in, he saw the place was nearly empty. He could see Kerrigan sitting at the end of the bar chewing on a sandwich as he read the newspaper. He glanced up and saw Treacy looking in the window and he waved to him to come in. He hesitated but he went in and sat at the bar before Kerrigan.

"I was on my way to see Darcy," he told him.

"Well, you missed him," Kerrigan said. "Passed by here a while ago with Bailey Walters. Looked like they were on their way to the hospital. The others were here but they all went off to the ballgame.

"You heard they booked the kid," Kerrigan said.

Treacy nodded.

"They're gonna move him to the house of detention. Want a cup of coffee?"

"Gimme a soda."

Kerrigan poured him a glass of ginger ale.

"I heard about you and Darcy going down to the precinct."

Treacy sipped his soda.

"You really didn't believe it was you that killed Annie Dahlgren?" he said.

"I know it sounds crazy, but when I saw the blood on my clothes it scared the hell out of me. I didn't know what to think. I mean I couldn't remember anything, for chrissake. Where I'd been, who I was with, or how the hell I got home. It's always like that. Who knows what the hell I could've done? So when I was at the funeral I talked to Darcy and he said the best way to relieve my mind was to go down to the station and have them test the blood. It was more to relieve my own mind. I was just desperate. And he offered to go down with me. He never believed it was me. He was asking them to just relieve my mind. I was in terrible shape coming off the bender and all. And then Arnie Meyers throws us both out on our asses. Jesus, I didn't mind for myself, but the way they treated Darcy was a bitch. He didn't deserve that. He's a good guy. First damn priest ever listened to me. He doesn't talk like he knows what it takes to get into heaven. And we're both kicked out on our asses. It was like they didn't want to know anything down there. I mean if we had brought in the confessed killer with all the proof in the world, they still would've thrown us out. They just didn't want to know."

"Yeah, they're gonna hang the kid and that's it. They figure he's it. Nothin's gonna change it. They ain't gonna look any further than him."

"Can't figure why they're so determined to hang it on the kid. I mean if he and Annie Dahlgren cared for each other the way they say, why would he want to kill her? It doesn't make any sense."

"And they're takin' Harry Cope's word for it about seeing him coming out of the alley. And no marks or scratches or a trace of blood on the kid's clothes. Yeah, just don't make sense. Maybe they're gettin' pressure from the DA and the pols. You know how it is with those guys. They've always got something going on. They want it over with, and they want someone to burn. So they go for the easy out: Toby Walters, a nigger kid. What the hell they gotta lose?"

"I tried to talk to Red about it. He don't wanna know nuthin'."

"Yeah—he just wants to marry that girl and get the hell away from here."

"Can't say as I blame him. I know how he feels, though. He ain't worryin' whether they got the right guy or not. His little sister's dead. That's all he knows."

Kerrigan nodded and took a bite out of his sandwich, then took a pull on his glass of beer. He leaned across the bar toward Treacy and spoke softly even though there were only a couple of old men sitting in the back.

"You know, Harry Cope came in here last night and got shitfaced. Never seen him like that in all the time I've been here. The guy hardly ever takes a drink. He stayed here for a long time, too. Sheila's expectin' any day now so they're stayin' over at her mother's so they can be close to the hospital. But he sat here all night drinking. Dooney and Raguso had to take him home in a taxi. So when they come back here they're telling me they think the poor sonofabitch is crazy. Breaks down and starts cryin' and everything. They said they were tryin' to shut him up but he just kept goin' on like he was crazy. I mean, Jack, the guy hardly ever takes a drink. You could count on one hand all the times he's been in here in all the years I've known him. So when Dooney and Rags is bringing him home he tells 'em he lost his job at the *Daily News* and he's afraid to tell Sheila."

"Guess he's nervous about her having the baby."

"But he don't say nuthin' about it or about being a father. Even had to put him in a booth before they took him home. He goes to sleep and then he sits up and lets a roar out of him like a stuck pig. I swear to Christ, Jack, I never heard anything like it in my life. It's like he saw Dracula or somethin'. Dooney says he was actin' like he was really crazy. Like it wasn't just the booze."

The *Daily News* was lying facedown on the bar. The sports headline read "Bums Down Bucs in Jersey City."

Treacy looked at the paper and shook his head.

"Jesus, can you believe this," he asked Kerrigan. "What the fuck's goin' on here? The Dodgers playin' in Jersey City. How the hell do you figure that?"

Kerrigan shook his head. "This guy O'Malley's got 'em all beat. Talk about crust. Holdin' the city over a barrel 'til he gets what he wants and the goddamn politicians standin' around with their fingers up their asses. They make a statement and O'Malley makes a statement, and they all belong down in the playground. He's tryin' to tell the city Ebbets Field ain't fit to play in, so he brings 'em over to that shitbox in Jersey City. Listen, the Dodgers are gonna leave and that's it. You can bet your ass on it. And all because one greedy sonofabitch says he ain't makin' enough money. He owns the bats and the balls and the park, and he'll tell you it's his right to take his team anywhere he wants even if it means fuckin' a million people. He ain't responsible to no one but himself. He'll turn around and tell you this is America and it's his right to do anything he wants to with his ball club. He shouts private property and free enterprise and he holds the city up to build him a brand-new stadium. That's the American way. You can be the biggest prick in the world but if you're a prick with money you're alright. You're a mogul.

"O'Malley's nuthin' but a fuckin' accountant. Couldn't swing a fuckin' bat to save his life. Sits up in the shadows of the grandstand countin' the house. Never shows his face. A goddamn accountant. You and I ever ask for a little help, they call us lazy bums and Commies. And you know what? Pretty soon the accountants are gonna be running it all. They're takin' the soul out of everything, believe me. We're losing somethin'. You can feel it right here in the neighborhood. Used to be we had what you could call a community here. Now look at it. What do they want? What are they all looking for? You know what I say? Fuck O'Malley. Let him go to Los Angeles. He'll fuck them, too. Somebody should knock the fuck off or break his legs. Damn accountant. Fight their fuckin' wars for them so they can have sales on Washington's birthday."

They fell silent, staring past each other, and they could feel the quiet sadness of something they knew was gone.

"Something not right about this whole Toby Walters thing," he said. "They really have nothin' on the kid 'cept what Harry told 'em and what's that? Even if they found the blood on my clothes was Annie's you just have the feeling they wouldn't do anything, anyway. I don't know, Johnny, there's somethin' up. I know I ain't anyone to be talkin', with my reputation around here, but you can feel it."

They were silent again as though they didn't know what to say. The traffic moved on the street outside and it looked like all of the glorious normal days they both had known for so long.

When the neighborhood seemed permanent and unchangeable.

When it was their haven.

When it was the place Treacy used to think about when he was close to death in Korea.

When it was the one true and sure place in their lives.

When they could read the papers and hear of the world outside and were sure it would never intrude.

Treacy's stomach leaped in fear as the thought surged through him again that maybe he had killed Annie Dahlgren.

"I was on my way to see Darcy," he told Kerrigan.

"I'm pretty sure he's at the hospital with Bailey Walters."

"Maybe I'll catch him down there. I'm sure he could use the company. You know the cops are gonna bust his balls."

"Yeah, Darcy's alright, but the whole neighborhood shuns him now. You shoulda seen him and Bailey Walters walking down the street. Everybody movin' out of their way like they were a couple of lepers. What the hell is it with people?"

"You're askin' the wrong guy," Treacy said.

Toby had begun to feel as though his strength had come back.

He was sure they were going to move him to the house of detention the next day and he knew his only chance of making a break was that night. He was hoping his father wouldn't let him down. If he didn't have clothes there was no way he could do it. Every time he heard footsteps in the hallway he expected to see his father walk through the door. His mind was made up. He was going to go down the drainpipe when it got dark and disappear into the night. It was off to the left of the window and he wanted to believe it would hold him. There was no other way. It was the only chance he had. He believed that if he could make it to the ground they would never catch him.

He had told himself that even if they had to kill him, he was never going to let them catch him. He didn't want to die and the thought of death terrified him. It was driving him. Escaping now was his only chance. Once they got him to the house of detention, it would be impossible to get away. He would have to wait for his trial. They were not going to allow him bail. But now he was feeling strong. He prayed his father would appear and bring him some clothes.

His strong young body had always given him confidence in himself. He believed it would take him to freedom. When he was on the track team at school, he knew he could win every race he ran in. He could pass anyone. Just leave them behind. The speed and the energy surged up in him as though it came from a bottomless well. No one could ever catch him. He knew that. No matter how hard they tried he had always found the strength and the speed to stay ahead and win.

He had stood at the window and looked down so many times, imagining himself climbing down. He felt he knew every step he would have to make on the descent. He knew he would head for Manhattan. Maybe head for the Village and lay low for a few days. He was sure he was going to make it just the way he had planned it.

He thought of Annie all the time.

Strange that they were holding him for murdering her and he still couldn't believe she was gone. He had even thought of how they would have planned his escape together.

Everything had happened so fast. They had buried her someplace now but she had come to him in his dreams. He could feel her presence and he had conversations with her.

She had told him not to be afraid. He had dreamed of walking in the park with her, finding their secret place together. She had smiled at him with that look he loved of wonder and excitement on her face. She had always been so sure of how life was going to be, and now he really believed she was trying to touch him even though she was gone. When he thought of how much he loved her he had cried hard into his pillow to muffle his sobs. He didn't understand how brokenhearted he was. She wanted to be a strength for him. To let him feel her closeness. He knew that no matter what happened, their closeness would never go away. They were to be together for all time. Nothing could come between them. He knew that if he died he would find her again. They were closer now than they had ever been.

Evening was coming now and he could see the amber glow of the sky through the top of the window. The day was beginning to slow down. He was beginning to think that maybe his father wouldn't come. And then he reminded himself that there was still plenty of time. If he came too early, there was a better possibility of the clothes being found. Better that he come late.

He and Bailey had sat in Ebbets Field so many times at this time of the day. They loved to get there to see batting practice and watch the infielders whip the ball around. There was something about the way they moved, making the most difficult plays look easy. They could make thirty thousand people come to their feet with one well-executed play. No showboating. No playing to the crowd. No need to show anything of themselves other than their skills. They would do it the same way even if the stands were empty. They were working-class men. The men of D-Day and Iwo Jima. They were sure of who they were and what they did, and they took the risk of being shown up every time a ball was hit their way.

All their strengths and all their flaws were on the field for everyone to see. Honorable men, and he wondered why the world outside of the ballpark wasn't like that. He was becoming more nervous now. Where was his father? It was time. Maybe he had decided at the last minute not to come.

Everything had quieted down. There were no sounds in the hallway now. It felt as though everyone had gone away. He strained to hear but the quietness was undisturbed. His heart began to beat in anticipation. They still had a cop standing outside the door, but he had gotten used to seeing Bailey come and go now. He even poked his head in the door once in a while and asked him how he was. There was no pain in his shoulder now and he stretched his legs out before him, tensing his muscles. He felt warm and he poured himself a glass of water from the pitcher on the bedside table. Then he reached for his wallet and pulled out a picture of Annie.

Her face smiled back at him. He had looked at it a thousand times, but now she looked different. Her face wasn't as bright. There was a sadness in her eyes. They had always had the feeling between them that they had been together in another life a long, long time ago and that they had simply met each other again. And now he didn't feel separated from her. He placed the picture back in his wallet and wondered if he was going crazy. He felt a stab of fear in his stomach and he lay back and closed his eyes to the terrible reality of what happened and where he was.

"Oh God, please don't let me down," he whispered. "Please don't let me down."

THIRTY-FIVE

Harry Cope drove toward the hospital. Sheila and her mother sat in the back. Sheila was groaning in pain and he was afraid he wouldn't get to the hospital in time. He was tired, his head was hurting, and his body ached. He never remembered feeling so sick and Sheila's mother was urging him go faster.

"The pains are coming quicker," Sheila said. He cursed the red lights and yelled out the window at the traffic. They had never seen him like this before. He wasn't the old Harry they had always known. He was always the guy they all turned to. So calm and sure of himself. Everything under control. Sheila was stretched out in the back and her mother was urging her to hold on. They held hands tightly.

"It's alright," her mother said. "We're nearly there. Everything's going to be alright. It was just like this when I had you. You were very anxious to come into the world. I barely got to the hospital on time and you came to us like an angel."

Sheila was convinced she was going to have a boy and she was going to call him Harry, after his father. He would always be called Harry and she would make sure no one ever called him Junior.

She believed that the baby would change everything for them, and now as the pains came quicker she kept telling herself that everything was going to be alright. When they brought the baby home to their house, into the nursery she had so lovingly prepared, it would be better than it had ever been and Harry would be so proud of his little boy.

Darcy and Bailey walked down the long corridor toward Toby's room. A large cop sat on a chair near the door. He looked up from his paper as they approached. It was the same cop who had been on duty the last time they had been up there. He nodded at them and stood up. He looked at the pass they had gotten from the cop at the reception desk and asked Bailey what was in the bag.

"Just some fruit and candy—change of underwear."

He waved them into the room and nodded to Darcy again with the reverence Irish cops have for priests and nuns. Darcy smiled at him. Toby looked up when he saw his father walk in, and he was surprised to see Darcy walk in behind him. He saw the brown shopping bag and wondered if his father had brought him the clothes.

"Did you bring the things?" he asked.

"Shush!" his father said, putting his finger to his lips and pointing toward the door.

"We don't want that guy hearin' us," he said quietly.

"How are you feeling?" Darcy asked him.

"I feel good. Real good," he said.

"You look a heck of a lot better."

"Are you plannin' to go through with this?" his father asked him.

"I don't have a choice."

"I feel like I'm sending you to your death. And you do have a choice. We can still get a good lawyer. Forget this. You're giving 'em an excuse to gun you down."

"No, Pop. I'm not waiting for a trial. I don't care what lawyer we get. I tell you I'm gonna make it. I feel strong."

Darcy walked over to the window and looked out. Then he opened it and leaned out. He saw the drainpipe. It was nearly four feet from the window. He doubted if Toby would be able to reach it by himself. Someone would have to hold him and let him reach for it, but there would be no one to do that. He looked down at the ground. It was a long drop to the street and he shivered at the thought of Toby falling that distance. He would never survive a fall. Even if he manages to reach the pipe, there was no guarantee it would hold his weight or that it wouldn't pull away from the building. He pulled his head back in and pulled the blind down, then he walked slowly across the bed.

"Are you sure you won't take another look at what you have to do? It's not a very good risk. The odds are all against you. That drainpipe is nearly four feet from the window. How are you going to reach it without someone holding on to you?"

"I'll make it. All I have to do is get one hand around it and then pull myself over."

"There's no guarantee it's going to hold. God knows how long it's been there. Thing could come right away from the wall. That's a helluva drop to the street."

"Then I won't have to worry about it."

The two men looked down at Toby. They knew that trying to stop him was useless. Bailey was tempted to go to the door and bring the cop in and tell him what was going on. His own heart was beating so fast it frightened him. He knew Toby wasn't going to make it. And he knew there was a good chance of him winding up in jail because they were sure to come looking for him. He wanted to pull Darcy into a corner of the room and tell him he wasn't going to let his son go through with it. He wanted the priest to stop him. He felt they were all crazy. It was all madness. Surely he would get a fair trial. He was sorry he had brought the clothes now. *I shouldn't have come*, he thought. *That's what I should've done. Just not come. What's the matter with us? The priest should've stopped me.*

He wanted to believe they wouldn't hurt his son if he were innocent. Could they really get away with it if they wanted him to be guilty? If that was true, then he wouldn't let them have him. It would be better if he made a run for it. At least they wouldn't have the pleasure of sitting him down in the electric chair. That was the way to think about it. Maybe Toby was right. Do whatever we can for the kid. Why should we let him be revenge for the whole neighborhood? Oh, they wanted their revenge. Eye for an eye. Didn't matter who they put in the chair because they hated what they couldn't understand and they couldn't afford to have doubts. It was too late to stop Toby now. He had to let him go through with it and hope to God he would get away. The cop opened the door and told them it was just about time up and closed the door behind him. Bailey pushed the shopping bag under the bed.

"Some cash in there, too," he told Toby.

They looked at each other not knowing what to say. Darcy walked over to the window and raised the blind. He looked down again and felt a bolt of fear run through him. He turned and looked at Toby. He wanted to stop him. To tell him there was no possibility of him making it down to the ground.

Whatever happened, he knew he was done in the parish. He wondered if he would even continue as a priest. What was it all about, anyway? People are going to do what they want to do. He had the urge to go to Toby and plead with him. He would make sure he got a fair trial. He wouldn't let them get away with lynching him. *My father's an important man. He knows a lot of people. He's connected. And the monsignor knows everyone, too, the mayor and the cardinal. They were the ones who could get things done in the city.*

But he knew in his heart what the monsignor would tell him.

And his father would never ruffle any feathers.

Something had been set in motion with Annie Dahlgren's death and it swept over them all with a terrible momentum. It was something not expected and it seemed to leave decent people powerless to stop it from taking them where it wanted.

Bailey Walters reached down and hugged his son. He clung to him as if he never wanted to let go and finally Toby pulled away and looked at him.

"Please don't worry, Pop. Everything's gonna be alright."

Bailey backed away, looking at his son, and moved toward the door. Darcy came to the edge of the bed and placed his hand on Toby's shoulder. He looked at him and he didn't know what to say. He wanted to take him out of there with him and his father. Reality was that pure obstacle that would never go away.

"Be careful," he said quietly. "If you need to come to me don't hesitate."

He turned away and he and Bailey left and closed the door behind them.

Harry and Sheila were told it was going to be some time before the delivery. They were disappointed because they had been sure she was going to have the baby in the car on the way to the hospital. "False alarm," the doctor told them. "Happens a lot, especially with the first baby."

They put Sheila in a room and the doctor told Mrs. Dolan and Harry to go home and come back later. He told them he would have them called when Sheila was ready to have the baby.

Mrs. Dolan told Harry to go home and get some sleep. She would stay at the hospital. She promised to call him the minute she got word. He was relieved to leave her there. The awful feeling of dread wouldn't leave him and he was fighting to keep himself from losing control. He mumbled something to Mrs. Dolan and walked down the corridor and out into the street.

It was nearly dark. The sky was still red, looking west toward the river. Even though it was cool and all the humidity of the past few days had gone, he felt clammy and he was sweating. He wiped his face as he was walking toward the car and he decided he didn't want to go home; he told himself he was going to Kerrigan's instead. I can call the hospital from there, he told himself. His mouth felt dry and the thought of a cool beer was delicious. He was surprised at himself because he had never had a yen for a beer before, but he was sure it was exactly what he needed. And they had been nice to him the other night. They had actually been nice to him. He still had no idea that Dooney and Raguso had brought him home. He had the feeling that someone or something else had come into his life and taken over. He knew he wasn't himself anymore.

"But who would believe me?" he heard his own voice asking out loud. "They still see me as Harry Cope, but he's gone. I don't feel like him anymore. Who would believe that some stranger has taken over my life?"

He parked the car across the street from Kerrigan's. They were all surprised to see him when he walked in. Dooney and Raguso looked at him, and then at each other. He nodded and sat next to them, then Kerrigan came over and asked him what he wanted to drink.

"Gimme the coldest beer you've got. Don't know what the hell it is but I never felt so thirsty in my life."

Kerrigan filled a Pilsner glass and placed it down before him. Harry lifted the glass and made a slight gesture toward the others. They were all looking at him as he drank and he downed it without a pause. He placed the glass back down on the bar as he finished.

"Gimme another one of these, Kerrigan, will you," he said.

Kerrigan filled the glass again and Harry gulped it down, not stopping until the glass was empty.

"That's a helluva thirst, alright," Kerrigan said, as he reached for the glass to fill it up again.

Harry was smacking his lips, savoring the taste of the beer, then he shuddered slightly as though it were flowing through him like a balm that would make feel like himself again.

He sipped his beer and smiled at Kerrigan as though a great weight had been lifted from him.

"Sheila's in the hospital. They told me it was gonna be a while before the baby comes. They said I should go home and wait 'til they call me. Nothing's ever easy, is it?"

He shook his head. "How do you figure these things? We didn't think she was gonna make it to the hospital. She had the pains all the way and she was really hurting. We thought she was gonna have the baby in the back of the car. And when we get her there, they tell us it's gonna be a while. How the hell do you figure it?"

Dooney and Raguso caught Kerrigan's eye and he winked quickly at them.

"So why didn't you go home and get some sleep?" Kerrigan asked him.

"Shit—how could I sleep at a time like this? I'd rather be here and have some company."

"You could be waitin' a long time," Dooney said. "Jeez, when my sister went in to have my nephew, we were waitin' nearly a day and a half. We started to figure she just wasn't gonna have it. You can never tell with a birth. And you know, sometimes they just want a little attention. That's the thing about women. Anything for attention."

"Yeah, that's a woman for you alright," Raguso said. "All ready to pop and then she just puts the brakes on. That's the way they are. I mean Jesus, how many times I figured I was onto a sure thing and nothin' happened. You know you can tell when a chick is ready to put out and then they get you off to someplace and they start playin' games. You been feelin' them up all night and then they won't let you lay a hand on 'em."

Harry looked at Raguso, then picked up his glass and finished his beer. He was beginning to have a vague recollection of he and Dooney taking him home in the taxi the night before. Or had he dreamed it? He was feeling a lot better now with the beer in him.

He asked Kerrigan for another, then he walked to the pay phone in the back of the place and called the hospital. Nothing had changed. He gave them Kerrigan's number and came back to the bar and sat down.

"Looks like it's gonna be a long night," he said. "Still nothing happening."

"So you better go easy on that stuff," Kerrigan said. "You don't wanna show up drunk and you better not forget go buy a box of cigars. You gotta hand 'em out after the baby comes. They got 'em down the candy store. They got a wrapper on 'em says whether it's a boy or a girl."

"Oh sure," Harry said. "I'll pick 'em up as soon as I know."

"You gotta do what a guy's expected to do or else they'll say Harry Cope's a cheap sonofabitch," Kerrigan said. They were all aware of Harry's reputation for being cheap.

"You don't have to worry about that. Soon as I know whether it's a boy or a girl, I'll pick up the cigars and I'll be happy to come back here and hand 'em out. And I'll buy everyone in the place a drink, too."

"Gonna cost you more than a box of cigars," Kerrigan said. "And they ain't gonna settle for beers."

"They can have whatever the hell they want," Harry said.

"I'll take out the good stuff. You know, the stuff I keep under the bar for special occasions."

"There ain't no good stuff in here, for chrissake," Dooney said. "Three-two beer and rotgut. Greenwood Cemetery is filled with old fucks used to drink in here. Jesus, Kerrigan, when Judgment Day comes you gonna have a lot of explainin' to do. All those guys gonna be lookin' for you."

"Kerrigan gets a rake-off from Katz down at the candy store for every sucker he sends over to buy cigars," Raguso said. "You know he's half Jew himself. He'll never tell you but his mother was Jewish."

"And the pity is my father wasn't, " Kerrigan said. "What the hell did we ever get for being Irish?"

"Don't worry about that," Dooney said. "You, Mr. Raguso, will never be included among the Irish. You might be mistaken for a nigger but never for a Mick."

"And fuck you, too, Dooney," Raguso said.

Kerrigan walked to the other end of the bar and poured himself a cup of coffee. Harry clasped his hands around his beer and smiled. He was staring into the mirror at the back of the bar and he saw his face staring back at him. The smile left him and all the anguish came back. He glanced at the others around him to see if they noticed, then he looked into the mirror again. He was remembering how Arnie Meyers had bit down into the wet stub of the cigar he held between his teeth and the way he had leaned over him when he wanted him to sign the statement saying he had seen Toby Walters come out of the alley. He could almost smell Arnie's breath, the awful cigar smell, and he remembered how he wanted to be sick. He lifted his glass and held it in front of him, obscuring the mirror, then he took a long pull from his beer. He glanced around him again as if he was afraid they could read his thoughts. He felt himself getting hot again and he began to sweat. He emptied his glass and tapped it on the bar, asking Kerrigan for another. He was mumbling to himself, unaware that the others could hear him.

He suddenly realized they were looking at him. They turned away when he looked at them and when he turned away Dooney nudged Raguso.

"I told you there's something wrong with that sonofabitch," he whispered. "And it ain't just that he's gettin' drunk."

Raguso nodded, then turned around and looked toward Harry. His face lit up when he saw Raguso looking at him as though he suddenly remembered where he was. He turned around on the bar stool and looked at them all.

"You can bet that as soon as I know whether it's a boy or a girl I'll be back here with the cigars. It won't matter what time it is. Even if I have to wake Katz up. That greedy bastard never closes, anyway. You can bet on it, and Kerrigan can break out the good stuff because we, my friends, are going to have a party."

"Go easy on the beer, Harry," Kerrigan said. "Slow down a little. You're not like these guys here. They could sit here and drink twenty-four hours a day and not have to get off the stool to take a piss. You don't have to keep up with them. When it comes to drinking, you belong to the amateur class and I mean that as a compliment. And, you don't want to go back to the hospital drunk. Take it easy now or I'll just have to cut you off. Now, I know how you feel, Harry. Having the first kid is always the hardest. When you're having your sixth you'll have it down pat. Listen— how about a sandwich. I'll make you a good roast beef sandwich. Good to have something in your stomach."

Harry nodded as if Kerrigan had made the decision for him.

He sat back on the stool and put his hands in his pockets. He clasped something and moved it around as he stared into the mirror again. Then he saw Arnie Meyers's face staring back at him.

He was smiling his leering smile as if he knew everyone's secrets just by looking at them, showing all of his yellow teeth with the stub of his cigar stuck in the center of his mouth.

Harry squeezed his eyes shut, trying to obliterate Arnie's face, but even with them closed the face was still smiling at him. He opened his eyes.

Kerrigan saw the terror in Harry's face.

"Jesus, Kerrigan, I think I need a shot. I'm coming down with something. Think I've got a bug."

"Come on, Harry, you're not coming down with anything. You're just nervous, that's all. You don't need a shot. Let me make you a cup of hot tea. Fix you right up."

"Look, Kerrigan—I don't want a sandwich and I don't want a cup of tea, got it? I want a shot. For Christ's sake, I know what I need."

They were all stunned and Kerrigan took a bottle of rye off the shelf and poured him a shot.

Harry grabbed it and drank it down in a gulp. He put the shot glass down and nodded to Kerrigan to pour him another.

"None of my business," Kerrigan said as he poured. Harry nodded as he drank the second shot.

"That's right," Harry said. "It's nobody's business but mine and I'll drink whatever the hell I want as long as I have the money to pay for it."

"Your custom is always welcome here, Harry," Kerrigan said as he turned and winked at the others.

"Oh yeah?" Harry said. "I really wonder about that. All of you tolerating me in here as if I'm some sort of an asshole. Who the hell do you all think you're dealing with? I know you guys. Don't you think I know all the things you say about me? You really think I give a shit. You're all jealous of me, that's all. And that's the truth of it. You're all goddamn jealous and you always have been."

He slid off the stool and placed his hands on the bar, trying to steady himself.

"I see the way you all look at me. Christ, you'd think I was some sort of criminal or something. What's the matter with all of you? I know what it is. You just can't stand to see a guy like me get ahead and that's the truth. And you can't stand that Sheila Dolan married me instead of Red Dahlgren."

"For God's sake, take it easy, Harry," Kerrigan said. "You're lettin' the booze do your talkin' for you. Now listen, you don't wanna be shitfaced when you go back to the hospital, do you? It's gonna be a long night for you. Why don't you do yourself a favor and go home and get some rest."

He stared back at Kerrigan as if trying to understand what he had said. Then he smiled his strange smile, his head moving slowly on his shoulders as if floating on water. All of the anger and defiance was gone now and he looked goofy. They had all been treading softly around him. They always had a grudging respect for him and now they were looking toward Kerrigan to set the tone for them.

There was something frightening about him. They all felt it from the night Dooney and Raguso had driven him home. Nobody said it, but there had to be more to his behavior than Sheila having the baby.

It just wasn't natural for him to be in Kerrigan's in the first place. The word had always been out that he wouldn't be caught dead in the place. Nobody becomes a drunk overnight.

Harry smiled at Kerrigan and climbed back up on the stool. He turned and looked at them again and his lips were moving as though he were trying to say something but he couldn't form the words.

"What's the matter, Harry?" Kerrigan asked him.

He closed his eyes and shook his head as if trying to clear it, and his mouth moved again but still nothing came out. He raised himself off the stool and held on to the bar, then he slowly turned himself around until his back was to the mirror.

He moved his mouth again and this time the words came out.

"You know what it is," he said. "I'm bored. I'm just goddamn bored."

"The best thing for boredom is sleep," Kerrigan told him.

"Bored," Harry said again. "Nothing here for me. Nothing for me anywhere."

Raguso and Dooney and the others were bored with him, too.

"He's fuckin' crazy," Raguso whispered to Dooney.

"Some guys should never drink," Charlie Wallace said in a voice a little louder than a whisper. "Some guys should never touch it. Thing is this guy really ain't had that much. Just can't handle it, that's all. Like I said, some guys should never touch it."

"It's always the same with you guys," Harry said. "Every time you see me, you whisper. I want to tell you it doesn't bother me because as the great man said, I'll be sober in the morning but all of you will still be assholes. Nothing ever gonna change that."

He grinned at them, nodding his head as though he had imparted a great truth. Then he started to walk unsteadily toward the door.

"I know now why I never come in here," he said. "The trouble is I forgot. Jesus, how could I forget something like that. You know, it's amazing what you forget. Same reason we moved out to the Island. Forgot just how much I wanted to get the hell away from here."

Dooney started to move off his stool toward him when he felt Kerrigan's hand on his shoulder.

He tried to shake it off but Kerrigan held him tighter.

"Stay here, Dooney. Let him be. He's still the same old Harry Cope. Why the hell should we be surprised?"

"That's right," Harry said. "I'm still the same and thank God I am."

"Harry, why don't you just get the hell outta here while the getting is good. Just leave and go and be there for your wife."

He looked back at them. His eyes were bulging in his head and his face was red. He stood by the door looking back at them and they all thought he was going to burst into tears.

"Maybe he just needs to take a shit," Dooney said.

"Takin' one dump won't empty that guy out," Charlie Wallace said.

"Somethin' up with that guy," Dooney said.

"Yeah—he's crazy, that's what's up with him. The guy's crazy," Dooney said.

"Gotta tell you I feel sorry for Sheila," Kerrigan said.

He refilled their glasses and they all turned back to the bar shaking their heads.

THIRTY-SIX

Toby lay in his bed under the sheet, waiting for darkness to come. His hands were clasped behind his head as he stared out into the gathering darkness. Outside it was clear and cool. There was a three-quarter moon coming up and it was one of those rare summer nights when it was going to be great for sleeping.

He could hear a radio playing somewhere off in the distance. The Dodgers were playing Pittsburgh. It wasn't close enough for him to make out the words but he could still recognize the voice of Red Barber. And he knew he was at Ebbets, sitting up in the booth, looking down on the magic of the field, and the crowd was looking on, moving like one on every play. Toby could hear them, that ballpark noise that was so normal, and nobody was thinking about anything but the Dodgers getting an out or scoring a run.

Toby had long realized what every Dodger fan knew, that no matter how good they were they would always have to deal with fate. They had been brought so close to victory so many times only to have it snatched away by some outrageous caprice that could only be the work of the gods set against them. No one would ever forget that most unjust blow in the long litany of bad breaks, the day Bobby Thompson had hit that terrible home run, depriving them of the pennant. Its cruelty had brought everyone together and they had learned since then to inflict small wounds upon themselves in the hope that major catastrophes could be averted.

There was no such thing as a sure thing.

He saw the door open and the cop on duty came into the room. He turned the light on and went over to the bed. Toby kept his eyes closed as if he were asleep and the cop stood over him for what seemed a long time. Then he heard his steps moving away and the door closing behind and the sound of him locking it. It was still too early to go. He still had to wait until he knew for sure the cop had nodded off outside the door. They still believed he was weak and the doctor was against them moving him to the house of detention. He had told them he still needed more time to heal. "He came very close to losing his life," he had said. "It wouldn't take a lot at this stage for that wound to open up again. He's still weak."

But Toby felt stronger than he had felt since they brought him in. He was sure he was going to make it. He didn't know what the doctor had told the cops. What he wanted more than anything was to be away from them. The sight of Arnie Meyers made him sick. Seeing him brought up something that was inexpressible. A hatred that smoldered white-hot. And they called him the best detective in Brooklyn. He wondered just how many of the people he had put away were guilty. And he knew it wasn't guilt or innocence with him. He was black and he was convenient. How easy it was for them. And everyone just wanted to go along as if there were nothing they could do about it, like Bobby Thompson's home run. He had purposely not let them see him out of bed at all.

Toby swung his legs over the side of the bed and placed his feet on the floor. His heart began to beat faster, and as he slowly rose and stood he felt light-headed and had to sit down again. He felt a stab of fear in his gut. He looked over toward the window and saw the blinds rattle softly in the breeze. He thought of how far away the drainpipe was from the window and he thought of maybe trying to go out through the door. He wondered if maybe the cop had mistakenly left it unlocked. He was always able to hear his rhythmic breathing when he fell asleep in his chair. He listened now but all he could hear was the beating of his own heart. Take it easy, take it easy, he told himself.

He sat for a moment, then slowly rose again. He was expecting the dizziness but it didn't come.

His legs felt alright and he walked barefoot around the room just to move. He was starting to feel better now.

He heard footsteps at the far end of the corridor but then they were gone and it was quiet again, and now he made his way slowly to the door and listened. He couldn't hear anything at first but then he was able to hear the faint sound of the cop's breathing, and as he continued to listen, it became more distinct and he knew for sure he was sleeping. He could even hear his wheezing and the way it became small snores. The cop was over six feet tall and he was heavy. So they gave him a job where he just had to sit all night.

Toby knew they never expected him to try an escape. They knew he had no clothes and he wondered if they had ever checked the window. He was sure they had and that they believed no one would ever be able to get to the drainpipe and make it down to the ground. He was sure now that if he could just make it to the pipe, he could get to the ground. There was no way of knowing if it would hold him. He didn't let himself think beyond getting to it.

He moved away from the door and tiptoed over to the window. He raised the blind slowly and raised the window. He felt the breeze waft in and it was cool and felt good on his face. He could smell the city smell, so familiar like an old friend, and his heart leaped in his chest at the thought of getting away. He looked straight down through the darkness and he couldn't see the bottom. It looked a lot further down than he thought. Then he looked toward the drainpipe. It was a lot further away than he thought. He was trying to figure out how to maneuver himself into position to make the leap for the pipe. He knew he would only get one chance and if he missed it was all over. He had to be able to balance himself, reach out as far as he could, and then make a lunge for it. There was the possibility that the force of his leap would pull it away from its casings.

He turned away from the window and went back to the bed. He could feel the perspiration on his brow and when he sat he felt it moving down, dropping like rain on the floor. His chest was heaving in anxiety and he wasn't able to swallow.

He looked at the window and he knew he was crazy to try it. He wondered if he was going mad. He wanted to go to the door and open it and scream out into the corridor. *Why can't I sleep in my own bed like everyone else and get up in the morning and get on with my life.* He wanted to punch the walls and cry out in frustration, to shout at all of the unseen people who were going about their lives who didn't know and didn't give a damn one way or the other. He wanted to turn to someone. Anyone who would listen. He wanted them to know what a terrible thing was happening and no one seemed to care.

That was the worst of it. No one seemed to care. It was just going to run its course, he would die one way or the other and it all would be forgotten. There were people who wanted him dead. He tiptoed over to the door once more and listened. The cop was still asleep. He wanted to try the door to see if by some chance it might be open. If it was he had decided he would try to make it that way. He reached down and clasped the doorknob as lightly as he could.

He listened again to make sure the cop hadn't wakened.

He turned it slowly, first one way and then the other. It was locked. He leaned his brow against the door and closed his eyes.

Give it one more try, just in case, he told himself.

He clasped it once more and again there was no movement either way.

It would have to be the window. He went to the bed and reached under it and pulled out the brown paper bag. He took the clothes out. A shirt and a pair of jeans, socks, and sneakers. He found the money his father had put in it and without looking he stuffed it into the pocket of his jeans. He dressed quickly. *No more thinking,* he told himself. Time to go. He had an overwhelming desire to look into the mirror and see himself and he went into the bathroom. He realized he dare not turn on the light. He stared into the mirror but he could only see a dark shadow of himself. He had wanted to look into his own face, to see his reflection staring back at him as if to make sure it was all real. There was still a part of him that could not bring itself to believe that the nightmare was real. He had wanted to see his own smile that always reassured him and let him know that he trusted himself. But all he saw was his own dark outline, unformed, waiting for the light so that it might reveal itself to him.

He smiled in the dark even though he couldn't see the reflection. He wanted to laugh and he didn't know why. He wondered again if he might be going crazy. The laughter welled up in him, making him clutch his sides and try to stifle it in case he might be heard. He grabbed a towel and held it to his face as the spasms of laughter shook his body.

He knew he must be crazy to be laughing at a time like this. Then at last it was gone and he felt tears in his eyes. He went back to the bed and pushed the paper bag under it. He took the pillows and set them lengthways under the sheet to make it look as if he were still in the bed sleeping. He looked around the room one more time to make sure he hadn't forgotten anything. He reached into his pocket and felt the roll of bills. They reminded him of his father and he wondered if he would ever see him again. He went to the door once more and listened. The cop was out like a light.

He came back and put on his sneakers. Time to go.

He went to the window and raised it slowly, pulling up the blind first. When he looked out he could see a patch of sky through the buildings. The three-quarter moon hung over the rooftops and he felt as though he could reach up with his hand and touch it. He could see the white clouds in front of it and it seemed as if the scene had been brought in for a show that was just about to begin.

He could see the tall spire of a church with a cluster of smaller buildings around it. More churches in Brooklyn than anyplace in the city, he remembered. The Borough of Churches, they called it. Then he looked to his left and saw the drainpipe and his mouth went dry. It seemed so far away. *Doesn't matter, have to try anyway*, he told himself.

He was tempted to close the window and climb back into bed.

Maybe there was another way.

He told himself he must not look down.

Now the window was raised as high as it would go; he threw one leg over the sill and he realized he would never be able to reach the pipe from the position he was in. He brought his other leg over now and moved until he was sitting on the sill, facing the room with his legs inside. He pushed the window up and raised himself until he was standing, looking back into the darkened room. He could see the bed and it looked as if he were still in it sleeping.

He edged across the sill until he was as close to the pipe as he could get. One chance to make the grab. The alley was below him, waiting in the dark. He would have to throw himself toward the pipe and let go of his hold on the window. Then he would have to hold on to it and hope it wouldn't pull away from the wall.

He was ready now. Nothing left to do but make the leap. He felt his body shiver and he felt cold. He took a deep breath and tried to steady himself. The pain was starting to come to his shoulder and his arms already felt tired from holding on to the window.

He began to realize that he was not as strong as he thought he was, but he knew he was not going to turn back now. He was holding on tightly to the window and his face was pressed against the glass. He was looking back into the room and he didn't know if he was going to be able to find it in himself to make the leap for the pipe. Fear began to take over him now and he could feel the panic come up in him. He heard an anguished whimper come out of his mouth and he closed his eyes in desperation.

When he opened them he was looking back into the room again and he saw a figure rise up out of the bed.

When it turned and looked at him he saw Annie's face looking toward him and she was smiling. He watched her get out of the bed and come slowly across the room toward him until her face was inches from the window, looking into his. She kissed him through the glass and he wanted to go back into the room and join her. He looked into her face as he had so many times. They had always loved to be close like that, just gazing at each closely without moving or saying anything, because it was enough for them just to see each other. They could talk without talking.

But now he wanted her to say something. To tell him that everything was alright. He looked into her eyes and they twinkled in the way they always did, and she opened her mouth and he saw her brush a strand of hair away from her face. She was so real and he wanted so much to be with her. He felt that she was so close to him, but suddenly she was gone and when he saw the room again it was the way he had left it.

He turned his head toward the pipe and without thinking he leapt for it. He was moving toward it and then he was clutching it, hanging on tightly. He had his arms wrapped around it and his legs grasped, too. It didn't budge from the wall and now there was only the long climb down to the ground. He caught his breath and began to move tentatively, one arm first, then the other.

Then he thought he felt the pipe move slightly out from the wall. He froze. Then he realized it was the wind that had touched him. There was a strong updraft from below and sometimes it gathered and howled around him.

He started to move again slowly. He was tempted to see if he could just slide all the way, but he knew it was the easiest way to lose his grip. *Just take it slow*, he told himself. He knew he had done the hardest part. Now all he needed was patience.

Treacy hadn't been able to sleep since he had stopped drinking. He longed for the blessed oblivion it would bring him but it wouldn't come. Now he dreaded the nights as he lay in bed trying to read, or staring into the darkness with all of his fears in the air around him. As much as he wanted sleep, the nightmares and the demons came to him as if they were intent on driving him insane. He had to find another way to pass the nights. When he had turned out the light that night he began to see the wispy outlines of gargoyled heads coming toward him in the dark. They came to him in the darkness and stopped, floating before his eyes, and he knew they were real. They were not coming from his imagination. They were his own personal demons, daring him to challenge them.

They came to him through the darkness in waves, one after another, dark, hollow, ugly faces, full of evil, determined to take him with them. This was the night he knew without a doubt that there was such a thing as evil. And it only had one purpose and that was to make everything around it evil, too.

He knew it had been with him for a long time. It was the part of him that told him he didn't deserve to live, that he was no good, that he should have died in Korea with all the others, that he was weak, that he didn't deserve happiness, that he was just bad, that it was useless to have hope or to believe that things could change.

And he tried to find the strength in himself to stare them down.

And he knew that night that evil was fear. The fear that dug itself deep inside of him hid in all of his deep, deep places and whispered to him that he wasn't worth it. But he stood up to them and they became angry and they had flung him out of the bed and he landed heavily on the floor.

He got up and quickly turned on the lights. He went to the bathroom and threw water on his face. He knew, too, that he didn't have to lie there and fight them all night. He got dressed and started to walk toward Brooklyn Heights. He sat on a bench on the promenade and looked across the river to Manhattan. And he watched the river traffic moving silently through the night with their running lights on. They always comforted him because he could tell they knew where they were going even in the deep, deep night.

He had often wished he could work on a tugboat or a small river tanker. It would be wonderful to go to work like that. He reminded himself that he would have to talk to Charlie Wallace about it. He knew everything there was to know about working on the docks or the river.

He started walking. The shakes and the sweats had left him for a while and he was beginning to get his appetite back. He was going to head for the diner after picking up the *News* and the *Mirror*. He would sit down, order bacon and eggs, and read the papers.

This is the best way to get through the night, he told himself. Drink some good coffee. He was going to stay sober and he was going to ask Darcy if he knew of anything he could do to help himself. Nothing worse than rolling around in bed with your head squawking like an untuned radio, body scrunched up tight like a ball, hands clasped between your knees saying the Twenty-third Psalm over and over the way he used to in Korea.

He was headed for the diner on Fourth Avenue when he saw a figure walking drunkenly toward him. When he got closer he was surprised to see it was Harry Cope. He weaved past Treacy, mumbling to himself, and didn't recognize him.

Treacy stopped and looked after him. Then he called out to him but Harry didn't hear him. Treacy walked back after him and when he caught up with him he put his arm across his shoulder. Harry looked at him, surprised.

"Can't stop," he said. "Have to get to the hospital."

"You sure you can make it?"

"Have to. Sheila's ready to deliver."

He swayed on his feet as he looked at Treacy.

"What the hell's the matter with you?" Treacy asked him.

He smelled of booze and he realized he had never seen Harry drunk before.

"I think I'm drunk," Harry said. "New thing for me. Looks like we've got this all wrong. You're the one's supposed to be drunk and you're asking me if I'm alright."

He was shaking with laughter and he had to lean against the side of a building to steady himself. He groped in his pocket for his cigarettes and when he found the pack he had trouble getting a cigarette out. He flung the pack away in disgust toward the curb and started to walk on again.

Treacy retrieved the pack and walked after Harry. He lit a cigarette and gave it to him and Harry tried to push him away. "Get the hell outta here," he shouted. "What the fuck do you want from me, anyway?"

"Nothin'. Just thought I'd tell you that if you're going to the hospital you're going in the wrong direction."

"What the hell do you know, for chrissake?"

"I know you're headed in the wrong direction."

"Oh, yeah?"

"For chrissake, Harry, do you know where you are?"

Harry looked at him and started to laugh. The goofy look came back to his face and he looked like a little boy caught stealing apples. He turned away and started to walk on again.

Treacy caught up with him and took his arm and guided him across the street.

"This way, Harry," he said.

"The good Samaritan," Harry said. "The drunken Samaritan leading the drunken husband. Sheila never saw me drunk, Jack. Nor her mother. She's waiting at the hospital, too. What do you think she's gonna say?"

"They'll be happy to see you. You won't be the first husband to show up drunk when his wife's about to give birth."

"The blind leading the blind," Harry said.

And he started to laugh. He was holding on to Treacy's arm now and the laughter came out of him in its mad way, echoing in the empty street.

There was nobody else to be seen and the three-quarter moon was high above them like a drawing in a children's coloring book. Treacy loved to see the soft amber light of the moon. He looked forward to the nights when it was over the river and the reflection made a golden path connecting Brooklyn and Manhattan.

Like all the others, he had never liked Harry. There was something about him. And he still wondered why Sheila Dolan had wound up marrying him. Harry had little time for Treacy and had made no bones about how he felt. He had succeeded in weaning Sheila away from the neighborhood and converted her to the joys of suburbia. He was proud he had made the great leap. He knew he would always be ahead of the others and he had nothing but disdain for the neighborhood and its ways. Made it clear he wanted no part of it, and it had no sentimental value for him, either. They had let him go.

Treacy guided him as Harry continued his mumbling and his dirge-like moans. He would be the last guy anyone expected to find drunk when his wife was about to give birth. But Treacy knew, too, that you could never count on how anyone was going to act under pressure. He had seen many a hotshot crumble when things got tough and saw guys everybody had written off become heroes when he was in Korea. There was never any sure way to tell. He had found out for himself that you could never tell what was going on inside of a man. We always figure we have a guy pegged but nobody ever knows. And he knew it wasn't about how well you did in business. There were always lots of phonies could stand up when they were risking money. What the hell was that? What about when your ass is really on the line. When you know for sure there's no way out and that you got a one-way ticket to the boneyard? Or when they tell you have to be part of the rear guard so that the other guys can make it out? And how about when you have no choice? And you can't go moaning to the senior officer and ask, *why me?* That's when you're lucky, you've got a little pride. When you can't let anyone know how scared you are. When you can't be free to show your feelings. When showing 'em ain't good for anyone. When you just have to swallow 'em.

Harry Cope's wife is about to have a baby and he's walking the streets too drunk to find his way to her, Treacy was thinking.

He was sorry he had run into him. He would much rather be alone in the diner, reading the papers and eating his bacon and eggs. *I gotta be here with this fuck,* he told himself.

The only connection he had to Harry was Sheila. He wondered how she was doing. He had always thought that he would be the proudest father standing in the delivery room if they would let him.

Treacy had always liked Sheila and he had been close to her when she and Red were together.

He had never told anyone how he felt about her. The truth was that he had been in love with her himself and he always had the feeling that she liked him, too. Sometimes when she and Red and he were together his eyes would meet hers and he always felt something coming back from her. It had always been like they were all playing roles and they had to stay in them because that was the way it had to be. He knew in his heart that she had a feeling for him. The thing was that she and Red had been together since grade school and no one had ever thought of them not being together. But Treacy had always known even before he and Red went to Korea that she wouldn't be waiting for him when he came back. They had all been shocked when she chose Harry over Red, but he knew that it was the only way for her to get away from him. He knew her mother had pushed her toward Harry. She wanted security in her old age and Harry was going to give it to her. She was always a shrewd bitch of a woman and Sheila was always under her thumb. Her beautiful only daughter.

Everyone knew she had started to see Harry when Red was in Korea and nobody had ever written to let him know. Who wants to get a letter like that? And they all waited for him to come home and find out for himself. Some of them said she would give Harry up when Red came home, but she didn't. Harry Cope was going to give her everything. They were the first couple to buy a house on the Island and it was as if he had lifted them both into another world.

But Harry Cope was not being shrewd this night, Treacy thought. He wondered what it was that brought people together. There are all sorts of things in the genes we just don't know about. What is it they think they are going to find? He couldn't get his mind off Sheila. He always had a feeling for her but he had never let himself dream of what could be, and he had often wondered why. He knew he wouldn't have had a chance with her and still he knew he had never given himself a chance. Even before he went to Korea he hadn't given himself much of a chance at anything. Going there was the out he wanted. It gave him the excuse to be a failure. He believed in his heart that what had happened to him really didn't have anything to do with the way he was now. He was beginning to be able to see that. He wondered why it had taken him so long to see it. He hadn't seen much of Sheila since he had come home from the war, but every time they were at the same gathering, she always came to him and gave him a warm hug and he was always surprised at the way she held on to him.

He knew that she, too, had lost something, no matter how wonderful her life with Harry seemed. It was her smile that always broke his heart. The look in the face is always much clearer than the words people say. That was the truth, but people hadn't learned to trust in it. He remembered the old gunny sergeant in the hospital telling him that it wasn't what happened that broke your heart but what could have been. He knew that well now. So many things he had never been able to see. So many things that could have been.

"Maybe we should stop and get a cup of coffee," Treacy said.

Harry didn't answer and he started to laugh quietly to himself.

"Coffee ain't gonna help me," he said.

"It couldn't hurt," Treacy answered.

"Jesus, you really are the good Samaritan," Harry said. "What the hell is it with you, anyway?"

He started to laugh again loudly and Treacy had the urge to smack him in the face. There was something about the way his mouth moved when he laughed, it was so clear he saw everyone else around him as fools. He thought he was in another league. Treacy wanted to grab his face and crush it.

"I hear you tried to tell Arnie Meyers that you killed Annie Dahlgren," Harry said.

He began to laugh even harder. He almost doubled over on the sidewalk and he could hardly walk.

"Musta been a fuckin' riot, you bringing those clothes in and throwing 'em down on Arnie's desk. Arnie musta loved it."

He was laughing hard and shaking his head.

Treacy was struggling to stop himself from taking a swing at him. He took his arm again and started to walk faster toward the hospital.

"Come on, Jack," he said. "Tell me. Do you really think it was you that killed Annie?"

"Just shut your mouth, Harry. Just shut the fuck up."

"And what about Red? What did he have to say about it? Must have been something. His asshole buddy from grade school and the war telling the cops he killed his little sister. Well, you don't have to worry, Jack. I told Arnie Meyers and Red that I saw Toby Walters coming out of the alley that night and that nails it. Open and shut, Arnie said. That's what he said. Open and shut. Just like Kerrigan's after hours. Open and shut. You, Jack Treacy, are off the hook."

Treacy stopped suddenly and grabbed Harry by the throat and pushed him up against the side of a building. Then he grabbed his jaw in one hand and forced his mouth shut.

"If Sheila wasn't in the hospital right now having that baby I'd kill you, you sonofabitch! Kill you and think nuthin' of it. Do you hear me?"

He slapped him hard across the face and the crack of the impact ran up and down the silent street.

Then he slapped him hard again.

Harry pulled his head back in to his chest and whimpered like a little boy. Harry grabbed his face with both hands, stunned by what had happened. The smile was gone now and his jaw hung slack and unmoving. He kept looking at Treacy like a dog unjustly punished, waiting to be petted so he could feel alright again. He couldn't find the words to say anything. Treacy turned him in the direction of the hospital and they started to walk again.

THIRTY-SEVEN

Toby was inching his way down the pipe. His arms felt like lead and the pain had come back to his shoulder. He wondered if the wound had opened up again. His arms wanted to let go of the pipe of their own accord. He didn't know if he could hang on much longer. He couldn't tell if it was blood or sweat that was making his clothes stick to his body. The bottom still seemed such a long way down. He was afraid that at any minute his arms would give out and he would go crashing down into the alley. He hung on and tried to move faster.

His body ached all over and all the pain seemed to move out from his shoulder. He was sure the old wound had opened up. He kept telling himself that he had to get away. It was the only thing that mattered, even if they killed him. At least he wouldn't be locked up waiting for a trial that was sure to find him guilty.

Arnie Meyers had never told him that it was Harry Cope who had identified him coming out of the alley, and he had asked himself a thousand times why someone would do it. Someone wanted him to be convicted and they had lied. There had to be a reason. It wasn't just that he was colored. It couldn't be just that.

He couldn't figure out why.

He asked himself who.

He had made lists in his head. Everyone he knew from the neighborhood. Men and women, young and old. He had never remembered anyone calling him a nigger, at least not to his face. He had never seen the kind of hatred that had landed him where he was now. It was all still so hard to be in the reality of what was happening.

As he was slowly, painfully making his way down, he moved his arms and legs, but it was as though he were hanging in the air looking at himself, detached because it was nearly impossible for him to accept that he really was trying to escape because he was thought to be the murderer of the girl he loved more than anything else in the world.

He managed to hang on and keep moving. Then, at last, his feet touched the ground. He could hardly stand and he leaned back against the wall and stared up into the darkness following the pipe until he could see it no more. Then he sat feeling the aches in his body. He had no energy and he knew he couldn't afford to sit for very long.

He knew he had to keep moving.

He was breathing heavily and he reached his hand under his shirt and he could feel the blood on his shoulder. The wound had opened up and he was bleeding. He raised himself slowly and leaned back again. He could hardly keep his eyes open. He wanted to stretch out where he was and fall asleep, but he knew they would soon discover he was gone and they would be out looking for him.

He made his way groggily out of the alley and into the street. It was deserted. There was a streetlight directly across from the alley casting a yellow arc of light. He looked up and down and he still saw no one.

Traffic was very light. An occasional car passed by, then a bus came down the street and made a stop a block away. It just stood for a while. Nobody got on or off. The driver was just killing time. He stayed close to the doorways and kept his head down. He was still surprised that he hadn't seen anyone. Then he heard a roar go up in the distance and he knew it came from Ebbets Field. Something terrific must be happening, he thought. Then it was almost silent again. It made him uneasy. He had the terrible feeling that he would be pounded on any minute and they would bring him back to Arnie Meyers.

He looked back in the direction of the hospital. It had been built before the turn of the century and it looked as if it would stand in the same place until the end of time. It had seen the neighborhood rise and it had cared for its people, the hardworking immigrants and their children. Many of them had been born there, the first generation born in the new land, and the old went there now in their last illnesses. There was an air of ancient impartiality about it, standing implacable in the midst of the constant change and the chaos of life around it. He was looking toward the area where his room was and all of the lights were still out. No trace of a light along the floor.

He hoped they still hadn't discovered that he was gone.

He thought about taking a cab to Manhattan. He'd be across the bridge in no time, but he wondered if he should take the risk of standing out and waving for a cab. There was always the chance he would be spotted. And there was also the possibility that a cab wouldn't stop for him. They didn't like to pick up coloreds late at night because they didn't want to risk going into colored neighborhoods.

He thought about the subway. Easy to get lost on the subway. That was a good bet, but if they knew he was gone that's the first place they would begin to look for him. They would start to watch the entrances and exits right away. He had read so many times of criminals trying to make an escape in New York, and it had always amazed him that in that huge place of eight million, they would always find the guy they were after, and he had often thought of what he would do if he had to try to get away. And now it was hard to think of anything except just not being caught. Worst of all was the feeling of having been cast out of the family of the city.

Of being totally alone.

Of having no place or no one to turn to.

No place to hide.

He thought it better to just keep making his way closer to the bridge, then maybe it would be easier to get a cab. Some guy who was eager to get back across the river to Manhattan after dropping someone off in Brooklyn. He was going to make his way through the quieter streets off Flatbush Avenue and if he couldn't get a cab, he would walk across the bridge and head for the Village. He believed that if he could just make it to the city, they would never find him. And he had decided that he would make it on foot because that way he was sure he would always be able to see what was happening around him.

Darcy was lying in bed with the light on. He hadn't been able to sleep. He had been reading, afraid that the phone would ring at any minute with the word that Toby had escaped and had just been caught.

He knew that when they discovered he was gone, Arnie Meyers would come looking for him. He would know that he had helped to get the clothes into the room with Bailey Walters. Irish cops were always suckers for priests. The ancient authority. Look at me, Father, aren't I a good boy? Arnie knew it very well.

Darcy thought of Bailey sitting at home by himself, waiting for the worst. They had known in their hearts that he would never get far but they knew there was no way to stop him. They hoped that he would be caught unharmed and that maybe his determination to escape would convince some people that he was innocent. That was crazy, too, Darcy knew. There was nothing anyone could count on in this situation except that the cops were determined to hang Annie's death on Toby. When all the world seems to be insane, what rules are there to play by? When decency and real morality is taken out of the equation, what takes their place? Where there is no justice, where do you go to find it? He knew just as well that in trying to escape, Toby would be seen to be making an admission of guilt, and if there was to be a trial his chances of acquittal were almost nil.

The vaunted justice system was administered by men who had often used it for their own ends, political and otherwise. It was always a precarious situation for the innocent accused. It didn't guarantee anything. Not a thing. It was never possible to be an accused innocent and have no fear. To take the chance of running away from the uncertainty of a justice that could not guarantee the acquittal of the innocent was after all not to be unexpected.

The priest lit a cigarette and tried to concentrate on his book. He knew the monsignor would get the word, too. And he would have a lot to say. He would have him transferred from the parish for sure. The people would want him sent away, too. Terrible thing for a priest to be mixed up in something like this. He would be sent to some remote parish and never be heard from again. Maybe that's what's best, he thought. Or maybe I'll leave the priesthood. I don't seem to be fitted for it.

He knew he would be an embarrassment to everybody. His family, the church, the parish, his friends. Especially his father. They would link him to this powerful man and he would take on all of the embarrassment he could carry and apologize for Darcy to the world.

Worst of all, his father's opinion of him would be confirmed. *A first-class fuck-up.* Then he would direct this anger at his mother and she would bear it stoically and attempt to defend him, but in her heart she would know it would be useless. *What the fuck's the matter with him?* the old man would say, and nobody would answer him. Darcy rose from the bed and he went to the window. He pulled the curtain aside and looked out into the night. He could hear a siren off in the distance. Could they be looking for Toby, he wondered.

He glanced at his watch. Eleven o'clock. He was sure he had gone by now.

Maybe he was in Manhattan already. He shuddered when he thought of him trying to make his way down the drainpipe. He knew he would never sleep until he knew for sure what had happened.

It was going to be a long night.

Treacy and Harry Cope arrived at the hospital. They hadn't spoken since Treacy had slapped Harry in the face. They found the waiting room where Sheila's mother was dozing in a chair. There were two young husbands in the room sitting side by side, smoking and staring straight ahead. They hardly glanced up when Treacy and Harry walked in. Mrs. Dolan opened her eyes and saw the two of them standing before her. A look of dismay came over her face and she shook her head in disgust when she saw them. She rose slowly from the chair and looked at them both, then she turned her attention to Harry and looked him up and down as if she were inspecting him.

"You've been drinking," she said. "You look awful."

"Yes, Mother dear, I've been drinking," he said sarcastically.

"And you've been with this drunk," she said as she turned her attention to Treacy. "I kept calling the house and I got no answer. I didn't know what happened to you. Where the hell were you?"

"I stopped into Kerrigan's on the way. Guess I was too nervous to sleep."

"My God, and you spent your time with this drunk. Of all the people to wind up with and your wife about to give birth. You should be ashamed of yourself, Harry Cope. Ashamed of yourself. The only thing he knows how to do is drink. Nearly driven his poor mother crazy since he came back."

Harry glanced at Treacy with a smirk on his face and began to shake his head.

"You got it all wrong," he said. "Jack here brought me to the hospital. And I can tell you for sure he's not drinking. You see, I was on the way to the hospital walking in the wrong direction, wasn't I, Jack?"

He looked at Treacy and then turned back to Mrs. Dolan.

"He brought me here because I might not have made it on my own. If I hadn't bumped into him, I'd still be walking in the wrong direction."

He looked at Treacy for confirmation.

"That's right. He'd still be walking in the wrong direction."

Mrs. Dolan turned away from them and sat down. Harry sat next to her and reached out for her hand. She pulled it back and he put his arm around her shoulder. She tried to move away but he wouldn't let her.

"For God's sake, Harry, what are you doing?" she said as she pushed him away. "What's the matter with you? You're all the same."

She looked at Treacy. "You must be proud of yourself, getting him drunk like this and his wife ready to deliver."

She was still trying to get Harry's arm from around her shoulder. He was trying to kiss her on the cheek and finally she stood up and moved to another seat. "Now Harry, you've got to behave yourself. Pull yourself together. I think they're ready to move Sheila to the delivery room. Please now, Harry."

He sat next to her again and reached out for her hand.

"It's alright, Harry. Just relax. Everything's going to be alright."

She looked across at Treacy.

"Thank God Sheila had the sense to marry Harry and not that Red Dahlgren. They were all around her like a pack of dogs, but thank God I never let any of them near her. They weren't going to ruin my daughter."

Treacy was looking at the two of them. He figured they were both crazy. He thought they really deserved each other. And he wondered how Sheila could have turned out the way she did with a mother like that. And he figured Red Dahlgren was lucky after all.

"Everything's going to be alright," she told Harry. "We should be getting word any minute now. She's been in labor for a while. I'm sure the baby's here by now. Oh, Harry, I can't wait to find out. And what a lucky baby, Harry. What a lucky child to have a father like you. Harry knows how to take care of those who love him, don't you, Harry?"

She kissed him on the cheek and as she did he stole a glance toward Treacy. He wasn't smiling now and there was fear in his eyes. Almost a pleading, as if he were asking him for something. He looked frightened, as though he were trapped, and then they heard shouts and the sound of running feet in the corridor outside the waiting room. Hard strong male voices sounding as though something terrible had happened. Then the door to the waiting room burst open and two cops came barging in with their guns drawn. They looked around the room and saw Treacy and the others.

"What the hell are you doing here?" one of them shouted at Treacy.

"My friend here's wife is about to deliver."

"You're the crazy guy came down the station with the clothes."

They could still hear shouting and the sound of running feet coming from the corridor.

"What the hell's goin' on?" Treacy asked.

"That colored kid killed that girl got away."

The cops looked around the room once more as if they believed that Toby had been hiding and would appear before them. Then they left.

Treacy and Harry were staring at each other.

Mrs. Dolan was standing now with her arm around Harry.

He looked stunned and his face was white. He looked sober all of a sudden and the goofiness was suddenly gone. He disengaged himself from Mrs. Dolan and stood trembling like he had the DT's. They could hear the sound of sirens in the street below them, one squad following another.

Treacy left the room and went down to the lobby. He stood watching the commotion. The place was full of cops and detectives. They were standing together in a huddle as more cops ran up and down the corridors. He could hear a voice coming out of the huddle and he knew it was Arnie Meyers.

"I want that kid, and I want him damn fast. Asses are gonna be hung for this. And I want him back here alive. You got me? Alive. We ain't gonna find him standing around here. Move it. Get going."

They made their way to the large front door and Treacy saw Red Dahlgren burst in. He headed straight for Arnie. He watched them as they talked, saw their heads nodding and moving, then he saw Arnie looking over to where he was standing. He could see that Red was angry and Arnie wanted him to go home.

"If you think I'm gonna go home and wait, you're crazy," Red said.

"Look, the only thing I care about is finding that kid. I can't get you involved in this. Got me?"

"I ain't going home."

"Tag along, but stay outta my sight. You really shouldn't be here and you know it. Anything happens and they know you're part of it. Then the papers get an angle for a crazy story."

"Don't worry, I ain't gonna talk to anyone."

"I just don't wanna know."

"How the hell did he get out?"

"Let's go and ask your friend Treacy over there. He's our walking martyr. Wants to take the rap for the shine. I mean, the balls of the guy to stand before you and say it was him murdered your sister. Jeez!"

"I never take him seriously. The guy's been whacked out since he came back. He ain't never gonna be straight. He's sick. You gotta know that, Arnie."

"Maybe whacked out enough to help the kid get outta here."

They were both looking at him and then they walked toward him. He saw them coming and he walked toward them. When they met, Red nodded and so did Treacy.

"What the fuck you doing here?" Arnie asked him.

"I came with Harry Cope. His wife's about to deliver."

"Yeah, but what are you doing here? What's that got to do with you?"

"As far as I know I can be any goddamn place I wanna be. I don't think I have to ask you for permission."

"Don't get smart with me or I'll run your ass in."

"For what?"

"Name it. Any damn thing I want to. Anything. Just go on bustin' my balls and you'll see."

"Who's bustin' whose balls?"

"Just tell me what you're doing here."

"I told you. I came here with Harry Cope. His wife's having a baby."

"You close to him?"

"Who?"

"Harry Cope, for God's sake."

Treacy shook his head. "Met him in the street. He was drunk and was having a hard time navigating. I walked him over here."

"Do you know Toby Walters escaped?"

"I just heard."

"It's still funny you should be here right now."

"I got no control over when babies choose to be born."

"When did you get here?"

"Ten minutes ago."

"Did you get over the DT's or do you still think you killed Annie?"

"Even if I could prove it to the two of you, you still wouldn't believe me."

"Think you can prove it?"

"What difference does it make? You've got your mind made up and you ain't gonna change it now."

"Did you confess it to your friend the priest? Did you tell him exactly how you did it?"

"That's between me and him."

"Jeez, you and that priest! What the hell's the matter with the two of you. Harry Cope himself swears he saw Walters coming out of the alley that night. And it fits because he's the only guy I can figure had a motive. He was jealous. He was in a jealous rage and he killed her, and you and your friend the priest can only think that we're not looking at anyone else. Well, Mr. Treacy, there ain't anyone else. You still think it could've been you?"

"Yeah—it coulda been me."

"Jesus, Jack, you really are crazy talkin' like that," Red said. "Christ, you could at least respect me. We're talkin' about my sister here."

"I know, Red. And the truth is there is just as much chance that I killed her as Toby Walters, because I don't remember anything that happened that night. I was boozin' for two weeks straight. I don't remember coming home. I don't remember anything except that my clothes were covered in blood when I woke up that Sunday morning. You don't think that's reason enough for me to have some doubts about myself?"

"You have anything to do with the kid breaking outta here?"

"I told you I wouldn't be here if it wasn't for Harry Cope. Ask him. He's over there in the waiting room with his mother-in-law."

"Sure you weren't here with the priest and Bailey Walters earlier on?" Arnie asked.

"I'm sure, but if they had asked me I would've come with them."

"You are one fuckin' bright boy, Mr. Treacy. You're convinced we've got the wrong guy, yet you were willing to help him escape and maybe be responsible for him being gunned down in the street. We know he's never gonna give himself up. There's a helluva good chance that he's gonna get himself killed. That what you want?"

"What makes you think he's gonna be killed?"

"Because it's gonna happen."

"Because you're gonna make sure it happens?"

"Look, smart-ass—I didn't help him get away from here."

"Sounds like you're glad he did, though."

Arnie looked at Red and shook his head.

"What the fuck's the matter with this guy?"

"I'll tell you what's the matter with me," Treacy said. "I've known guys like you. Guys who were certain. Guys who were convinced they knew what was best. Guys who never wanted to hear anything that would upset their take on things. And they got a helluva lot of good men killed in Korea."

"This ain't Korea. This is Brooklyn."

"What's the difference?"

Arnie looked at him. "Get the fuck outta here before I run you in as an accessory."

"Accessory to what?"

"Accessory to any fuckin' thing I want."

Treacy looked him in the eye and he could only shake his head. Then he reached his hand into his pocket and pulled it out again. He held it out toward Red, his hand still closed, then he opened it.

"Recognize that, Red?" he said.

Red looked down into his open hand and nestling in it was a silver Celtic cross and chain.

Treacy then reached across and held it up before the two of them.

"That belonged to Annie," Red said. "Charlie Gallucci gave it to her."

"Not Charlie Gallucci. Toby Walters. Take a look at the back of it."

He turned it over in his hand so that they could see the inscription on the back.

Love Forever—Toby.

They lifted their heads in unison and looked at Treacy.

"Where did you get this?" Red asked him.

"What difference does it make?"

"What the hell do you mean?" Arnie growled at him. "Makes a helluva difference. Where did you get it?"

"You're sure it makes a difference?"

"Where did you get it?" Arnie asked him again.

"I found it in the pocket of the trousers I was wearing the night Annie was killed. Same pair you threw back at me when I brought them to the station."

"Why didn't you show us the cross then?"

"I didn't know it was there. I found it when I went through the pockets before I was going to bring 'em to the cleaners."

"She wore that cross all the time," Red said.

He took it from Treacy's hand and held it by the chain and looked at it. Then he saw his eyes cloud with tears.

THIRTY-EIGHT

Toby stood in a doorway on Flatbush Avenue near the Long Island Railroad station. There wasn't much traffic on the avenue but he could hear the sound of sirens all around him and he had the feeling they were looking for him.

He wasn't far from the entrance to the Brooklyn Bridge and he could hear a train rumbling its way across to Manhattan. He wanted to be on it, but he knew they would have the station covered now. He knew he was going to have to walk across without them seeing him. He told himself they would never expect him to walk and that was his hope. They would not think of looking on the bridge itself for him.

He moved back into the doorway as a squad car sped past him toward the bridge, and he watched it turn off just before it got to the entrance. Then he saw another one coming in the opposite direction and he wondered if he would be able to move at all. His shoulder was hurting now, throbbing, it was bleeding again. He was starting to feel weak. He knew that no matter what happened, he was not going to let them take him back. He wasn't going to stop for them even if they saw him.

He had made up his mind to just keep going no matter what.

He could see the huge tower of the bridge reaching up into the sky like the spire of a great cathedral. His eyes followed it upward and he could see the stars in the clear summer night.

He saw lengthy streaks of white clouds stretching across the sky like veils caught in the wind and he thought of all the nights he and Annie used to sit on the old pier under the bridge and stare across the river to Manhattan and talk about the possibilities. He still couldn't believe she was gone and he wanted so much to talk to her.

The street was nearly clear now. Just a handful of people moving back and forth, hurrying through the night. He left the doorway and looked up and down, then started to walk quickly toward the bridge. He stayed close to the buildings and kept his head bowed.

As he was passing the railroad station a crowd of people suddenly emerged and he found himself caught up with them. Nobody looked at him. He saw two cops standing near the station entrance but they were looking the other way. He walked on quickly, moving with the crowd. He was getting closer to the bridge now. He had to stop himself from running toward it. He made himself walk casually, slowly toward it. He left the sidewalk and he knew he would have to be out in the open until he got on the bridge. He was walking diagonally now and he looked in each direction. He could hear the sound of sirens all around him. Then he saw a cab speeding toward the entrance and he wondered if he should try to flag it down. That would make it all so easy. Just ride it to the other side and he knew for sure they would never find him. Three minutes and he'd be there. But he decided against it at the last minute and he hung back, letting it speed past him. He watched its red taillights moving toward the city and cursed himself for not taking it.

Then, just as he was nearing the entrance to the walkway, he saw two cops walking toward him from the other side of the street. He didn't know if they had seen him and he ducked back into a doorway and stood rigid. He wasn't sure if they were looking for him or if they were just the regular cops walking the beat. He knew something was up. They had to know by now that he had escaped, he thought.

He wondered if he would be able to make his way onto the bridge. The cops were coming closer, and he thought for sure they would see him, but just before they got to the doorway they turned and began to walk back in the opposite direction.

He waited until he could no longer hear their footsteps, then looked out and saw that at last his way was clear to the walkway. He started to walk toward it quickly, trying not to attract attention. There was still traffic moving back and forth on the bridge. He knew it never stopped. Twenty-four hours a day, relentlessly, trip after trip after trip. It would be great if he could hitch a ride across but nobody hitchhikes in Brooklyn. In just fifteen minutes, if he moved fast, he would walk across. Come out by City Hall and move west toward the Village. Hang out there for a while until things cooled down and then head south, maybe toward New Orleans, where nobody would ever find him. Then he would find a ship and work his way over to France. Wind up in Paris. Jesus, Paris, where he could walk down the Champs Elysee with any woman he wanted, white or black, and nobody would even look at him.

He wished that woman could be Annie.

A squad car pulled up outside the rectory of the church and two cops got out and headed for the door. They rang the bell and waited, then rang it again. They saw the light go on and then heard the approaching steps of the housekeeper. She opened the door and looked out at the two men with a look of disbelief on her face.

"What do you want?" she asked quickly.

"Is Father Darcy here?" one of them asked.

She nodded toward them and turned as though she were going to get him, but then he appeared and stood before the two cops.

"It's alright, Mrs. Flanagan," he told her. "Go on back to bed."

"We have to ask you to come with us, Father," one of them said.

"What's the matter?"

"That Negro kid we were holding at the hospital got away."

"And what can I do for you?"

"Well, Father, Arnie Meyers thinks you and the kid's father helped him. He wants us to bring the two of you down to the hospital. Figures you might know where he was headed."

Darcy looked at the two men and nodded.

"I don't know where he was headed but just let me get my jacket."

He went back inside and came back with his jacket and collar on. He followed them to the car and they started toward Bailey Walters's house.

Harry Cope was sitting beside Mrs. Dolan in the waiting room. Despite the coolness of the evening he was sweating and he wiped his forehead constantly with a soaking handkerchief.

He had heard one of the cops say that Toby Walters could still be hiding in the hospital somewhere. The lobby area was still full of cops and they had set up a command post near the reception desk. A tall captain was on the phone, calling out orders to the squad cars.

"This had to happen on the night Sheila is about to deliver," he said.

"It's a terrible thing to have happen. All these policemen and all the activity. I just hope they don't disrupt anything," Mrs. Dolan said. "I hope they're not running around in the maternity wing. What an awful thing to have happen. Isn't that the Negro boy Annie Dahlgren was supposed to be going out with? My God, how could she? What's the matter with the young girls today. Why are they all surprised she wound up dead?"

"That's just what I say," Harry said. "What could've been the matter with her?"

Mrs. Dolan sat shaking her head.

A white-clad nurse appeared in the doorway and asked for Mr. Cope. Mrs. Dolan stood up and Harry followed her example as though she had shown him what to do.

"This is Mr. Cope," his mother-in-law said.

"Congratulations," the nurse said, smiling. "Your wife has just given birth to a seven-pound four-ounce baby girl, and they're both doing very well."

Mrs. Dolan threw her arms around Harry and started to cry. He stared blankly over her shoulder toward the wall. He was numb. Then Mrs. Dolan had pulled back and she was looking into his face.

"Well, well. Say something, Harry. A little girl. Oh, a little girl! Oh, Harry!"

She wiped her tears of joy with a small handkerchief.

"Can we go up and see them?" she asked the nurse.

"In a little while. I'll come and get you."

"And are you sure they're both alright?"

"They are both wonderful. Mrs. Cope is very tired. Right now she should rest but you can certainly come and see the baby. I'll come get you."

They both sat down, suddenly feeling tired themselves. They stared out expressionless. Then Harry stood and started to walk slowly toward the door.

"Where are you going?" Mrs. Dolan asked.

"I want to find Jack Treacy and tell him."

"What do you need to tell him for?"

"He brought me here. I just want to tell him everything's alright so he can go home."

Harry looked across the lobby and saw Arnie Meyers and Red talking to Treacy. He walked toward them and stood. They didn't notice him at first.

"Sheila just had a baby girl," he said quietly. They didn't hear him and he said it again.

"Sheila just had a baby girl."

They turned and looked at him.

"What's that, Harry," Arnie said.

"My wife just gave birth to a baby girl. Everything's alright."

"That's great, Harry," Treacy said.

"A little girl," Arnie said.

Harry nodded. He caught Red's eye and they looked at each other.

"What's wrong, Red?" he asked.

He shook his head.

"Harry, why don't you go back to the waiting room," Arnie said. "We got some business here."

"What about Toby Walters?" Harry asked.

"What about him?"

"I keep thinking about him. Did they find him yet?"

"You got other things to worry about."

"They gonna find him?"

"He ain't goin' nowhere."

"What will they do when they catch him?"

"Lock him up again."

"Will they bring him back here?"

"I don't think so."

Treacy had turned around now and was looking directly at Harry.

"You don't have to wait any longer, Jack," Harry said. "You can go home now. Thanks for getting me here."

Treacy nodded.

"I want to ask you something, Harry," Treacy said.

"Sure."

"Did you really see Toby Walters coming out of the alley the night Annie was killed?"

He hesitated, then looked at Arnie.

"Yeah—I saw him."

"How did you know it was him?"

"I knew."

"How far away from the alley were you when you saw him?"

"I was up the block."

"Where—how far up the block."

"Not far from Red's house."

"And you could tell for sure from where you were it was Toby?"

"Sure."

"What was he wearing?"

"I don't know. I couldn't tell."

"Why not?"

"It was too dark and he was too far away."

"But you could tell it was Toby Walters?"

"Yes."

Treacy looked toward Arnie.

"For Christ's sake, the guy just became a papa," Arnie said. "What are you doing bustin' his balls?"

"Bustin' his balls. What about the truth? You don't know who the fuck he saw coming out of that alley, do you, Mr. Meyers?"

He turned back to Harry. "I know who you saw coming out of the alley and it wasn't Toby Walters, was it?"

Harry didn't answer.

"Was it? Why did you say it was Toby Walters?"

"Who else could it have been? He was her boyfriend, wasn't he?"

"But you didn't know it was him. Why did you say it was him?"

Harry looked toward Arnie.

"You didn't really know if it was him, did you?"

Harry shook his head.

"Who told you to say it was Toby?"

"Nobody."

"Bullshit—who brought his name up?"

Mrs. Dolan came out of the waiting room and called Harry.

"They want us to go see the baby now."

"I gotta go," Harry said.

"Harry—did the cops mention Toby's name to you?" Treacy asked.

He nodded again.

"What did they say."

"They said it had to be Toby."

"And what did you tell 'em?"

"I said that if they thought it was Toby, who else could it be? I thought they knew."

"So you never knew for sure it was him."

"I thought they knew who it was. Look, I have to go see the baby."

Harry walked toward the waiting room and Mrs. Dolan took his arm and led him away.

Treacy turned back to Arnie Meyers and Red.

"Chances are it was me he saw that night."

They were both looking at him and they didn't say anything.

"And you still don't want it to be me," Treacy said. "You still want Toby Walters."

"For God's sake Jack, do you really want me to believe you killed Annie," Red said. "I mean, do you realize what the hell you're saying? Do you know what you're asking me to believe?"

"Do you think I want to believe it? I don't want to believe it, but how the hell did I come up with that cross in my pocket? Either of you got an answer for that?"

"You could've found it in the street," Arnie said.

"What were the chances of me finding it in the street? You think someone stuck it in my pocket?"

"Jesus, you really want to be the killer," Red said.

Arnie turned away and called out to the captain at the reception desk.

"Any word on the Walters kid yet?"

The captain looked at him and shook his head.

"There's more to connect me with Annie's death than Toby Walters," Treacy said.

THIRTY-NINE

Toby was on the bridge high above the river, walking fast. The moon was still up looking down on the lower bay and shining toward the bridge. It was the flood tide and the river was at its highest, a spring tide that raised its way above the high watermark. There was a golden path reaching from the harbor all the way up the river, reflecting the moonlight, and when he looked down he felt as though he could walk on it. He was nearly halfway across. He had seen no one else on the bridge coming or going but the flow of traffic remained constant as though it couldn't turn itself off. He could feel the pain in his shoulder and he still felt weak. He allowed himself to slow down a little.

He felt sure he was going to make it across. Nothing to stop him now. He felt the breeze blowing up from the bay and he could smell the sea air. He thought of a ship that would take him far, far away. He thought of himself standing at the bow, riding up and down on the waves, the foam hitting his face. There was a vast sunlight sea ahead of him with the light dancing on the water. Light and water and warmth. He was the bedlamite of the poem escaping the madness of the pursuit. Life looking for a cause.

He didn't pay any attention to the siren because he had been hearing them all night. But then he realized it was coming closer, and when he looked back he could see the headlights speeding toward him. He wondered if they knew he was on the bridge. He ducked down on the walkway and watched as the squad car sped across the bridge toward the city. Didn't make sense for Brooklyn cops to be going to Manhattan he thought. They wouldn't try to block the other end themselves. They would've called Manhattan.

He began to realize that he had not seen any regular traffic for a while. It had all stopped. They had pulled the plug.

He knew they were looking for him on the bridge. Someone had to see him getting on at the Brooklyn end. When he looked back he saw a car with a flashing light moving slowly. He knew they were checking the walkway. It had to be one of the brightest nights he could ever remember. He heard fast-moving footsteps on the walkway behind him. They were cops, for sure.

There was no place to hide. It was hard for him to run and the pain in his shoulder throbbed. He walked on as fast as he could, and when he looked back he could see that the squad car was moving faster. He heard shouts but the breeze carried the voices away from him and he didn't know what they were saying. A car was suddenly alongside him and a cop was yelling at him to stop and raise his hands in the air. He kept moving as fast as he could and the car moved with him.

"We've got the bridge covered on both ends," the cops shouted. "There's no way you can make it. Stand still and put your hands in the air."

The cop had a gun pointed at him. He kept moving and looking toward the cop in the car, waiting for him to fire. He was not going to stop. They were going to have to kill him.

The car suddenly stopped and two cops jumped out with their guns drawn. He glanced desperately at them, climbed over the railing and held on. They ran to where he was and reached for him, but he climbed down until he was below them and all they could see was his head and shoulders.

"Anyone comes any closer, I jump," he shouted.

They stopped in their tracks. They all had their guns drawn, pointing at him. They were shouting at him to climb back, assuring him that nothing would happen to him. They tried to reach down and grab him but every time they came close to him he threatened to jump. One of them ran back to the car and called the captain on the radio.

"We've got him trapped on the Brooklyn Bridge," he said. "But he's climbed over the rail and he's threatening to jump if we come close to him. The kid is serious. He's not going to let us take him."

The captain slammed down the phone and walked quickly to where Arnie Meyers and Red were standing.

"They got the Walters kid trapped on the bridge," he told Arnie.

"He's threatening to jump if anyone goes near him. He's over the railing, holding on."

Arnie looked at Treacy, then at Red.

"Get on that phone and tell them we got the killer. Have 'em tell the kid he don't have to worry. He can give himself up. We got the guy who did it."

The captain ran back to the phone and made the call.

"Better get this guy cuffed," Arnie told Red.

Red called one of the cops over and Treacy held out his wrists. The cop put the cuffs on him and Red was standing in front of him now, staring into his face. Treacy bowed his head.

"I really didn't want it to be me Red," he said. "I'm so sorry. So sorry. I don't remember anything. My God, Red, how could I ever do something like that to Annie? Oh God."

"Just shut up, Jack. Just shut up. You have nothin' to say. If it was just the two of us here I'd kill you myself."

"I wish the fuck you would."

"Just shut up."

"Better get him down to the station," Arnie said.

"And tell the captain to have those guys bring the kid back here to the hospital."

Toby was clinging to the railing just out of the reach of the cops, who were calling out to him, telling him they had found the real killer. "We just don't want you to jump. Please come on back up. Arnie Meyers says they have the real killer in custody. There's no reason for you to run anymore."

Toby didn't answer them.

He knew for sure it had to be a trick. Still, he wondered if it might be true. If they had found the killer, who could it be? He was feeling weaker and the pain in his shoulder was getting worse. He knew he couldn't take the chance of letting them grab him. One of the cops came closer to him and kneeled down.

Toby was looking up into his Irish face made even more red by the magnifying light of the moon. The breeze was coming up stronger and his white shirt billowed out and rippled like a flag.

"Come on up kid," the cops said. "They got the guy who did it. No reason for you to be out there. I got orders to bring you right back to the hospital. You need treatment and you ain't gonna be able to hang on there for too long. I can see the blood coming through your shirt."

"You're lying. They don't have the killer," Toby said. "Think I'm crazy? You guys want to kill me. That's what you're gonna have to do. I ain't coming up there. They got no other guy."

"Look, I ain't lyin'. Come on, kid, give yourself a break. You don't look too good. We coulda shot you anytime if we wanted to."

"Who they got? Tell me that. Who they got? They never even looked for anyone else. Somebody walk in and confess? They wouldn't believe him, anyway. Just quit bullshittin' me."

"Listen, kid, I'm telling you the truth. I got no reason to lie to you."

"Yes, you do."

"Why would I lie to you?"

"Because you guys want to hang me. Give me a fair trial and then hang me. No thanks."

"Look, you ain't gonna be able to hang on there much longer. Come on up. Every cop here got his weapon in his holster. I don't wanna see you kill yourself. Believe me, if Arnie Meyers says he has the killer he has him."

"Just tell me who they got."

"I don't know, kid. They didn't tell us."

"They're lyin', then."

The cop saw Toby's eyes close.

"Please, kid," he pleaded. "Come on up and we'll talk about it. You can talk to the captain himself."

Toby didn't answer him. The cop ran back to the squad car and got on the radio.

"Captain, that kid's not getting back up on the bridge because he doesn't believe us. He thinks we're trying to pull something on him."

"You can't let anything happen to him," the captain said.

"Somebody's got to convince him we ain't lyin'. You really got the killer?"

"Yeah, we got him. For Christ's sake do I have to send you an affidavit."

"Whatever it takes, captain. The kid is really weak. He's over the rail. I don't know how the hell he's holding on."

"They got Jack Treacy—the guy brought the clothes to the precinct."

"Jesus, he ain't gonna believe it's him. Everyone knows that story. That's who they got? I mean is this on the level? We're talking about the guy Arnie threw out of the precinct?"

"It's on the level, goddamnit. Now do whatever the hell you have to do, but get his ass back here."

The captain hung up and walked across to Arnie. The circle around him and Red had grown larger. Some of the cops still didn't realize why they had arrested Treacy.

His arms were handcuffed in front of him and they were about to have him brought to the precinct.

"Jimmy Ryan says the kid's really spooked. He wants to know who we've taken in."

"Did you tell him?"

"I told Jimmy. He says he'll never believe it's Treacy. He knows you threw him out of the precinct. He's getting weaker too. He's bleeding from the wound in his shoulder."

"Why don't you bring me down there?" Treacy said.

"And what the hell would you do?" Arnie asked.

"I'll show him the cross and tell him I found it in my pocket. Jesus, you can't let the kid kill himself."

Arnie was looking at the captain, then he looked at Red.

"What do you think?"

"What the hell do we have to lose?"

"I'll tell you what we have to lose. If he kills himself we're all in goddamn trouble. Damn newspapers will have a field day with it."

"Alright, let's get down there and bring Mr. Treacy along. And Captain, send the priest and Bailey Walters after us when they get here."

FORTY

Treacy sat with a cop next to him in the backseat of a squad car. Arnie Meyers chewed on the stub of his cigar as Red drove them toward the Brooklyn Bridge. Red could not bring himself to believe that Treacy was the killer. He was still thinking that it had to be Toby.

When they stopped at a red light he turned around quickly and looked at Treacy. It was hard to see his face in the darkness of the car, but he was amazed that with all of the drinking and the hospitalizations, his face still held its youthfulness. He wasn't sure if Arnie really believed it was Treacy or if he was just using him to get Toby.

Treacy was thinking of the retreat from the Chosin Reservoir. The bitter cold when it was so hard to walk, the howling wind that never ceased, and the endless attacks. The red blood on the snow and the terrified face of the young Chinese soldier he had bayoneted over and over until he was covered in blood himself and they had to pry him away. And the smell of the blood on him that wouldn't go away. Wearing the same clothes for weeks until the blood, frozen and hardened, seemed like paint. He had been afraid ever since that the black anger that was at the very bottom of his despair would rise up in him like a virus. The volcano within him that had been stoked by the pain of senseless deaths that had taken place thousands of miles away in places everyone forgot. He could still see the fir trees on the snowy Korean hillsides with all of their tears frozen on them like icicles. The terrible consequences in the remotest lives brought on by distant men's decisions.

He kept trying to remember that Saturday night. Something that would come back . . . or was it that he just wouldn't let himself.

All he could remember of his bender was Clyde. The warmth he had felt when they were together and how frightening it was. It kept coming back to him. It was the one part he wanted to keep away from himself. He wanted the feeling so much but he was ashamed of it. He had never felt that kind of closeness before. He had carried a torn and battered paperback of *Leaves of Grass* with him all through Korea. He loved the words, but there was so much in it he just didn't understand; they gave him comfort, anyway. Some of them scared him.

That I was I knew was of my body, and what I should be I knew I should be of my body.

. . . nor is it you alone who knows what it is to be evil, I am he who knew what it was to be evil.

Soon he would be crossing the same East River that old Walt crossed, who had told all those who would be born in the future that he had been there before them and had had all of the same anguish that they had, and he was still there with them looking from someplace along the river, telling them not to be afraid. Let no man be the arbiter of the struggle between any other man and his soul. Who knows of the battle any man has holding on in ignorant desperation until the mystery he is forced to cling to turns in distraction and offers a blessing.

They were coming close to the bridge and when he looked out of the window, the moon was still shining its light down, holding its place in the sky as if waiting for them to come together at the place where Toby was still hanging on. They made their way through a lane kept open for the cops and the emergency service people. There was an ambulance on the scene already and a crowd of newspaper people who were being held back from getting closer to where Toby was. They were all screaming at the cops, pleading with them to let them get to the rail to get pictures.

"Jesus, what a mess," Arnie said. "Who let all those goddamn newspaper guys get this close?"

"Guess the story is out all over the place now," Red said.

"Front page of the *News* and the *Mirror* tomorrow, for sure," Arnie said. "Jesus, this better be done right. Can't afford a fuck-up here. It'll be all our asses."

They pulled up as close as they could and Arnie called out to Jimmy Ryan. He came over to their car and nodded at Arnie.

"What's the story?" he asked him.

"Same as before."

"We got Mr. Treacy with us," Arnie said, nodding toward the back-seat.

Ryan looked in and Treacy stared back at him.

"Don't know that he's gonna go for this," Ryan said.

"Yeah, well, we got proof now it was him. Look, Jimmy, if you need reinforcements to keep those newspaper guys back, then let's get 'em here right now. This thing's gotta be over in the next five minutes or that kid is gone. Get 'em back now as far as you can. Pull your weapons on 'em if you have to."

Arnie started to get out of the car, then he stopped and looked at Red.

"Those newspaper guys know who you are, Red. They'll be all over you. Stay here until we get the kid back."

He looked at the cop and Treacy and nodded to the cop to follow him. The cop opened the door and helped Treacy, who was still handcuffed, get out of the car. Jimmy Ryan was about to lead them over to where Toby was when Arnie stopped suddenly.

"Hold on a minute," he said.

He went back to the car and looked in at Red.

"Let me have the cross," he said.

Red reached into his pocket and pulled it out. He held it up by the chain for an instant before he gave it to Arnie. He took it from him and put it in Treacy's hand.

"You are the only one can get him back up here. You've gotta tell him about the cross. He won't believe us. He knows nothing about it. Let's go."

More police had arrived and they formed a barrier to keep the news-papermen back. They shouted out to Arnie as he and Treacy moved to where Toby was.

There were flashing camera lights all around them. Some of the photographers had climbed onto girders and were perched precari-ously as they tried to hold on and take pictures at the same time. There was a continual banter among them and someone was giving a running commentary from on top of a car. Toby was hanging on unseen below the railing. They wondered why Arnie had a hand-cuffed man with him as they approached the place where Toby was. Most of the cops didn't know, either.

"Arnie, Arnie," they shouted. "What the hell's going on? That the killer you got there? Turn him around so we can get a picture."

Arnie ignored them as Jimmy Ryan brought them to the edge where they were looking down at Toby. The three of them knelt down as though they had come before an altar. They heard Arnie grunt as he forced himself into this unfamiliar position. He quickly pulled his large crumpled white handkerchief from his pocket, put it on the ground, and knelt on it.

They could see Toby's face looking up at them and saw the ghostly paleness of his dark face and the bloodstains on his white shirt.

The moon was higher in the sky, moving toward the west, and the path its reflection made bridged the river. The three men could see all the way down to the river itself under the bridge, dark and ominous as though waiting benignly for someone to drop or fall into its bosom, casting no judgment one way or the other.

Toby looked at them and he could see that Treacy was handcuffed. He believed it was a trick to get him back up on the bridge and he was determined he wasn't going to do it. He had reached that place where he was ready to let go and plunge down into the river. He had kept telling himself that he would find Annie on the other side waiting for him. They could be together and no one would be there to say a word about it. It was a far better option than being brought back to a holding cell and going though a trial he knew he was sure to lose.

"Get back up here, kid," Arnie said. "We know you didn't kill Annie Dahlgren. We've got the guy who did it."

Toby was staring up through the railing at Treacy, who was looking down at him.

"Who did it?" Toby asked.

"Jack Treacy," he said, turning to where Treacy was kneeling beside him. Jimmy Ryan reached down and urged Toby to take his hand.

"My father told me the story about you and Treacy and now you bring him here and he's supposed to be the killer."

"Let me tell you, kid," Arnie said. "We'd be justified right now in shooting you if we wanted to for attempting to escape and resisting arrest."

"Why don't you, then," Toby heard himself say.

"Because we'd be killing the wrong guy."

"You telling me that Jack Treacy killed Annie?"

"That's what we're saying, kid. Why do you think we went to all this trouble?"

They were leaning down closer to Toby now because they were having trouble hearing him.

He could barely speak above a whisper.

"Listen, kid," Arnie said. "You don't have the strength to hold on down there much longer. Let us pull you up here and I'll prove to you it was Treacy."

"Jeez, you must have been really disappointed," Toby said. "I know you wanted so much for it to be me."

"My job is to find the killer and it ain't you. I mean, I got witnesses here to what I'm telling you. I don't want to deceive you, kid. Why don't you climb back up here?"

They heard shouts and curses behind them and when they looked back they saw Darcy and Bailey Walters trying to fight their way through to where Toby was.

"For God's sake, let us through," they heard Darcy shout. Then a cop came to where Arnie was.

"What about these two?" he asked. "It's the kid's father and a priest."

"Let them through," Arnie said.

The cop led them over and they got as close as they could. They hunched down and saw Toby below them.

"Oh my God, son," Bailey said. "Don't do it. Please, Toby. Don't let them make you do this."

"There's no reason for him to do it," Arnie said. "We've got the guy who killed Annie Dahlgren right here. We been trying to convince him it's over."

Darcy looked up at Arnie and for the first time his eyes fell on Treacy. He really hadn't noticed him standing there before. He saw the handcuffs and he looked from him to Arnie.

"What's going on here?" he asked.

"I have to admit, Father, we were a little premature in not following up on what Treacy here came to see us about."

"I don't care about that now. For God's sake, can't we get this boy back up here? I mean, look at him. How much longer do you think he can hold on?"

"Jesus, Father, with all due respect what the hell do you think we've been trying to do here? We can't help him unless he wants to be helped. It's up to him."

Treacy had risen to his feet now. He was looking down the river toward the lower bay, which he could see clearly. The moon had moved west and was casting its pale light on the mouth of the river. He could see the Statue of Liberty rising up like a specter, its torch held high in the midst of the stars. He could hear the voices pleading and arguing all around him and he wondered why they hadn't asked him to show the cross to Toby.

He couldn't take his gaze away from the pale, peaceful light sitting over the harbor like a balm. And he remembered he had had the same peaceful feeling before and he was sure it would never come back to him again. It had happened when they were retreating from the Chosin and they were all sure that none of them were going to make it. They all seemed to realize at the same time that there was nothing to fear anymore and in that instant it left them. All of the barriers that had ever been between them were gone. The hate, the resentments, the annoyances. There was no black or white. They were all one. There was the soft feeling of unhurried love for one another. There was no past or future, only the peace that held them together in the instant of the present. They knew they were men and there was no need to hide anything. They were devoid of all the trappings of the world. They didn't apply anymore. It was the clear white truth of all of their vulnerability and they all knew that in this pure truth there was no need for the thing called honor. There was only the purity of their divine camaraderie.

He could feel the cross in his hand and he knew he had to move forward now and reach down to Toby. He moved until he was directly above him, then reached his handcuffed hands through the railing, holding the cross by the chain until it was dangling above Toby. The others looked at him. Darcy and Bailey Walters wondered what he was doing. It was hard for Toby to see.

"Anybody got a flashlight?" Treacy asked.

Jimmy Ryan moved close to him and shone the flashlight down through the darkness under the bridge.

"Shine it on my hands," Treacy said.

They were all looking down now and they saw that Treacy was holding the cross as close as he could get it to Toby's hand.

"What's he doing?" Darcy asked.

No one answered him.

"Look at my hands," Treacy told Toby. "Look at what I'm holding."

Toby stared up through the darkness toward the light focused on Treacy's hands. He saw the cross hanging from the chain, spinning slowly. He still wasn't sure what it was, then it slowly came to a stop. He could see it clearly now and it looked familiar. He immediately thought of Annie.

"Do you recognize the cross?" Arnie shouted.

"Looks like the cross I gave Annie," Toby said.

"Read him what's on the back of it," Arnie told Treacy.

"It says, 'Love forever, Toby.'"

"Is that the cross you gave Annie Dahlgren?" Arnie asked.

Toby was stunned but there was no doubt about it.

"Yes," Toby said. "Where did you get it?"

"Treacy found it in the pocket of the pants he was wearing on the night she was killed."

"Was it you, Treacy?" Toby shouted up at him.

Treacy nodded.

"Will you come up here now?" Arnie asked.

Treacy stood up and moved back as Jimmy Ryan got as close as he could, reached down with both hands, and pulled Toby back up onto the bridge.

Bailey Walters rushed to him and held him as they both cried. Toby was so weak it was hard for him to stand.

They were all gathered around them and even the newspaper men had somehow managed to get through the cordon of cops. They were snapping pictures as fast as they could and calling out dozens of questions that were ignored.

"Better get him back to the hospital," Jimmy Ryan said. "He can't afford to lose any more blood."

With Darcy and Bailey on either side of him, Toby began to move slowly toward the ambulance.

Nobody noticed that Treacy had moved closer to the railing.

He was standing against it, and then he leaned out over it.

He peered down through the darkness to the river below. The moon had moved on, taking its pale light with it as though there were no more need of it.

The press and the photographers were taking pictures of Toby from all sides and throwing questions at Arnie. They wanted to know how he had been able to figure out that Toby Walters wasn't the murderer.

Bailey Walters and Darcy climbed into the back of the ambulance with Toby. He lay down and the young doctor was standing over him, taking his vital signs. It felt so good to lie down, and he closed his eyes. He remembered Annie's cross and wanted to have it with him. He opened his eyes and looked at his father.

"The cross," he said. "Annie's cross. I forgot to take it. Can I get it before we go?"

"I don't know that they would let you have it now. I'm sure they need it for evidence," Darcy said.

"Please—see if you can get it."

Darcy left the ambulance and saw Arnie still surrounded by the newsmen. He went over to where he stood and told him Toby wanted the cross. Arnie looked around him as though he suddenly remembered Treacy. He knew he still had it. He looked toward the railing, and Darcy followed his gaze. They saw Treacy standing by the railing, still leaning over it.

"Stop him. For God's sake, stop him!" Arnie cried.

Everyone turned around, startled, and some of the cops rushed toward Treacy. Darcy called out to him.

"Jack, for God's sake don't. Don't."

Just as they reached him he managed to tumble over the railing. They saw him fall and disappear into the darkness.

They didn't see him hit the water.

He was gone as though he had never stood on the bridge.

Darcy stared down, his mind blank. He was numb. Even the newsmen hadn't realized what had happened. He brushed past them all and walked toward the car. Red was standing outside.

They looked at each other and neither of them knew what to say.

Arnie climbed into the car.

Red stayed outside and told him he was going to walk home.

Darcy looked down into the blackness.

He felt an aching despair that was beyond the reality of everything that had happened. He couldn't move himself. The ambulance had gone. *My God, my God, why have you forsaken us,* he thought.

Beyond the blankness there was a terrible sense of betrayal that he didn't want to acknowledge. To acknowledge it would be to not believe, and he was afraid of what it would mean not to believe. The darkness he gazed into was so inviting. It said there was nothing to work out. Just fall down into me and it will all be over. And he knew that he was just as capable of falling down into it as Treacy. It has all been explained so easily for so long. Just as men would explain the incomprehensibility of the mystery by scriptures and aphorisms and wealth, technology and science. If we keep pecking away we will someday crack the thing. We will get to the heart of the mystery and no one will ever jump off a bridge again. Is that it?

Is that what we're aiming for?

Traffic was moving on the bridge again and the cops and the newspapermen had left. Darcy didn't know how long he had been standing there, staring down the river to the mouth of the harbor. He was so tired he could hardly stand and now he had no choice but to walk home. Or maybe he'd be lucky and find a cab when he got to Flatbush. He finished his cigarette and flicked the butt over the railing and watched as the wind caught it, held it up for a while, then let it fall down through the darkness. He couldn't find the words to pray but he found his arm reaching out over the railing, making the sign of the blessing.

As he turned to move away his eye caught something gleaming on the railing.

He took a step closer and saw that it was Annie's cross and chain sitting where Treacy must have left it before he jumped.

He picked it up and let it dangle before him.

The breeze blowing up the river moved it. He turned the cross over and saw the inscription on the back. *Love Forever, Toby.*

As he walked back to Brooklyn, Darcy couldn't help but feel that. Sometimes there is no honor in the truth. And sometimes a man kills himself not from despair or avoidance. Sometimes it is a choice made out of love and the very simple longing for it.